SIR HEREWARD and FITZ

MISTER

By Garth Nix:

THE OLD KINGDOM SERIES
Sabriel

Lirael

Abhorsen

Clariel

Goldenhand

Terciel and Elinor

Newt's Emerald

To Hold the Bridge: An Old Kingdom Novella and Other Tales

A Confusion of Princes

Across the Wall: A Tale of the Abhorsen and Other Stories

The Ragwitch

One Beastly Beast: Two Aliens, Three

Inventors, Four Fantastic Tales

Shade's Children

Angel Mage

Sir Hereward and Mister Fitz: Stories of the

Witch Knight and the Puppet Sorcerer

The Left-Handed Booksellers of London

The Sinister Booksellers of Bath

SIR HEREWARD *and* MISTER FITZ

STORIES OF THE WITCH KNIGHT AND THE PUPPET SORCERER

GARTH NIX

First published in Great Britain in 2023 by Gollancz
an imprint of The Orion Publishing Group Ltd
Carmelite House, 50 Victoria Embankment
London EC4Y 0DZ

An Hachette UK Company

1 3 5 7 9 10 8 6 4 2

Copyright © Garth Nix 2023
Map illustration © Mike Hall

A CIP catalogue record for this book is
available from the British Library.

ISBN (HB) 978 1 399 60635 6
ISBN (ETPB) 978 1 399 60636 3
ISBN (eBook) 978 1 399 60638 7
ISBN (audio) 978 1 399 60639 4

Printed in Great Britain by Clays Ltd, Elcograf S.p.A.

MIX
Paper from
responsible sources
FSC® C104740

www.gollancz.co.uk

To Eric Flint, in memoriam.
He published the first of these stories;
without his encouragement there
might never have been more.
And
To Anna, Thomas, Edward, and
all my family and friends.

CONTENTS

INTRODUCTION

IT IS ALWAYS DIFFICULT TO LOOK BACK and identify the genesis of a story. I can't recall what prompted me to begin the first "Sir
H and Mister F" story (as I tend to call them). A lot of the short
fiction I write is in response to a particular invitation, when an
editor asks me to submit something for consideration, usually to a
themed anthology. But "Sir Hereward and Mister Fitz Go to War
Again" was not written for any particular anthology or editor.

Looking back through my emails and files (not all of which
have survived multiple migrations over the last seventeen years
or so) it seems I wrote the first story in late 2005 and early 2006
and then didn't know what to do with it.

But I had earlier sold a SF story called "Dog Soldier" to Eric
Flint for the then-new online magazine *Jim Baen's Universe*. He
had expressed a general interest in seeing more from me, and I
liked both his own work and what he was doing with the magazine. It struck me that this new story might well be right up his
alley. So on Wednesday, 2nd August 2006, I sent an email to
Eric, which included this key passage:

> I have an approx. 11,000 word new fantasy story called
> SIR HEREWARD AND MISTER FITZ GO TO
> WAR AGAIN which I think is a *Jim Baen's Universe*
> kind of story, and I wondered if you'd like to see it.
> It's kind of a pike and shot sword and sorcery heroic
> military fantasy, I guess. If you do want to see it I can
> e-mail it over. Or not, as the case may be.

"Kind of a pike and shot sword and sorcery heroic military fantasy" is perhaps not my strongest sales pitch ever, but it does capture some of the essence of what I was trying to achieve, and it also gives some clues to the genesis of that story.

A literary DNA test would very quickly identify some obvious ancestors, including the "Fafhrd and Gray Mouser" stories by Fritz Leiber; *Don Quixote* by Cervantes; and books and stories by Rafael Sabatini; Robert Louis Stevenson; Alexandre Dumas; Michael Moorcock; Edgar Rice Burroughs; and many others.

However, any such test would not reveal another very important influence from my childhood: papier-mâché and puppet-making. My mother, Katharine Nix, a papermaker and artist, made many puppets for and with my brothers and I (and numerous costumes which were often essentially child-inhabited puppets). I have vivid memories of the painstaking application of torn paper and glue to a balloon, over and over again in layers, to make the head of a puppet. Once we even made the head of a giant, on a chicken wire frame, for a fifth-grade production of *The Amiable Giant*. It was a three-child puppet, I operated the left arm. The extensive papier-mâché-making apprenticeship of my primary school years is, I am sure, where the first faint idea of someone like Mister Fitz was implanted in my subconscious.

Back to that first story. Eric's response was immediate:

Yes, I would very much like to see it. I'm generally not
buying for the moment, but I do have a slot open for
a lead fantasy story in the sixth issue, coming out next
April. I was wondering how I was going to fill it . . . :)

I sent Eric the story. He said he didn't have time to read it because he was off to Anaheim for the 2006 Worldcon the next week. Coincidentally, I was too, it was the first Worldcon for me outside Australia, and only my second Worldcon at all. We arranged to catch up and say hello, and I had no expectation he would have read the story. I presumed it would simply wait its turn in the queue until he got back.

I caught up with Eric on the Sunday morning. He told me he read the story on the flight over, he loved it and he wanted to publish it in *Jim Baen's Universe*. I'd sent it in three weeks earlier, it was one of the fastest acceptances ever.

I didn't write the story expressly for Eric, but without his immediate enthusiasm simply to see the story and then his swift embrace of it, it is likely the first outing of Sir Hereward and Mister Fitz would have taken much longer to find a home, or perhaps might never even have been published, and then the others would not have been written either.

After that first story, I found the duo often in my thoughts when I wanted to write a new story. When asked to write something for a pirate anthology for Ann and Jeff Vandermeer, Hereward and Fitz immediately popped up on the horizon in their skiff. Similarly, when Jonathan Strahan and Lou Anders approached me for *Swords and Dark Magic*, the title instantly said to me "Sir H and Mister F"; and so it went on, for what is now nine stories. I suspect any editorial querying in my direction that mentions "sorcery," "swords," "gunpowder," "godslaying," "swashbuckling," or improbably "papier-mâché," would have me once again summoning these two companions in arms to the forefront of my writing mind.

THE WORLD OF
SIR HEREWARD AND MISTER FITZ

High Steppe

KAPOMAN RANGE

Shezak

Mt Alastra

Alastran Valley

Jeminero

• *Field of Fallen Foe*

Konqwal   Ryzha °

○ Pecall-Torin

THE SYNDICAL SEA

Hrorst   *The Shallows*   *Low Steppe*

Lesemb   Junum °   Trimgol

Kahaon

Hurshell

KAHAON EMPIRE   Perridel   Kquq   Karrilinion

Lazzarenno   Lundol   New Aruth

The Game Wall   Kallink   Aruth   *GREAT ARUTHIAN FOREST*

Hunterhorn

KAHAONESE IMPERIAL FOREST   Simiril   *Smallest Sea*   Fulwek °

○ Durlal

Ashagah   Orthaon

Asantra–Lurre   Ingmal °

RORGRIM FASTNESS   *HRYKEN BAY*   ○ Jinqu

Therelle

Hryk   Shrivet   Kaz

Diamond Fort   Yarken

Fort Largin

Arotha   Balkash   *Larnuk-Agre*   Shundalar

BALKASH DESERT   *Jungle*

Herenclos   *River Coradon*

🜂 *Hruria*

Gebrak

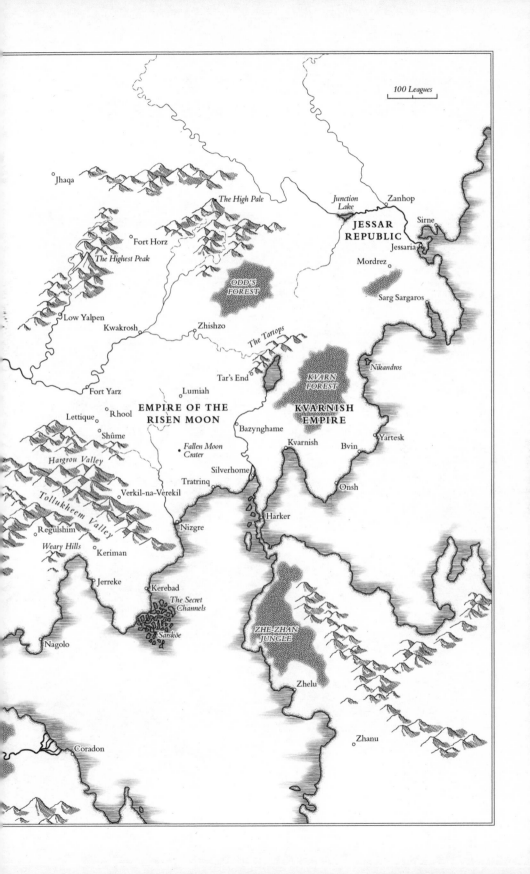

100 Leagues

Jhaqa

The High Pale

Junction
Lake

Zanhop

**JESSAR
REPUBLIC**

Sirne

Jessaria

Fort Horz

The Highest Peak

Mordrez

ODD'S
FOREST

Sarg Sargaros

Low Yalpen

Kwakrosh

Zhishzo

The Tartops

Nikandros

Tar's End

KVARN
FOREST

Fort Yarz

Lumiah

**EMPIRE OF THE
RISEN MOON**

**KVARNISH
EMPIRE**

Lettique

Rhool

Shûme

Bazynghame

Kvarnish

Bvin

Yartesk

Hargrou Valley

• *Fallen Moon
Crater*

Onsh

Silverhome

Tollukheem Valley

Verkil-na-Verekil

Tratrinq

Regulshim

Nizgre

Harker

Weary Hills

Keriman

Jerreke

Kerebad

*The Secret
Channels*

**ZHE-ZHAN
JUNGLE**

Nagolo

• *Sarsköe*

Zhelu

Zhanu

Coradon

SIR HEREWARD and MISTER FITZ

SIR HEREWARD AND MISTER FITZ GO TO WAR AGAIN

O YOU EVER WONDER ABOUT THE NATURE OF the world, Mister Fitz?" asked the foremost of the two riders, raising the three-barred visor of his helmet so that his words might more clearly cross the several feet of space that separated him from his companion, who rode not quite at his side.

"I take it much as it presents itself, for good or ill, Sir Hereward," replied Mister Fitz. He had no need to raise a visor, for he wore a tall, lacquered hat rather than a helmet. It had once been taller and had come to a peak, before encountering something sharp in the last battle but two the pair had found themselves engaged in.

This did not particularly bother Mister Fitz, for he was not human. He was a wooden puppet given the semblance of life by an ancient sorcery. By dint of propinquity, over many centuries a considerable essence of humanity had been absorbed into his fine-grained body, but attention to his own appearance or indeed vanity of any sort was still not part of his persona.

Sir Hereward, for the other part, had a good measure of vanity and in fact the raising of the three-barred visor of his helmet almost certainly had more to do with an approaching apple seller of comely appearance than it did with a desire for clear communication to Mister Fitz.

The duo were riding south on a road that had once been paved and gloried in the name of the Southwest Toll Extension of the Lesser Trunk. But its heyday was long ago, the road being even older than Mister Fitz. Few paved stretches remained, but the tightly compacted understructure still provided a better surface than the rough soil of the fields to either side.

The political identification of these fallow pastures and the occasional once-coppiced wood they passed was not clear to either Sir Hereward or Mister Fitz, despite several attempts to ascertain said identification from the few travelers they had encountered since leaving the city of Rhool several days before. To all intents and purposes, the land appeared to be both uninhabited and untroubled by soldiery or tax collectors and was thus a void in the sociopolitical map that Hereward held uneasily, and Fitz exactly, in their respective heads.

A quick exchange with the apple seller provided only a little further information, and also lessened Hereward's hope of some minor flirtation, for her physical beauty was sullied by a surly and depressive manner. In a voice as sullen as a three-day drizzle, the woman told them she was taking the apples to a large house that lay out of sight beyond the nearer overgrown wood. She had come from a town called Lettique or Letiki that was located beyond the lumpy ridge of blackish shale they could see a mile or so to the south. The apples in question had come from farther south still, and were not in keeping with their carrier, being particularly fine examples of a variety Mister Fitz correctly identified as emerald brights. There was no call for local apples, the young woman reluctantly explained. The fruits and vegetables from the distant oasis of Shûme were always preferred, if they could be obtained. Which, for the right price, they nearly always could be, regardless of season.

Hereward and Fitz rode in silence for a few minutes after parting company with the apple seller, the young knight looking back not once but twice as if he could not believe that such a vision of loveliness could house such an unfriendly soul. Finding the young woman did not bother to look back at all, Hereward cleared his throat and, without raising his visor, spoke.

"It appears we are on the right road, though she spoke of Shumey and not Shome."

Fitz looked up at the sky, where the sun was beginning to lose its distinct shape and ooze red into the shabby grey clouds that covered the horizon.

"A minor variation in pronunciation," he said. "Should we stop in Lettique for the night, or ride on?"

"Stop," said Hereward. "My rear is not polished sandalwood, and it needs soaking in a very hot bath enhanced with several soothing essences . . . ah . . . that was one of your leading questions, wasn't it?"

"The newspaper in Rhool spoke of an alliance against Shûme," said Mister Fitz carefully, in a manner that confirmed Hereward's suspicion that didactic discourse had already begun. "It is likely that Lettique will be one of the towns arrayed against Shûme. Should the townsfolk discover we ride to Shûme in hope of employment, we might find ourselves wishing for the quiet of the fields in the night, the lack of mattresses, ale, and roasted capons there notwithstanding."

"Bah!" exclaimed Hereward, whose youth and temperament made him tend towards careless optimism. "Why should they suspect us of seeking to sign on with the burghers of Shûme?"

Mister Fitz's pumpkin-sized papier-mâché head rotated on his spindly neck, and the blobs of blue paint that marked the pupils of his eyes looked up and down, taking in Sir Hereward from toe to head: from his gilt-spurred boots to his gold-chased helmet. In between boots and helm were Hereward's second-best buff coat, the sleeves still embroidered with the complicated silver tracery that proclaimed him as the Master Artillerist of the city of Jeminero. Not that said city was any longer in existence, as for the past three years it had been no more than a mass grave sealed with the rubble of its once-famous walls. Around the coat was a frayed but still quite golden sash, over that a rare and expensive Carnithian leather baldric and belt with two beautifully ornamented (but no less functional for that) wheel-lock pistols thrust through said belt. Hereward's longer-barreled and only slightly less ornamented cavalry pistols were holstered on either side of his saddle horn, his sabre with its sharkskin grip and gleaming hilt of gilt brass hung in its scabbard from the rear left quarter of his saddle, and his sighting telescope was secured inside its leather case on the right rear quarter.

Mister Fitz's mount, of course, carried all the more mundane items required by their travels. All three feet six and a half inches of him (four foot three with the hat) was perched upon a yoke across his mount's back that secured the two large panniers that were needed to transport tent and bedding, washing and shaving gear, and a large assortment of outdoor kitchen utensils. Not to mention the small but surprisingly expandable sewing desk that contained the tools and devices of Mister Fitz's own peculiar art.

"Shûme is a city, and rich," said Fitz patiently. "The surrounding settlements are mere towns, both smaller and poorer, who are reportedly planning to go to war against their wealthy neighbor. You are obviously a soldier for hire, and a self-evidently expensive one at that. Therefore, you must be en route to Shûme."

Hereward did not answer immediately, as was his way,

while he worked at overcoming his resentment at being told what to do. He worked at it because Mister Fitz had been telling him what to do since he was four years old and also because he knew that, as usual, Fitz was right. It would be foolish to stop in Lettique.

"I suppose that they might even attempt to hire us," he said, as they topped the low ridge, shale crunching under their mounts' talons.

Hereward looked down at a wasted valley of underperforming pastures filled either with sickly-looking crops or passive groups of too-thin cattle. A town—presumably Lettique—lay at the other end of the valley. It was not an impressive ville, being a collection of perhaps three or four hundred mostly timber and painted-plaster houses within the bounds of a broken-down wall to the west and a dry ravine, that might have once held a river, to the east. An imposing, dozen-spired temple in the middle of the town was the only indication that at some time Lettique had seen more provident days.

"Do you wish to take employment in a poor town?" asked Mister Fitz. One of his responsibilities was to advise and positively influence Hereward, but he did not make decisions for him.

"No, I don't think so," replied the knight slowly. "Though it does make me recall my thought . . . the one that was with me before we were interrupted by that dismal apple seller."

"You asked if I ever wondered at the nature of the world," prompted Fitz.

"I think what I actually intended to say," said Hereward, "is 'do you ever wonder why we become involved in events that are rather more than less of importance to rather more than less people?' As in the various significant battles, sieges, and so forth in which we have played no small part. I fully comprehend that in some cases the events have stemmed from the peculiar responsibilities we shoulder, but not in all cases. And that being so, and given my desire for a period of quiet, perhaps I should consider taking service with some poor town."

"Do you really desire a period of quiet?" asked Mister Fitz.

"Sometimes I think so. I should certainly like a time where I might reflect upon what it is I do want. It would also be rather pleasant to meet women who are not witch-agents, fellow officers, or enemies—or who have been pressed into service as powder monkeys or are soaked in blood from tending the wounded."

"Perhaps Shûme will offer some relative calm," said Mister Fitz. "By all accounts it is a fine city, and even if war is in the offing, it could be soon finished if Shûme's opponents are of a standard that I can see in Lettique."

"You observe troops?" asked Hereward. He drew his telescope, and carefully leaning on his mount's neck to avoid discomfort from the bony ridges (which, even though regularly filed down and fitted with leather stocks, were not to be ignored), looked through it at the town. "Ah, I see. Sixty pike and two dozen musketeers in the square by the temple, of no uniform equipment or harness. Under the instruction of a portly individual in a wine-dark tunic who appears as uncertain as his troops as to the drill."

"I doubt that Shûme has much to fear," said Mister Fitz. "It is odd, however, that a town like Lettique would dare to strike against such a powerful neighbor. I wonder . . ."

"What?" asked Hereward as he replaced his telescope.

"I wonder if it is a matter of necessity. The river is dry. The wheat is very thin, too thin this close to harvest. The cattle show very little flesh on their ribs. I see no sign of any other economic activity. Fear and desperation may be driving this mooted war, not greed or rivalry. Also . . ."

Mister Fitz's long, pale blue tongue darted out to taste the air, the ruby stud in the middle of what had once been a length of stippled leather catching the pallid sunlight.

"Their godlet is either asleep or . . . mmm . . . comatose in this dimension. Very strange."

"Their god is dead?"

"Not dead," said Mister Fitz. "When an other-dimensional entity dies, another always moves in quickly enough. No . . . definitely present, but quiescent."

"Do you wish to make a closer inquiry?"

Hereward had not missed the puppet's hand tapping the pannier that contained his sewing desk, an instinctive movement Mister Fitz made when contemplating sorcerous action.

"Not for the present," said Mister Fitz, lifting his hand to grasp once again his mount's steering chains.

"Then we will skirt the town and continue," announced Hereward. "We'll leave the road near those three dead trees."

"There are many trees that might be fairly described as dead or dying," remarked Fitz. "And several in clumps of three. Do you mean the somewhat orange-barked trio over yonder?"

"I do," said Hereward.

They left the road at the clump of trees and rode in silence through the dry fields, most of which were not even under attempted cultivation. There were also several derelict farmhouses, barns, and cattle yards, the level of decay suggesting that the land had been abandoned only in recent years.

Halfway along the valley, where the land rose to a slight hill that might have its origin in a vast and ancient burial mound, Hereward reined in his mount and looked back at the town through his telescope.

"Still drilling," he remarked. "I had half thought that they might dispatch some cavalry to bicker with us. But I see no mounts."

"I doubt they can afford the meat for battlemounts," said Mister Fitz. "Or grain for horses, for that matter."

"There is an air gate in the northeastern temple spire," said Hereward, rebalancing his telescope to get a steadier view. "There might be a moonshade roost behind it."

"If their god is absent, none of the ancient weapons will serve them," said Mister Fitz. "But it would be best to be careful, come nightfall. Lettique is reportedly not the only town arrayed against Shûme. The others may be in a more vigorous condition, with wakeful gods."

Hereward replaced his telescope and turned his mount to the north, Mister Fitz following his lead. They did not speak further, but rode on, mostly at the steady pace that Hereward's Zowithian riding instructor had called "the lope," occasionally urging their mounts to the faster "jag." In this fashion, several miles passed quickly. As the sun's last third began to slip beneath the horizon, they got back on the old road again, to climb out of the wasted valley of Lettique and across yet another of the shale ridges that erupted out of the land like powder-pitted keloid scars, all grey and humped.

The valley that lay beyond the second ridge was entirely different from the faded fields behind the two travelers. In the warm twilight, they saw a checkerboard of green and gold, full fields of wheat interspersed with meadows heavily stocked with fat cattle. A broad river wound through from the east, spilling its banks in several places into fecund wetlands that were rich with waterfowl. Several small hillocks in the valley were covered in apple trees, dark foliage heavily flecked with the bright green of vast quantities of emerald fruit. There were citrus groves too, stone-walled clumps of smaller trees laden with lemons or limes, and only a hundred yards away, a group of six trees bearing the rare and exquisite blue-skinned fruit known as *serqa*, which was normally only found in drier climes.

"A most pleasant vista," said Hereward. A small smile curled his lip and touched his eyes, the expression of a man who sees something that he likes.

Shûme itself was a mile away, built on a rise in the ground in the northwestern corner of the valley, where the river spread into a broad lake that lapped the city's western walls. From the number of deep-laden boats that were even now rowing home to the jetties that thronged the shore, the lake was as well stocked with fish as the valley was with livestock and produce.

Most of the city's buildings were built of an attractively pale yellow stone, with far fewer timber constructions than was usual for a place that Hereward reckoned must hold at least five thousand citizens.

Shûme was also walled in the same pale stone, but of greater interest to Hereward were the more recent earthworks that had been thrown up in front of the old wall. A zigzag line of re-vetments encircled the city, with respectably large bastions at each end on the lakeshore. A cursory telescopic examination showed several bronze demicannon on the bastions and various lesser pieces of ordnance clustered in groups at various strong points along the earthworks. Both bastions had small groups of soldiery in attendance on the cannon, and there were pairs of sentries every twenty or thirty yards along the earthen ramparts and a score or more walked the stone walls behind.

"There is certainly a professional in charge here," observed Hereward. "I expect . . . yes . . . a cavalry piquet issues from yonder orchard. Twelve horse troopers under the notional com-mand of a whey-faced cornet."

"Not commonplace troopers," added Mister Fitz. "Dercian keplars."

"Ah," said Hereward. He replaced his telescope, leaned back a little and across, and, using his left hand, loosened his sabre so that an inch of blade projected from the scabbard.

"They are in employment, so they should give us the benefit of truce."

"They should," conceded Mister Fitz, but he reached inside his robe to grasp some small item concealed under the cloth. With his other hand he touched the brim of his hat, releasing a finely woven veil that covered his face. To casual inspection he now looked like a shrouded child, wearing peculiar papery gloves. Self-motivated puppets were not great objects of fear in most quarters of the world. They had once been numerous, and some few score still walked the earth, almost all of them entertainers, some of them long remembered in song and story.

Mister Fitz was not one of those entertainers.

"If it comes to it, spare the cornet," said Hereward, who remembered well what it was like to be a very junior officer, whey-faced or not.

Mister Fitz did not answer. Hereward knew as well as he that if it came to fighting, and the arts the puppet employed, there would be no choosing who among those who opposed them lived or died.

The troop rode towards the duo at a canter, slowing to a walk as they drew nearer and their horses began to balk as they scented the battlemounts. Hereward raised his hand in greeting and the cornet shouted a command, the column extending to a line, then halting within an easy pistol shot. Hereward watched the troop sergeant, who rode forward beyond the line for a better look, then wheeled back at speed towards the cornet. If the Dercians were to break their oath, the sergeant would fell her officer first.

But the sergeant halted without drawing a weapon and spoke to the cornet quietly. Hereward felt a slight easing of his own breath, though he showed no outward sign of it and did not relax. Nor did Mister Fitz withdraw his hand from under

his robes. Hereward knew that his companion's molded papier-
mâché fingers held an esoteric needle, a sliver of some arcane
stuff that no human hand could grasp with impunity.

The cornet listened and spoke quite sharply to the sergeant,
turning his horse around so that he could make his point forcefully to the troopers as well. Hereward only caught some of
the words, but it seemed that despite his youth, the officer was
rather more commanding than he had expected, reminding the
Dercians that their oaths of employment overrode any private
or societal vendettas they might wish to undertake.

When he had finished, the cornet shouted, "Dismount! Sergeant, walk the horses!"

The officer remained mounted, wheeling back to approach
Hereward. He saluted as he reined in a cautious distance from
the battlemounts, evidently not trusting either the creatures'
blinkers and mouth-cages or his own horse's fears.

"Welcome to Shûme!" he called. "I am Cornet Misolu. May
I ask your names and direction, if you please?"

"I am Sir Hereward of the High Pale, artillerist for hire."

"And I am Fitz, also of the High Pale, aide de camp to Sir
Hereward."

"Welcome . . . uh . . . sirs," said Misolu. "Be warned that
war has been declared upon Shûme, and all who pass through
must declare their allegiances and enter certain . . . um . . ."

"I believe the usual term is 'undertakings,'" said Mister Fitz.

"Undertakings," echoed Misolu. He was very young. Two
bright spots of embarrassment burned high on his cheekbones,
just visible under the four bars of his lobster-tailed helmet, which
was a little too large for him, even with the extra padding, some
of which had come a little undone around the brow.

"We are free lances, and seek hire in Shûme, Cornet Misolu," said Hereward. "We will give the common undertakings

if your city chooses to contract us. For the moment, we swear to hold our peace, reserving the right to defend ourselves should we be attacked."

"Your word is accepted, Sir Hereward, and . . . um . . ."

"Mister Fitz," said Hereward, as the puppet said merely, "Fitz."

"Mister Fitz."

The cornet chivvied his horse diagonally closer to Hereward, and added, "You may rest assured that my Dercians will remain true to *their* word, though Sergeant Xikoliz spoke of some feud their . . . er . . . entire people have with you."

The curiosity in the cornet's voice could not be easily denied, and spoke as much of the remoteness of Shûme as it did of the young officer's naïveté.

"It is a matter arising from a campaign several years past," said Hereward. "Mister Fitz and I were serving the Heriat of Jhaqa, who sought to redirect the Dercian spring migration elsewhere than through her own prime farmlands. In the last battle of that campaign, a small force penetrated to the Dercians' rolling temple and . . . ah . . . blew it up with a specially made petard. Their godlet, thus discommoded, withdrew to its winter housing in the Dercian steppe, wreaking great destruction among its chosen people as it went."

"I perceive you commanded that force, sir?"

Hereward shook his head.

"No, I am an artillerist. Captain Kasvik commanded. He was slain as we retreated—another few minutes and he would have won clear. However, I did make the petard, and . . . Mister Fitz assisted our entry to the temple and our escape. Hence the Dercians' feud."

Hereward looked sternly at Mister Fitz as he spoke, hoping to make it clear that this was not a time for the puppet to exhibit his tendency for exactitude and truthfulness. Captain Kasvik had in fact been killed before they even reached the rolling temple, but it had served his widow and family better for Kasvik to be a hero, so Hereward had made him one. Only Mister Fitz and one other survivor of the raid knew otherwise.

Not that Hereward and Fitz considered the rolling temple action a victory, as their intent had been to force the Dercian godlet to withdraw a distance unimaginably more vast than the mere five hundred leagues to its winter temple.

The ride to the city was uneventful, though Hereward could not help but notice that Cornet Misolu ordered his troop to remain in place and keep watch, while he alone escorted the visitors, indicating that the young officer was not absolutely certain the Dercians would hold to their vows.

There was a zigzag entry through the earthwork ramparts, where they were held up for several minutes in the business of passwords and responses (all told aside in quiet voices, Hereward noted with approval), their names being recorded in an enormous ledger and passes written out and sealed allowing them to enter the city proper.

These same passes were inspected closely under lantern light, only twenty yards farther on by the guards outside the city gate—which was closed, as the sun had finally set. However, they were admitted through a sally port and here Misolu took his leave, after giving directions to an inn that met Hereward's requirements: suitable stabling and food for the battle-mounts; that it not be the favourite of the Dercians or any other of the mercenary troops who had signed on in preparation for Shûme's impending war; and fine food and wine, not just small beer and ale. The cornet also gave directions to the citadel, not that this was really necessary as its four towers were clearly visible, and advised Hereward and Fitz that there was no point going there until the morning, for the governing council was in session and so no one in authority could hire him until at least the third bell after sunrise.

The streets of Shûme were paved and drained, and Hereward smiled again at the absence of the fetid stench so common to places where large numbers of people dwelt together. He was looking forward to a bath, a proper meal, and a fine feather bed, with the prospect of well-paid and not too onerous employment commencing on the morrow.

"There is the inn," remarked Mister Fitz, pointing down one of the narrower side streets, though it was still broad enough for the two battlemounts to stride abreast. "The sign of the golden barleycorn. Appropriate enough for a city with such fine farmland."

They rode into the inn's yard, which was clean and wide and did indeed boast several of the large iron-barred cages used to stable battlemounts complete with meat canisters and feeding chutes rigged in place above the cages. One of the four ostlers present ran ahead to open two cages and lower the chutes, and the other three assisted Hereward to unload the panniers. Mister Fitz took his sewing desk and stood aside, the small rosewood-and-silver box under his arm provoking neither recognition nor alarm. The ostlers were similarly incurious about Fitz himself, almost certainly evidence that self-motivated puppets still came to entertain the townsfolk from time to time.

Hereward led the way into the inn, but halted just before he entered as one of the battlemounts snorted at some annoyance. Glancing back, he saw that it was of no concern, and the gates were closed, but in halting he had kept hold of the door as someone else tried to open it from the other side. Hereward pushed to help and the door flung open, knocking the person on the inside back several paces against a table, knocking over an empty bottle that smashed upon the floor.

"Unfortunate," muttered Mister Fitz, as he saw that the person so inconvenienced was not only a soldier, but wore the red sash of a junior officer, and was a woman.

"I do apolog—" Hereward began to say. He stopped, not only because the woman was talking, but because he had looked at her. She was as tall as he was, with ash-blond hair tied in a queue at the back, her hat in her left hand. She was also very beautiful, at least to Hereward, who had grown up with women who ritually cut their flesh. To others, her attractiveness might be considered marred by the scar that ran from the corner of her left eye out towards the ear and then cut back again towards the lower part of her nose.

"You are clumsy, sir!"

Hereward stared at her for just one second too long before attempting to speak again.

"I am most—"

"You see something you do not like, I think?" interrupted the woman. "Perhaps you have not served with females? Or is it my face you do not care for?"

"You are very beautiful," said Hereward, even as he realized it was entirely the wrong thing to say, either to a woman he had just met or an officer he had just run into.

"You mock me!" swore the woman. Her blue eyes shone more fiercely, but her face paled, and the scar grew more livid. She clapped her broad-brimmed hat on her head and straightened to her full height, with the hat standing perhaps an inch over Hereward. "You shall answer for that!"

"I do not mock you," said Hereward quietly. "I have served with men, women . . . and eunuchs, for that matter. Furthermore, tomorrow morning I shall be signing on as at least colonel of artillery, and a colonel may not fight a duel with a lieutenant. I am most happy to apologize, but I cannot meet you."

"Cannot or will not?" sneered the woman. "You are not

yet a colonel in Shûme's service, I believe, but just a mercenary braggart."

Hereward sighed and looked around the common room. Misolu had spoken truly that the inn was not a mercenary favourite. But there were several officers of Shûme's regular service or militia, all of them looking on with great attention.

"Very well," he snapped. "It is foolishness, for I intended no offence. When and where?"

"Immediately," said the woman. "There is a garden a little way behind this inn. It is lit by lanterns in the trees, and has a lawn."

"How pleasant," said Hereward. "What is your name, madam?"

"I am Lieutenant Jessaye of the Temple Guard of Shûme. And you are?"

"I am Sir Hereward of the High Pale."

"And your friends, Sir Hereward?"

"I have only this moment arrived in Shûme, Lieutenant, and so cannot yet name any friends. Perhaps someone in this room will stand by me, should you wish a second. My companion, whom I introduce to you now, is known as Mister Fitz. He is a surgeon—among other things—and I expect he will accompany us."

"I am pleased to meet you, Lieutenant," said Mister Fitz. He doffed his hat and veil, sending a momentary frisson of small twitches among all in the room save Hereward.

Jessaye nodded back but did not answer Fitz. Instead she spoke to Hereward.

"I need no second. Should you wish to employ sabres, I must send for mine."

"I have a sword in my gear," said Hereward. "If you will allow me a few minutes to fetch it?"

"The garden lies behind the stables," said Jessaye. "I will await you there. Pray do not be too long."

Inclining her head but not doffing her hat, she stalked past and out the door.

"An inauspicious beginning," said Fitz.

"Very," said Hereward gloomily. "On several counts. Where is the innkeeper? I must change and fetch my sword."

THE GARDEN WAS VERY PRETTY. RAILED IN IRON, IT WAS not gated, and so accessible to all the citizens of Shûme. A wandering path led through a grove of lantern-hung trees to the specified lawn, which was oval and easily fifty yards from end to end, making the centre rather a long way from the lantern light, and hence quite shadowed. A small crowd of persons who had previously been in the inn were gathered on one side of the lawn. Lieutenant Jessaye stood in the middle, naked blade in hand.

"Do be careful, Hereward," said Fitz quietly, observing the woman flex her knees and practice a stamping attack ending in a lunge. "She looks to be very quick."

"She is an officer of their temple guard," said Hereward in a hoarse whisper. "Has their god imbued her with any particular vitality or puissance?"

"No, the godlet does not seem to be a martial entity," said Fitz. "I shall have to undertake some investigations presently, as to exactly what it is—"

"Sir Hereward! Here at last."

Hereward grimaced as Jessaye called out. He had changed as quickly as he could, into a very fine suit of split-sleeved white showing the yellow shirt beneath, with gold ribbons at the cuffs, shoulders, and front lacing, with similarly cut bloomers of yellow showing white breeches, with silver ribbons at the knees, artfully displayed through the side-notches of his second-best boots.

Jessaye, in contrast, had merely removed her uniform coat and stood in her shirt, blue waistcoat, leather breeches, and unadorned black thigh boots folded over below the knee. Had the circumstances been otherwise, Hereward would have paused to admire the sight she presented and perhaps offer a compliment.

Instead he suppressed a sigh, strode forward, drew his sword, and threw the scabbard aside.

"I am here, Lieutenant, and I am ready. Incidentally, is this small matter to be concluded by one or perhaps both of us dying?"

"The city forbids duels to the death, Sir Hereward," replied Jessaye. "Though accidents do occur."

"What, then, is to be the sign for us to cease our remonstrance?"

"Blood," said Jessaye. She flicked her sword towards the onlookers. "Visible to those watching."

Hereward nodded slowly. In this light, there would need to be a lot of blood before the onlookers could see it. He bowed his head but did not lower his eyes, then raised his sword to the guard position.

Jessaye was fast. She immediately thrust at his neck, and though Hereward parried, he had to step back. She carried through to lunge in a different line, forcing him back again with a more awkward parry, removing all opportunity for Hereward to riposte or counter. For a minute they danced, their swords darting up, down and across, clashing together only to move again almost before the sound reached the audience.

In that minute, Hereward took stock of Jessaye's style and action. She was very fast, but so was he, much faster than anyone would expect from his size and build, and, as always, he had not shown just how truly quick he could be. Jessaye's wrist was strong and supple, and she could change both attacking and defensive lines with great ease. But her style was rigid, a variant of an old school Hereward had studied in his youth.

On her next lunge—which came exactly where he anticipated—Hereward didn't parry but stepped aside and past the blade. He felt her sword whisper by his ribs as he angled his own blade over it and with the leading edge of the point, he cut Jessaye above the right elbow to make a long, very shallow slice that he intended should bleed copiously without inflicting any serious harm.

Jessaye stepped back but did not lower her guard. Hereward quickly called out, "Blood!"

Jessaye took a step forward and Hereward stood ready for another attack. Then the lieutenant bit her lip and stopped, holding her arm towards the lantern light so she could more clearly see the wound. Blood was already soaking through the linen shirt, a dark and spreading stain upon the cloth.

"You have bested me," she said, and thrust her sword point first into the grass before striding forward to offer her gloved hand to Hereward. He too grounded his blade, and took her hand as they bowed to each other.

A slight stinging low on his side caused Hereward to look down. There was a two-inch cut in his shirt, and small beads of blood were blossoming there. He did not let go Jessaye's fingers, but pointed at his ribs with his left hand.

"I believe we are evenly matched. I hope we may have no cause to bicker further?"

"I trust not," said Jessaye quietly. "I regret the incident. Were it not for the presence of some of my fellows, I should not have caviled at your apology, sir. But you understand . . . a reputation is not easily won, nor kept . . ."

"I do understand," said Hereward. "Come, let Mister Fitz attend your cut. Perhaps you will then join me for a small repast?"

Jessaye shook her head.

"I go on duty soon. A stitch or two and a bandage is all I have time for. Perhaps we shall meet again."

"It is my earnest hope that we do," said Hereward. Reluctantly, he opened his grasp. Jessaye's hand lingered in his palm for several moments before she slowly raised it, stepped back, and doffed her hat to offer a full bow. Hereward returned it, straightening up as Mister Fitz hurried over, carrying a large leather case as if it were almost too heavy for him, one of his standard acts of misdirection, for the puppet was at least as strong as Hereward, if not stronger.

"Attend to Lieutenant Jessaye, if you please, Mister Fitz," said Hereward. "I am going back to the inn to have a cup . . . or two . . . of wine."

"Your own wound needs no attention?" asked Fitz as he set his bag down and indicated to Jessaye to sit by him.

"A scratch," said Hereward. He bowed to Jessaye again and walked away, ignoring the polite applause of the onlookers, who were drifting forward either to talk to Jessaye or gawp at the blood on her sleeve.

"I may take a stroll," called out Mister Fitz after Hereward. "But I shan't be longer than an hour."

MISTER FITZ WAS TRUE TO HIS WORD, RETURNING A FEW minutes after the citadel bell had sounded the third hour of the evening. Hereward had bespoken a private chamber and was dining alone there, accompanied only by his thoughts.

"The god of Shûme," said Fitz, without preamble. "Have you heard anyone mention its name?"

Hereward shook his head and poured another measure from the silver jug with the swan's beak spout. Like many things he had found in Shûme, the knight liked the inn's silverware.

"They call their godlet Tanesh," said Fitz. "But its true name is Pralqornrah-Tanish-Kvaxixob."

"As difficult to say or spell, I wager," said Hereward. "I commend the short form, it shows common sense. What of it?"

"It is on the list," said Fitz.

Hereward bit the edge of his pewter cup and put it down too hard, slopping wine upon the table.

"You're certain? There can be no question?"

Fitz shook his head. "After I had doctored the young woman, I went down to the lake and took a slide of the god's essence—it was quite concentrated in the water, easy enough to yield a sample. You may compare it with the record, if you wish."

He proffered a finger-long, inch-wide strip of glass that was striated in many different bands of color. Hereward accepted it reluctantly, and with it a fat, square book that Fitz slid across the table. The book was open at a hand-tinted color plate, the illustration showing a sequence of color bands.

"It is the same," agreed the knight, his voice heavy with regret. "I suppose it is fortunate we have not yet signed on, though I doubt they will see what we do as being purely a matter of defense."

"They do not know what they harbor here," said Fitz.

"It is a pleasant city," said Hereward, taking up his cup again to take a large gulp of the slightly sweet wine. "In a pretty valley. I had thought I could grow more than accustomed to Shûme—and its people."

"The bounty of Shûme, all its burgeoning crops, its healthy stock and people, is an unintended result of their godlet's predation upon the surrounding lands," said Fitz. "Pralqornrah is one of the class of cross-dimensional parasites that is most dangerous. Unchecked, in time it will suck the vital essence out of all the land beyond its immediate demesne. The deserts of Balkash are the work of a similar being, over six millennia. This one has only been embedded here for two hundred years—you have seen the results beyond this valley."

"Six millennia is a long time," said Hereward, taking yet another gulp. The wine was strong as well as sweet, and he felt the need of it. "A desert might arise in that time without the interference of the gods."

"It is not just the fields and the river that Pralqornrah feeds upon," said Fitz. "The people outside this valley suffer too. Babes unborn, strong men and women declining before their prime . . . this godlet slowly sucks the essence from all life."

"They could leave," said Hereward. The wine was making him feel both sleepy and mulish. "I expect many have already left to seek better lands. The rest could be resettled, the lands left uninhabited to feed the godlet. Shûme could continue as an oasis. What if another desert grows around it? They occur in nature, do they not?"

"I do not think you fully comprehend the matter," said Fitz. "Pralqornrah is a most comprehensive feeder. Its energistic threads will spread farther and faster the longer it exists here, and it in turn will grow more powerful and much more difficult to remove. A few millennia hence, it might be too strong to combat."

"I am only talking," said Hereward, not without some bitterness. "You need not waste your words to bend my reason. I do not even need to understand anything beyond the salient fact: this godlet is on the list."

"Yes," said Mister Fitz. "It is on the list."

Hereward bent his head for a long, silent moment. Then he pushed back his chair and reached across for his sabre. Drawing it, he placed the blade across his knees. Mister Fitz handed him a whetstone and a small flask of light, golden oil. The knight oiled the stone and began to hone the sabre's blade. A repetitive rasp was the only sound in the room for many minutes, till he finally put the stone aside and wiped the blade clean with a soft piece of deerskin.

"When?"

"Fourteen minutes past the midnight hour is optimum," replied Mister Fitz. "Presuming I have calculated its intrusion density correctly."

"It is manifest in the temple?"

Fitz nodded.

"Where is the temple, for that matter? Only the citadel stands out above the roofs of the city."

"It is largely underground," said Mister Fitz. "I have found a side entrance, which should not prove difficult. At some point beyond that there is some form of arcane barrier—I have not been able to ascertain its exact nature, but I hope to unpick it without trouble."

"Is the side entrance guarded? And the interior?"

"Both," said Fitz. Something about his tone made Hereward fix the puppet with an inquiring look.

"The side door has two guards," continued Fitz. "The interior watch is of ten or eleven . . . led by the Lieutenant Jessaye you met earlier."

Hereward stood up, the sabre loose in his hand, and turned away from Fitz.

"Perhaps we shall not need to fight her . . . or her fellows."

Fitz did not answer, which was answer enough.

THE SIDE DOOR TO THE TEMPLE WAS UNMARKED AND AP-peared no different than the other simple wooden doors that lined the empty street, most of them adorned with signs marking them as the shops of various tradesmen, with smoke-grimed night lamps burning dimly above the sign. The door Fitz indicated was painted a pale violet and had neither sign nor lamp.

"Time to don the brassards and make the declaration," said the puppet. He looked up and down the street, making sure that all was quiet, before handing Hereward a broad silk armband five fingers wide. It was embroidered with sorcerous thread that shed only a little less light than the lantern above the neighboring shop door. The symbol the threads wove was one that had once been familiar the world over but was now unlikely to be recognized by anyone save a historian . . . or a god.

Hereward slipped the brassard over his left glove and up his thick coat sleeve, spreading it out above the elbow. The suit of white and yellow was once again packed, and for this expedition the knight had chosen to augment his helmet and buff coat with a dented but still eminently serviceable back- and breastplate, the steel blackened by tannic acid to a dark grey. He had already primed, loaded, and spanned his two wheel-lock pistols, which were thrust through his belt; his sabre was sheathed at his side; and a lozenge-sectioned, armour-punching bodkin was in his left boot.

Mister Fitz wore his sewing desk upon his back, like a wooden backpack. He had already been through its numerous small drawers and containers and selected particular items that were now tucked into the inside pockets of his coat, ready for immediate use.

"I wonder why we bother with this mummery," grumbled Hereward. But he stood at attention as Fitz put on his own brassard, and the knight carefully repeated the short phrase uttered by his companion. Though both had recited it many times, and it was clear as bright type in their minds, they spoke carefully and with great concentration, in sharp contrast to Hereward's remark about mummery.

"In the name of the Council of the Treaty for the Safety of the World, acting under the authority granted by the Three Empires, the Seven Kingdoms, the Palatine Regency, the Jessar

Republic, and the Forty Lesser Realms, we declare ourselves agents of the Council. We identify the godlet manifested in this city of Shûme as Pralqornrah-Tanish-Kvaxixob, a listed entity under the Treaty. Consequently, the said godlet and all those who assist it are deemed to be enemies of the World and the Council authorizes us to pursue any and all actions necessary to banish, repel, or exterminate the said godlet."

Neither felt it necessary to change this ancient text to reflect the fact that only one of the three empires was still extant in any fashion; that the seven kingdoms were now twenty or more small states; the Palatine Regency was a political fiction, its once broad lands under two fathoms of water; the Jessar Republic was now neither Jessar in ethnicity nor a republic; and perhaps only a handful of the Forty Lesser Realms resembled their antecedent polities in any respect. But for all that the states that had made it were vanished or diminished, the Treaty for the Safety of the World was still held to be in operation, if only by the Council that administered and enforced it.

"Are you ready?" asked Fitz.

Hereward drew his sabre and moved into position to the left of the door. Mister Fitz reached into his coat and drew out an esoteric needle. Hereward knew better than to try to look at the needle directly, but in the reflection of his blade, he could see a four-inch line of something intensely violet writhe in Fitz's hand. Even the reflection made him feel as if he might at any moment be unstitched from the world, so he angled the blade away.

At that moment, Fitz touched the door with the needle and made three short plucking motions. On the last motion, without any noise or fuss, the door wasn't there anymore. There was only a wood-paneled corridor leading down into the ground and two very surprised temple guards, who were still leaning on their halberds.

Before Hereward could even begin to move, Fitz's hand twitched across and up several times. The lanterns on their brass stands every six feet along the corridor flickered and flared violet for a fraction of a second. Hereward blinked, and the guards were gone, as were the closest three lanterns and their stands.

Only a single drop of molten brass, no bigger than a tear, remained. It sizzled on the floor for a second, then all was quiet.

The puppet stalked forward, cupping his left hand over the needle in his right, obscuring its troublesome sight behind his fingers. Hereward followed close behind, alert for any enemy that might be resistant to Fitz's sorcery.

The corridor was a hundred yards long by Hereward's estimation, and slanted sharply down, making him think about having to fight back up it, which would be no easy task, made more difficult as the floor and walls were damp, drops of water oozing out between the floorboards and dripping from the seams of the wall paneling. There was cold, wet stone behind the timber, Hereward knew. He could feel the cold air rippling off it, a chill that no amount of fine timber could cloak.

The corridor ended at what appeared from a distance to be a solid wall, but closer to was merely the dark back of a heavy tapestry. Fitz edged silently around it, had a look, and returned to beckon Hereward in.

There was a large antechamber or waiting room beyond, sparsely furnished with a slim desk and several well-upholstered armchairs. The desk and chairs each had six legs, the extra limbs arranged closely at the back, a fashion Hereward supposed was some homage to the godlet's physical manifestation. The walls were hung with several tapestries depicting the city at various stages in its history.

Given the depth underground and the proximity of the lake, great efforts must have been made to waterproof and beautify the walls, floor, and ceiling, but there was still an army of little dots of mold advancing from every corner, blackening the white plaster and tarnishing the gilded cornices and decorations.

Apart from the tapestry-covered exit, there were three doors. Two were of a usual size, though they were elaborately carved with obscure symbols and had brass, or perhaps even gold, handles. The one on the wall opposite the tapestry corridor was entirely different: it was a single ten-foot-by-six-foot slab of ancient marble veined with red lead, and it would have been better situated sitting on top of a significant memorial or some potentate's coffin.

Mister Fitz went to each of the carved doors, his blue tongue flickering in and out, sampling the air.

"No one close," he reported, before approaching the marble slab. He actually licked the gap between the stone and the floor, then sat for a few moments to think about what he had tasted.

Hereward kept clear, checking the other doors to see if they could be locked. Disappointed in that aim as they had neither bar nor keyhole, he sheathed his sabre and carefully and quietly picked up a desk to push against the left door and several chairs to pile against the right. They wouldn't hold, but they would give some warning of attempted ingress.

Fitz chuckled as Hereward finished his work, an unexpected noise that made the knight shiver, drop his hand to the hilt of his sabre, and quickly look around to see what had made the puppet laugh. Fitz was not easily amused, and often not by anything Hereward would consider funny.

"There is a sorcerous barrier," said Fitz. "It is immensely strong but has not perhaps been as well thought-out as it might have been. Fortuitously, I do not even need to unpick it."

The puppet reached up with his left hand and pushed the marble slab. It slid back silently, revealing another corridor, this one of more honest bare, weeping stone, rapidly turning into rough-hewn steps only a little way along.

"I'm afraid you cannot follow, Hereward," said Fitz. "The barrier is conditional, and you do not meet its requirements. It would forcibly—and perhaps harmfully—repel you if you tried to step over the lintel of this door. But I would ask you to stay here in any case, to secure our line of retreat. I should only be a short time if all goes well. You will, of course, know if all does not go well, and must save yourself as best you can. I have impressed the ostlers to rise at your command and load our gear, as I have impressed instructions into the dull minds of the battlemounts—"

"Enough, Fitz! I shall not leave without you."

"Hereward, you know that in the event of my—"

"Fitz. The quicker it were done—"

"Indeed. Be careful, child."

"Fitz!"

But the puppet had gone almost before that exasperated single word was out of Hereward's mouth.

It quickly grew cold with the passage below open. Chill, wet gusts of wind blew up and followed the knight around the room, no matter where he stood. After a few minutes trying to find a spot where he could avoid the cold breeze, Hereward took to pacing by the doors as quietly as he could. Every dozen steps or so he stopped to listen, either for Fitz's return or the sound of approaching guards.

In the event, he was mid-pace when he heard something. The sharp beat of hobnailed boots in step, approaching the left-hand door.

Hereward drew his two pistols and moved closer to the door. The handle rattled, the door began to move and encountered the desk he had pushed there. There was an exclamation and several voices spoke all at once. A heavier shove came immediately, toppling the desk as the door came partially open.

Hereward took a pace to the left and fired through the gap.

The wheel locks whirred, sparks flew, then there were two deep, simultaneous booms, the resultant echoes flattening down the screams and shouts in the corridor beyond the door, just as the conjoining clouds of blue-white smoke obscured Hereward from the guards, who were already clambering over their wounded or slain companions.

The knight thrust his pistols back through his belt and drew his sabre, to make an immediate sweeping cut at the neck of a guard who charged blindly through the smoke, his halberd thrust out in front like a blind man's cane. Man and halberd clattered to the floor. Hereward ducked under a halberd swing and slashed the next guard behind the knees, at the same time picking up one edge of the desk and flipping it upright in the path of the next two guards. They tripped over it, and Hereward stabbed them both in the back of the neck as their helmets fell forward, left-right, three inches of sabre point in and out in an instant.

A blade skidded off Hereward's cuirass and would have scored his thigh but for a quick twist away. He parried the next thrust, rolled his wrist, and slashed his attacker across the stomach, following it up with a kick as the guard reeled back, sword slack in his hand.

No attack—or any movement save for dulled writhing on the ground—followed. Hereward stepped back and surveyed the situation. Two guards were dead or dying just beyond the door. One was still to his left. Three lay around the desk. Another was hunched over by the wall, his hands pressed uselessly against the gaping wound in his gut, as he moaned the god's name over and over.

None of the guards was Jessaye, but the sound of the pistol shots at the least would undoubtedly bring more defenders of the temple.

"Seven," said Hereward. "Of a possible twelve."

He laid his sabre across a chair and reloaded his pistols,

taking powder cartridges and shot from the pocket of his coat
and a ramrod from under the barrel of one gun. Loaded, he
wound their wheel-lock mechanisms with a small spanner that
hung from a braided-leather loop on his left wrist.

Just as he replaced the pistols in his belt, the ground trembled beneath his feet, and an even colder wind came howling
out of the sunken corridor, accompanied by a cloying but not
unpleasant odor of exotic spices that also briefly made Hereward
see strange bands of color move through the air, the visions fading as the scent also passed.

Tremors, scent, and strange visions were all signs that Fitz
had joined battle with Pralqornrah-Tanish-Kvaxixob below.
There could well be other portents to come, stranger and more
unpleasant to experience.

"Be quick, Fitz," muttered Hereward, his attention momentarily focused on the downwards passage.

Even so, he caught the soft footfall of someone sneaking in,
boots left behind in the passage. He turned, pistols in hand, as
Jessaye stepped around the half-open door. Two guards came
behind her, their own pistols raised.

Before they could aim, Hereward fired and, as the smoke
and noise filled the room, threw the empty pistols at the trio,
took up his sabre, and jumped aside.

Jessaye's sword leapt into the space where he'd been. Hereward landed, turned, and parried several frenzied stabs at his
face, the swift movement of their blades sending the gun smoke
eddying in wild roils and coils. Jessaye pushed him back almost
to the other door. There, Hereward picked up a chair and used
it to fend off several blows, at the same time beginning to make
small, fast cuts at Jessaye's sword arm.

Jessaye's frenzied assault slackened as Hereward cut her badly
on the shoulder near her neck, then immediately after that on
the upper arm, across the wound he'd given her in the duel. She

cried out in pain and rage and stepped back, her right arm useless, her sword point trailing on the floor.

Instead of pressing his attack, the knight took a moment to take stock of his situation.

The two pistol-bearing guards were dead or as good as, making the tally nine. That meant there should only be two more, in addition to Jessaye, and those two were not immediately in evidence.

"You may withdraw, if you wish," said Hereward, his voice strangely loud and dull at the same time, a consequence of shooting in enclosed spaces. "I do not wish to kill you, and you cannot hold your sword."

Jessaye transferred her sword to her left hand and took a shuddering breath.

"I fight equally well with my left hand," she said, assuming the guard position as best she could, though her right arm hung at her side and blood dripped from her fingers to the floor.

She thrust immediately, perhaps hoping for surprise. Hereward ferociously beat her blade down, then stamped on it, forcing it from her grasp. He then raised the point of his sabre to her throat.

"No, you don't," he said. "Very few people do. Go, while you still live."

"I cannot," whispered Jessaye. She shut her eyes. "I have failed in my duty. I shall die with my comrades. Strike quickly."

Hereward raised his elbow and prepared to push the blade through the so-giving flesh, as he had done so many times before. But he did not. Instead he lowered his sabre and backed away around the wall.

"Quickly, I beg you," said Jessaye. She was shivering, the blood flowing faster down her arm.

"I cannot," muttered Hereward. "Or rather I do not wish to. I have killed enough today."

Jessaye opened her eyes and slowly turned to him, her face
paper white, the scar no brighter than the petal of a pink rose.
For the first time, she saw that the stone door was open, and she
gasped and looked wildly around at the bodies that littered the
floor.

"The priestess came forth? You have slain her?"

"No," said Hereward. He continued to watch Jessaye and
listen for others as he bent and picked up his pistols. They were
a present from his mother, and he had not lost them yet. "My
companion has gone within."

"But that . . . that is not possible! The barrier—"

"Mister Fitz knew of the barrier," said Hereward wearily.
He was beginning to feel the aftereffects of violent combat, and
strongly desired to be away from the visible signs of it littered
around him. "He crossed it without difficulty."

"But only the priestess can pass," said Jessaye wildly. She was
shaking more than just shivering now, as shock set in, though
she still stood upright. "A woman with child! No one and nothing else! It cannot be . . ."

Her eyes rolled back in her head, she twisted sideways, and
fell to the floor. Hereward watched her lie there for a few seconds while he attempted to regain the cold temper in which he
fought, but it would not return. He hesitated, then wiped his
sabre clean, sheathed it, then despite all better judgment, bent
over Jessaye.

She whispered something and again, and he caught the
god's name, "Tanesh," and with it a sudden onslaught of cin-
namon and cloves and ginger on his nose. He blinked, and in
that blink, she turned and struck at him with a small dagger
that had been concealed in her sleeve. Hereward had expected
something, but not the god's assistance, for the dagger was in
her right hand, which he'd thought useless. He grabbed her wrist

but could only slow rather than stop the blow. Jessaye struck true, the dagger entering the armhole of the cuirass, to bite deep into his chest.

Hereward left the dagger there and merely pushed Jessaye back. The smell of spices faded, and her arm was limp once more. She did not resist, but lay there quite still, only her eyes moving as she watched Hereward sit down next to her. He sighed heavily, a few flecks of blood already spraying out with his breath, evidence that her dagger was lodged in his lung, though he already knew that from the pain that impaled him with every breath.

"There is no treasure below," said Jessaye quietly. "Only the godlet, and his priestess."

"We did not come for treasure," said Hereward. He spat blood on the floor. "Indeed, I had thought we would winter here, in good employment. But your god is proscribed, and so . . ."

"Proscribed? I don't . . . who . . ."

"By the Council of the Treaty for the Safety of the World," said Hereward. "Not that anyone remembers that name. If we are remembered, it is from the stories that tell of . . . god-slayers."

"I know the stories," whispered Jessaye. "And not just stories . . . we were taught to beware the god-slayers. But they are always women, barren women, with witch-scars on their faces. Not a man and a puppet. That is why the barrier . . . the barrier stops all but gravid women . . ."

Hereward paused to wipe a froth of blood from his mouth before he could answer.

"Fitz has been my companion since I was three years old. He was called Mistress Fitz then, as my nurse-bodyguard. When I turned ten, I wanted a male companion, and so I began to call him Mister Fitz. But whether called Mistress or Master, I believe

Fitz is nurturing an offshoot of his spiritual essence in some
form of pouch upon his person. In time he will make a body for
it to inhabit. The process takes several hundred years."

"But you . . ."

Jessaye's whisper was almost too quiet to hear.

"I am a mistake . . . the Witches of Har are not barren, that
is just a useful tale. But they do only bear daughters . . . save
the once. I am the only son of a witch born these thousand
years. My mother is one of the Mysterious Three who rule the
Witches, last remnant of the Council. Fitz was made by that
Council, long ago, as a weapon to fight malignant gods. The
more recent unwanted child became a weapon too, puppet and
boy flung out to do our duty in the world. A duty that has
carried me here . . . to my great regret."

No answer came to this bubbling, blood-infused speech.
Hereward looked across at Jessaye and saw that her chest no longer rose and fell, and that there was a dark puddle beneath her
that was still spreading, a tide of blood advancing towards him.

He touched the hilt of the dagger in his side, and coughed,
and the pain of both things was almost too much to bear; but
he only screamed a little, and made it worse by standing up and
staggering to the wall to place his back against it. There were
still two guards somewhere, and Fitz was surprisingly vulner-
able if he was surprised. Or he might be wounded too, from the
struggle with the god.

Minutes or perhaps a longer time passed, and Hereward's
mind wandered and, in wandering, left his body too long. It
slid down the wall to the ground and his blood began to mingle
with that of Jessaye, and the others who lay on the floor of a
god's antechamber turned slaughterhouse.

Then there was pain again, and Hereward's mind jolted back
into his body, in time to make his mouth whimper and his eyes
blink at a light that was a color he didn't know, and there was

Mister Fitz leaning over him and the dagger wasn't in his side anymore and there was no bloody froth upon his lips. There was still pain. Constant, piercing pain, coming in waves and never subsiding. It stayed with him, uppermost in his thoughts, even as he became dimly aware that he was upright and walking, his legs moving under a direction not his own.

Except that very soon he was lying down again, and Fitz was cross.

"You have to get back up, Hereward."

"I'm tired, Fitzie . . . can't I rest for a little longer?"

"No. Get up."

"Are we going home?"

"No, Hereward. You know we can't go home. We must go onward."

"Onward? Where?"

"Never mind now. Keep walking. Do you see our mounts?"

"Yes . . . but we will never . . . never make it out the gate . . ."

"We will, Hereward . . . leave it to me. Here, I will help you up. Are you steady enough?"

"I will . . . stay on. Fitz . . ."

"Yes, Hereward."

"Don't . . . don't kill them all."

If Fitz answered, Hereward didn't hear, as he faded out of the world for a few seconds. When the world nauseatingly shivered back into sight and hearing, the puppet was nowhere in sight and the two battlemounts were already loping towards the gate, though the leading steed had no rider.

They did not pause at the wall. Though it was past midnight, the gate was open, and the guards who might have barred the way were nowhere to be seen, though there were strange splashes of color upon the earth where they might have stood. There were no guards beyond the gate, on the earthwork bastion

either, the only sign of their prior existence a half-melted belt
buckle still red with heat.

To Hereward's dim eyes, the city's defenses might as well be
deserted, and nothing prevented the battlemounts continuing
to lope, out into the warm autumn night.

The leading battlemount finally slowed and stopped a mile
beyond the town, at the corner of a lemon grove, its hundreds of
trees so laden with yellow fruit they scented the air with a sharp,
clean tang that helped bring Hereward closer to full consciousness. Even so, he lacked the strength to shorten the chain of his
own mount, but it stopped by its companion without urging.

Fitz swung down from the outlying branch of a lemon tree,
onto his saddle, without spilling any of the fruit piled high in
his upturned hat.

"We will ride on in a moment. But when we can, I shall
make a lemon salve and a soothing drink."

Hereward nodded, finding himself unable to speak. Despite
Fitz's repairing sorceries, the wound in his side was still very
painful, and he was weak from loss of blood, but neither thing
choked his voice. He was made quiet by a cold melancholy that
held him tight, coupled with a feeling of terrible loss, the loss of
some future, never-to-be happiness that had gone forever.

"I suppose we must head for Fort Yarz," mused Fitz. "It is
the closest likely place for employment. There is always some
trouble there, though I believe the Gebrak tribes have been
largely quiet this past year."

Hereward tried to speak again, and at last found a croak that
had some resemblance to a voice.

"No. I am tired of war. Find us somewhere peaceful, where
I can rest."

Fitz hopped across to perch on the neck of Hereward's mount
and faced the knight, his blue eyes brighter than the moonlight.

"I will try, Hereward. But as you ruminated earlier, the

world is as it is, and we are what we were made to be. Even should we find somewhere that seems at peace, I suspect it will not stay so, should we remain. Remember Jeminero."

"Aye." Hereward sighed. He straightened up just a little and took up the chains as Fitz jumped to his own saddle. "I remember."

"Fort Yarz?" asked Fitz.

Hereward nodded, and slapped the chain, urging his battle-mount forward. As it stretched into its stride, the lemons began to fall from the trees in the orchard, playing the soft drumbeat of a funerary march, the first sign of the passing from the world of the god of Shûme.

BEYOND THE SEA GATE OF THE SCHOLAR-PIRATES OF SARSKÖE

EMIND ME WHY THE PIRATES WON'T SINK US with cannon fire at long range," said Sir Hereward as he lazed back against the bow of the skiff, his scarlet-sleeved arms trailing far enough over the side to get his twice folded–back cuffs and hands completely drenched, with occasional splashes going down his neck and back as well. He enjoyed the sensation, for the water in these eastern seas was warm, the swell gentle, and the boat was making a good four or five knots, reaching on a twelve-knot breeze.

"For the first part, this skiff formerly belonged to Annim Tel, the pirate's agent in Kerebad," said Mister Fitz. Despite being only three feet six and a half inches tall and currently lacking even the extra height afforded by his favourite hat, the puppet was easily handling both tiller and main sheet of their small craft. "For the second part, we are both clad in red, the color favoured by the pirates of this archipelagic trail, so they

will account us as brethren until proven otherwise. For the
third part, any decent perspective glass will bring close to their
view the chest that lies lashed on the thwart there, and they will
want to examine it, rather than blow it to smithereens."

"Unless they're drunk, which is highly probable," said
Hereward cheerfully. He lifted his arms out of the water and
shook his hands, being careful not to wet the tarred canvas bag
at his feet that held his small armory. Given the mission at hand,
he had not brought any of his usual, highly identifiable weapons. Instead the bag held a mere four snaphance pistols of quite
ordinary though serviceable make, an oiled leather bag of powder, a box of shot, and a blued steel main gauche in a sharkskin
scabbard. A sheathed mortuary sword lay across the top of the
bag, its half-basket hilt at Hereward's feet.

He had left his armour behind at the inn where they had
met the messenger from the Council of the Treaty for the Safety
of the World and though he was currently enjoying the light air
upon his skin, and was optimistic by nature, Hereward couldn't
help reflect that a scarlet shirt, leather breeches, and sea boots
were not going to be much protection if the drunken pirates
aboard the xebec they were sailing towards chose to conduct
some musketry exercise.

Not that any amount of leather and proof steel would help if
they happened to hit the chest. Even Mister Fitz's sorcery could
not help them in that circumstance, though he might be able to
employ some sorcery to deflect bullets or small shot from both
boat and chest.

Mister Fitz was currently dressed in the puffy-trousered rai-
ment of one of the self-willed puppets that were made long ago
in a gentler age to play merry tunes, declaim epic poetry, and
generally entertain. This belied his true nature and most people
or other beings who encountered the puppet other than casually
did not find him entertaining at all. While his full sewing desk

was back at the inn with Hereward's gear, the puppet still had
several esoteric needles concealed under the red bandanna that
was tightly strapped on his pumpkin-size papier-mâché head,
and he was possibly one of the greatest practitioners of his chosen
art still to walk—or sail—the known world.

"We're in range of the bow chasers," noted Hereward. Casually, he rolled over to lie on his stomach, so only his head was
visible over the bow. "Keep her straight on."

"I have enumerated three excellent reasons why they will
not fire upon us," said Mister Fitz, but he pulled the tiller a little
and let out the main sheet, the skiff's sails billowing as it ran
with the wind, so that it would bear down directly on the bow
of the anchored xebec, allowing the pirates no opportunity for
a full broadside.

"In any case, the bow chasers are not even manned."

Hereward squinted. Without his artillery glass he couldn't
clearly see what was occurring on deck, but he trusted Fitz's
superior vision.

"Oh well, maybe they won't shoot us out of hand," he said.
"At least not at first. Remind me of my supposed name and
title?"

"Martin Suresword, Terror of the Syndical Sea."

"Ludicrous," said Hereward. "I doubt I can say it, let alone
carry on the pretense of being such a fellow."

"There is a pirate of that name, though I believe he was
rarely addressed by his preferred title," said Mister Fitz. "Or perhaps I should say there was such a pirate, up until some months
ago. He was large and fair, as you are, and the Syndical Sea is extremely distant, so it is a suitable cognomen for you to assume."

"And you? Farnolio, wasn't it?"

"Farolio," corrected Fitz. "An entertainer fallen on hard
times."

"How can a puppet fall on hard times?" asked Hereward.

He did not look back, as some movement on the bow of the xebec fixed his attention. He hoped it was not a gun crew making ready.

"It is not uncommon for a puppet to lose their singing voice," said Fitz. "If their throat was made with a reed, rather than a silver pipe, the sorcery will only hold for five or six hundred years."

"Your throat, I suppose, is silver?"

"An admixture of several metals," said Fitz. "Silver being the most ordinary. I stand corrected on one of my earlier predictions, by the way."

"What?"

"They *are* going to fire," said Fitz, and he pushed the tiller away, the skiff's mainsail flapping as it heeled to starboard. A few seconds later, a small cannonball splashed down forty or fifty yards to port.

"Keep her steady!" ordered Hereward. "We're as like to steer into a ball as not."

"I think there will only be the one shot," said the puppet. "The fellow who fired it is now being beaten with a musket stock."

Hereward shielded his eyes with his hand to get a better look. The sun was hot in these parts, and glaring off the water. But they were close enough now that he could clearly see a small red-clad crowd gathered near the bow, and in the middle of it, a surprisingly slight pirate was beating the living daylights out of someone who was now crouched—or who had fallen—on the deck.

"Can you make out a name anywhere on the vessel?" Hereward asked.

"I cannot," answered Fitz. "But her gunports are black, there is a remnant of yellow striping on the rails of her quarterdeck, and though the figurehead has been partially shot off, it is clearly a rampant sea-cat. This accords with Annim Tel's description, and is the vessel we seek. She is the *Sea-Cat,* captained by one Romola Fury. I suspect it is she who has clubbed the firer of the bow chaser to the deck."

"A women pirate," mused Hereward. "Did Annim Tel mention whether she is comely?"

"I can see for myself that you would think her passing fair," said Fitz, his tone suddenly severe. "Which has no bearing on the task that lies ahead."

"Save that it may make the company of these pirates more pleasant," said Hereward. "Would you say we are now close enough to hail?"

"Indeed," said Fitz.

Hereward stood up, pressed his knees against the top strakes of the bow to keep his balance, and cupped his hands around his mouth.

"Ahoy, *Sea-Cat!*" he shouted. "Permission for two brethren to come aboard?"

There was a brief commotion near the bow, most of the crowd moving purposefully to the main deck. Only two pirates remained on the bow: the slight figure, who now they were closer they could see was female and so was almost certainly Captain Fury, and a tub-chested giant of a man who stood behind her. A crumpled body lay at their feet.

The huge pirate bent to listen to some quiet words from Fury, then filling his lungs to an extent that threatened to burst the buttons of his scarlet waistcoat, answered the hail with a shout that carried much farther than Hereward's.

"Come aboard then, cullies! Portside if you please."

Mister Fitz leaned on the tiller and hauled in the main sheet, the skiff turning wide, the intention being to circle in off the port side of the xebec and then turn bow first into the wind and drop the sail. If properly executed, the skiff would lose way and bump gently up against the pirate ship. If not, they would run into the vessel, damage the skiff, and be a laughingstock.

This was the reason Mister Fitz had the helm. Somewhere in his long past, the puppet had served at sea for several decades, and his wooden limbs were well-salted, his experience clearly remembered, and his instincts true.

Hereward, for his part, had served as a gunner aboard a frigate of the Kahlian Mercantile Alliance for a year when he was fifteen, and though that lay some ten years behind him, he had since had some shorter-lived nautical adventures and was thus well able to pass himself off as a seaman aboard a fair-size ship. But he was not a great sailor of small boats and he hastened to follow Mister Fitz's quiet commands to lower sail and prepare to fend off with an oar as they coasted to a stop next to the anchored *Sea-Cat*.

In the event, no fending off was required, but Hereward took a thrown line from the xebec to make the skiff fast alongside, while Fitz secured the head- and mainsail. With the swell so slight, the ship at anchor, and being a xebec low in the waist, it was then an easy matter to climb aboard, using the gunports and chain-plates as foot- and handholds, Hereward only slightly hampered by his sword. He left the pistols in the skiff.

Pirates sauntered and swaggered across the deck to form two rough lines as Hereward and Fitz found their feet. Though they did not have weapons drawn, it was very much a gauntlet, the men and women of the *Sea-Cat* eyeing their visitors with suspicion. Though he did not wonder at the time, presuming it the norm among pirates, Hereward noted that the men in particular were ill-favoured, disfigured, or both. Fitz saw this too, and marked it as a matter for further investigation.

Romola Fury stepped down the short ladder from the forecastle deck to the waist and stood at the open end of the double line of pirates. The red waistcoated bully stood behind, but Hereward hardly noticed him. Though she was sadly lacking in the facial scars necessary for him to consider her a true beauty, Fury was indeed comely, and there was a hint of a powder burn on one high cheekbone that accentuated her natural charms. She wore a fine blue silk coat embroidered with leaping sea-cats, without a shirt. As her coat was only loosely buttoned, Hereward found his attention very much focused upon her. Belatedly, he remembered his instructions, and gave a flamboyant but unstructured wave of his open hand, a gesture meant to be a salute.

"Well met, Captain! Martin Suresword and the dread puppet Farolio, formerly of the *Anodyne Pain*, brothers in good standing of the chapter of the Syndical Sea." Fury raised one eyebrow and tilted her head a little to the side, the long reddish hair on the unshaved half of her head momentarily catching the breeze. Hereward kept his eyes on her, and tried to look relaxed, though he was ready to dive aside, headbutt a path through the gauntlet of pirates, circle behind the mizzen, draw his sword, and hold off the attack long enough for Fitz to wreak his havoc . . .

"You're a long way from the Syndical Sea, Captain Suresword," Fury finally replied. Her voice was strangely pitched and throaty, and Fitz thought it might be the effects of an acid or alkaline burn to the tissues of the throat. "What brings you to these waters, and to the *Sea-Cat*? In Annim Tel's craft, no less, with a tasty-looking chest across the thwarts?"

She made no sign, but something in her tone or perhaps in the words themselves made the two lines of pirates relax and the atmosphere of incipient violence ease.

"A proposition," replied Hereward. "For the mutual benefit of all."

Fury smiled and strolled down the deck, her large enforcer at her heels. She paused in front of Hereward, looked up at him, and smiled a crooked smile, provoking in him the memory of a cat that always looked just so before it sat on his lap and trod its claws into his groin.

"Is it riches we're talking about, Martin Sure . . . sword? Gold treasure and the like? Not slaves, I trust? We don't hold with slaving on the *Sea-Cat,* no matter what our brothers of the Syndical Sea may care for."

"Not slaves, Captain," said Hereward. "But treasure of all kinds. More gold and silver than you've ever seen. More than anyone has ever seen."

Fury's smile broadened for a moment. She slid a foot forward like a dancer, moved to Hereward's side and linked her arm through his, neatly pinning his sword arm.

"Do tell, Martin," she said. "Is it to be an assault on the Ingmal Convoy? A cutting-out venture in Hryken Bay?"

Her crew laughed as she spoke, and Hereward felt the mood change again. Fury was mocking him, for it would take a vast fleet of pirates to carry an assault on the fabulous biennial convoy from the Ingmal saffron fields, and Hryken Bay was dominated by the guns of the justly famous Diamond Fort and its red-hot shot.

"I do not bring you dreams and fancies, Captain Fury," said Hereward quietly. "What I offer is a prize greater than even a galleon of the Ingmal."

"What then?" asked Fury. She gestured at the sky, where a small turquoise disc was still visible near the horizon, though it was faded by the sun. "You'll bring the blue moon down for us to plunder?"

"I offer a way through the Secret Channels and the Sea Gate of the Scholar-Pirates of Sarsköe," said Hereward, speaking louder with each word, as the pirates began to shout, most in angry disbelief, but some in excited greed.

Fury's hand tightened on Hereward's arm, but she did not speak immediately. Slowly, as her silence was noted, her crew grew quiet, such was her power over them. Hereward knew very few others who had such presence, and he had known many kings and princes, queens and high priestesses. Not for the first time, he felt a stab of doubt about their plan, or more accurately Fitz's plan. Fury was no cat's-paw, to be lightly used by others.

"What is this way?" asked Fury, when her crew was silent, the only sound the lap of the waves against the hull, the creak of the rigging, and to Hereward at least, the pounding of his own heart.

"I have a dark rutter for the channels," he said. "Farolio here is a gifted navigator. He will take the star sights."

"So the Secret Channels may be traveled," said Fury. "If the rutter is true."

"It is true, madam," piped up Fitz, pitching his voice higher than usual. He sounded childlike, and harmless. "We have journeyed to the foot of the Sea Gate and returned, this past month."

Fury glanced down at the puppet, who met her look with his unblinking, blue-painted eyes, the sheen of the sorcerous varnish upon them bright. She held the puppet's gaze for several seconds, her eyes narrowing once more, in a fashion reminiscent of a cat that sees something it is not sure whether to flee or fight. Then she slowly looked back at Hereward.

"And the Sea Gate? It matters not to pass the channels if the gate is shut against us."

"The Sea Gate is not what it once was," said Hereward. "If pressure is brought against the correct place, then it will fall."

"Pressure?" asked Fury, and the veriest tip of her tongue thrust out between her lips.

"I am a Master Gunner," said Hereward. "In the chest aboard our skiff is a mortar shell of particular construction—and I believe that not a week past you captured a Harker-built bomb vessel, and have yet to dispose of it."

He did not mention that this ship had been purchased specifically for his command, and its capture had seriously complicated
their initial plan.

"You are well-informed," said Fury. "I do have such a craft,
hidden in a cove beyond the strand. I have my crew, none better
in all this sea. You have a rutter, a navigator, a bomb, and the
art to bring down the Sea Gate. Shall we say two-thirds to we
Sea-Cats and one-third to you and your puppet?"

"Done," said Hereward.

"Yes," said Fitz.

Fury unlinked her arm from Hereward's, held up her open
hand, and licked her palm most daintily before offering it to
him. Hereward paused, then spat mostly air on his own palm,
and they shook upon the bargain.

Fitz held up his hand, as flexible as any human's, though it
was dark brown and grained like wood, and licked his palm
with a long blue-stippled tongue that was pierced with a silver
stud. Fury slapped more than shook Fitz's hand, and she did not
look at the puppet.

"Jabez!" instructed Fury, and her great hulking right-hand
man was next to shake on the bargain, his grip surprisingly light
and deft, and his eyes warm with humour, a small smile on his
battered face. Whether it was for the prospect of treasure or
some secret amusement, Hereward could not tell, and Jabez did
not smile for Fitz. After Jabez came the rest of the crew, spitting
and shaking till the bargain was sealed with all aboard. Like every ship of the brotherhood, the Sea-Cats were in theory a free
company, and decisions made by all.

The corpse on the forecastle was an indication that this was
merely a theory and that in practice, Captain Fury ruled as she
wished. The spitting and handshaking was merely song and
dance and moonshadow, but it played well with the pirates,
who enjoyed pumping Hereward's hand till his shoulder hurt.

They did not take such liberties with Fitz, but this was no sign
they had discerned his true nature, but merely the usual wari-
ness of humans towards esoteric life.

When all the hand-clasping was done, Fury took Hereward's arm again and led him towards the great cabin in the
xebec's stern. As they strolled along the deck, she called over her
shoulder, "Make ready to sail, Jabez. Captain Suresword and I
have some matters to discuss."

Fitz followed at Hereward's heels. Jabez's shouts passed over
his head, and he had to weave his way past pirates rushing to
climb the ratlines or man the capstan that would raise the anchor.

Fury's great cabin was divided by a thick curtain that separated her sleeping quarters from a larger space that was not quite
broad enough to comfortably house both the teak-topped table
and the two twelve-pounder guns. Fury had to let go of Hereward to slip through the space between the breech of one gun
and the table corner, and he found himself strangely relieved
by the cessation of physical proximity. He was no stranger to
women, and had dallied with courtesans, soldiers, farm girls,
priestesses, and even a widowed empress, but there was something about Fury that unsettled him more than any of these past
lovers.

Consequently, he was even more relieved when she did not
lead him through the curtain to her sleeping quarters, but sat at
the head of the table and gestured for him to sit on one side. He
did so, and Fitz hopped up onto the table.

"Drink!" shouted Fury. She was answered by a grunt from
behind a half-door in the fore bulkhead that Hereward had
taken for a locker. The door opened a fraction and a scrawny,
tattooed, handless arm was thrust out, the stump through the
leather loop of a wineskin which was unceremoniously thrown
up to the table.

"Go get the meat on the forecastle," added Fury. She raised the wineskin and daintily directed a jet of a dark, resinous wine into her mouth, licking her lips most carefully when she finished. She passed the skin to Hereward, who took the merest swig. He was watching the horribly mutilated little man who was crawling across the deck. The pirate's skin was so heavily and completely tattooed that it took a moment to realize he was an albino. He had only his left hand, his right arm ending at the wrist. Both of his legs were gone from the knee, and he scuttled on his stumps like a tricorn beetle.

"M' steward," said Fury, as the fellow left. She took another long drink. "Excellent cook."

Hereward nodded grimly. He had recognized some of the tattoos on the man, which identified him as a member of one of the cannibal societies that infested the decaying city of Coradon, far to the south.

"I'd invite you to take nuncheon with me," said Fury, with a sly look. "But most folk don't share my tastes."

Hereward nodded. He had in fact eaten human flesh, when driven to extremity in the long retreat from Jeminero. It was not something he wished to partake of again, should there be any alternative sustenance.

"We are all but meat and water, in the end," said Fury. "Saving your presence, puppet."

"It is a philosophic position that I find unsurprising in one of your past life," said Fitz. "I, for one, do not think it strange for you to eat dead folk, particularly when there is always a shortage of fresh meat at sea."

"What do you know of my 'past life'?" asked Fury and she smiled just a little, so her sharp eyeteeth protruded over her lower lip.

"Only what I observe," remarked Fitz. "Though the mark

is faded, I perceive a Lurquist slave brand in that quarter of the skin above your left breast and below your shoulder. You also have the characteristic scar of a Nagolon manacle on your right wrist. These things indicate you have been a slave at least twice, and so must have freed yourself or been freed, also twice. The Nagolon cook the flesh of their dead rowers to provide for the living, hence your taste—"

"I think that will do," interrupted Fury. She looked at Hereward. "We all need our little secrets, do we not? But there are others we must share. It is enough for the crew to know no more than the song about the Scholar-Pirates of Sarsköe and the dangers of the waters near their isle. But I would know the whole of it. Tell me more about these Scholar-Pirates and their fabled fortress. Do they still lurk behind the Sea Gate?"

"The Sea Gate has been shut fast these last two hundred years or more," Hereward said carefully. He had to answer before Fitz did, as the puppet could not always be trusted to sufficiently skirt the truth, even when engaged on a task that required subterfuge and misdirection. "The Scholar-Pirates have not been seen since that time and most likely the fortress is now no more than a dark and silent tomb."

"If it is not now, we shall make it so," said Fury. She hesitated for a second, then added, "For the Scholar-Pirates," and tapped the table thrice with the bare iron ring she wore on the thumb of her left hand. This was an ancient gesture, and told Fitz even more about the captain.

"The song says they were indeed as much scholars as pirates," said Fury. "I have no desire to seize a mound of dusty parchment or rows of books. Do you know of anything more than legend that confirms their treasure?"

"I have seen inside their fortress," said Fitz. "Some four hundred years past, before the Sea Gate was . . . permanently

raised. There were very few true scholars among them even
then, and most had long since made learning secondary to the
procurement of riches . . . and riches there were, in plenty."

"How old are you, puppet?"

Fitz shrugged his little shoulders and did not answer, a for-
bearance that Hereward was pleased to see. Fury was no common pirate, and anyone who knew Fitz's age and a little history
could put the two together in a way that might require adjustment, and jeopardize Hereward's current task.

"There will be gold enough for all," Hereward said hastily.
"There are four or five accounts extant from ransomed captives
of the Scholar-Pirates, and all mention great stores of treasure.
Treasure for the taking."

"Aye, after some small journey through famously impassable
waters and a legendary gate," said Fury. "As I said, tell me the
whole."

"We will," said Hereward. "Farolio?"

"If I may spill a little wine, I will sketch out a chart," said
Fitz.

Fury nodded. Hereward poured a puddle of wine on the
corner of the table for the puppet, who crouched and dipped
his longest finger in it, which was the one next to his thumb,
then quickly sketched a rough map of many islands. Though he
performed no obvious sorcery, the wet lines were quite sharp
and did not dry out as quickly as one might expect.

"The fortress itself is built wholly within a natural vastness
inside this isle, in the very heart of the archipelago. The pirates
called both island and fortress Cror Holt, though its proper name
is Sarsköe, which is also the name of the entire island group."

Fitz made another quick sketch, an enlarged view of the
same island, a roughly circular land that was split from its eastern shore to its centre by a jagged, switchbacked line of five
turns.

"The sole entry to the Cror Holt cavern is from the sea, through this gorge which cuts a zigzag way for almost nine miles through the limestone. The gorge terminates at a smooth cliff, but here the pirates bored a tunnel through to their cavern. The entrance to the tunnel is barred by the famed Sea Gate, which measures one hundred and seven feet wide and one hundred and ninety-seven feet high. The sea abuts it at near forty feet at low water and sixty-three at the top of the tide. The gorge is narrow, only broad enough for three ships to pass abreast, so it is not possible to directly fire upon the Sea Gate with cannon. However, we have devised a scheme to fire a bomb from the prior stretch of the gorge, over the intervening rock wall and into the top of the gate.

"Once past the gate, there is a harbor pool capacious enough to host a dozen vessels of a similar size to your *Sea-Cat*, with three timber wharves built out from a paved quay. The treasure houses and storehouses of the Scholar-Pirates are built on an inclined crescent above the quay, along with residences and other buildings of no great note."

"You are an unusual puppet," said Fury. She took the wineskin and poured another long stream down her throat. "Go on."

Fitz nodded, and returned to his first sketch, his finger tracing a winding path between the islands.

"To get to the Cror Holt entry in the first place, we must pick our way through the so-called Secret Channels. There are close to two hundred islands and reefs arrayed around the central isle, and the only passage through is twisty indeed. Adding complication to difficulty, we must pass these channels at night, a night with a clear sky, for we have only the dark rutter to guide us through the channels, and the path contained therein is detailed by star sights and soundings.

"We will also have to contend with most difficult tides. This is particularly so in the final approach to the Sea Gate, where the shape of the reefs and islands—and I suspect some sorcer-ous tinkering—funnel two opposing tidewashes into each other. The resultant eagre, or bore as some call it, enters the mouth of the gorge an hour before high water and the backwash returns some fifteen minutes later. The initial wave is taller than your topmasts and very swift, and will destroy any craft caught in the gorge.

"Furthermore, we must also be in the Cror Holt gorge just before the turn of the tide, in order to secure the bomb vessel ready for firing during the slack water. With only one shot, He . . . Martin, that is, will need the most stable platform pos-sible. I have observed the slack water as lasting twenty-three minutes and we must have the bomb vessel ready to fire.

"Accordingly, we must enter after the eagre has gone in and come out, anchor and spring the bomb vessel at the top of the tide, fire on the slack and then we will have some eight or nine hours at most to loot and be gone before the eagre returns, and without the Sea Gate to block it, floods the fortress completely and drowns all within."

Fury looked from the puppet to Hereward, her face impas-sive. She did not speak for at least a minute. Hereward and Fitz waited silently, listening to the sounds of the crew on deck and rigging above them, the creak of the vessel's timbers and above all that, the thump of someone chopping something up in the cap-tain's galley that lay somewhat above them and nearer the waist.

"It is a madcap venture, and my crew would mutiny if they knew what lies ahead," said Fury finally. "Nor do I trust either of you to have told me the half of it. But . . . I grow tired of the easy pickings on this coast. Perhaps it is time to test my luck again. We will join with the bomb vessel, which is called *Strongarm*, by nightfall and sail on in convoy. You will both stay aboard the *Sea-Cat*. How long to gain the outer archipelago, master navigator puppet?"

"Three days with a fair wind," said Fitz. "If the night then is clear, we shall have two of three moons sufficiently advanced to light our way, but not so much they will mar my starsights. Then it depends upon the wind. If it is even passing fair, we should reach the entrance to the Cror Holt gorge two hours after midnight, as the tide nears its flood."

"Madness," said Fury again, but she laughed and slapped Fitz's sketch, a spray of wine peppering Hereward's face. "You may leave me now. Jabez will find you quarters."

Hereward stood and almost bowed, before remembering he was a pirate. He turned the bow into a flamboyant wipe of his wine-stained face and turned away, to follow Fitz, who had jumped down from the table without any attempt at courtesy.

As they left, Fury spoke quietly, but her words carried great force. "Remember this, Captain Suresword. I eat my enemies— and those who betray my trust I eat alive."

That parting comment was still echoing in Hereward's mind four days later, as the *Sea-Cat* sailed cautiously between two lines of white breakers no more than a mile apart. The surf was barely visible in the moonlight, but all aboard could easily envision the keel-tearing reefs that lay below.

Strongarm wallowed close behind, its ragged wake testament to its inferior sailing properties, much of this due to the fact it had a huge mortar sitting where it would normally have a fore-mast. But though it would win no races, *Strongarm* was a beautiful vessel in Hereward's eyes, with her massively reinforced decks and beams, chain rigging, and of course, the great iron mortar itself.

Though Fury had not let him stay overlong away from the *Sea-Cat*, and Fitz had been required to stay on the xebec, Hereward had spent nearly all his daylight hours on the bomb vessel, familiarizing himself with the mortar and training the crew he had been given to serve it. Though he would only have one

shot with the special bomb prepared by Mister Fitz, and he
would load and aim that himself, Hereward had kept his gunners busy drilling. With a modicum of luck, the special shot
would bring down the Sea Gate, but he thought there could
well be an eventuality where even commonplace bombs might
need to be rained down upon the entrance to Cror Holt.

A touch at Hereward's arm brought his attention back to
Fitz. Both stood on the quarterdeck, next to the helmsman,
who was peering nervously ahead. Fury was in her cabin, possibly to show her confidence in her chosen navigator—and in
all probability, dining once more on the leftovers of the unfortunate pirate who had taken it on himself to fire the bow chaser.

"We are making good progress," said Fitz. He held a peculiar
device at his side that combined a small telescope and a tiny,
ten-line abacus of screw-thread beads. Hereward had never seen
any other navigator use such an instrument, but by taking sights
on the moons and the stars, and with the mysterious aid of
the silver chronometric egg he kept in his waistcoat, Fitz could
and did fix their position most accurately. This could then be
checked against the directions contained with the salt-stained
leather bindings of the dark rutter.

"Come to the taffrail," whispered Fitz. More loudly, he
said, "Keep her steady, helm. I shall give you a new course presently."

Man and puppet moved to the rail at the stern, to stand near
the great lantern that was the essential beacon for the following
ship. Hereward leaned on the rail and looked back at the *Strongarm* again. In the light of the two moons the bomb vessel was a
pallid, ghostly ship, the great mortar giving it an odd silhouette.
Fitz, careless of the roll and pitch of the ship, leapt to the rail.
Gripping Hereward's arm, he leaned over and looked intently
at the stern below.

"Stern windows shut—we shall not be overheard," whispered Fitz.

"What is it you wish to say?" asked Hereward.

"Elements of our plan may need reappraisal," said Fitz. "Fury is no easy dupe and once the Sea Gate falls, its nature will be evident. Though she must spare me to navigate our return to open water, I fear she may well attempt to slay you in a fit of pique. I will then be forced into action, which would be unfortunate as we may well need the pirates to carry the day."

"I trust you would be 'forced into action' before she killed me . . . or started eating me alive," said Hereward.

Fitz did not deign to answer this sally. They both knew Hereward's safety was of *almost* paramount concern to the puppet.

"Perchance we should give the captain a morsel of knowledge," said Fitz. "What do you counsel?"

Hereward looked down at the deck and thought of Fury at her board below, carving off a more literal morsel.

"She is a most uncommon woman, even for a pirate," he said slowly.

"She is that," said Fitz. "On many counts. You recall the iron ring, the three-times tap she did on our first meeting below? That is a grounding action against some minor forms of esoteric attack. She used it as a ward against ill-saying, which is the practice of a number of sects. I would think she was a priestess once, or at least a novice, in her youth."

"Of what god?" asked Hereward. "A listed entity? That might serve us very ill."

"Most probably some benign and harmless godlet," said Fitz. "Else she could not have been wrested from its service to the rowing benches of the Nagolon. But there is something about her that goes against this supposition . . . it would be prudent to confirm which entity she served."

"If you wish to ask, I have no objection . . ." Hereward began. Then he stopped and looked at the puppet, favouring his long-time comrade with a scowl.

"I have to take many more starsights," said Fitz. He jumped down from the rail and turned to face the bow. "Not to mention instruct the helmsman on numerous small points of sail. I think it would be in our interest to grant Captain Fury some further knowledge of our destination, and also endeavor to discover which godlet held the indenture of her youth. We have some three or four hours before we will reach the entrance to the gorge."

"I am not sure—" said Hereward.

"Surely that is time enough for such a conversation," interrupted Fitz. "Truly, I have never known you so reluctant to seek private discourse with a woman of distinction."

"A woman who feasts upon human flesh," protested Hereward as he followed Fitz.

"She merely does not waste foodstuffs," said Fitz. "I think it commendable. You have yourself partaken of—"

"Yes, yes, I remember!" said Hereward. "Take your starsight! I will go below and speak to Fury."

The helmsman looked back as Hereward spoke, and he realized he was no longer whispering.

"Captain Fury, I mean. I will speak with you anon, Mister . . . Farolio!"

Captain Fury was seated at her table when Hereward entered, following a cautious knock. But she was not eating and there were no recognizable human portions upon the platter in front of her. It held only a dark glass bottle and a small silver cup, the kind used in birthing rites or baptismal ceremonies. Fury drank from it, flicking her wrist to send the entire contents down her throat in one gulp. Even from a few paces distant, Hereward could smell the sharp odor of strong spirits.

"Arrack," said Fury. "I have a taste for it at times, though it does not serve me as well as once it did. You wish to speak to me? Then sit."

Hereward sat cautiously, as far away as he dared without giving offence, and angled his chair so as to allow a clean draw of the main gauche from his right hip. Fury appeared less than sober, if not exactly drunk, and Hereward was very wary of the trouble that might come from the admixture of a pirate with cannibalistic tendencies and a powerfully spirituous drink.

"I am not drunk," said Fury. "It would take three bottles of this stuff to send me away, and a better glass to sup it with. I am merely wetting down my powder before we storm the fortress."

"Why?" asked Hereward. He did not move any closer.

"I am cursed," said Fury. She poured herself another tot. "Did you suppose 'Fury' is my birth name?"

Hereward shook his head slowly.

"Perhaps I am blessed," continued the woman. She smiled her small, toothy smile again, and drank. "You will see when the fighting starts. Your puppet knows, doesn't it? Those blue eyes . . . it will be safe enough, but you'd best keep your distance. It's the tall men and the well-favoured that she must either bed or slay, and it's all I can do to point her towards the foe . . ."

"Who is she?" asked Hereward. It took some effort to keep his voice calm and level. At the same time he let his hand slowly fall to his side, fingers trailing across the hilt of his parrying dagger.

"What I become," said Fury. "A fury indeed, when battle is begun."

She made a sign with her hand, her fingers making a claw. Her nails had grown, Hereward saw, but not to full talons. Not yet. More discolored patches—spots—had also appeared on her face, making it obvious the permanent one near her eye was not a powder-burn at all.

"You were a sister of Chelkios, the Leoparde," stated Hereward. He did not have Fitz's exhaustive knowledge of cross-dimensional entities, but Chelkios was one of the more prominent deities of the old Kvarnish Empire. Most importantly from his point of view, at least in the longer term, it was not proscribed.

"I was taken from Her by slavers when I was but a novice, a silly little thing who disobeyed the rules and left the temple," said Fury. She took another drink. "A true sister controls the temper of the beast. I must manage with rum, for the most part, and the occasional . . ."

She set down her cup, stood up, and held her hand out to Hereward and said, "Distraction."

Hereward also stood, but did not immediately take her hand. Two powerful instincts warred against each other, a sensuous thrill that coursed through his whole body versus a panicked sense of self-preservation that emanated from a more rational reckoning of threat and chance.

"Bed or slay, she has no middle course," said Fury. Her hand trembled and the nails on her fingers grew longer and began to curve.

"There are matters pertaining to our task that you must hear," said Hereward, but as he spoke all his caution fell away and he took her hand to draw her close. "You should know that the Sea Gate is now in fact a wall . . ."

He paused as cool hands found their way under his shirt, muscles tensing in anticipation of those sharp nails upon his skin. But Fury's fingers were soft pads now, and quick, and Hereward's own hands were launched upon a similar voyage of discovery.

"A wall," gulped Hereward. "Built two hundred years ago

by the surviving Scholar-Pirates . . . to . . . to keep in something they had originally summoned to aid them . . . the treasure is there . . . but it is guarded . . ."

"Later," crooned Fury, close to his ear, as she drew him back through the curtain to her private lair. "Tell me later . . ."

Many hours later, Fury stood on the quarterdeck and looked down at Hereward as he took his place aboard the boat that was to transfer him to the *Strongarm*. She gave no sign that she viewed him with any particular affection or fondness, or indeed recalled their intimate relations at all. However, Hereward was relieved to see that though the lanterns in the rigging cast shadows on her face, there was only the one leopard patch there and her nails were of a human dimension. Fitz stood at her side, his papier-mâché head held at a slight angle so that he might see both sky and boat. Hereward had managed only a brief moment of discourse with him, enough to impart Fury's nature and to tell him that she had seemed to take the disclosure of their potential enemy with equanimity. Or possibly had not heard him properly, or recalled it, having been concerned with more immediate activities.

Both *Sea-Cat* and *Strongarm* were six miles up the gorge, its sheer, grey-white limestone walls towering several hundred feet above them. Only the silver moon was high enough to light their way, the blue moon left behind on the horizon of the open sea. Even so, a bright three-quarters of the disc shone down, and the sky was clear and full of stars, so on one score at least the night was ideal for the expedition. But the wind had been dropping by the minute, and now the air was still, and what little sail the *Sea-Cat* had set was limp and useless. *Strongarm*'s poles were bare, as she was already moored in the position Fitz had chosen on their preliminary exploration a month before, with three anchors down and a spring on each line. Hereward would adjust the vessel's lie when he got aboard, thus training the mortar exactly on the Sea Gate, which lay out of sight on the other side of the northern wall, in the next turn of the gorge.

In consequence of the calm, recourse had to be made to oars, so a longboat, two gigs, and Annim Tel's skiff were in line ahead of the *Sea-Cat*, ready to tow her the last mile around the bend in the gorge. Hereward would have preferred to undertake the assault entirely in the small craft, but they could not deliver sufficient force. There were more than a hundred and ninety pirates aboard the xebec, and he suspected they might need all of them and more.

"High water," called out someone from near the bow of the *Sea-Cat*. "The flow has ceased."

"Give way!" ordered Hereward and his boat surged forward, six pirates bending their strength upon the oars. With the gorge so narrow it would only take a few minutes to reach the *Strongarm*, but with the tide at its peak and slack water begun, Hereward had less than a quarter hour to train, elevate, and fire the mortar. Behind him, he heard Jabez roar, quickly followed by the splash of many oars in the water as the boats began the tow. It would be a slow passage for the *Sea-Cat*, and Hereward's gig would easily catch them up.

The return journey out of the gorge would be just as slow, Hereward thought, and entailed much greater risk. If they lost too many rowers in battle, and if the wind failed to come up, they might well not make it out before the eagre came racing up the gorge once more.

He tried to dismiss images of the great wave roaring down the gorge as he climbed up the side of the bomb vessel and quickly ran to the mortar. His crew had everything ready. The chest was open to show the special bomb, the charge bags were laid on oil-cloth next to it and his gunner's quadrant and fuses were laid out likewise on the opposite side.

Hereward looked up at the sky and at the marks Fitz had sorcerously carved into the cliff the month before, small things that caught the moonlight and might be mistaken for a natural pocket of quartz. Using these marks, he ordered a minor adjustment of the springs to warp the bomb vessel around a fraction, a task that took precious minutes as the crew heaved on the lines.

While they heaved, Hereward laid the carefully calculated number and weight of charge bags in the mortar. Then he checked and cut the fuse, measuring it three times and checking it again, before pushing it into the bomb. This was a necessary piece of misdirection for the benefit of the pirates, for in fact Fitz had put a sorcerous trigger in the bomb so that it would explode exactly as required.

"Load!" called Hereward. The six pirates who served the mortar leapt into action, two carefully placing the wadding on the charge-bags while the other four gingerly lifted the bomb and let it slide back into the mortar.

"Prepare for adjustment," came the next command. Hereward laid his gunner's quadrant in the barrel and the crew took a grip on the two butterfly-shaped handles that turned the cogs that would raise the mortar's inclination. "Up six turns!"

"Up six turns!" chorused the hands as they turned the handles, bronze cogs ticking as the teeth interlocked with the thread of the inclination screws. The barrel of the mortar slowly rose, till it was pointing up at the clear sky and was only ten degrees from the vertical.

"Down one quarter turn!"

"Down one quarter turn!"

The barrel came down. Hereward checked the angle once more. All would depend upon this one shot.

"Prime her and ready matches!"

The leading hand primed the touchhole with fine powder

from a flask, while his second walked back along the deck to
retrieve two linstocks, long poles that held burning lengths of
match cord.

"Stand ready!"

Hereward took one linstock and the leading gunner the
other. The rest of the gun crew walked aft, away from the mortar, increasing their chances of survival should there be some
flaw in weapon or bomb that resulted in early detonation.

"One for the sea, two for the shore, three for the match,"
Hereward chanted. On three he lit the bomb's fuse and strode
quickly away, still chanting, "Four for the gunner, and five for
the bore!"

On "bore" the gunner lit the touchhole.

Hereward already had his eyes screwed shut and was
crouched on the deck fifteen feet from the mortar, with his back
to it and a good handhold. Even so, the flash went through his
eyelids and the concussion and thunderous report that followed
sent him sprawling across the deck. The *Strongarm* pitched and
rolled too, so that he was in some danger of going over the side,
till he found another handhold. Hauling himself upright, Hereward looked up to make sure the bomb had cleared the rim of
the gorge, though he knew that if it hadn't there would already
be broken rock falling all around. Blinking against the spots
and luminous blurring that were the aftereffects of the flash, he
stared up at the sky and a few seconds later, was rewarded by
the sight of another, even brighter flash, and hard on its heels, a
deep, thunderous rumble.

"A hit, a palpable hit!" cried the leading gunner, who was
an educated man who doubtless had some strange story of how
he had become a pirate. "Well done, sir!"

"It hit something, sure enough," said Hereward, as the other
gunners cheered.

"But has it brought the Sea Gate down? We shall see. Gunners, swab out the mortar and stand ready. Crew, to the boat. We must make haste."

As expected, Hereward's gig easily caught the *Sea-Cat* and its towing boats, which were making slow progress, particularly as a small wave had come down from farther up the gorge, setting them momentarily aback, but heartening Hereward as it indicated a major displacement of the water in front of the Sea Gate. This early portent of success was confirmed some short time later as his craft came in sight of the gorge's terminus. Dust and smoke still hung in the air, and there was a huge dark hole in the middle of what had once been a great wall of pale green bricks.

"Lanterns!" called Hereward as they rowed forward, and his bowman held a lantern high in each hand, the two beams catching spirals of dust and blue-grey gunsmoke which were still twisting their way up towards the silver moon. The breach in the wall was sixty feet wide, Hereward reckoned, and though bricks were still tumbling on either side, there were none left to fall from above. The *Sea-Cat* could be safely towed inside, to disgorge the pirates upon the wharves or if they had rotted and fallen away, to the quay itself.

Hereward looked aft. The xebec was some hundred yards behind, its lower yardarms hung with lanterns so that it looked like some strange, blazing-eyed monster slowly wading up the gorge, the small towing craft ahead of it low dark shapes, lesser servants lit by duller lights.

"Rest your oars," said Hereward, louder than he intended. His ears were still damped from the mortar blast. "Ready your weapons and watch that breach." Most of the pirates hurried to prime pistols or ease dirks and cutlasses in scabbards, but one woman, a broad-faced bravo with a slit nose, laid her elbows on her oars and watched Hereward as he reached into his boot and removed the brassard he had placed there. A simple armband, he had slid it up his arm before he noticed her particular attention, which only sharpened as she saw that the characters embroidered on the brassard shone with their own internal light, far brighter than could be obtained by any natural means.

"What's yon light?" she asked. Others in the crew also turned to look.

"So you can find me," answered Hereward easily. "It is painted with the guts of light-bugs. Now I must pray a moment. If any of you have gods to speak to, now is the time."

He watched for a moment, cautious of treachery or some reaction to the brassard, but the pirates had other concerns. Many of them did bend their heads, or close one eye, or touch their knees with the backs of their hands, or adopt one of the thousands of positions of prayer approved by the godlets they had been raised to worship.

Hereward did none of these things, but spoke under his breath, so that none might hear him.

"In the name of the Council of the Treaty for the Safety of the World, acting under the authority granted by the Three Empires, the Seven Kingdoms, the Palatine Regency, the Jessar Republic, and the Forty Lesser Realms, I declare myself an agent of the Council. I identify the godlet manifested in this fortress of Cror Holt as Forjill-Um-Uthrux, a listed entity under the Treaty. Consequently, the said godlet and all those who assist it are deemed to be enemies of the World and the Council authorizes me to pursue any and all actions necessary to banish, repel, or exterminate the said godlet."

"Captain Suresword! Advance and clear the channel!"

It was Fury calling, no longer relying on the vasty bellow of Jabez. The xebec was closing more rapidly, the towing craft rowing faster, the prospect of gold reviving tired pirates. Hereward could see Fury in the bow of the *Sea-Cat*, and Fitz beside her, his thin arm aglow from his own brassard.

Hereward touched the butts of the two pistols in his belt and then the hilt of his mortuary sword. The entity that lay in the darkness within could not be harmed by shot or steel, but it was likely served by those who could die as readily as any other mortal. Hereward's task was to protect Fitz from such servants, while the puppet's sorcery dealt with the god.

"Out oars!" he shouted, loud as he could this time. "Onward to fortune! Give way!"

Oars dipped, the boat surged forward, and they passed the ruins of the Sea Gate into the black interior of Cror Holt.

Out of the moonlight the darkness was immediate and disturbing, though the tunnel was so broad and high and their lantern-light of such small consequence that they had no sense of being within a confined space. Indeed, though Hereward knew the tunnel itself was short, he could only tell when they left it and entered the greater cavern by the difference in the sound of their oar-splashes, immediate echoes being replaced by more distant ones.

"Keep her steady," he instructed, his voice also echoing back across the black water. "Watch for the wharves or submerged piles. It can't be far."

"There, Captain!"

It was not a wharf, but the spreading rings of some disturbance upon the surface of the still water. Something big had popped up and sank again, off the starboard quarter of the boat.

"Pull harder!" instructed Hereward. He drew a pistol and cocked the lock. The *Sea-Cat* was following, and from its many lanterns he could see the lower outline of the tunnel around it.

"I see the wharf!" cried the bowman, his words immediately followed by a sudden thump under the hull, the crack of broken timber, and a general falling about in the boat, one of the lanterns going over the side into immediate extinguishment.

"We've struck!" shouted a pirate. He stood as if to leap over the side, but paused and looked down.

Hereward looked too. They had definitely hit something hard and the boat should be sinking beneath them. But it was dry. He looked over the side and saw that the boat was at rest on stony ground. There was no water beneath them at all. Another second of examination, and a backward look confirmed that rather than the boat striking a reef, the ground below them had risen up. There was a wharf some ten yards away but its deck was well above them, and the harbor wall a barrier behind it, that they would now need to climb to come to the treasure houses.

"What's that?" asked the gold-toothed pirate uncertainly.

Hereward looked and fired in the same moment, at a seven-foot-tall yellow starfish that was shuffling forward on two points. The bullet took it in the midsection, blasting out a hole the size of a man's fist, but the starfish did not falter.

"Shoot it!" he shouted. There were starfish lurching upright all around and he knew there would be even more beyond the lantern-light. "*Sea-Cat*, ware shallows and enemy!"

The closer starfish fell a second later, its lower points shot to pulp. Pirates swore as they reloaded, all of them clustering closer to Hereward as if he might ward them from this sudden, sorcerous enemy.

Louder gunfire echoed in from the tunnel. Hereward saw flashes amid the steady light of the xebec's lanterns. The *Sea-Cat*'s bow chasers and swivel guns were being fired, so they too must be under attack. He also noted that the ship was moving no closer and in fact, might even be receding.

"Cap'n, the ship! She's backing!" yelled a panicked pirate. He snatched up the remaining lantern and ran from the defensive ring about the boat, intent on the distant lights of the *Sea-Cat*. A few seconds later, the others saw pirate and lantern go under a swarm of at least a dozen starfish, and then it was dark once more, save for the glow of the symbols on Hereward's arm.

"Bowman, get a line over the wharf!" shouted Hereward. The mortuary sword was in his hand now, though he could not recall drawing it, and he hacked at a starfish whose points were reaching for him. The things were getting quicker, as if, like battlemounts, they needed to warm their blood. "We must climb up! Hold them back!"

The six of them retreated to the piles of the wharf, the huge, ambulatory starfish pressing their attack. With no time to re-load, Hereward and the pirates had to hack and cut at them with sword, cutlasses, and a boarding axe, and kick away the pieces that still writhed and sought to fasten themselves on their en-emies. Within a minute, all of them had minor wounds to their lower legs, where the rough suckers of the starfish's foul bodies had rasped away clothing and skin.

"Line's fast!" yelled the bowman and he launched himself up it, faster than any topman had ever climbed a ratline. Two of the other pirates clashed as they tried to climb together, one kick-ing the other in the face as he wriggled above. The lower pirate fell and was immediately smothered by a starfish that threw itself over him. Muffled screams came from beneath the writh-ing, five-armed yellow monster, and the pirate's feet drummed violently on the ground for several seconds before they stilled.

"Go!" shouted Hereward to the remaining pirate, who needed no urging. She was halfway up the rope as Hereward knelt down, held his sword with both hands, and whirled on his heel in a complete circle, the fine edge of his blade slicing through the lower points of half a dozen advancing starfish. As they fell over, Hereward threw his sword up to the wharf, jumped on the back of the starfish that was hunched over the fallen pirate, leapt to the rope, and swarmed up it as starfish points tugged at his heels, rasping off the soles of his boots.

The woman pirate handed Hereward his sword as he reached the deck of the wharf. Once again the surviving quartet huddled close to him, eager to stay within the small circle of light provided by his brassard.

"Watch the end of the wharf!" instructed Hereward. He looked over the side. The huge starfish were everywhere below, but they were either unable or unwilling to climb up, so unless a new enemy presented itself there was a chance of some respite.

"She's gone," whispered one of his crew.

The *Sea-Cat* was indeed no longer visible in the tunnel, though there was still a great noise of gunfire, albeit more distant than before.

"The ground rising up has set her aback," said Hereward. "But Captain Fury will land a reinforcement, I'm sure."

"There are so many of them evil stars," whispered the same man.

"They can be shot and cut to pieces," said Hereward sternly. "We will prevail, have no fear."

He spoke confidently, but was not so certain himself. Particularly as he could see the pieces of all the cut-up starfish wriggling together into a pile below, joining together to make an even bigger starfish, one that could reach up to the wharf.

"We'll move back to the quay," he announced, as two of the five points of the assembling giant starfish below began to flex. "Slow and steady, keep your wits about you."

The five of them moved back along the wharf in a compact huddle, with weapons facing out, like a hedgehog slowly retreating before a predator. Once on the quay, Hereward ordered them to reload, but they had all dropped their pistols, and Hereward had lost one of his pair. He gave his remaining gun to the gold-toothed pirate. "There are stone houses above," he said, gesturing into the dark. "If we must retreat, we shall find a defensible position there."

"Why wait? Let's get behind some walls now."

"We wait for Captain Fury and the others," said Hereward. "They'll be here any—"

The crack of a small gun drowned out his voice. It was followed a second later by a brilliant flash that lit up the whole cavern and then hard on the heels of the flash came a blinding horizontal bolt of forked lightning that spread across the whole harbor floor, branching into hundreds of lesser jolts that connected with the starfish in a crazed pattern of blue-white sparks.

A strong, nauseatingly powerful stench of salt and rotted meat washed across the pirates on the quay as the darkness returned. Hereward blinked several times and swallowed to try and clear his ears, but neither effort really worked. He knew from experience that both sight and sound would return in a few minutes, and he also knew that the explosion and lightning could only be the work of Mister Fitz. Nevertheless he had an anxious few minutes till he could see enough to make out the fuzzy globes that must be lanterns held by approaching friendly forces, and hear his fellows well enough to know that he would also hear any enemy on the wharf or quay.

"It's the captain!" cried a pirate. "She's done those stars in."

The starfish had certainly been dealt a savage blow. Fury and Fitz and a column of lantern-bearing pirates were making their way through a charnel field of thousands of pieces of starfish meat, few of them bigger than a man's fist.

But as the pirates advanced, the starfish fragments began to move, pallid horrors wriggling across the stony ground, melding with other pieces to form more mobile gobbets of invertebrate flesh, all of them moving to a central rendezvous somewhere beyond the illumination of the lanterns.

Hereward did not pause to wonder exactly what these disgusting starfish remnants were going to do in the darker reaches of the harbor. He ran along the wharf and took Fitz's hand, helping the puppet to climb the boarding nets that Fury's crew were throwing up. Before Fitz was on his feet, pirates raced past them both, talking excitedly of treasure, the starfish foe forgotten. Hereward's own boat crew, who might have more reason than most to be more thoughtful, had already been absorbed into this flood of looters.

"The starfish are growing back," said Hereward urgently, as he palmed off a too-eager pirate who nearly trod on Fitz.

"Not exactly," corrected Fitz. "Forjill-Um-Uthrux is manifesting itself more completely here. It will use its starfish minions to craft a physical shape. And more importantly—"

"Captain Suresword!" cried Fury, clapping him on the back. Her eyes were bright, there were several dark spots on her face and her ears were long and furred, but she evidently had managed to halt or slow the full transformation. "On to the treasure!"

She laughed and ran past him, with many pirates behind her. Up ahead, the sound of ancient doors being knocked down was already being replaced by gleeful and astonished cries as many hundredweight of loose gold and silver coinage poured out around the looter's thighs.

"More importantly, Um-Uthrux is doing something to manipulate the sea," continued Fitz. "It has tilted the harbor floor significantly, and I can perceive energistic tendrils extending well beyond this island. I fear it is raising the tide ahead of time and with it—"

"The eagre," said Hereward. "Do we have time to get out?"

"No," said Fitz. "It will be at the mouth of the gorge within minutes. We must swiftly deal with Um-Uthrux and then take refuge in one of the upper buildings, the strongest possible, where I will spin us a bubble of air."

"How big a bubble?" asked Hereward, as he took a rapid glance around. There were lanterns bobbing all about the slope above the quay, and it looked like all two hundred odd of Fury's crew were in amongst the scholar-pirates' buildings.

"A single room, sufficient for a dozen mortals," said Fitz. "Ah, Um-Uthrux has made its host. Please gather as many pirates as you can to fire on it, Hereward. I will require some full minutes of preparation."

The puppet began to take off his bandanna and Hereward shielded his face with his hand. A terrible, harsh light filled the cavern as Fitz removed an esoteric needle that had been glued to his head, the light fading as he closed his hand around it. Any mortal who dared to hold such a needle unprotected would no longer have hand or arm, but Fitz had been specifically made to deal with such things.

In the brief flash of light, Hereward saw a truly giant starfish beginning to stand on its lower points. It was sixty feet wide and at least that tall, and was not pale yellow like its lesser predecessors, but a virulent color like infected pus, and its broad surface was covered not in a rasping, lumpy structure of tiny suckers but in hundreds of foot-wide puckered mouths that were lined with sharp teeth.

"Fury!" roared Hereward as he sprinted back along the wharf, ignoring the splinters in his now bare feet, his ruined boots flapping about his ankles. "Fury! Sea-Cats! To arms, to arms!"

He kept shouting, but he could not see Fury, and the pirates in sight were gold-drunk, bathing uproariously in piles of coin and articles of virtu that had spilled out of the broken treasure houses and into the cobbled streets between the buildings.

"To arms! The enemy!" Hereward shouted again. He ran to the nearest knot of pirates and dragged one away from a huge gold-chased silver cup that was near as big as he was. "Form line on the quay!"

The pirate shrugged him off and clutched his cup.

"It's mine!" he yelled. "You'll not have it!"

"I don't want it!" roared Hereward. He pointed back at the harbor. "The enemy! Look, you fools!"

The nearer pirates stared at him blankly. Hereward turned and saw . . . nothing but darkness.

"Fitz! Light up the cursed monster!"

He was answered by a blinding surge of violet light that shot from the wharf and washed across the giant starfish, which was now completely upright and lifting one point to march forward.

There was silence for several seconds, the silence of the shocked. Then a calm, carrying voice snatched order from the closing jaws of panic.

"Sea-Cats! First division form line on the quay, right of the wharf! Second to load behind them! Move, you knaves! The loot will wait!"

Fury emerged from behind a building, a necklace of gold and yellow diamonds around her neck. She marched to Hereward and placed her arm through his, and together they walked to the quay as if they had not a care in the world, while pirates ran past them.

"You have not become a leoparde," said Hereward. He spoke calmly but he couldn't help but look up at the manifested godlet. Like the smaller starfish, it was becoming quicker with every movement, and Fitz stood alone before it on the end of the wharf. There was a nimbus of sorcerous light around the puppet, indicating that he was working busily with one or more energistic needles, either stitching something otherworldly together or unpicking some aspect of what was commonly considered to be reality.

"Cold things from the sea, no matter their size, do not arouse my ire," replied Fury. "Or perhaps it is the absence of red blood . . . Stand ready!"

The last words were for the hundred pirates who stood in

line along the quay, sporting a wide array of muskets, muske-
toons, blunderbusses, pistols, and even some crossbows. Behind
them, the second division knelt with their own firearms ready
to pass on, and the necessaries for reloading laid out at their feet.

"Fire!" shouted Fury. A ragged volley rang out and a cloud
of smoke rolled back across Hereward and drifted up towards
the treasure houses. Many shots struck home, but their effect
was much less than on the smaller starfish, with no visible holes
being torn in the strange stuff of Um-Uthrux.

"Firsts, fire as you will!" called Fury. "Seconds, reload!"

Though the shots appeared to have no effect, the frantic
movement of the pirates shooting and reloading did attract
Um-Uthrux's attention. It swiveled and took a step towards the
quay, one huge point crashing down on the middle wharf to
the left of Mister Fitz. Rather than pulling the point out of the
wreckage it just pushed it forward, timber flying as it bulled
its way to the quay. Then with one sweep of a middle point, it
swept up a dozen pirates and, rolling the point to form a tight
circle, held them while its many mouths went to work.

"Fire and fall back!" shouted Fury. "Fire and fall back!"

She fired a long-barreled pistol herself, but it too had no
effect. Um-Uthrux seized several more pirates as they tried to
flee, wrapping around them, bones and bloody fragments falling upon shocked companions who were snatched up themselves by another point seconds later.

Hereward and Fury ran back to the corner of one of the
treasure houses. Hereward tripped over a golden salt-boat and
a pile of coins and would have fallen, had not Fury dragged
him on even as the tip of a starfish point crashed down where
he had been, flattening the masterwork of some long-forgotten
goldsmith.

"Your sorcerer-puppet had best do something," said Fury.

"He will," panted Hereward. But he could not see Fitz, and

Um-Uthrux was now bending over the quay with its central torso as well as its points, so its reach would be greater. The quay was crumbling under its assault, and the stones were awash with the blood of many pirates. "We must go higher up!"

"Back, Sea-Cats!" shouted Fury. "Higher up!"

The treasure house that had sheltered them was pounded into dust and fragments as they struggled up the steep cobbled street. Panicked pirates streamed past them, most without their useless weapons. There was no screaming now, just the groans and panting of the tired and wounded, and the sobbing of those whose nerve was entirely gone.

Hereward pointed to a door at the very top of the street. It had already been broken in by some pirate, but the building's front appeared to be a mere facade built over a chamber dug into the island itself, and so would be stronger than any other.

"In there!" he shouted, but the pirates were running down the side alleys as one of Um-Uthrux's points slammed down directly behind, sending bricks, masonry, and treasure in all directions. Hereward pushed Fury towards the door, and turned back to see if he could see Fitz.

But there was only the vast starfish in view. It had slid its lower body up on to the quay and was reaching forth with three of its points, each as large as an angled artillery bastion. First it brought them down to smash the buildings, then it used the fine ends to pluck out any pirates, like an anteater digging out its lunch.

"Fitz!" shouted Hereward. "Fitz!"

One of Um-Uthrux's points rose up, high above Hereward. He stepped back, then stopped as the godlet suddenly halted, its upper points writhing in the air and lower points staggering. A tiny, glowing hole appeared in its middle, and grew larger. The godlet lurched back still farther and reached down with its points, clawing at itself as the glowing void in its guts yawned wider still. Then, with a crack that rocked the cavern and knocked Hereward over again, the giant starfish's points were sucked through the hole, it turned inside out, and the hole closed taking with it all evidence of Um-Uthrux's existence upon the earth and with it most of the light.

"Your puppet has done well," said Fury. "Though I perceive it is called Fitz and not Farolio."

"Yes," said Hereward. He did not look at her, but waved his arm, the brassard leaving a luminous trail in the air. "Fitz! To me!"

"It has become a bloody affair after all," said Fury. Her voice was a growl and now Hereward did look. Fury still stood on two legs, but she had grown taller and her proportions had changed. Her skin had become spotted fur, and her skull transformed, her jaw thrust out to contain savage teeth, including two incisors as long as Hereward's thumbs. Long curved nails sprouted from her rounded hands, her eyes had become bright with a predatory gleam, and a tail whisked the ground behind.

"Fury," said Hereward. He looked straight at her and did not back away. "We have won. The fight is done."

"I told you that I ate my enemies," said Fury huskily. Her tail twitched and she bobbed her head in a manner no human neck could mimic. Hereward could barely understand her, human speech almost lost in growls and snarls. "You did not tell me your name, or your true purpose."

"My name is Hereward," said Hereward and he raised his open hands. If she attacked, his only chance would be to grip her neck and break it before those teeth and nails did mortal damage. "I am not your enemy."

Fury growled, speech entirely gone, and began to crouch.

"Fury! I am not your—"

The leoparde sprang. He caught her on his forearms and felt the nails rake his skin. Fending her off with his left hand, he

seized hold of the necklace of yellow diamonds with his right
and twisted it hard to cut off her air. But before he could apply
much pressure, the beast gave a sudden, human gasp, strange
and sad from that bestial jaw. The leoparde's bright eyes dulled
as if by sea mist, and Hereward felt the full weight of the animal
in his hands.

The necklace broke, scattering diamonds, as the beast slid
down Hereward's chest. Fitz rode on the creature's shoulders
all the way down before he withdrew the stiletto that he had
thrust with inhuman strength up through the nape of her neck
into her brain.

Hereward closed his hand on the last diamond. He held it
just for a second, before he let that too slip through his fingers.

"Inside!" called Fitz and the puppet was at his companion's
knees, pushing Hereward through the door. The knight fell
over the threshold as Fitz turned and gestured with an esoteric
needle, threads of blinding white whipping about faster than
any weaver's shuttle.

His work was barely done before the wave hit. The ground
shook and the sorcerous bubble of air bounced to the ceiling
and back several times, tumbling over Hereward and Fitz in a
mad crush. Then as rapidly as it had come, the wave receded.
Fitz undid the bubble with a deft twitch of his needle and
cupped it in his hand. Hereward lay back on the sodden floor
and groaned. Blood trickled down his shredded sleeves, bruises
he had not even suspected till now made themselves felt, and his
feet were unbelievably sore.

Fitz crouched over him and inspected his arms.

"Scratches," he proclaimed. He carefully put the esoteric
needle away inside his jerkin and took off his bandanna, ripping
it in half to bind the wounds. "Bandages will suffice."

When the puppet was finished, Hereward sat up. He cupped

his face in his hands for a second, but his rope-burned palms made him wince and drop them again.

"We have perhaps six hours to gather materials, construct a raft, and make our way out the gorge," said Fitz. "Presuming the eagre comes again at the usual time, in the absence of Um-Uthrux. We'd best hurry."

Hereward nodded and lurched upright, holding the splintered doorframe for support. He could see nothing beyond Fitz, who stood a few paces away, but he could easily envision the many corpses that would be floating in the refilled harbor pool, or drifting out to the gorge beyond.

"She was right," he said.

Fitz cocked his head in question.

"Meat and water," replied Hereward. "I suppose that *is* all we are, in the end."

Fitz did not answer, but still looked on, his pose unchanged.

"Present company excepted," added Hereward.

A SUITABLE
PRESENT FOR
A SORCEROUS
PUPPET

SIR HEREWARD LICKED HIS FINGER AND TURNED the page of the enormous tome that was perched precariously on a metal frame next to his sickbed. It was not a book he would have chosen to read—or rather to fossick through like a rook searching for seed in a new-sown field—but as it was the only book in the lonely tower by the sea, he had little choice. Having broken two small but important bones in his left foot, he could not range farther afield for other amusements, so reading it had to be. This particular book was entitled *The Compendium of Commonplaces* and presented itself as a collection of knowledge that should be at the command of every reasonably educated gentleman of Jerreke, a country that had ceased to exist some thousand years before, shortly after the book was printed.

The demise of Jerreke and the publication of the book were not likely to be connected, though Sir Hereward did notice that

the pages were often bound out of order, or the folios were in-
correct, and that there was a general carelessness with numbers.
Together, these might be symptomatic of the somewhat unusual
end of Jerreke, a city-state which had defaulted on its debts so
enormously that its entire population had to be sold into slavery.

The finger licking was required by the book's long, dark
hibernation inside a chest up in the attic of the tower. A thor-
oughly damp finger was a necessary aid to the separation of the
sadly gummed-together pages.

Sir Hereward sighed as he turned another page. His enthusiasm for reading had diminished in the turning of several
hundred pages, with its concomitant several hundred finger
lickings, for he had found only two entries worth reading: one
on how to cheat at a board game that had changed its name but
was still widely played in the known world; and another on the
multiplicity of uses of the root spice cabizend, some surprising
number of which fell into Hereward's professional area of expertise as an artillerist and maker of incendiaries.

In fact, Hereward was about to give up and bellow to the
housekeeper who kept the tower to bring him some ale, when
the title of the next commonplace caught his eye. It was called
"On the Propitiation of Sorcerous Puppets."

As Sir Hereward's constant companion, comrade-in-arms,
and one-time nanny was a sorcerous puppet known as Mister
Fitz, this was very much of interest to the injured knight. He
eagerly read on, and though the piece was short and referred
solely to the more usual kind of sorcerous puppet—one made to
sing, dance, and entertain—he did learn something new.

According to Doctor Professor Laxelender Prouzin, the au-
thor of this particular, far-from-commonplace entry, all sorcerous puppets shared a common birthday, much in the manner
of the priests of a number of particularly jealous godlets, who
allowed no individuality among their chosen servants (some of

them even going as far as the Xarwashian god of bookkeeping and warehouses, who not only refused his servants individual birthdays but referred to them all by the same name).

Sir Hereward quickly calculated this shared birthday of the puppets, transposing the Tramontic calendar that had been used in Jerreke with the more modern Adjusted Celestial, and discovered that it would occur in a matter of days, depending on whether it was currently the first or the second day of what the Adjusted Celestial calendar prosaically called "Second Month" and the Tramontics had termed "Expialomon."

As Sir Hereward had been laid up for a week already, and had no urgent matters to attend to, he had rather lost track of the date.

"Sister Gobbe!" called out Sir Hereward. "Sister Gobbe!"

Sister Gobbe was the priestess-housekeeper who looked after the tower and its guests as a representative of the Cloister of Narhalet-Narhalit. Colloquially known as Nar-Nar, it was a gentle and kindly deity whose slow but potent healing powers had aided tens of thousands of petitioners over the last several millennia. This particular tower was one of the more remote bastions of Nar-Nar's presence upon the earth, and likely to be abandoned in the not-too-distant future. Hence it was staffed only by Sister Gobbe and an as yet unseen novice Sir Hereward believed might be called "Sisterling Lallit"—a name he had overheard being hissed by Sister Gobbe outside his door the previous evening. There was also a guard, a small but broad-shouldered fellow with a very large axe, who doubtless could call upon Nar-Nar's rather less well-known powers to open wounds that hadn't even happened yet, rather than heal ones that had.

Fortunately for all concerned, Narhalet-Narhalit was far from a proscribed entity, but a welcome extrusion into the world, so the god and its followers were not an item of business

for Sir Hereward and Mister Fitz. Consequently, their discovery
of the tower en route from Tar's End to Bazynghame had been
a welcome opportunity for the lame and hobbling knight to
rest up and let the bones in his foot knit faster than they would
anywhere else.

Mister Fitz had also taken their forced rest as an opportunity to engage in some activity that he said had hitherto been
impracticable on their travels, though Sir Hereward was not
entirely sure what that meant. The sorcerous puppet was up to
something. He had taken to exploring the sea caves that ate into
the cliffs near the tower, and he returned each evening covered in a layer of what looked like salt, suggesting immersion
in the ocean and subsequent drying. This was odd in a creature who usually avoided complete submersion, being made of
papier-mâché and carved timber, albeit sorcerously altered, but
Sir Hereward had not made enquiry. He knew that Mister Fitz
would tell him of his activities in due course, if there was any
need for Sir Hereward to know.

"Sir?"

It was not Sister Gobbe who appeared in the doorway, red-
faced and puffing as she always was from the tightly spiraling
stair, but a considerably younger and far more attractive atten-
dant, who might have wafted her way upstairs on a beam of
sunlight, for she was neither out of breath, nor was her habit or
broad-brimmed hat in any disarray.

"I am Sisterling Lallit," said the vision. "Sister Gobbe has
had to go into the village, to speak to Boll about the veal to go
with the crayfish sauce for Your Honor's dinner. Is there anything you need?"

Sir Hereward continued to stare and failed to answer. It had
been some months since he had even the slightest conversation
with a beautiful woman, and he was both surprised and sadly
out of practice. But as she continued to stand in the door, with

her head down and her face shadowed by her hat, he recovered himself.

"My companion, Mister Fitz," he began. "The puppet, you know . . ."

"Yes, sir," said Sisterling Lallit. "A most wondrous puppet, and so wise."

"Yes . . . just so," said Sir Hereward. He wondered what Mister Fitz had been talking about with Sisterling Lallit, but pressed on. "It is his birthday on the fourth of Second Month—"

"Tomorrow!" exclaimed Lallit, proving Sir Hereward had been even more careless about the passage of time than he'd thought. She raised her hands and inadvertently looked up, to show Hereward a face of great charm and liveliness, though sadly marred by the lack of the old and faded facial scars he had been brought up to regard as necessary to true beauty. "You should have said! It will be a doing to manage a feast—"

"Mister Fitz does not eat, so a feast is superfluous," said Sir Hereward, with a dismissive wave of his hand. "However, I wish to give him a present. Given that we are leagues from any shop or merchant, and in any case, I cannot for the moment leave my bed . . . I wondered if there might be something suitable in the tower that I might purchase for Mister Fitz."

"Something suitable?" asked Lallit. She tugged her earlobe and frowned, a gesture Sir Hereward found irresistible. "I don't know . . ."

"Come and sit by me," said Sir Hereward. He slid over and patted the mattress by his side. "To begin with, you can tell me what is in the attic above. Most particularly, a musical instrument would meet the need."

Doctor Professor Laxelender Prouzin had written that musical instruments were the usual gift to an entertainer puppet, and Sir Hereward supposed that one might be of interest to Mister Fitz, who was quite capable of appearing to be an entertainer puppet. He could sing most sweetly and seemingly play any musical instrument, and dance fascinatingly as well. But Mister Fitz was not an entertainer puppet, and usually only deployed these talents as a ruse or deception, shortly before unleashing his other, even more greatly developed skills as a practitioner of arcane arts that were not generally the province of puppets. Or of people, for that matter.

"Oh, I'm not allowed to come into your room, sir," exclaimed Lallit. "Sister Gobbe is most strict about who may handle patients, and Mister Fitz told me of your vow, and I would not wish to accidentally—"

"My vow?" asked Sir Hereward suspiciously. He thought for a moment, then asked, "Ah, which one? I have . . . made several."

"To not share the breath of a woman, by intent or accident—save a consecrated priestess of course—till you have finished your pilgrimage to the Rood of Bazynghame," said Lallit innocently. "Don't worry, I shall breathe ever so softly, and stay in the doorway."

"I am grateful," said Sir Hereward, though he felt quite the opposite emotion.

"About this present for Mister Fitz . . ."

"Perhaps it is all too difficult," said Sir Hereward, whose affection for the puppet had encountered a sudden reverse. He turned his head to the side and sighed heavily. "I shall simply wish him a happy birthday and leave it at that."

"But there is an instrument in the attic," said Lallit. "In the same chest your book came from, there is a mandora . . . or a gallichon . . . of five strings, such as my uncle plays. Though it is perhaps too large and heavy for Mister Fitz."

Sir Hereward thought of several occasions when Mister Fitz had shown his true strength. He remembered those spindly wooden puppet arms inside Mister Fitz's thin coat, the cuffs sliding back as he lifted the Arch-Priest of Larruk-Agre above his bulbous head and threw him into the mouth of the volcano; or the time when Fitz had beheaded a slave gladiator below the arena pits of Yarken. The look of surprise on the fellow's face had matched Sir Hereward's own expression, for Mister Fitz had been standing on the gladiator's head at the time, and had pulled the tip of the man's own blade back . . .

"I can fetch it down," said Lallit, interrupting his reminiscences. "Sister Gobbe would set a fair price, I'm sure."

"Very well," said Hereward. "A fine mandora might be the very thing. If it is not too much trouble, I would like to see it. When is Sister Gobbe returning?"

"Oh, I will fetch it for you now," said Lallit. "Sister Gobbe won't be back for hours yet."

"My thanks," said Sir Hereward. "But how will you hand it to me, if we must not share our breath?"

"Oh, I can hold my breath for ages," said Lallit innocently. She demonstrated, taking a deep breath that thrust out her chest. Sir Hereward watched in admiration, tempered by his annoyance at Mister Fitz. It was uncharacteristic of the puppet to preemptively meddle in Hereward's amorous affairs, and it galled no less to know it was almost certainly for a good reason.

Lallit held her breath for quite some time, before suddenly exhaling, turning her head so her breath went up the stairs. She smiled and followed it up to the attic. A minute later, Hereward heard her footsteps as she looked around, the oak-planked floor of the attic being the ceiling of his room.

The novice returned a few minutes later, carrying a stringed instrument that looked to Sir Hereward like an oversized lute. He could play the lute somewhat, and sing passably, as Mister Fitz graded his voice, but the knight had done neither for some years.

Lallit paused for an intake of breath and the resultant inflation of her habit at the door, then nimbly crossed the room,

deposited the mandora on the end of Hereward's bed, and retreated as swiftly back to the stair.

Hereward leaned forward and took up the instrument. The
mandora was made of ash with an open rose of ebony inlaid
around the sound hole. It was still strung, which surprised him,
for it had presumably been there for some lengthy time, and the
strings were of a material other than gut, one that he could not
immediately recognize.

He was about to pluck a note when he saw that the sound
hole was obstructed, and that there was something inside the
body of the mandora. Closer investigation revealed it to be a
parchment folded into a triangle, which was sealed with wax at
each corner. It could not be removed without de-stringing the
instrument, which meant that it had been put there on purpose,
and the mandora strung thereafter.

"Aha," said Sir Hereward. "A mystery within the mandora."

"What is it?" asked Lallit. The novice stood on tiptoe,
craned her elegant neck, and took several steps closer.

"A parchment," said Sir Hereward. He held the mandora
up to the nearer window, so the light fell more clearly through
the sound hole. "Sealed three ways, and stuck to the body with
a red tape and three further seals . . . I think perhaps this is a
matter for . . ."

He had been going to say "Mister Fitz," for the sealed parchment smacked of sorcery, but as the true nature of the puppet
was best not revealed even to the servants of friendly gods, he
fell silent.

"Oh, it is exciting!" said Lallit. She clapped her hands together and took a further step towards him. "What is written
on the parchment?"

Sir Hereward carefully rested the mandora across his knees
and thought. There was something not quite right about Lallit's
enthusiasm, the parchment, and the mandora. He noticed that

the instrument's strings were humming slightly, though he had not struck them. They appeared to be aping Lallit's enthusiasm, and Sir Hereward did not like this at all.

Nor on closer examination was he sure that it was the same Lallit who had returned from the attic. She looked a little taller, and thinner, and now that he studied her, he could see that her eyes were too far apart, and her hat was on backward.

"I shall have to remove the strings," said Sir Hereward. "To get the parchment out. I believe there is a spanner in my saddlebag . . . I shall just fetch it."

Sir Hereward's saddlebags were propped against the far wall, under the shuttered window on that side, as were his sabre and two holstered wheel-lock pistols, though unfortunately these were neither primed nor loaded.

"Allow me," said Lallit.

Sir Hereward held up his hand as he swung his legs off the bed. "No, no, remember my vow."

He hopped over on his right foot, and caught hold of the shutter bolt.

"Might as well have a little more sunshine, while the weather holds," said Sir Hereward. He did not think that the thing that had assumed the shape of Lallit would be deterred by sunlight, given that the other window was already open, but more might help. He opened the shutter, knelt down by his saddlebag, and cast a smiling glance back over his shoulder.

The light from the second window had no visible effect upon his visitor, but it did allow him to see very clearly that the woman in the door was neither Lallit, nor actually a woman. It was some kind of other-dimensional entity that had assumed the shape of Lallit, and stolen her clothes. Hereward hoped Lallit was still alive in the attic, just as he hoped he would live through whatever was about to occur.

"It's very good of your god Narhalet-Narhalit to look after

me so well," added Sir Hereward. He leaned into the window
alcove, and looked out as if idly surveying the ground beneath.
Saying the god's name might help bring its attention to this
intruder in its temple. "Narhalet-Narhalit is good to look after
my companion, Mister Fitz, as well."

He said "Mister Fitz" quite loudly, for the puppet's senses
were extraordinarily sharp. If he was anywhere nearby, he
would be alerted. But he was probably off in his sea cave, which
meant Sir Hereward must manage on his own.

"The spanner," said Lallit. The thing was having trouble
keeping its voice human. "The strings. The parchment."

"Ah yes," said Sir Hereward. He bent down to his saddlebag, and began to rummage through it, removing items as he
went, as if to make it easier.

"Let me see. A dagger, needs a bit of sharpening . . . another
dagger, this one's not too bad . . . where is that—"

He sensed a sudden movement behind him, and spun about
on his good foot, the daggers in his hands. The thing was in
front of him, losing its human form as it moved, its claws reaching for his arms. Hereward parried with the daggers, felt the
shock of impact, and was borne back to the window and almost
thrown out of it.

"You will get the parchment for me!" shrieked the thing.
Flesh was melting off it, revealing the scaly, skeletal beast within,
a creature not wholly present on the earth, for Hereward's daggers, ensorcelled as they were, were slowly sinking through its
wrists, the scales reforming behind the passage of the steel.

"Never!" shouted Hereward, quickly followed by, "Mister
Fitz! To me! Narhalet-Narhalit, aid me!"

"You will obey!" shrieked the beast, and bit at Hereward's
shoulder. He twisted away, but its teeth raked through his
nightshirt and tore flesh. At the same time, his daggers lost all
purchase on the creature's wrists. Instantly, it went for him again,

and he only managed to avoid its grasp by suddenly slipping down the wall and sliding between the creature's legs. He was attempting to roll away when it latched on to his back, dragged him up, and threw him on the bed.

"Remove the strings and open the parchment," it instructed him. "Or you shall be hurt, and hurt again, until you obey!"

Hereward gaped. It was not in response to the creature's command, but an inadvertent reaction to the sudden arrival of a completely naked yet literally radiant Lallit. Surrounded by a nimbus of the violet hue favoured by her god, she burst into the room and made a swatting motion in the air, as if crushing a mosquito.

A hole appeared in the creature's chest, followed by a geyser of greenish ichor that splashed the end of Sir Hereward's bed, the stained linen immediately beginning to send up small tendrils of evil-smelling smoke.

Despite what would be a mortal injury to a human, the beast was not distressed. It turned away from Sir Hereward and tensed to spring at Lallit.

Before it could do so, Hereward jumped up and smashed it on the head with *The Compendium of Commonplaces,* it being the only makeshift weapon close at hand. The huge, brass-and-leather-bound book boomed like a gong as it struck the monster, and most of the tome turned to ash in Hereward's hands, leaving him clutching a ragged folio of loosely bound pages, without any binding or brass accoutrements.

Hereward dropped the newly slim volume and dove for his sabre. He drew it and spun about, ready to slash, but there was nothing there to hit. The creature had also turned to ash, had been picked up by a doubtlessly divine wind, and was being carried out the closest window, to be spread to the four corners of the earth.

The nimbus around Lallit faded, her knees buckled, and Hereward was just able to hop forward and catch her as she fell.

However, he could not hold her weight with his injured foot, so both of them toppled back into the bed, just as Mister Fitz peered cautiously around the doorway, a sorcerous needle held in his cupped hand, its inhuman brilliance quickly dulled as he took in the situation.

But as the puppet replaced the needle inside his pointy hat, the small guard with the large axe leapt up the last step, his weapon held ready to use on anyone who violated the purity of the temple's novices.

"But I haven't . . ." protested Sir Hereward. He reluctantly released Lallit, and started patting out the incipient fire at the end of the bed. "We didn't . . ."

"What am I doing here?" asked Lallit wonderingly. She had the look of someone still waking from a dream. "I felt the god . . ."

"Narhalet-Narhalit has been here," confirmed Mister Fitz. He looked at the guard, his little blue-painted eyes sharp on his papier-mâché head. "This is the god's business, Jabek, however it may appear."

"Aye, I feel it so," said Jabek. He smiled, and added, "But I'll ask you to explain it to Sister Gobbe."

"Oh, the mandora is broken!" exclaimed Lallit. She picked up the instrument, whose neck was broken, and cradled it to her. "Sir Hereward wanted to give it to you for your birthday, Mister Fitz."

"A birthday present?" asked Mister Fitz. "For me?"

"According to the book I was reading, sorcerous puppets have a common birthday," said Sir Hereward. "The fourth day of the Second Month."

"But I am not a common puppet," said Mister Fitz. "Nor can it be said that I was born on any particular day, given my gradual ascent to full sentience over the course of my making. Besides, those other puppets have their birthday on the fifth day of the Second Month."

Hereward shrugged, grimacing as he felt a pang from the wound in his shoulder and a renewed ache in his foot.

"I appreciate the thought," said Mister Fitz. "Now tell me. This broken mandora doubtless figures in the strange events that have just come to pass?"

"There is a triangle-folded, thrice-sealed missive inside," said Hereward. "Which is strange enough, and stranger still when you consider yonder book, which until I hit that shade-walker, or whatever it was, was a much larger volume."

"I remember opening the chest to pick up the mandora, and nothing since," said Lallit. "Perhaps I may take your second blanket for a robe, Sir Hereward?"

"Pray do not cloak your beauty on my account . . ." began Sir Hereward, then, as Jabek of the Axe shifted noisily behind him, hastily added, "I mean, please do."

Mister Fitz crouched over the remnants of the book, flipping the pages with one of Sir Hereward's daggers. He then examined the mandora.

"It is simple enough," he said. "The book—which I am surprised you did not note is set in that type called Sorcery and thus highly suspect—is part of the revenge upon their creditors set in play by the sorcerer-merchants of Jerreke. Forced into slavery by their own economic ineptitude, they contrived to bind twinned otherworldly entities to their service. One would be constrained within a book or some such household item, the other in an instrument, or perhaps a game set. The items would be sent separately to the chosen target, in the hope that this would enable them to bypass any sorcerous protections. When both were in proximity, the bonds would release the entities, who would slay everyone within reach."

"But only one entity came forth," said Sir Hereward. "And it didn't try to kill me, at least not at first. It wanted me to open the parchment that was inside the mandora."

"The sorcerer-merchants of Jerreke were famous as inept merchants and ineffective sorcerers," sniffed Mister Fitz. "In this case, the spell was set off long ago, but due to the botched execution, only one entity was released. Realizing its twin was still entrapped within the mandora, it had to wait inside the chest for the opportunity to make someone else release its companion. Neither Sister Gobbe, who initially brought you the book, nor Lallit, both being in the eye of her god, would be suitable persons to release the twin, so it came down to you. However, by breaking the item that had once held it in bond—the book, or rather the outer pages bound around these remains—you immediately banished it."

"But the twin is still trapped inside the mandora?" asked Sir Hereward.

"Indeed," said Mister Fitz. "And as, of course, it is a listed entity, albeit a minor one . . ."

"Yes," said Sir Hereward. "Lallit, Jabek, if you would excuse us for a few minutes?"

"Certainly, Sir Hereward," said Jabek. He turned and left at once. Hereward helped Lallit to stand, holding her perhaps a little closer than was necessary. She looked him in the eye as she stood up, and smiled.

"I am sorry about your vow, Sir Hereward," she said. Her breath was very sweet, and the blanket very loose upon her body. "I have a vow also, as do all the novices of Narhalet-Narhalit . . . that until we are consecrated, we shall not . . ."

"I know," said Sir Hereward, with a glance at Mister Fitz. "I mean, I know now. Best you be going, Lallit."

"If it were not for the god's presence, reminding me of what I will become, I might have forgotten that vow," whispered Lallit. Then she was gone, wafting past him.

Hereward sighed, hopped over to his saddlebag, and got out a silk armband, a brassard embroidered with sorcerous symbols that shone with their own light, though this was faint under the sun's bright shaft that came in through the northern window.

"Should I fix your shoulder first?" asked Mister Fitz, as he took his own brassard out from under his hat, and slid it up his arm.

"It's only a trifle. I think that Nar-Nar has already stopped it bleeding," said Sir Hereward. He gave a grunt of pain that lessened the effect of this statement, twitching his shoulder as he settled the brassard above his elbow. "I may well get another wound in the next few minutes, to keep you busy. Now, will you open the parchment and I shall strike it on the head with the mandora?"

"Yes," said Mister Fitz, his slim puppet fingers reaching in through the now-slack strings to pull out the sealed triangle. He held it ready, and looked at Sir Hereward. "But first . . ."

"I know, I know," grumbled Sir Hereward. "What's the thing's name? Or do I just say 'Summoned Antagonist'?"

Mister Fitz looked at the parchment for a long second. His painted eyes could see many more things than any human gaze, both in and beyond the ordinary world.

"Hypgrix the Second."

"Right."

Sir Hereward picked up his sabre and set it ready on the bed, just in case, before holding the mandora high above the parchment. Then he spoke, the words coming as they always did, familiar and strong, the symbols on his and Mister Fitz's brassards growing brighter with every word.

"In the name of the Council of the Treaty for the Safety of the World, acting under the authority granted by the Three Empires, the Seven Kingdoms, the Palatine Regency, the Jessar Republic, and the Forty Lesser Realms, we declare ourselves agents of the Council. We identify the godlet manifested in this parchment of Jerreke, as Hypgrix the Second, a listed entity under the Treaty. Consequently, the said godlet and all those who assist it are deemed to be enemies of the World and the Council authorizes us to pursue any and all actions necessary to banish, repel, or exterminate the said godlet."

Mister Fitz broke the seals on the parchment of "godlet," and even as the creature within boiled up like smoke and began to coalesce into something resembling flesh, Sir Hereward brought the mandora down upon it. Both beast and instrument immediately turned to dust, Mister Fitz gestured, and the dust blew out the window and was gone.

Sir Hereward winced as he sat back down on the bed, and looked at Mister Fitz.

"Now, tell me," he said. "Why are you covered in salt?"

"Salt?" asked Mister Fitz. "It is not salt, but powdered bone and chalk. I have been digging in the tomb of some ancient, vasty creatures. It has been most interesting. Though not, it is clear, as exciting as your reading."

"Perhaps not," said Sir Hereward. He lay back on the bed, and pointed at a long wooden case that lay on the floor near his saddlebag. "If you can spare yourself from your digging, what say you to a game of kings and fools?"

Mister Fitz's pumpkin-size head slowly rotated on his ridiculously thin neck, and his blue eyes peered at Sir Hereward's face.

"So soon after your last defeat? You are transparent, Hereward, but I doubt you have found some real advantage. The better player always wins."

"We shall see," said Sir Hereward. "Please lay out the set, and if you would be so kind, call down for ale.

"Oh, and put this back in its place." Hereward stripped the brassard from his arm. "I trust that I will not need it, at least until we reach Bazynghame?"

"Best keep it near," said Mister Fitz as he picked up the game box. "There is the small matter of what I was digging for—and what I have found . . ."

LOSING HER
DIVINITY

T WAS A YEAR AGO, OR SLIGHTLY MORE, AS I RECALL.
I was coming back from Orthaon, I had been there to
discuss the printing works at the original monastery,
they had a very old press and, though it worked well
enough, it had been designed to be driven by slaves, and since
the most recent emancipation a number of the mechanical en-
couraging elements needed to be removed, quite a difficult task
as the original drawings for the machine were long lost and
some parts of it were very obscure.

What? Oh, no, I was not present as a mechanician, I was
there to write an account of the reworking. I thought it might
prove to be of some interest, for one of the city gazettes, or perhaps as a selection in a book that I have begun, observations of
curious machines, sorceries, and the like.

You might yourself make an interesting dozen pages, Master Puppet. I have heard of you, of course. Read about you too,
unless I miss my guess. That is to say, I have read about a certain
sorcerous puppet who bears a striking similarity, in the works of
Rorgulet and in Prysme's Annals—oh, of course, Sir Hereward,
you would rate at least as many pages, I should think. But you

desire discretion, and I respect that. No, no, I *will* be discreet, I do not write about *everything*. Yes, I am aware of the likely consequences, so there is no need for that, good knight . . . please, allow me to withdraw my throat a little from that . . . it looks exceedingly sharp. Really? Every morning, without fail, one hundred times each side, and then the strop? I had no idea. I do not treat my razor so well, though perhaps it gets less shall we say . . . use . . . no, no, I am getting on with it. Have patience. You should know that I am not a man who can be spurred by threats.

As I said I was coming back from Orthaon, traveling on the Scheduled Unstoppable Cartway, in the third carriage, as I do not like the smell of the mokleks. Speaking of razors, what a job it must be to shave a moklek, though I have heard it said it is required only once, and the handlers rub in a grease that inhibits the regrowth. Done at the same time as the unkindest cut of all, though nothing needed there to prevent the regrowth, of course. It is interesting that the wild mammoths treat the occasional escaped moklek well, as if it were a cousin who had fallen on unfortunate circumstances. Better than many of us treat our cousins, as I can attest.

Yes. I was on the Cartway, in the third carriage, through choice, not primarily through lack of funds, though it is true both fare and luxury reduce from the front. We had stopped, as is common, despite the name of the conveyance. My compartment was empty, save for myself, and though the afternoon light was dim, I had been correcting some pages that the dunderheaded typesetter of the *Regulshim Trumpet-Zwound* had messed up, a piece on the recent trouble with the nephew of the Archimandrite of Fulwek and his attempt to . . . ouch!

I told you I need no such encouragement, and it would have been a very short digression. You might even have learned something. As I was saying, the light suddenly grew much brighter. I

thought the sun had come out from behind the skulking clouds
that had bedeviled us all day, but in fact it was a lesser and much
closer source of illumination, a veritable glow that came from
the face of a remarkably beautiful woman who had stepped up
to the door of my compartment and was looking in through the
window. A very good window; they know how to make a fine
glass in Orthaon, no bubbles or obscuration, so I saw her clear.

"Pray stay there, for a moment!" I called out, because the
light was extremely helpful, and the proofs were such a mess
and set quite small, and there was this one footnote I couldn't
quite read. But she ignored me, opening the door and entering
the compartment. Rather annoyingly, she also dimmed the radiance that emitted not only from her beautiful face, but from
her exposed skin. Of which there was quite a lot, as she was clad
only in the silken garment that is called a rhuskin in these re-
gions, but is also known as a coob-jam or attanousse. I am sure
you know it, a very long, broad piece of silk wound around the
breast and tied at the front and back so that the trailing pieces
provide a form of open tabard covering the nethers, save when
a wind blows or the wearer attempts a sudden movement, as in
entering the compartment of a carriage on the Scheduled Unstoppable Cartway.

She had very fine legs. I may have admired them for a
moment or two, before she interrupted the direction of my
thoughts, which I must confess were running along the lines of
the two of us being alone in the compartment, and the interior
blinds, which could be drawn, and why such a beautiful, shining woman would intrude upon my compartment in particular,
even though of course it is not entirely unusual that beautiful
women throw themselves upon . . . why do you chuckle, Sir
Knight? Not all women favour height and splendid mustaches,
and the obvious phallic overcompensation and fascination with
swords . . . and yes, daggers like that one, which I do not want

thrust through my hand, thank you. This hand that has written a hundred . . . well, ninety books . . . and has many more to write! Thank you, Master Puppet. I would be grateful if you could keep your . . . your comrade contained.

So. She was in the compartment, beautiful, illuminated, and semi-naked. Obviously a sorceress of some kind, I presumed, or a priestess, perhaps of Daje-Onkh-Arboth, they tend to be lit up in a similar fashion. I had no idea then what she actually was, you understand.

She smiled at me, winked, and sat down on the cushions opposite.

"Tell them you haven't seen me, and put me in your pocket," she said, very sultry and promising. "It shall be to your advantage."

"Tell who—" I started to ask, but she shrank away before my very eyes, and in a matter of moments there was no longer a shining woman on the cushion, but a small figurine of jade, or some similar greenstone, no taller than my thumb. Now, as you can plainly see, I am a man of the world who has seen a great deal more than most, but never anything like that. I picked up the figure, and was further surprised to find it very cold, as cold as a scoop of ice from the coolth-vendors you may have seen along the street here, offering their wares to chill a drink or a feversome brow.

I put her in my pocket, the deep inner one of my outer coat, where I keep a selection of pencils, an inkstone, and other odds and ends of the writer's trade. It was none too soon, for there was a commotion outside only a few seconds later, with a great clattering of armour and the usual unnecessary shouting of military folk, the roar of battle mounts and the like, all of which I understood immediately to be the sudden arrival of some force bent on intercepting the conveyance, which meant more stopping and greater delay. I was not pleased, I tell you, and even less so when two rude troopers flung open the compartment door, waved a pistol and a sword in my face, and by means of emphatic gestures and strange, throat-deep grunts, demanded that I alight.

Naturally, I refused, pointing out to them that there were numerous treaties guaranteeing the inviolate nature of the Unstoppable Cartway, and that by interfering with it they were risking war with no fewer than three city-states, and the Kingdom of Aruth, admittedly a great distance away at the terminus, and not only these polities but also the parent company of the Cartway, which they might not know was the Exuberant Order of Holy Commerce, well known for its mercenary company business, in addition to its monopoly on Hrurian nutmeg, the original source of the order's wealth, which by curious chance—

Your interruptions, sir, delay matters far more than my minor educational digressions. Yet I protest in vain, as in fact occurred with these other soldiers. After they had dragged me out quite forcibly, I ascertained that in fact they were deaf-mutes, directed solely by a sign language that I did not know, involving numerous finger flicks from their officer. This fellow, from his ill-fitting gun-metal cuirass and the crushed plumes of his helmet, was clearly more priest than soldier, the armour worn over robes of an aquamarine hue flecked with silver bristles, here and there showing silver buttons that were embossed with the heads of two women, one gazing left, the other right, and apparently sharing the same neck. I did not immediately recognize this outfit, but then there are many gods in the Tollukheem Valley, some with multiple orders of followers.

"Have you seen Her?" asked the officer, the capital *H* readily apparent in his speech.

"Who?" I asked.

"The Goddess," said the officer. The capital *G* was also very evident.

"What goddess?"

"Our Goddess. Pikgnil-Yuddra the Radiant One."

I must admit that upon hearing this description the jade figurine felt suddenly very much heavier in my pocket, and I felt a similar chill around my heart. But I gave no sign of this, nor of the slight unease that was beginning to spread in the region of my bowels.

"Am I to understand you have lost a goddess?" I said to the officer, with a yawn. "I am afraid I have never heard of your Pikgnil-Yuddra. Now, I trust you will not be delaying the Cartway for very long?"

"Pikgnil-Yuddra the Radiant," corrected the officer, with a frown. "You are very ignorant, for our Goddess is the light that does not fail, the illuminatrix of the city of Shrivet, and verily for leagues and leagues about the city!"

"Shrivet . . . Shrivet . . ." I pondered aloud. "But that is at least a hundred leagues from here. I take it the illumination does not extend that far? I believe here we fall under the aegis of the god of Therelle, the molerat-digger Gnawtish-Gnawtish?"

I made up the molerat godlet, of course, for my own amusement. That part of the world is so infested with little godlets that no one could know them all, and as the soldiers were from Shrivet, which was indeed a great distance away, they would have no clue.

"Other gods do not concern us," said the officer. "Only our own. She must be here somewhere; we were only an hour at most behind her chariot."

"Chariot?" I asked. I looked around, hoping to see it, for I was naturally curious about what style of chariot a luminous goddess might drive, and what manner of locomotion might propel it, or beasts draw it.

"Crashed half a league back," said the officer. "But near the track of this . . . this . . ."

He gestured at the carriages of the Cartway, and the ten

mokleks harnessed in line, with their mahouts standing by their heads and the guards in the howdahs watching the temple soldiers search with surprising equanimity or possibly cowardice—certainly they had made no attempt to intervene. There were more guards by the rear carriage, and the conductor-major herself, but they were even more relaxed, offering wine to another priestly officer.

"It is called the Unstoppable Cartway," I said. "Though clearly it is neither unstoppable nor do the mokleks draw carts, but luxurious carriages. I believe in its infancy, carts were drawn, carrying a regular cargo of foodstuffs from Durlal to Orthaon, and manufactured goods on the return—"

The officer was, as might have been expected, uninterested in learning more. He interrupted me most rudely.

"Have you seen the Goddess?"

"I don't know," I countered. "I am traveling alone in my compartment, a blessed luxury, but I confess I have looked out the window from time to time, and upon several occasions have seen women."

"You would not mistake her for a mortal woman," snapped the officer. "She is bright with virtue, her light constant, a shining star to guide correct behavior."

"No, I can't say I've seen anyone like that," I said. By this point I had noticed that while everyone had been rousted from their compartments, there were no individual searches taking place and the general ambience had become more relaxed as the Goddess was not found within the carriages. There seemed only a small chance that the jade figurine would be found upon my person, and I must confess that I was intrigued by this search for a goddess, even more than I was interested in her physical charm.

"Does your Goddess regularly take . . . ah . . . unscheduled journeys?"

"Pikgnil-Yuddra the Radiant does not leave the city ever," said the officer firmly. "Only Yuddra-Pikgnil the Darkness may leave the city."

I confess that a slight frown may have moved across my brow at this point. Discussing godlets with their priests is often fraught with difficulty, and this search for a goddess who had not left, or who possibly had, but under a different name, was very much in keeping with the tradition of godlets who did not at all correspond to their priesthood's teachings or texts.

"I'm not sure I follow," I said. "You are searching a hundred leagues from Shrivet for a goddess who does not leave the city ever, and there is another goddess who does leave the city but you are not searching for her?"

"They are the twin Goddesses of Day and Night," said the officer. "Pikgnil-Yuddra the Radiant may not leave the city, and Yuddra-Pikgnil the Darkness may not enter, save at certain festivals. A week ago, the temple was discovered to be empty, the warders slain, the bounds broken, and Pikgnil-Yuddra the Radiant was no longer housed there."

"So it is Pikgnil-Yuddra the Radiant you are looking for?"

"We seek the Goddess in both aspects," said the officer. "For it may be the doing of Yuddra-Pikgnil the Darkness that has unhoused Pikgnil-Yuddra the Radiant, in their eternal struggle for the souls of the people of our city."

"I see," I said, though to be accurate, the only thing I saw was yet another idiotic priest, a member of a hierarchy that was preserving their authority by drawing upon the power of an imprisoned extra-dimensional intrusion that had become anthropomorphized by long association with mortals. Yes, unlike the great majority of the deluded people who populate this world, I do not think of them as gods or godlets. Indeed, it has been theorized that should a mortal here be somehow introduced to some other plane of existence, there they too would have the powers and attributes seen here as godlike. But I speak to those who know far more than I, if indeed you are as I believe you to be, agents of that ancient treaty—ah, you are a barbarian, Sir Knight, to so interrupt civilized discourse in the interest of what you like to call the bare facts. I will continue.

Suffice to say that after some show of searching and questioning, the priestly soldiers departed and the Cartway continued. Shortly after the cries of the mahouts had ceased and the mokleks had stretched out to their full shamble, our conveyance traveling at a remarkable speed only slightly slower than a battlemount's lope, I felt a stirring in my coat pocket. Reaching in, I withdrew the jade figurine and set it upon the seat at my side, whereupon a few moments later it once again became an alluring woman, or rather goddess, though this time she kept her radiance dimmed to the extent that she merely glowed with the luster one finds inside the better kind of oyster shell, one likely to provide a pearl.

"So, you are a runaway goddess, to wit, one Pikgnil-Yuddra the Radiant," I said conversationally as she rearranged her rhuskin, not for modesty, I might add, but rather to show off those beautiful limbs to even greater advantage.

"Don't be silly," she said. "I am, of course, Yuddra-Pikgnil the Darkness. But you can call me Yuddra."

"I am slightly confused," I replied. "The priest-officer said that it was your, ahem, counterpart—"

"Sister," corrected Yuddra. "You might say we are twins."

"Your sister, then, who had become unhoused and traveling. Also, if you are the Darkness, why are you illuminated?"

"There is no difference between us," replied Yuddra, stretching her arms up towards the padded ceiling—padded these last twelve years, I might add, since the unfortunate overturning of a carriage that was inhabited by the Prince-Incipient of Enthemo, resulting in his crown being forced down over his ears, the ceiling back then being considerably harder—a stretch that made me catch my breath, I confess. I reached out to her, and to my extreme disappointment, found my hand passing through the waist I had hoped to encircle, Yuddra proving no more substantial than a wisp of steam.

"There is no difference between us," repeated Yuddra. "In fact, we have swapped roles many times over the past millennia. Sometimes I stay in the temple, sometimes Pikgnil does."

"But now you are both wandering," I said, essaying to lift her hand to plant a courteous kiss, but with the same result as my previous attempt. "Out of your temple, far from your power, and pursued by your priesthood. What has brought you to this pass?"

She smiled at me and leaned in close, with just as much effect as if she were normal flesh and blood, perhaps even more so, given that the tantalization of not being able to touch is well known as an erotic accentuator, one employed to great effect in the theater of . . . yes, yes, you know what I'm talking about, I'm sure, puppet excepted.

"Just such a matter as now concerns us both," she said. "I am jade and air, and have always been so, save for brief periods of corporeality. My sister, as always, is the same, and both of us . . . want more."

"So you are able to assume a fleshly form?" I asked, this being the chief part of her speech that I had taken in. "For some short time?"

"Yes," said Yuddra. "But it is difficult. Pikgnil and I want to permanently assume mortal form, so that we may experience in full the experiences we have heretofore only . . . tasted."

"What do you require to assume a mortal form?" I asked, being driven by curiosity as always. "For those short periods, I mean."

"Blood," said Yuddra, and smiled again, showing her delicate, finely pointed teeth. "Mortal blood. A few clavelins might grant me an hour, but where to find a willing donor? It must be given freely, you see."

A clavelin? A small bottle, about so tall, so round, commonly used here for young wine. Not an excessive amount and, though I am no barber-surgeon, I knew that a man could lose more blood than that without fear of faintness.

"I should be happy to oblige Your Divinity," I said. Long caution caused me to add, "Two clavelins of blood and no more, I can happily spare, and indeed I would welcome a charming and *touchable* companion to lessen the drear of this journey."

She smiled again and agreed that such a diversion would be pleasant, that in fact a great part of her desire to assume a permanent mortal form was to engage in just such activities as I suggested, but on a more regular basis. I must confess that I had expected her to use those sharp teeth to draw my blood in the manner of those creatures some call the vampire, but rather she had me use my penknife to make a cut on my hand, and allow blood to drip into the saucer of one of the teacups provided by the Cartway, along with the samovar that had been bubbling away since Orthaon. As I let the drops of blood fall, Yuddra licked the liquid from the saucer, very daintily, after the fashion of a cat. As she consumed the blood, I saw her grow more corporeal, the pearly light fading and her skin becoming . . . real, I suppose, though still extraordinarily beautiful.

I shall draw the shades on the window of this retelling, as I drew the actual shades in the carriage. Suffice to say that time passed all too quickly, and far too soon I found her growing once again incorporeal, though there was a curious pleasure to be derived when she was neither truly there nor entirely not. I believe she also found the time well spent, Sir Knight, so you can wipe that small smirk from your face. I have studied the works of the great lover Hiristo of Glaucus, and practiced much therein, up to page one hundred and seventy-seven, and there is a young widow who resides near me who has agreed that we shall together essay the matter of pages one hundred and seventy-eight to eighty-four—

Yes! I am getting on with it. The blinds were drawn up, the Goddess sat opposite, the sun shone in, and we had got another dozen leagues closer to Durlal. I made a cup of tea—the black leaf from the Kaz coast, not the green from Jinqu—and made further inquiries of Yuddra, if indeed she was that sister.

"So you wish to no longer be a goddess, but to become permanently mortal?"

"I do," said Yuddra, eyeing my steaming cup of tea with a wolfish, hungry look. "I have not, for example, ever tasted that drink you have. There are so many tastes, so many experiences that are beyond the purely energistic to savor, as I would do!"

"But tell me, how is it that you will become mortal?" I asked. "Surely not by the imbibing of blood, for if two clavelins amounts to but an hour, then the supply required to maintain corporeality would be . . . monstrous, and not likely to be freely given."

She laughed and tossed her head back.

"Pikgnil has found a way, or so she said in her last missive. I am to meet her at Halleck's Cross, and then we are to make our way to . . . but perhaps I should not tell you, for despite our embraces, I fear you are not entirely sympathetic to my cause."

There she glanced at the ring I wear, which, as you see, shows the sign of the compass, the mark of my order. I was a little surprised that she should be so worldly as to recognize the sign, and beyond that, have some understanding of the strictures, yet only a little, else she would have understood that I would have no wish to stand in the way of a god who desired mortality, believing as I do that we mortals must be paramount over gods, that it is our works that will endure, when the last godlet is thrust back to whence it came. I believe this is a more extreme view than you share yourselves, for I understand you have fooled yourselves with definitions, gods deemed beneficial or trivial, and gods malevolent and harmful, to be destroyed or banished. We consider them all a pest, to be gotten rid of at any opportunity. Though use may be made of them first, of course.

"It is true I do not care for gods," I told her. "But as you wish to become mortal, I shall consider you a mortal and not my enemy. Provided your aim does not require the exsanguination of many people by trickery, for example."

"No, it does not involve blood," said Yuddra. She shifted near the window, and looked out. "I think we near Halleck's Cross and here I must leave you. Please, do not speak of our tryst, indeed even of our meeting, for we must remain free of the temple, and they have many spies and paid informants."

"I will not speak of it, nor write of it," I said. "I hope that one day we might meet again, when you are but a mortal woman and not a fleeing goddess. Should you wish to, my house in Durlal is easily found, it has a roof of yellow tiles, the only such in the street of the Waterbear."

There is little more to tell of that first encounter. As we drew up at Halleck's Cross, she turned once more into that cold jade figurine and, at her instruction, I carried her from the platform and across the street, depositing her in the branches of the ancient harkamon tree that marks some ancient battle. I turned back after I crossed the street, and saw a cloaked and hooded figure swoop upon the tree, take up the figurine, and be gone, a person that though shrouded, I reckoned to be the sister goddess.

And that, I presumed, was that. A curious encounter, a brief and no less curious tryst, and an odd tale that I had promised not to tell. I had work to do, pages to be corrected, stories to be written. I soon forgot Pikgnil-Yuddra the Radiant and Yuddra-Pikgnil the Darkness, save in some half-remembered dreams, in which the two of them happened to come by . . . ah . . . such dreams are sweet, though sadly oft ill-remembered . . .

Please! I continue. Yes, I did see the Goddess again, as I am sure you know or you would not be here, taking up time I had allocated to write a denunciation of the guild of parodists' most recent stupidity. I saw her a few days ago I think . . . What? It is not easy to be exact when one works as much at night as in the day. Very well, it was last night, but already this one is almost at the dawn, so it is not so far to say two days ago.

I was working here, in my study, sitting in this very chair. I heard a faint knock at that door, though no visitor had been announced and indeed my goblin had long gone to bed and so would not have answered the front door in any case. Having some respectable number of enemies, I took up the pistol from the drawer, that same pistol you have confiscated, Sir Knight, though I know not the reason, any more than you should take my paper knife, for all it looks like a dagger. I assure you the sharpness is required to swiftly slit a signature of this rough paper I use for notes, that my neighborly printer sells me very cheap as being offcuts and remainders. A blunt knife will tear and rip, and is no use at all.

"Come in," I called out, my voice steady, for all that my finger was upon the trigger and my heart beat a little more rapidly than was usual.

The door opened slowly, and a bent figure entered, to all appearances some aged crone, so covered in shawls and scarves that I could not make out a face at all, until she shuffled closer and straightened, so that the light of my lamp fell upon her face. An aged and withered face, a woman twice my age or more but yet . . . there was something familiar there. Her eyes were bright, and younger, and I knew her.

It was Pikgnil-Yuddra, or her sister. No longer radiant, no longer young, rather greatly aged and very clearly mortal.

"You know me, then?" she croaked. Her voice still retained something of her former self, but her appearance astounded me. It was no more than a year since we had met on the Cartway.

"Yuddra-Pikgnil the Darkness," I said quietly, but inside I felt a new excitement, for I suspected there was a story here such as few might ever hear, a story that having heard, I might then remake in writing and call my own.

"Yes. I was once Yuddra-Pikgnil the Darkness," said the old woman, and creaking, she sat where you sit now, Sir Puppet, and set her bag, a shabby cloak-bag of boiled leather, upon the seat you occupy, Sir Knight. "And you once expressed a desire to see me again, and so I have come."

I was a trifle alarmed by this, sensing some undercurrent of permanent residence being suggested, but that could be dealt with later, I felt. The important matter was the story; the story was the thing!

"But tell me, how have you come to be as you are now?" I asked. "What of your sister? Where did you go?"

"After Halleck's Cross," said the old woman. She looked past me as she spoke, her old eyes seeing things that were not there, at least not for me to see. "Where did we not go? It was my sister's plan, she was the one who had thought upon it longest, and it was she who found the way. Not the blood drinking, for that would not answer, not for very long. If we could have drunk blood taken forcefully, that would have been a different road, and we did try that, when we were very young. But it did not work, and we could not discover why it did not work, save that it was a stricture of our making, when first we came.

"We tried other things, sought wisdom from sorcerers and priests, wizards and wise folk. None of them could help us. In the end it was Pikgnil who found the answer, a decade or more ago, when she was being me, outside the temple, wandering in search of how we might escape our godhood.

"There is a place far to the northwest, beyond Keriman and the Weary Hills, beyond even Fort Largin and the Rorgrim Fastness, up in the mountains beyond the Valley of the Hargrou, just below the peaks where the Diminished Folk dwell. A place called Verkil-na-Verekil, a ruined city, yet where some mortals still live, eking out their simple lives.

"Pikgnil had found an ancient text that spoke of Verkil-na-Verekil, of the city before it was ruined, of the king who ruled there, and of his crown. It was his crown that interested us, for the text spoke of its singular property, that it could make a man a god . . . or . . ."

She smiled, her teeth no longer white and shining, but gray with age, and broken at the edges.

"Or make a god a man.

"It was a long way to Verkil-na-Verekil, a difficult way, for our powers were greatly reduced with every league we traveled from Shrivet, the locus of our extension from the otherworld. By the time we passed Rorgrim Fastness and began to climb into the mountains, I could not take the jade shape, and it took both of us together to conjure some little light. Worse than that, we were fading, our energistic presences weakening. It became doubtful that we could even reach Verkil-na-Verekil, it might be simply too far . . . but we resolved to press on. We did not know what would happen if we did overextend ourselves, whether our existence would be terminated, or the stretched energistic threads that led back to the temple would contract, and we would find ourselves once again imprisoned in Shrivet. By then, we did not fear termination and should we end up back in the temple, we would simply try again. So we pressed on.

"We did reach Verkil-na-Verekil in the end, albeit as thinly

painted caricatures, little more than half-caught reflections in a
mirror . . . which in some ways was helpful, for the people there
were still loyal to ancient ideals, and guarded the ruins well,
some of them armed with weapons that could slay even such as
we were . . . yet thin as shadows, we slipped past them, and went
deep into the ruins and there, in the deep of the mountain, yes,
we did find the crown."

She fell silent then, her eyes downcast, her ancient hands
trembling with the import of what she told.

"Go on," I said. "You found the crown . . . Did you put
it on?"

"Pikgnil put it on," whispered the old woman. "Even as she
raised it to her head, I felt a presentiment of doom and the flash
of a long-forgotten memory. I screamed at her to wait, but she
would not wait."

"It made her mortal?" I asked.

"Yes. It made her mortal, with the full weight of all our
years," said the woman who had been a god. "I saw her turn
to flesh, and smile in triumph, and then the smile twisted, fear
shone in her eyes as that flesh sank upon her bones, the smile
became a rictus grin, and then she decayed before my eyes,
turned to charnel meat and thence to bare, fleshless bones, and
I felt the magic flow from the crown, and I too became mortal
and my shadowed shape took flesh, and I remembered that long
ago, when we first burst out upon this world, we were one, a
single thing, and it was called Pikgnilyuddra, that only became
two as the centuries passed and the priests wove stories that
shaped us, the twins of day and night . . . and all of those thousands of years we had been upon this earth, all of them came
pouring into me from the crown!

"I lunged forward and slapped the crown from the skull
that wore it . . . saving some scant few years of life, but too late,
for I am as you see me now. Mortal but ancient, too old for the

simplest pleasures that I hoped to taste, too old even for those who guarded the crown to consider an enemy, so that they let me by, thinking me only a crazed old biddy of their own people. And so I came, in many weary steps and by weary ways, to Durlal. I remembered a scribbler, who I had some fondness for, and so here I am and here I would rest, before I go on to Shrivet and my rightful place."

So there you have it. I gave her some supper, a bed, a cloak. In the morning I added some money to her purse, enough for the fifth carriage on the Cartway to Orthaon, and from there she would have an easy way to Shrivet.

That is all I can tell you. I suppose you would catch her easily if you took the next Cartway, she won't have gotten far from Orthaon. I presume you do wish to catch her, that she must be . . . tidied up, the books made correct? Even if she is no longer a rogue goddess, but mortal, still your business, if as I presume your business is indeed the dispatch of such unhoused and irregular godlets?

Other business? What other business could we possibly have? I have told you everything. Yuddra was here, she left, she is no longer a god. I am a busy man, I have much to write, look at this desk—

The bag? Her bag? Yes, I did mention a bag, boiled leather, with bronze clasps. I have no idea what was . . . Why are you putting on those armbands? What does the writing on them mean? It is no text that I recognize. I do not like this, though you are guests in my house I think I shall leave, at once!

Ah, that hurt, and is quite unnecessary. Yes, I shall sit quietly, though I do not like your mumbling, it smacks of priestly doings and, as you know, I am by reason of principle opposed to priests and gods.

Mister Fitz, you unnerve me, as a puppet you are alarming enough, but if that is what I think it is, sorcery is forbidden within this precinct, and there is no need for it, none at all.

What are you doing, Sir Knight? That is a particularly ancient casket, most precious, where I store my old manuscripts; there is no occasion to open it, and in any case I have lost the key. Though now I think of it, perhaps the key is in the pocket of my other coat, which I left at the Dawn-Greeter's Club after some revels the other day. You know of the club, I'm sure, frequented by night workers, particularly printers and the like. I shall just slip over there and fetch my coat, and the key—

How now! There's no need, you might have merely asked me to take my seat again. I shall not get the key, then, and so your curiosity about my old parchments and scribblings will not be answered. Why should I shield my eyes? I shall do no—

I see, or rather, I see with some difficulty. That was a most remarkably bright flash, Master Puppet. As I mentioned, that is . . . or was . . . a very ancient casket, and melting off the lock will have damaged its value considerably. I fear I must ask you to pay for it, a matter of at least ten, no a dozen, guilders of this city, none of your sham coin. And I must forbid you to ransack my papers . . . yes, I have laid an old cloak upon them to keep out the damp. I must suppose that the smell is from some vellum that has grown a noxious mold, or an inadequately scraped calfskin, I write upon various materials. I am in the middle of an important piece now as it happens, and so must require solitude to continue, please . . .

A corpse? An old woman's corpse? I have no conception how that might have gotten there. You are playing some complex joke upon me, perhaps? I shall call for the Watch! Help! Help! Help! Heeeelp!

I presume from the lack of muffling, smothering, or other restraint that you have already paid off the Watch? Such foresight

indicates men . . . a man and a puppet . . . attuned to pecuniary
advantage. I have some wealth, and would happily pay a suitable
sum so that this matter may remain confidential. Shall we say
twenty guilders? No? Fifty, then? A hundred guilders! It is all
that I have, take it and leave me . . .

The bag under her feet? With bronze clasps? As you can see,
untouched by me. I didn't kill her, she just died in her sleep, she
was old. I put her in the casket for now, to avoid trouble. Her
bag likewise, see, the crown is there. I hid it so that it could not
be used by others who might be tempted!

What? Of course I didn't wear the crown! How dare you
make such a suggestion. I wear the compass, I am on the square.
"Men before gods" is my creed. Such a crown is worthless to
a true man. Take it, and go, and I shall not swear a complaint
against you. It is against my beliefs, but I shall not stop another
from becoming a god, clearly I cannot stop you in any case.

You do not want to become a god, Sir Knight? And you,
Master Puppet, with your sorcerous needle, what are you doing? Yes, yes, this time I shall shield my eyes, but that crown is
valuable in itself . . .

I should not have believed it if I had not seen it myself.
To destroy such a beautiful thing, even though it be tainted
with . . . with evil magic. But I presume that completes your
business here. Allow me to show you to the door, and I trust
that we shall not meet again.

Another needle, Master Puppet? What can you need with
another needle? The crown is destroyed, the old goddess is dead,
all is right with the world, or will be once I am finally left alone!

What? I told you I would never put on the crown. How can
you see signs of . . . I don't understand . . . energistic tendrils . . .
unlawful protrusion of entities . . . it is all Khokidlian to me,
pure nonsense, so upsetting in fact that I need a drink. I will
fetch a bottle and we might share it as a stirrup cup for your

departure . . . ah . . . that really did hurt and was quite, quite unnecessary. We are all friends here, are we not?

Yes, I confess, I am a curious fellow. I collect oddments, ancient jewelry, that sort of thing. Perhaps I did just touch the crown to my forehead, but nothing happened, nothing much, and anyway, how could you know? I tell you I am not a godlet, I am just a man, I will cause no trouble, I am just a—

A CARGO OF
IVORIES

"W E SHOULD HAVE PURCHASED THE MONKEY," whispered Sir Hereward as he balanced precariously on the ridge of the tiled roof, which was shining bright under the moon and had become extremely slippery, the result of the squall of needle-sharp rain that had just blown through and over the erstwhile knight and his puppet-sorcerer companion, Mister Fitz.

Neither looked the part of knight or sorcerer this night. Sir Hereward was garbed in the soot-stained leather vest and breeches of a chimney sweep, the latter cut short at the knee, with a coil of rope over his shoulder and a dagger at his belt rather than a sword; and Mister Fitz had assumed the disguise of a sweep's boy by putting a ragged and filthy hood over his pumpkin-shaped papier-mâché head and child-sized leather gauntlets on his wooden hands.

"The monkey was insufficiently trained, and its mind not well formed enough for the impressing of sorcerous commands," Fitz whispered back.

"It stole my purse easily enough," countered Sir Hereward.

"If we had bought it, then it would be here, and I wouldn't be wet and cold and—"

"The matter is moot, as we did not purchase the monkey, and furthermore we have arrived at our point of ingress."

Sir Hereward glanced ahead at the huge brick chimney stack that protruded six or seven feet from the roof. Halfway up the stack, a thin ribbon of gold had been affixed to the brickwork, the metal etched with many malevolent-looking runes and sorcerous writings.

"The monkey could have jumped straight to the top of the stack and avoided those curses," said Sir Hereward. He shuffled forward a pace or two, wincing as his bare feet found a sharp edge to the copper that sheathed the ridge.

"Jumping to the top would not avoid them," said Mister Fitz. His piercing blue eyes reflected brightly in the moonlight as he studied the gold ribbon. "The architect-sorcerer who made this place was well versed in her art."

"I trust you can counter the spells?" asked Sir Hereward.

"It were best to leave them in place but render them less efficacious," replied the puppet sorcerer. He rummaged in the pouch at his belt as he spoke, withdrawing a number of long pieces of onionskin paper that were heavily inscribed with runes, written in an ink the color of dried blood, in close lines.

"Less efficacious?" asked Sir Hereward. "In exactly what proportion? Those are death curses, are they not?"

"Indeed," said Fitz. He licked the roof with his long, blue, fabriclike tongue, picking up the moisture he would need in lieu of the saliva his mouth did not make, moistened one of the pieces of paper, and carefully pasted it over the gold ribbon, pressing it hard against the brickwork of the chimney. The runes in the gold began to glow hotly, before being soothed and quieted by the counterspells on the paper. "They will now merely cause a pang, an ache, or something of that order."

"There are many degrees and varieties of ache," said Sir Hereward gloomily. But he took the coil of rope off his shoulder and pressed the catch on the grapnel that extended its three barbed arms. "Shall I fix this in place now?"

"Not yet," said the puppet, who was peering closely at the lip of the chimney. He took another paper, wet it in the same manner, and stuck it over the cornice. "A clever mage. There were hidden spells upon the top bricks. But I believe it is now safe enough to proceed. Are you confident of the plan?"

"If everything is as we have been told, and as you have scried," said Sir Hereward. "Which, of course, is almost certainly not the case. But I do not think Montaul suspects our coming, which is something."

The house whose ensorcelled roof they were perched upon belonged to the aforementioned Montaul, commonly known as "Flatpurse"—not because of his poverty but because of his vast riches, which he denied existed and did not easily spend. He had drawn the attention of Sir Hereward and Mister Fitz, who were only house-robbers upon occasion, because two days previously he had secretly taken delivery of a cargo of ivory figurines, seventy-four finger-high carvings that represented the godlets of the far kingdom of Asantra-Lurre. Possibly unbeknownst to Montaul, fourteen of the figurines were not merely representations of godlets but energistic anchors that secured the actual deities to this mortal plane and could be used to summon them into renewed existence. As the said godlets were all proscribed for various reasons, usually their inimical nature, the destruction of the ivories had long been sought by the Council of the Treaty for the Safety of the World, the possibly mythical, often thought defunct, and generally surprising sisterhood that Sir Hereward had been born into, his male gender a surprise that had not been allowed to interfere with his usefulness. Mister Fitz, on the other hand, was both male and female, or neither, or whichever he wished to be, and had served the Council in various roles almost since its establishment by a number of now mostly vanished polities several millennia gone.

In other places, or perhaps other times, it would not have been necessary for Sir Hereward and Mister Fitz to climb over the rooftops and make entry into Montaul's house through a death charm–warded chimney. But the city of Kwakrosh was far from any of the Council's traditional allies who might exert some influence or force. Here, Montaul was not only a councillor and a colonel of the city's trained bands, he also reluctantly but wisely paid good, fine-minted money to a great number of judges, advocates, watchmen, and thief-takers to ensure that if any criminal activity was going on, it would be done *by* him rather than *to* him or to his exceedingly valuable property.

Hence the rooftop in the rain and the descent down the chimney.

Sir Hereward gritted his teeth as he lifted one leg over the papered charms to straddle the chimney stack, expecting something like a dagger strike to the groin, this being the kind of thing Mister Fitz might call an ache. But there was only a faint tingle, reminiscent of the sensation usually called pins and needles, that came from sitting too long in one spot.

Fastening the grapple to the lip of the chimney, he let down the rope as slowly and quietly as he could, till it hung slack. If the plans they had bribed the chimney-tax inspector to provide were accurate, the rope should now be hanging a foot or so above the top of the open hearth. Close enough to drop easily but hidden from view.

"Considering the quantity of Alastran wine you drank last night, I think we should take a moment to recapitulate the plan," said Mister Fitz quietly. "I go first, to take care of any additional sorcerous defenses. You follow on the count of eight . . ."

"Ten. I thought we agreed ten," whispered Sir Hereward.

"What if there is something that takes you more than a moment to dispel? I don't want to blunder into a death spell or skin separator or the like."

"Very well. You follow upon the count of ten. We emerge in the Great Hall, likely deserted—"

"Hmmpf," said Hereward, which was not exactly disagreement but a certain hedging of bets.

"Likely deserted due to Montaul's parsimony, apart from the hounds who have free range of the interior," continued Mister Fitz. "If they are present, we throw the soporific bone I prepared earlier . . . I trust you have that somewhere easy to reach?"

Sir Hereward indicated the left leg of his breeches, where there was an unusually large bulge that extended almost to his knee, marking the position of the segmented bone that Mister Fitz had imbued with a sleeping spell for dogs. The bone itself was jointed in quarters, to allow each of the four lurchers, grippers, alaunts, or whatever breed of guard dog there was inside to tear off and secure its own portion. The merest lick would then send them to sleep. Fortunately, the soporific bone only worked on dogs, so it was safe to handle. Mister Fitz knew many variations for other species, though when he prepared it for humans, the spell was normally emplaced in confectionary or sweetmeats, unless intended for cannibals such as the terrible inhabitants of the ruined city of Coradon.

"We turn right, along the hall, up the steps, and through the inner door to the countinghouse," said Mister Fitz. "Scrying suggests that this inner way is not locked when Montaul is in residence, he likes to come and go, but in any case I have two remaining curiosities, which should suffice to pick the lock if it proves necessary."

"We grab the ivories, open the main door of the countinghouse from the inside, go across the courtyard, fight the gate guards who won't be expecting us, go out the night postern, and run away," picked up Hereward. "Simple, elegant, straight-forward."

"I would not describe it as elegant," said Mister Fitz. "However, it should serve the purpose. Shall we proceed?"

"Please do," said Sir Hereward, inclining his head as if ac-knowledging someone of importance at a ball or court levee.

Mister Fitz gripped the rope with both gauntleted hands and began to climb down the rope headfirst, his blue-pupiled eyes staring down into the sooty darkness.

Hereward counted to twelve before he followed. His move-ments were not as fluid as the puppet's, but he climbed with a spare efficiency, the technique learned years before as a super-numerary aboard the pirate chaser *Termagant Biter* returning to him without conscious thought.

The chimney, though rarely used, in accordance with Mon-taul's cheeseparing ways that begrudged the purchase of any fuel, was still caked with soot. Though Hereward tried to keep to the rope and only touch the side with his feet, he swung a few times on the way down, and his back and elbows dislodged a considerable quantity of choking, black dust. Much of it blew up as well as sinking down, so that by the time he gently low-ered himself down next to Mister Fitz, they were both entirely blackened, their chimney sweep disguises much enhanced.

The hall was not only empty, but very dark. Montaul did not approve of candles or lanterns in rooms where he was not present. Mister Fitz could see perfectly well, but Sir Hereward had to depend upon his ears alone, and he didn't like what he was hearing. A wet, slobbery snuffling that sounded likely to precede the crunch of large teeth, and it was much closer than he deemed secure. It also did not sound particularly like a dog. It was louder and just . . . different.

"Hand me the bone," said Mister Fitz, who seemed calm

enough, though this was little indication of the seriousness of the situation. Mister Fitz was always calm.

"What is it?" whispered Sir Hereward, moving very slowly to pull the soporific bone out of his trousers. He moved slowly because he was deeply concerned that a sudden movement might hasten the transition from slobbering noises to crunching ones, with his hand or arm featuring as the source of the crunching.

"A basilisk," said Mister Fitz. "It's licking my glove right now."

"A basilisk!" hissed Sir Hereward, instinctively screwing his eyes tight at the very mention of the petrifying beast. "Will the bone work on a basilisk?"

"We shall see," replied Mister Fitz. Hereward felt the puppet take the bone and a second later the slobbering noise increased, followed by the hideous crunching sounds he had feared. Almost immediately they then ceased and were punctuated by a very loud thud, a strong vibration through the floor, and the cessation of the munching and crunching.

"Remind me to amend my treatise on soporific bones," said Mister Fitz. "I thought there was a slim chance it would prove efficacious, as Plontarl's Index states there was dog in the original hybrid made by Kexil-Ungard when it created the first basilisks. A gaze-hound, perhaps, though there is clearly a preponderance of reptile in the creature—"

"Is there?" asked Sir Hereward, with no small degree of sarcasm apparent in his voice. "Given I can't see a thing, I must trust to your opinion. Could we perhaps continue? With a little light?"

"Indeed," replied Mister Fitz.

The puppet did not resort to an esoteric needle for something as simple as shedding a little light. Instead Sir Hereward noticed two faint blue sparks appear, as if a copperized wick had been lit. Slowly they grew brighter as Fitz increased the luminosity of his eyes, an old trick of his that had more than

once proven to be of great value, most famously when the
hasty reading of a map at midnight had resulted in Hereward's
leading a rear guard to safety, rather than certain defeat and a
lingering death, since the enemy in question were devotees of
Pozalk-Nimphenes, a god whose concept of prisoners of war
was indistinguishable from that of food, so anyone captured
was invariably fed into its insatiable but toothless maw, expiring
days later in the god's otherworldly stomach or whatever organ
processed things so devoured.

Fitz did not make his eyes shine very brightly, so Hereward
squinted as he poked his head out of the hearth and looked
around the hall. The basilisk was a dark shape on the floor just
beyond the bronze firedogs. As far as he could tell from its silhouette, it looked entirely like an ugly lizard, which is what he
had always thought they were, albeit ones with the power to
mesmerize their prey into statue-like stillness.

"Why would there be a basilisk here?" asked Sir Hereward
as he slowly looked around the room. "Unless there is some trap
to set lights going, it would be entirely wasted in the dark."

"I do not think it is an intentional inhabitant of the house,"
said Mister Fitz.

"There is something else near the door to the counting-
house," said Hereward. He could make out a silhouette that at
first he had thought some very large piece of furniture, but it
was moving slightly, suggesting breathing. "The door behind
it is ajar. Can you see what it is?"

The puppet edged out next to him, holding Hereward's
knee for a moment as he leaned around the marmorealized foot
of a moklek, the shorn and domesticated cousins of the wild
mammoth. This hollowed-out foot served to hold several pok-
ers and other useful fireplace implements, including a six-tined
toasting fork.

"Yes . . . I can," said Mister Fitz. "Curious."

"What is it, if you don't mind?"

"A pygmy moklek. An albino, I should think. Which is surprising, but also presents us with an opportunity."

"A basilisk and an albino pygmy moklek were most definitely not part of the plan," said Sir Hereward. "Nor do I consider the presence of said creatures to be an 'opportunity.' That moklek is lying in front of the door. Does it have tusks?"

"Short tusks jeweled at the tips," confirmed Mister Fitz. "It is asleep."

"Even a moklek can lose its temper, and even short tusks can disembowel," said Sir Hereward. "The jewels might even help. The question is, how did it get here?"

"The 'why' may also be relevant," suggested Mister Fitz, his tone educational. He had never really given up his early role as Sir Hereward's nurse and tutor.

"Lord Arveg, whose house lies adjacent to the perimeter wall here, has a private menagerie . . ." mused Sir Hereward, after a moment's thought. "If breaches were made in the west wall of his house, and then the eastern wall of this . . . but there has been no explosion, no petard blast . . ."

"Stone may be dissolved by sorcery," said Mister Fitz. "Animals transported energistically through solid matter. Sound may be dulled, or sent elsewhere, via a number of magical instruments."

"Someone else is after the ivories," concluded Sir Hereward. He drew his dagger, turning it so the light from Fitz's eyes did not reflect from the bright steel blade. "Presumably a sorcerer."

"Or someone equipped with sorcerous apparatus," agreed Mister Fitz. He reached inside his sooty robe and withdrew an energistic needle from some hidden interior pocket, holding it tightly inside his gloved fist so that its shocking light could not escape, nor the energies within curdle Sir Hereward's mind or vision. "They might also have a different aim in mind, apart from the ivories. Montaul has many riches, and many enemies. In any case, it is doubly unfortunate, for use of sorcery may . . . wake something in one of the ivories. They tremble on the verge of immanence at the best of times. We had best hurry."

Sir Hereward nodded, stepped out of the fireplace, and began to walk cautiously towards the door out to the counting-house, his bare feet silent on the flagstones. Mister Fitz rustled at his side, the light of his eyes like a hooded lantern in a mine, illuminating the way just enough for safe movement while creating shadows at every side that hinted at terrible things.

"Are you sure the moklek is asleep?" whispered Hereward as they drew closer.

"No, I think it is merely resting," said Mister Fitz. "Don't tread on its tail."

As they ascended the four steps to the door to the counting-house, skirting the pygmy moklek, it suddenly stood up, turned about very daintily on the spot, and made a plaintive whuffling noise with its trunk.

Sir Hereward stopped in midstep and tightened his grip on his dagger. It was fine Trevizond steel, and very sharp, but whether he could punch it through the weak spot in a moklek's head above and between its eyes was very much a moot question. Particularly if it had to be done while trying not to be disemboweled.

"There, there," said Mister Fitz, reaching out to stroke the trunk that came questing out to them. "All will be well."

"Are you talking to me or the moklek?" whispered Sir Hereward.

"Both," said Mister Fitz. "It is a youngster, and scared. There, there. All will be well. Say hello to the moklek, Hereward."

"Hello," said Sir Hereward. He reached out gingerly with his left hand and joined Mister Fitz in gently stroking the moklek's trunk.

"You had better come with us," said Mister Fitz. "Follow along."

The moklek made a soft trumpeting noise and took a step forward. Sir Hereward hastily jumped up a step and bent down to whisper in Mister Fitz's ear.

"Why are we bringing the moklek? You didn't want a monkey. Surely a moklek is no better?"

"It is a very smart moklek," said Mister Fitz. "As opposed to a particularly stupid monkey. And it may prove useful. As I said, its presence provides an opportunity. One that may be lost if we don't procure the ivories quickly."

Sir Hereward sighed, hefted his dagger, and sidled through the open doorway and along a short corridor into the countinghouse proper. He had expected this large chamber to also be dark, but it was filled with moonlight, courtesy of a large, ragged round hole in the eastern wall where something sorcerous or immensely acidic had melted through a three-foot thickness of good red brick.

The person presumably responsible for this absence of wall was in the middle of the room, opening drawers in Montaul's trading desk, a massive piece of powerful but ugly furniture that had dozens of drawers in great columns of polished mahogany on the left and right of the actual writing surface, a slab of Perridel marble characteristically veined with gold.

She whirled around as Hereward took another step though he thought he'd been extremely stealthy, and, in the next instant, he had to parry away not one but two thrown daggers, which flew clattering to the wall and the floor. She followed that up by jumping to the desk and then to the ceiling, running along it upside down by virtue of Ikithan spider-slippers, dropping on Hereward from above in a move that he fortunately recognized as the vertical shearing scissor-leg attack of the long-defunct but still influential warrior nuns of the Red Morn Convent, and so was able to adopt the countermove of swaying aside and delivering two quick punches to the head as she descended. One of the punches was with the pommel of his dagger, and so particularly efficacious. The thief, as she must be, dropped to the floor long enough for Sir Hereward to press a knee on her back and place the point of his dagger in the nape of her neck, angled so that it would strike through to the brain with little effort.

"Move and you die," he rasped. "Also, we are not guards, but visitors like yourself, so there is no profit in employing any unusual stratagem or sorcery you may be considering."

"You are trespassers, then," said the woman coolly. She was dressed in thieves' garb, entirely in dark grey, a single suit of it like a cold-weather undergarment, complete with a padded hood. Even prone, she was clearly tall and lightly built, but as evident from her jumping, made of corded muscle and sinew.

"As are you," said Sir Hereward. "What are you looking for?"

"Trespassing against the guild, I mean," said the woman impatiently. "I have bought the license to steal here. But if you release me and go now, I will not take you to the Thief-Mother's court for the doubtless inevitable separation of thumbs from hands."

"Ah, a *professional* thief," said Mister Fitz. "We are not, however, here to rob Montaul. We are reclaiming stolen property."

"Oh," said the woman. "You are agents, then?"

Sir Hereward grew still and his grip on his dagger tightened, ready to drive it home. A human's brain was so less well protected than a moklek's as he knew well. It would be an easy and quick death. Not that his and Mister Fitz's occupation was necessarily secret, it was simply that only their enemies tended to know who they were.

"Agents?" asked Sir Hereward, his voice flat and dull.

"Of the Barcan Insurance? Or the Association of Wealth Protection?"

"Insurance agents," said Mister Fitz. "Yes . . . but from far away. We have been tracking a stolen cargo for some considerable time. Now we believe it has arrived here."

"Then we can come to an agreement," said the thief. "My name is Tira, Thief of the Seventh Circle of the Guild of Thieves in Kwakrosh, Lesemb, and Navilanaganishom. Who might you be?"

"I am Sir Hereward," said Hereward, though he did not ease off with his knee or remove his dagger. "My companion is known as Mister Fitz. Where are the guards from the courtyard outside, before we get to talking about agreements?"

"Asleep," said Tira. "I sprinkled Nighty Dust down on them from my shadow-stilts, as they gathered to gossip about tomorrow's battlemount races."

"And the wall here, was it dissolved with a spray of Argill's Discontinuance of Stone, or something else?" asked Mister Fitz.

"Argill's," confirmed Tira. "And the wall of Arveg's menagerie across the courtyard, though I must confess that was an error. The mixture was stronger than I thought and the wind came up. But the creatures are docile, I presume made to be that way. There is nothing to fear from them."

"You have invested considerable coin to enter here, on stilts and dust and dissolving," said Mister Fitz. "You seek some particular treasure?"

"Montaul is known as a very warm man," said Tira.

"Please answer the question," said Sir Hereward.

"The new ivories," she said, after a moment's pause. "The Guild has a buyer for them. But I guess that's what you are after too, is it not, arriving so soon on their heels?"

"Yes," said Sir Hereward. "But not all of them. Only fourteen are . . . covered by our contract. You can have the others. Agreed?"

"Agreed," said Tira.

Hereward removed his dagger, leaned back, and stood up.
Tira rolled over and looked up at him. Her hood was drawn
close about her face, and though her skin was dark, her nose and
cheekbones had also been painted with a grey stuff almost the
same color as her curious garment, to dull any shine. As far as
Hereward could tell, she seemed fair, or as fair as could be without facial scars, and she looked younger than he had expected.
Her eyes were hidden behind a strip of a dark red gauzy cloth
loose-woven with hundreds of tiny holes, allowing her to see
while offering some protection against such things as a basilisk's
gaze, unless it got nose to nose, by which time its petrifying
properties would be of the least concern. The fact she was wearing it suggested that she had not spoken the truth about dissolving the wall to the menagerie by accident.

"I could have got free, you know," she said.

"Doubtless," agreed Sir Hereward politely, though he
thought quite the opposite. "Where are the ivories?"

"Not here," said Tira. "Or so I had just discovered when
you came."

Sir Hereward looked around the room. Apart from Montaul's trading desk with its drawers askew, there were three lesser
perching desks for his clerks, a cabinet whose doors were open to
show the papers and parchments piled within, and a great chest
with its padlock awry and its lid back. Mister Fitz was already
inside the chest, rummaging around.

"Nothing of consequence," said the puppet. "A fallen coin
or two in the corners. I should say it was emptied in some hurry.
Hereward, go and see if Montaul is in his rooms upstairs."

Hereward nodded and ran up the circular stair in the corner, returning a scant minute later with a shake of his head.

"Chamber's empty. Like a monk's cell up there, thin blanket
and all. But our watchers . . . they were supposed to blow their
screech-whistles if anyone left, damn them!"

"Oh," said Tira. She made a motion with her fingers, indicating the sprinkling of dust. "They were *your* watchers . . ."

Mister Fitz jumped out of the chest and went to the door that led out to the gatehouse, his back bent from the waist, his round head close to the ground. At the door itself, he sniffed the ground, dust swirling around his papier-mâché nose, though its carefully molded nostrils did not inflate.

"One of the godlets has begun to manifest," he said shortly. "Some hours ago, I judge. We must presume it now controls Montaul's actions and follow before it can fully emerge upon this plane and ease the way of its fellows from the pantheon of ivories."

"Godlet?" asked Tira. "What godlet?"

"The ivories are not simply treasure," said Hereward, as he went to the door and unbarred it, using only his left hand, the dagger ready in his right. "At least the fourteen we seek. Did you make the gate guards sleep as well as those in the western court?"

"No," said Tira. She retrieved her thrown knives and went to stand by the knight, Mister Fitz bringing up the rear, his sorcerous needle still hidden in his gauntleted hand.

"You would think they would enter," said Sir Hereward, "given the noise within. Moklek and basilisk, and all your rummaging about. Ready?"

"They are not valiant, nor young," said Tira, readying her knives to throw. "Go!"

Sir Hereward pulled the door back. Tira stood with knives poised, then slowly lowered them. Sir Hereward moved past her, and looked down at the two desiccated bodies that lay on the steps. They were more vaguely human-shaped parcels of dust wrapped in mail than bodies, their swords lying next to withered hand-and-arm bones that would have not disgraced some revenant a thousand years dead.

"It needed life to stabilize its presence," said Mister Fitz, bending down to sniff again at the bodies of the guards. "They were convenient."

"Do you know which one it is?" asked Sir Hereward. There were fourteen ivories, and fourteen godlets, but of that number, one was far more to be feared than any of the rest.

"No," answered Mister Fitz. "It has left no obvious signs or declarations, and we cannot spare the time to take a sample of whatever essence it may have excreted."

"I like not this talk," said Tira. "If I had not seen these two, I might think you sought to scare me from my rightful theft."

"You need not come with us, lady," said Sir Hereward over his shoulder as he ran to the gate, ignoring the small night postern they had planned to use, for it would not be broad enough to permit the moklek's passage. Mister Fitz ran after him but jumped to one of the torch brackets above, and peered through an arrow slit, taking care not to draw too close to another ensorcelled band of gold set there to slay any child, monkey, or ensorcelled rat that might otherwise be able to creep inside.

Behind them, the pygmy moklek gingerly investigated the wizened bodies with its trunk, gave a snort of disgust, and trotted after the knight, thief, and puppet.

"I am no lady," said Tira as she helped Sir Hereward lift the bar of the gate. "I am a Thief of the Sixth Circle of the Guild of Thieves in Kwakrosh, Lesemb, and Navilanaganishom!"

"I thought you said the Seventh Circle," said Sir Hereward.

"When I return with the ivories," said Tira. "I merely anticipated my elevation. In truth, I did not expect any complications with godlets."

Mister Fitz dropped down as they opened the postern.

"There is some commotion by the harborside," he said. "It will be the godlet. Quickly!"

Montaul's house lay on a low hill directly above the harbor, so that he could watch the arrival and departure of his ships, the foundation of his riches. A cobbled road ran down to the long, semicircular quay where four ships were tied up at the jetties that thrust out from the quay like fingers from a hand. A few other vessels were some distance away, bulky trading cogs lying at anchor under the shelter of the mole, a long breakwater of great stones that protected the harbor from wind and wave, with a hexagonal fort at its seaward end, built to protect the port against pirates and naval foes. The fort could fire forge-heated red-hot shot from the cannons on its walls, and explosive bombs the size of a puncheon from the great mortar that squatted in the centre of the fort like a fat spider in a hole. Except that, as with many other civic buildings in Kwakrosh, it was somewhat neglected, and only fully manned in time of obvious threat, the good worthies of the town council not wanting to recognize that by that point it would be too late.

Sir Hereward, Mister Fitz, Tira, and the pygmy moklek ran down the harbor road, fleet shadows in the night. The moon lit the street in stark relief, casting silver shadows and reflecting off the puddles left by the earlier rainstorm, illuminating the drunks asleep in the doorways of the warehouses closer to the quay—drunks who upon inspection in the morning would be found to be no more than husks within their layers of rags.

"It must be after a ship," called out Sir Hereward. "But the wind is against the mole and the tide on the flood, no ship can leave harbor tonight."

"Not under sail," answered Mister Fitz. He pointed ahead to the most distant jetty, where there was the sound of screaming, suddenly cut short, and a yellow lantern winked out. Behind it, the dim outline of a long but relatively low ship with only a single stubby mast could be seen.

"The hexareme?" asked Sir Hereward, sidestepping a particularly deep-looking puddle in an area of missing cobbles. He referred to the state ship of Kwakrosh, a relic of the past, that was rowed out once a year for the Grand Mayor to perform the ritual throwing of the flotsam, a floating basket of spices, wine, cloth, smoked herring, and a very small amount of silver currency. This was then fought over by all the bum-boaters, fisherfolk, and semiaquatic layabouts of the harbor in joyous anarchy, a mark of respect for the ancient days when the town had been no more than a village of wreckers.

"But it has no rowers, no crew," said Tira, who ran easily at Sir Hereward's side.

"If the godlet is strong enough, it will bend the oars by energistic means," said Mister Fitz. "I am heartened by this."

"You are heartened?" asked Sir Hereward. "If it is strong enough to row a hexareme of sixty benches against this wind and tide, it is too strong by my measure!"

"It indicates a certain stupidity, a singleness of purpose," said Mister Fitz. "It wants to return to Asantra-Lurre, not knowing or caring that the kingdom is no more, and a thousand leagues distant besides."

"What is *it*?" asked Tira. "Do you mean Montaul?"

"Montaul lives no more, save as a vessel for the godlet," said Mister Fitz.

They reached the quay as he spoke, cobbles giving way to the smooth planks of the boardwalk. Two watchmen in the livery of the town guard stared at them nervously, their lantern-adorned halberds held high over the starched and dehydrated body of one of their companions, her arms frozen in the act of trying to fend off some horror that had come upon her.

"Who . . . who goes there?" stuttered one of them.

"Friends," called out Sir Hereward easily as he ran past, momentarily forgetting he was covered from head to toe in soot, was barefoot, had a dagger bare in his hand, and was ac-

companied by a sorcerous puppet, an obvious thief, and an albino pygmy moklek.

"Oh good," said the watchman nervously to their backs. He
raised his voice to add, "Uh, pass, friends."

Up ahead, there was a great squeal of long-unused timber
moving against bronze, and the splash of water as the hexareme's
starboard oars all came out at once, the port side being up against
the jetty.

"We must board before it shoves off," said Sir Hereward,
increasing his pace, bare feet pounding across quayside to
jetty. The hexareme's oars were tumbled together for the moment, but were already lifting and shifting, energistic tendrils of
bright violet visible through the oar ports as the godlet sought
to properly organize the rowing benches, like a team of octopi
sorting toothpicks.

"Do we *want* to be on board with whatever is doing that?"
asked Tira.

"The godlet's mind and power is bent upon moving the
ship," said Mister Fitz, who had jumped to Sir Hereward's
shoulder as the sprint became too fast for his short legs. "While
it is focused upon that task, we have a better chance of dispatch-
ing it to whence it came."

"Almost there!" panted Sir Hereward. He jumped to the
gangway and ran up it even as the starboard oars dug deep and
the hexareme groaned and moved diagonally away from the
jetty, mooring ropes at stern and bow singing as they stretched
taut. There was a great crash as the gangway fell, the pygmy
moklek jumping the last few feet, the deck resounding like an
enormous drum as it landed.

"Why is that moklek still following us?" asked Sir Hereward, who had narrowly avoided being crushed by the pachy-
derm's leap.

"I asked her to," said Mister Fitz. "As I said, she could be very useful. Time for the declaration. We have a few minutes now, I doubt the godlet is aware of our presence, it being fixated on a swift exit from the harbor."

The starboard oars sank in and pushed again. The mooring ropes snapped with cracks like gunshots, and the hexareme wallowed far enough away from the jetty for the portside oars to come out, again propelled by energistic tendrils.

Sir Hereward and Mister Fitz reached into pocket and pouch and brought out silk armbands, which they slipped over their arms, above the elbow. Sorcerous symbols began to shine upon the cloth, brighter than the moon. Then man and puppet spoke together:

"In the name of the Council of the Treaty for the Safety of the World, acting under the authority granted by the Three Empires, the Seven Kingdoms, the Palatine Regency, the Jessar Republic, and the Forty Lesser Realms, we declare ourselves agents of the Council. We identify the godlet manifested . . . uh . . ."

Sir Hereward paused and looked at Mister Fitz, who carried on, the man echoing the puppet's words a moment later.

"Aboard this vessel as an unknown, but listed entity under the Treaty, as proven by its dire actions upon innocents. Consequently, the said godlet and all those who assist it are deemed to be enemies of the World and the Council authorizes us to pursue any and all actions necessary to banish, repel, or exterminate the said godlet."

"You're not insurance agents," said Tira. Her hood had come slightly unstuck in the race to the ship and slipped backward, showing more of her face. She looked even younger than she had previously.

"You could say we are," replied Mister Fitz. "After a fashion."

"In any case, you'll get your share of the ivories," said Hereward, thinking he correctly judged the fleeting expression that crossed Tira's eyes and flattened her mouth. "Presuming we survive."

The ship lurched sternward as the oars on both sides moved in unison, a clumsy, lurching progress that made the deck tilt one way and then the other, with every part of the old ship groaning and screeching in turn.

"We won't get far like this," said Sir Hereward. "I doubt this tub has been out in anything but a dead calm for years, and going in the right direction at that. Where is the godlet? And what's to stop its sucking the life out of us as we approach?"

"It is underneath us," said Mister Fitz. "In the centre of the ship, on the middle deck. As long as it keeps rowing, it will have no energy to spare for dehydrative assaults."

"And if it stops rowing?" asked Tira.

"The ship will probably sink," said Sir Hereward, who didn't like the feel of the deck under his feet. The planks were shifting sideways, the hull clearly lacked rigidity, and it was already down a foot or more at the stern, not so much piercing the small harbor waves as plowing into them. "It is moot whether it will turn turtle as soon as we pass the mole, or be driven under stern first."

"We must get the ivories before then," said Mister Fitz. "If the ship does sink, the godlet will realize that it can simply walk on the floor of the sea. For the moment, it is still imprinted with Montaul's view of the world and his human limitations."

"Is it weak enough for you to banish it with your needle?" asked Sir Hereward. "We distract it, while you get close enough?"

"I fear not," said Mister Fitz. "Rather we must secure the ivory figurine that anchors it, bring it up here, and have Moonray Pallidskin Helterskelter III step on it."

Sir Hereward followed the flick of the puppet's eyeballs to the left, indicating their animal companion.

"You mean the moklek?"

"It is one sure means of destruction for such things," said Mister Fitz. "To be trodden on by an albino moklek. That is why I said it was an opportunity. Considerably more convenient than our original plan to take the ivories to the fire pools of Shundalar, and cheaper than committing them to the priests of the Infallible Index to be stored without hope of retrieval. Though it would be even better if our friend here had silver shoes, that speeds the process—"

"How you do know her name?" interrupted Sir Hereward.

"It is carved on her right tusk," said the puppet. "That is her pedigree name. But there is a name on her left tusk, which I suspect she prefers. Rosie."

The moklek raised her trunk and gave a short, soft trumpet. Almost as if in answer, a red rocket suddenly shot up from the fort on the mole, followed by two cannon blasts.

"Not so swift on the alarm," said Sir Hereward, eyeing the rocket's trajectory with professional interest. When not engaged directly in the elimination of inimical godlets, he was a mercenary officer of artillery. "And their powder is damp. That rocket should have gone twice as high."

"Even with damp powder, the idiots in the fort might hit us if they decide to shoot," said Tira. "It is close enough."

"So how *do* we get to the ivories?" asked Sir Hereward, grabbing at a rail and wincing as the oars sank again to drive the ship backward, and a particularly nasty groan came from the timbers below, the vessel shivering down its whole length as it was propelled too fast into the swell. They were already a good hundred yards out from the quay and heading into brisker waters away from the protection of the mole. "I presume it keeps them close, and even if the thing is rowing for dear life, I don't fancy just strolling in on a desiccating inimical godlet."

"I suggest you and Tira climb over the sides and go in through the oar ports on the deck above it—"

"There are huge *oars* going up and down in those ports," interrupted Tira. "We would be crushed."

"It has already broken a number of oars, or they were broken before, so there are empty ports," said Mister Fitz. "Choose carefully, climb down, swing in. I will cast a nimbus on your weapons that will allow them to engage the energistic tendrils of the godlet. As you hack and slash them away from the oars, it will disrupt the rowing, and the entity will have to fight back. While it is distracted fighting you on the upper deck, I will sneak in on the middle deck where it lies, gather the ivories, and bring them up here, where Rosie will stomp on them."

"The fourteen ivories you mentioned," said Tira. "Not the others."

"Indeed," said Mister Fitz, who did not lie but did not always tell the truth.

"So there will be a few inches of rotten, worm-eaten oak between us and the main presence of the godlet?" mused Sir Hereward. "That is better than I feared. Do you wish to take the port or starboard side, Tira?"

"Neither," said the thief. "But having come this far, and waiting a year already for my Fifth Circle testing—"

"Fifth Circle?" asked Sir Hereward. "At this rate we will discover you were only apprenticed yesterday."

"Fifth, Sixth, Seventh, a haul such as these ivories will grant me rapid advancement," said Tira nonchalantly. "I will take the port side."

"Hold out your weapons and look away," said Mister Fitz.

They did so. The sorcerous needle flared, a flash of light illuminating the deck as if lightning had struck the stumpy mast above them. When they looked back, the needle was once again closed in Fitz's hand, and the blades of dagger and knives glowed with shimmering blue light, like a Wintertide pudding in burning brandy, only somewhat more impressive.

"A word of advice," said Sir Hereward to Tira. "Ikithan spider silk does not stick when subjected to seawater."

Tira looked surprised, but quickly schooled her face, and stripped the slippers from her feet. The nails of her big toes were clad in bronze, darkened at the tips with some kind of poison.

"Watch the oars through at least two strokes before you choose your port," added Sir Hereward. "Make sure you won't be caught by those forr'ard or behind."

Tira nodded. She looked scared, and Hereward thought he heard her suppress a whimper.

"You're really just an apprentice, aren't you?" asked Sir Hereward suddenly. "How old are you?"

Tira shrugged, then nodded her head again.

"Fifteen," she whispered. "And a half."

"Gods help us," muttered Sir Hereward, from the lofty height of his twenty-five years. "Stay here with the moklek. Please."

Hereward turned away from her and so did not see the smile that so briefly flickered across her face. He looked over the side, his head jerking back in momentary startlement at how low the hexareme was in the water, so low that the bottom tier of oar ports was only a handsbreadth above the sea, with the taller waves slopping in. If there had been any hope the ship would weather a turn past the protective mole, it was now extinguished.

It was the matter of only a few seconds to find a suitable gap, where no oars extended. He briefly considered holding the dagger with its energistic flames in his teeth but instead put it through his belt, climbed swiftly over the side, and, wasting no time, went feetfirst through the port below.

It was brighter belowdecks than above, the moonbeams through the ports faint beside the bright violet light of the energistic tendrils that worked the oars, tendrils that came up like a great trunk from below, through the gridded hatch in the lane between the empty benches, and then broke into branches extending to every oar.

Sir Hereward slashed at the closest tendril, severing it from the oar, and had to duck and dodge as the iron-shod shaft kicked up. He stayed low, crawling forward to hack at the next tendril, with similar results, and this time that oar crossed with the one in front, with a rending and splintering that spread along the deck as the oars in motion tangled with those suddenly stopped. The hexareme yawed broadside to the wind, and almost immediately listed to port, the lowest oar ports two decks below now fully submerged, water cascading in with unstoppable force.

Sir Hereward felt the list and heard the fateful gurgling. Leaping back from a tendril that came questing for him, not for an oar, he cut it in two and retreated to the port where he'd come in.

"Fitz!" he roared, in full sea captain's shout. "Do you have them?"

More tendrils came towards him, from both sides and in the front, and many more were giving up their useless, broken oars and reorienting themselves to attack. Hereward cut and slashed at them while he hung half out of the port. His bare foot touched the crest of a wave, and he felt the hexareme shudder with every wave. It was sinking, and sinking fast.

"Fitz! Do you have them?"

"Yes! Come up!"

The puppet's thin, reedy voice came clear and high through the bass groans of breaking timber and the drowning gurgles of the ship. Sir Hereward hacked at a tendril that was trying to grasp him by the throat, threw the dagger at another that almost had his ankle, and exited through the port faster than the monkey he had almost bought earlier had disappeared with his purse when demonstrating its abilities.

He was none too soon. The sea poured in under him as he climbed, and there was already water washing halfway up the main deck, which was inclined at an angle of some twenty degrees, perhaps halfway to turning over. Rosie the albino pygmy moklek was leaning against the mainmast, one foot raised, and Mister Fitz was placing a wooden case with a bronze handle and reinforced edges under that foot. The case containing the ivories.

Then the puppet was suddenly caught up in a glowing net of bright *blue* energistic spiracules and dragged away from the case, which was snatched up by Tira. Letting the netted puppet roll down the deck, she sprang to the port gunwale, the case in her right hand.

Sir Hereward swarmed up the slanted deck on all fours. Tira held up the case, smiled at him, and shouted, "Asantra-Lurre may no longer be, but we Asantrans live on!"

She turned to dive into the sea, just as Hereward drew his short, three-barreled pepperbox pistol from the secret pocket under his vest, cocked it, and shot her in one swift motion. Only two barrels fired, but at least one ball struck the thief, low on her right arm above the wrist. Blood and fragments of bone sprayed out. Tira dropped the case and fell over the side, her scream of anguish cut short by the green wave that caught her.

The case slid down towards Hereward. He bent and grabbed it, swinging it over to the moklek even as lurid violet tendrils broke out through the deck in a dozen places and shot towards him, and a hulking, vaguely man-shaped mass of sickening energies erupted from the aft companionway, its inhuman voice shrieking in some incomprehensible language that hurt Hereward's ears. The godlet staggered along the deck, and its farthermost tendrils reached with snakelike speed to grip Hereward around the bare ankles, his skin sizzling from the touch till he let himself slide down the deck to plunge into the great wash of sea that was roiling about above the already submerged gunwales.

As he fell, Sir Hereward cried out: "Crush the case, Rosie! Crush the case!"

The pygmy moklek trumpeted in response and brought her foot down on the case. It splintered, but did not break. A wave crashed in, sending Hereward, struggling amidst tendrils, back up towards the mast. The wash caught the case and threatened to push it away, till Rosie gripped the handle with her trunk. The godlet, or that portion of it within the remnant body of Montaul, staggered towards the ivories, reaching out, only to be seized by an energistic lash, white as lightning, that emanated from a needle in the hand of Mister Fitz, who had escaped the blue net and was now some ten feet up the mainmast backstay.

"Crush—" Sir Hereward called again, but a tendril closed around his throat, and his shout was curtailed, the breath stopped from his lungs. He tried to prize the noose open, but his fingers burned and could get no purchase, and more and more tendrils were wrapping themselves around every part of his body, squeezing and tugging, so that he was as like to be torn apart as strangled, or even drowned, as in their viciousness the tendrils kept shoving him underwater.

Rosie the moklek, her broad rear wedged against the mainmast, did not need to be told again. She raised her foot and brought it down with all her strength, smashing the lid of the case. Treading down, she ground the case and all the ivories within to dust, continuing to stomp and crush till there was nothing left larger than a tiny splinter.

The energistic tendrils grew flaccid and shrank back from Hereward, who crawled coughing and spluttering up the slanted deck, emerging from the froth of broken water just in time to see the tendrils withdraw into the corpse of Montaul. There, they dimmed to become small lights that flickered within the cadaver's eyes, mouth, and open ribs. Then there was a dull pop, a sudden rush of air against the wind, and the lights went out.

The remnants of Montaul fell to the deck and were whisked away by the roiling sea, for the hexareme had now settled so far that only a small part of its deck was above the surface.

"Abandon ship!" called out Hereward weakly. "She's foundering!"

Mister Fitz nodded, but instead of jumping to the sea from the backstay, he climbed up it, and then swung down on a rope to Rosie's back, where he perched easily atop her head. The moklek raised her trunk, ready for use as a breathing tube, shifted away from the mast, and plunged into the sea.

Hereward swam to them. Seeing that Rosie was at home even in the sea, and her broad back, though smaller than a regular moklek's, offered considerable room, he pulled himself aboard with a little help from Mister Fitz. Though the moklek's back offered only inches of freeboard, Rosie floated with the waves, and wind and tide were already carrying them back to the quay, aided by her four strong legs paddling vigorously below.

"Well shot," said Mister Fitz. "Somewhat making up for your misjudgment of the woman, though I should have come to expect that."

"She fooled you too," said Sir Hereward, grimacing as he felt his burned throat. "You, to be caught like a novice in an Ikithan net."

"True," mused the puppet. "It was fortunate she did not have one resistant to seawater. But I suspected her from the first, for she had too much sorcerous gear for any thief of Kwakrosh, even she be the Thief-Mother herself."

"Then why did you not—" said Sir Hereward hotly before a great crack sounded behind them, and man and puppet turned to see a gout of flame leap up from the fortress on the mole.

"Mortar bomb," said Sir Hereward, watching fuse sparks

trail across the sky. "They are poor aimers . . . if you have a needle left, Fitz . . ."

"None to hand," said the puppet. "My sewing desk is back at the inn."

"Or perhaps their aim is good," said Sir Hereward, as the spark trail plummeted towards the almost completely submerged hulk of the hexareme, only its stumpy mast now visible above the white tops of the waves, a hundred yards behind them. "But if the fuse is too long, the bomb will be drowned . . ."

A yellow-red flash lit the sky, followed a moment later by the shock of force through the water, and a moment later still by a great boom. As Hereward blinked to clear the flash from his eyes, he saw that there was no longer a mast or any other indication of the hexareme.

"I thought they were shooting at us," he said.

"Perhaps they were," said Mister Fitz.

"In any case, it will take them some time to load another bomb," said Sir Hereward, looking back again. "We will be ashore before then. It is a sad end for a famous vessel. One of the last surviving hexaremes of Ashagah, I believe. It will be difficult to explain to the worthies of the town, who I perceive are amongst the notable force gathering on the quay as our reception."

"Perhaps not so difficult, should we provide a suitable scapegoat," said Mister Fitz. He stood up on Rosie's head, held on to Hereward's shoulder, and pointed ahead.

Tira the thief, or priestess, or whatever she was, was floating on her back ahead of them, feebly kicking her legs. As the moklek drew closer, Hereward reached out and half slid her, half dragged her onto Rosie's back.

"Curse you," she whispered. "May Pixalten-Qockril send—"

Mister Fitz leaned across and pressed one wooden finger

against the middle of her forehead, his gauntlets being long since swept away. Tira stopped talking, her eyes rolled back, and Hereward had to turn her head so her mouth and nose weren't in the water.

"And we have money for bribes," continued Mister Fitz. He reached to his arm and pulled off the brassard, the letters fading. "All will be well."

"So I suppose," said Sir Hereward. He took off his own armband, slapped his hand lightly on the moklek's back, and added, "We have much to thank you for, Rosie."

"Indeed, she is a princess amongst mokleks," said Mister Fitz. "Quite literally, albinism is a mark of the royal line."

"Hexareme of Ashagah and mokleks," said Hereward thoughtfully. "It reminds me of a poem. Let me see . . .

Hexareme of Ashagah
From far-off Panas
Drumming down the sea-lanes
In search of easy prey
Seeking a cargo of ivories, gold, and mokleks . . .

"Bah!" protested Mister Fitz. "That is doggerel, a murder of the original poem. If you must recite, Hereward, you should do honor to the poet, not commit a crime!"

"It is a later translation, true, but nonetheless I stand by it!" protested Sir Hereward. "You and your heart of cypress have no feeling for verse!"

The moklek trumpeted, spraying them with a little seawater. A wave lifted her, and the east wind blew against Hereward's back, taking them shoreward, knight and puppet bickering all the way.

HOME IS THE
HAUNTER

THE CANNON WAS ONE HUNDRED AND TWENTY-five feet long and its rifled bore tapered from six feet in diameter at the breech to two foot nine and three quarter inches at the muzzle, using the old measures of the Mergantz system. Cast in bronze, the vast weapon's entire length was adorned with cryptic writings and fevered drawings of tormented souls, acid-etched into the metal. Never designed to be moved at all, the great gun was currently being transported upon a dozen carefully lashed-together ox carts, the whole being drawn by six mokleks, the shorn and gentled draft animals that were not to be confused with their wild cousins, the hairy mammoths of the icy wastes.

Sir Hereward was seated inside the howdah of the lead moklek, resting uncomfortably on the slightly padded shelf that was supposed to be a seat, and might have served as such for a shorter and slighter man. He would have preferred to be astride a battlemount or a horse, but their last horse had died the week before, and their last battlemount a few days after its final meal of horse.

The mokleks would go next, Hereward thought, though

their most pressing need was for water rather than food. He could then survive on moklek meat and blood for a considerable time thereafter, but without the draft animals the cannon would have to be abandoned here on the featureless steppe, the interminable grassy plain that he had loathed from the start of this ill-fated journey.

They were taking a route that his companion Mister Fitz had claimed would cut weeks from the more usual way between Low Yalpen and Jeminero. That followed the switch-backed road up and through the passes of the Kapoman Range. Though they would have needed even more mokleks to make the grade, the high road had no shortage of springs and wells and even several well-spaced and highly hospitable caravanserais.

Hereward's dry throat instinctively swallowed at the thought of arriving at one of those grand hostels, to be met at the gate with a silver ewer of chilled wine, as was the traditional welcome to important travelers. But the high Kapoman passes, the caravanserais, and the chilled wine were regrettably far distant. Here, there was only the sea of yellow grass that stretched ahead of him so monochromatically, till at the horizon it met with the downwards-curving expanse of an equally featureless sky of endless blue.

The knight sighed and shifted the carbine off his legs, so that he could stretch out and push his feet against the front wall. But the thin, pink-lacquered timber, hardly thicker than parchment, promptly splintered under his boot heels and the rear of the howdah began to bend behind him, requiring him to sit up straight again.

"Please do not destroy our accommodation," called out Mister Fitz as he climbed up the ear of the moklek. The ears were the only parts of the animal left unshorn, and a plaited and knotted rope of hair hung from each lobe to allow their mahouts an easy way to climb aboard.

"You will be glad of it when the rains begin," continued the puppet as he continued up onto the high roof of the howdah, which was made of thick canvas, painted with an oily concoction—also pink—that supposedly would repel any rain short of a tropical cloudburst. Not that there had been any rain, and in fact there was not even a single cloud to take the sting out of the sun. Even this late in the afternoon it still burned fiercely hot.

"What rain?" asked Hereward. He spoke to the puppet's shadow directly above him, showing through the pink canvas roof like a dark stain. "I keep hearing promises of rain, but I believe there is some requirement for clouds to be in the sky first."

"The rains are some days late, it is true," agreed Mister Fitz. "However, I do not believe it is a matter of concern."

"Possibly because you do not need to drink. However, I and the mokleks do, so if you have any thoughts about finding water, I would welcome them."

Above Sir Hereward, Mister Fitz's pumpkin-shaped papier-mâché head slowly swiveled around a full three hundred and sixty degrees before finally stopping as his gaze focused ahead and somewhat to the right of their line of march.

"I do not believe it is a matter of concern," repeated Mister Fitz, "because we shall shortly be wading through the stuff. I expect you will then curse the abundance of water, rather than the lack."

"Wading? Through what?" asked Sir Hereward. He shielded his eyes with his hand, and looked where the shadow of Fitz's arm pointed, but all he could see was the heat haze shimmering off the yellow grass.

"The Shallows, as the folk hereabouts call them," said Mister Fitz. "You will see them in a few more minutes, when we reach the crest of this rise."

"Rise?" asked Sir Hereward. He looked behind and scowled. He had thought they were making slow progress for flat country, but now he saw that the ground behind did slope away, albeit very gently. The ubiquity of the yellow grass and the heat haze had disguised the lay of the land, and he was disappointed in himself that he had not noticed it. As a soldier he prided himself on his awareness of any advantages or disadvantages the ground might offer if, as was often the case, battle was suddenly joined.

"Yes, a rise," said Mister Fitz. "We have climbed some sixty-eight paces in the last league. Assisted by the haze, an increase in altitude sufficient to mask the Shallows, even from the back of a moklek. Ah, look ahead now."

Hereward grunted as he turned about again and put another dent in the howdah with his elbow.

"Do be careful," chided Mister Fitz.

Hereward did not answer. He was gaping at the suddenly transformed vista that lay ahead. It was like one of the trompe l'oeil shows of the Participatory Theatre of Hurshell, where backdrop after backdrop slid away to reveal new scenes and worlds. Admittedly, the panorama of clear water and reedy islands ahead lacked the fornicating nymphs and satyrs of the Hurshell, which were possibly the real reason the theatre flourished, not the scenery behind the frolics.

"It seems unusual, topographically speaking," said Hereward. "A freshwater lake shallow enough to wade through—why does it not dry up?"

"It is the relic of a god," said Mister Fitz, in his instructional voice. "Some two thousand years ago, a benign entity known as Ryzha the Twelve-Wheeled, who since time immemorial had roamed the steppe, was partially subsumed by a much more aggressive intruder from the Beyond. The resulting entity, which became known as Yeogh-Yeogh the Two-Headed, was driven mad by its conflicting natures and wreaked great destruction before, with a little assistance, Ryzha managed to assert itself for the several minutes required to irretrievably cut its throat with one of its own sharpened hooves. A vast quantity of the godlet's blood spread across the steppe, and yet another struggle occurred as the dying godlets fought to render it into either acid or poison or something beneficial. I believe Ryzha tried to make it fermented goat milk, but instead achieved sweet water, which is preferable in any case, and certainly an improvement over the lake of extreme toxicity which Yeogh-Yeogh favoured. The sweet water has remained ever since, and so the Shallows were made."

"You mentioned Ryzha had a little help . . ." said Hereward, with a knowing glance at the puppet.

"Yes," said Mister Fitz. "Though not, in this case, from me. One of our own was involved, a distant relative of yours as it happens. You remind me of her sometimes."

"Oh?" asked Hereward. He smiled and sat up a little straighter. "In what fashion?"

"A certain similarity of facial hair," said Mister Fitz. "That, and an unfortunate tendency to lack forethought and allow un-warranted enthusiasms to distract you from the most pressing matters at hand. In fact, perhaps if I were to tell you of some of her more egregious follies, it might benefit your own—"

"Facial hair?" interrupted Sir Hereward. "A female ancestor of mine had a *beard*?"

"Whatever gave you that notion?" asked Mister Fitz. "Your *eyebrows* are identical, and incidentally, you have proven my statement about enthusiasms distracting you. You should have asked an improving question, not one about hair."

"An improving question?" asked Sir Hereward slowly. He was looking to the front, once again shading his eyes with his hand. "How about, 'What is that fortification that lies ahead?'"

"Interesting . . . ," came the puppet's musing reply. Sir Hereward saw Fitz's shadow lengthen as the puppet stood up on the
roof. "I have no knowledge of any habitation here. It is a manor
house of some kind, perhaps four or five hundred years old if I
am any judge. A little newer than the most recent map in my
collection."

The manor house in question was a squat, rectangular fortress some one hundred and fifty feet long, perhaps eighty wide
and five stories high, all but the highest two floors presenting a
blank expanse of tightly fitted ashlar stone. Even those top levels
only had arrow slits, and there were no battlements, the whole
being topped by a low-pitched roof of greenish copper.

The house was built upon hundreds of log piles, Hereward
surmised, the evidence for this being a burned and destroyed
lesser building some distance from the main structure, where
the remnants of the piles that had once been its foundation stuck
out of the water like a row of heavily decayed dragon teeth.

"A lonely house," remarked the knight. "Who would build
such a place here?"

"It is not so strange," said Mister Fitz. "One moment."

He jumped down from the roof of the howdah and went
to the head of the moklek, leaning down to whisper something
near its ear, before he turned to continue talking to Hereward.

The moklek, who was the lead animal by virtue of being the
smartest of the six, changed direction slightly, aiming towards
the right of the manor house. The others followed dutifully, and
the cannon trundled behind on its many well-greased wheels.
Though the gun carriage was jury-rigged from common ox
carts and resembled a kind of articulated reptile of multiple segments, it had been carefully designed by Sir Hereward and put
together by expert artisans, and the purely mechanical nature
of its joints and bindings had been bolstered by the sorcerous
intervention of Mister Fitz. No mere hole, bump, mound, or

minor obstacle could deter its passage, provided the mokleks continued to pull it with their full strength.

"It is not so strange," continued the puppet. "The Shallows abound with fish and other comestible aquatic life, including a weed that is dried and blended into a smoking mixture by the people of Kquq, which lies no more than a hundred and fifty leagues away. The Kquqers come three or four times a year, to harvest the weed, or at least they used to within recent memory. I would surmise that this fortification was built by some enterprising bandit with a view to exacting a suitable toll or impost upon that trade, eventually legitimizing themselves as an aristocrat."

"A weed-taxer," grunted Hereward. His bottom hurt and he was not inclined to be charitable. "Hardly a noble calling. Is there not some greater authority hereabouts who would take amiss such carryings-on?"

"None is known," said Mister Fitz. "Long ago, this was part of the demesne of the Exclusiarch of Ryzha, the godlet's principal servant, who was a semi-independent vassal of the Emperor in Kahaon. Since Ryzha's fall and the unrelated but consequent decline of the Kahaonese, dozens of petty states have temporarily exerted their control. No significant political entity claims these lands now, at least not in any active fashion."

"The house, however, is inhabited," said Sir Hereward. "Look, to the top left, there is the flash of a perspective glass in the second arrow slit."

"Indeed," said Mister Fitz, whose odd blue orbs were keener than any mere mortal eyes. "We are being observed by a woman. Several other women cluster tight behind her, hoping for a turn at the glass, yet judging by their posture, cannot clamor or snatch, and must wait for the current wielder who doubtless is their superior . . . perhaps even the mistress of the house."

Hereward leaned forward in sudden attention, accidentally damaging yet more of the howdah, and searched through the saddlebags at his feet for his own spyglass, a fine instrument originally owned by a famous general of artillery. It was so well-constructed that it was the only item to survive the general's death, when the rather too short fuse of the petard he was inspecting was lit by his own cigarillo. The lenses, of course, had needed to be replaced, as did the outer case of sharkskin-covered bronze, but it was in all other respects the same.

But by the time Hereward had found it, snapped it fully open, and raised it to his eye, there was only an empty arrow slit to look at. The womenfolk had gone.

"Did they appear friendly?" asked Hereward. "Should we . . . ah . . . skirt the place?"

Mister Fitz leaned over the edge of the howdah's roof, and neatly flipped himself over to land at Hereward's side.

"Spare me your attempts at wordplay," said the puppet. "I would adjudge the occupants as being welcoming, even receptive. Furthermore, I suggest that we stop this night within, if they offer hospitality."

"Did I hear you correctly?" asked Sir Hereward with no small suspicion. It was not like Mister Fitz to think of comfortable beds or the chance of something more interesting to eat than dry biscuit and horsemeat. After all, he did not sleep or eat.

"There is something in the air, or perhaps the water . . . ," said the puppet slowly. He swiveled his head around in a full circle again, very slowly. "Some arcane presence is close by, though I cannot exactly place it. And as you know, I have but a single energistic needle left in my sewing desk and so I am . . . we are . . . ill-prepared for any sorcerous foe. We may need to be behind stout walls come nightfall."

Hereward scowled and also looked around, but all he could see was blue sky, the endless yellow grass of the steppe, the reflection of the sun on the water of the Shallows, and the tall manor house.

"I will load my pistols with silver shot," he said. The carbine was merely charged with lead. He hesitated, then added, "How serious is this threat? Should I get the old dagger out of the . . . ah . . . howdah-bag?"

Mister Fitz turned his head a little way to the left and then back again to the right, still questing for the source of his disquiet.

"Yes," he said finally. "It may well prove a greater help than hindrance, for once."

The old dagger was one of the two items they had been charged to deliver to Jeminero, a great and ancient city that was readying for war. The other item was the cannon, and it was not certain which of the two weapons might be more useful when the time came. Particularly as there was some question whether either of them would be any use at all. The cannon had its peculiarities, perhaps the most significant being that it was breech-loaded via a rotating chamber, and required either sorcery or two score mightily-thewed gunners and a thirty-foot high shear-legs to open the chamber, load the cartridge and shot, and then rotate it back into place within the barrel again.

The old dagger, while not needing any such muscular preparation, was an entrapped extra-dimensional entity that tended towards a less than useful relationship with its various wielders. It had unique powers and, unfortunately, a mind of its own. A not very improved or civilized mind, which made it an unreliable and often unpleasant companion even when not being actively employed. When it *was* used, it became extraordinarily dangerous. Fortunately, some three centuries after its initial forging, some long-forgotten sorcerer had made the dagger a scabbard which put it into a comfortable and apparently very satisfying sleep, quietening its complaints, insults, and attempts at solo forays.

Like the cannon, the dagger was a weapon of last resort.

Sir Hereward thought of this as he reached over the side and undid the straps on the topmost of the six large bags that hung down the side of the moklek in a nested cascade of pink canvas. The old dagger was the sole item in the top bag. He pulled it out, and carefully checked that the peace strings and accompanying wax seals were still in place, and the weapon secure in its scabbard.

It was a surprisingly small dagger. The blade measured less than the distance from his wrist to the tip of his index finger, and the hilt appeared to have been made to fit a child's hand. Yet in its own way, the dagger was as dangerous a weapon as the vast cannon the mokleks dragged behind them . . .

Tucking the dagger through his belt, Sir Hereward took out a mahogany box from a howdah bag on the other side of the moklek. It contained two dueling pistols, ready-made paper cartridges of powder, a dozen perfectly-round silver pistol balls, priming powder in a patented triangular applicator that was far less useful than its inventor imagined, precut wads of thick felt that had been printed with curses and imprecations, and a serviceable ramrod that had replaced the uselessly ornate one that had been in the original set.

Hereward quickly loaded and primed the pistols and settled them in his broad leather belt. Only then did he take up his spyglass again and focus it upon the large and imposing gate of the manor house ahead, just in time to catch a flash of color and movement.

The flash came from the wine-red dress of a woman as she hitched it up at the thighs so that it wouldn't drag in the ankle-deep water that surrounded the house. Through the glass, she appeared to be no more than forty, and comely, though Hereward could not yet make out whether she bore the facial scarifications that to him would elevate her from mere prettiness to true beauty.

She had a hand-and-a-half sword slung on her back, the bronze cross-piece almost as wide as her shoulders and the blade stretching from neck to knees. Hereward looked at the corded muscle in her wrists and knew that she could use the massive sword. The weapon was not just for show.

A dozen women followed half a dozen yards behind the tall one with the oversized sword. They wore serviceable boiled leather cuirasses over plain linen shifts and several of them, Sir Hereward noted, carried racked crossbows with bolts in place, and all of them bore dirks in tinned iron sheaths tied to their thighs.

"Halt the mokleks," said Sir Hereward. "I would lief as not stay out of range of those arbalests."

"They will not shoot," said Mister Fitz. "Look, their chief advances alone, greatsword sheathed upon her back. You should descend and meet her."

Sir Hereward could walk faster than the mokleks' steady pace, at least when they were dragging the giant cannon, but he was not overly keen to do so. The extremely thick, wrinkled skin of moklek might turn a crossbow bolt, but he wore no armour in the heat, his linen shirt offering no protection against anything but the sun.

"I think we need to get inside soon," said Mister Fitz slowly, once again surveying the land around them. "It is also likely these women have knowledge of . . . whatever is going to happen."

"Which is what?" asked Sir Hereward crossly, as he clambered out of the howdah and cautiously crawled over the flat, broad head of the moklek.

"I do not know," said Mister Fitz slowly. "Something is coming. From some other plane that intersects here, where it should not."

Sir Hereward heard the tone in the puppet's voice. Though

Mister Fitz was never afraid as such, there was a certain amount of what could only be described as dread in his words.

The knight grabbed the highest knot of the dozen or so that ran the length of the strand of ear-hair, swung so as to place his feet on a lower knot, and descended knot by knot to the ground. There, he matched his pace to the moklek's, and looked back up to Mister Fitz.

"Throw down my sabre," he said. "If you would be so kind."

Mister Fitz easily lifted the weapon from the howdah, and pitched it down. Sir Hereward caught it and buckled on the scabbard, drawing out the blade a few inches and back again, to ensure that it moved freely. His hand was slightly sweaty, but the sabre's sharkskin grip was never slippery, be it inundated in sweat, blood, or other fluids. Mister Fitz had ensorcelled it long ago, together with several other minor enchantments that made it a most valuable blade.

"You're sure these women are friendly?" asked Sir Hereward.

"Moderately so," replied Mister Fitz. His hand was tightly closed, but even so there was now the hint of some horrible brightness beneath his wooden fist, indicating he held his last sorcerous needle there. "I stand ready in the event I am mistaken."

Taking a deep breath, Sir Hereward settled his pistols for a quick draw, and splashed forward to meet the woman in the deep red dress, thinking that if her cohorts did raise their arbalests it would be a tricky thing to dive under the bolts without his pistols taking in rather too much water, and a sodden dash forward with his sabre would also be rather slower than desired, perhaps even allowing them time to reload and re-tension their weapons. In which case, he would have to use the old dagger, and this was potentially more dangerous than meeting a fusillade of crossbow bolts, even with Mister Fitz standing by with his sorcerous needle to protect him . . .

As he drew closer, Sir Hereward observed the women handled their weapons well and were watching carefully. But their attentions were not exclusive to him. Most of them were actually looking out across the Shallows to the left and right, as if some enemy might emerge from the waters. Nevertheless, Sir Hereward took care to keep himself in line with their leader, so that only the flankers would get a decent shot. When he was half a dozen paces away, the swordswoman stopped, and Sir Hereward followed suit.

"Well met, good sir," said the woman, her voice evidently trained for authority and projection. "I am the Archimandress Withra. You are a most welcome guest, for this Wedding Night."

Sir Hereward instinctively took a step backward at the mention of a wedding. But his natural good manners did not desert him, and he managed to incorporate this backward step into a sweeping bow, though his eyes never left the Archimandress or the crossbows of her companions.

"Sir Hereward of the High Pale," he said. He gestured back at the lead moklek, where Mister Fitz could be seen perched on the howdah. "And my companion, Mister Fitz."

"A self-willed puppet," said the Archimandress, raising her eyebrows. The tiny jewels pasted there caught the sunlight as they moved. "It is long since we have been fortunate enough to welcome a puppet entertainer. I hope he will play and sing for us at our feast."

Sir Hereward kept his face immobile, not wanting to reveal any hint that unlike the vast majority of self-willed puppets, Mister Fitz was not an entertainer.

"We bid you both welcome, Sir Hereward, and invite you to take refuge within our convent."

"Refuge?" asked Sir Hereward.

"Indeed," said the Archimandress. She cast a glance towards

the western horizon, where the sun was beginning to settle. "As a man, you have chosen an inopportune time to cross the Shallows."

"As a man?" asked Hereward.

"Tonight the Hag of the Shallows seeks a husband," said Withra. "She roams the Shallows looking for suitable candidates till the dawn. But I expect we can keep you safe inside our house."

"What precisely is this 'Hag of the Shallows'?" asked Sir Hereward. "And what does she do with her . . . ahem . . . husbands?"

"She rises from the Shallows this one day of the year, a thing of impenetrable darkness wreathed in fog and rain," said Withra, not really answering the question. "Her chosen husbands are found soon after dawn, or rather the chewed remnants of them are found . . ."

"I see," said Sir Hereward. He looked back at the lead moklek, which was ambling forward again. This was a conversation that Mister Fitz needed to be involved in, and the sooner the puppet *was* involved, the happier Sir Hereward would be. "And what exactly do you ladies do here, may I ask?"

"We belong to the Sacred Order of the Sisters of Mercantile Fairness of the Goddess Lanith-Eremot," said Withra. "Our convent here was established with a perpetual endowment from the Council of Seven in the city of Kquq, in order that we might protect their weed-gatherers from competitors, predators, and unfortunate events. But come, the light already fails. We must all withdraw inside."

Sir Hereward hesitated. Mister Fitz had said they should seek shelter, but uncharacteristically he felt more cautious than he usually did when conversing with an attractive woman who was inviting him indoors. He had no knowledge of the goddess Lanith-Eremot, so there was a possibility she was proscribed and thus no friend to the likes of the knight and his puppet companion. Nor had he ever heard of the Sisters of Mercantile Fairness.

"I hesitate to ask," he said. "But I trust that in accepting your kind and gracious invitation, we will not be incurring any debt or entering into any arrangement beyond the mere acceptance of customary shelter, and that we will be free to leave unhindered and unharmed in the morning?"

"The Sisterhood has no ill intentions towards anyone save weed-stealers or other criminals, and it is part of the charter of the Sisters of Mercantile Fairness to offer hospitality to travelers. In some other convents there is a small charge for this, but not here, the Kquq Council of Seven having provided sufficient funds for the purpose in the original endowment. Ah, your puppet friend closes. Greetings, Master Puppet."

"Greetings," replied Mister Fitz from atop the moklek. He inclined his pumpkin-shaped head stiffly, moving slowly with small jerks and tics. This was a common practice with him, to instill in strangers a false notion of his flexibility and speed.

"This is the Archimandress Withra of the Sisters of Mercantile Fairness, who follow the goddess Lanith-Eremot," said Sir Hereward quickly, only half turning towards Mister Fitz, at the same time calculating that he could shoot the two closer crossbow priestesses, throw his pistols down, draw his sabre, and run Withra through before she could get the greatsword off her back, and then retreat holding her body up as a shield—

"I know of your order," said Mister Fitz. He pitched his voice higher and softer than usual, to enhance the impression he was one of the entertaining type of self-willed puppets. "Your good reputation travels far, and I am very pleased that we should meet such noble sisters here."

Sir Hereward's thoughts made a sharp turn away from the consideration of imminent combat and he relaxed a little. Mister

Fitz would not speak so fulsomely if Lanith-Eremot was proscribed, or the Sisters an outlawed organization. But while he
was less worried about the women, he was growing ever more
concerned at the gathering dusk and the threat of this creature
that sought a husband, or as seemed more accurate to say, a meal
to be made of a male personage.

"The Archimandress invites us inside," said Hereward. "Apparently there is a . . . thing . . . called the Hag of the Shallows
that will rise tonight and seek a husband, and I fear I am the
only eligible prospect."

"A situation not to be envied, I apprehend," said Mister Fitz
gravely. He looked around again, his tongue of blue stippled
leather tasting the air, as if it had slipped out by accident.

"Perhaps if we continued on apace," said Sir Hereward. Fitz
seemed undecided, and he wanted to distract the priestess from
the puppet. "We might remove ourselves from this Hag's hunting grounds in time?"

"I fear she ranges very widely," said Withra. "There is less
than an hour until full dark, and already I feel her emanations
gathering."

"Perhaps we should take shelter, Sir Hereward," said Mister
Fitz, adding a quaver to his voice. "What might this Hag do to
a puppet of the masculine persuasion? I am called 'Mister' after
all!"

"True, true," said Sir Hereward, relieved that Fitz had come
to a decision. "But first we must relieve the mokleks of their
harness and let them forage and bathe. That is . . ."

He paused.

"Does this Hag of the Shallows molest animals as well?"
he continued, thinking of their mission to deliver the cannon,
which would be impossible without the mokleks.

"If they are male, of a certainty," said Withra. "However,
having suffered the cut, they should be safe enough."

Hereward suppressed a wince at the thought of that cut. He had seen the thing done upon one occasion, which was more than enough. However, he did not want to reveal a weakness in front of the priestess and her womenfolk.

"If you will grant us a little time, milady, we will tend to our mokleks and then accept your kind invitation and enter your fortress," said Sir Hereward.

"Certainly," replied Withra. "Our doors are open to you, and you are welcome guests. But do be sure you come within before night falls. The gate will be locked then, and not re-opened until well after the dawn."

Sir Hereward bowed and backed away. Withra inclined her head and did an about turn to slosh back to the manor house, her followers in two files behind. The sun, now setting behind the fortification, cast a red glint across everything and made the priestesses' shadows long and thin and predatory, rippling across the shallow water.

It took Sir Hereward and Mister Fitz only twenty minutes to lift down the essential items they wished to carry inside, unbuckle the mokleks from their harness, and slide the howdah off the back of the lead beast by means of its cunning system of blocks and lines. After a word with Mister Fitz, the massive creatures trod farther into the Shallows, into a deeper pool. There, they took up water in their trunks and sprayed them-selves and one another with all the gravity and deliberation that tired human workers might show upon taking a long-awaited bath after a weary day.

The cannon lay on its wagons, pointing at the northwestern corner of the manor house. Sir Hereward hadn't noticed this at first, and it now irritated his professional instincts. The gun was charged, because this was the safest way to transport the arcane powder, a massive five-hundred weight cartridge bag made of seven thicknesses of calico, designed to keep out both water and stray sparks. But the cannon was not loaded with shot. In fact, it was unlikely anywhere within a thousand leagues could supply a ball of the prodigious size necessary to fit the bore, let alone one with the required sorcerous properties to complement the magic that had been infused in the weapon.

The chamber that held the charge was also kept open rather than being rotated shut in the firing position, so in the event of accidental discharge, there would be a lesser effluxion of flame and bits of calico out the business end of the barrel. But even without shot and the chamber open, Sir Hereward considered that in the event of accident the concussive and fiery force delivered would be extremely detrimental to the fabric of the building. The cannon really should not be aimed at anything but sky.

However, as the sun was now but a reddish blur on the horizon and the mokleks loosed, there was no time to put it right. He dismissed his uneasiness as mere parade ground soldiering, the kind of rigid thinking that desired everything to be just so at all times regardless of circumstance, a form of thought that he despised.

Going towards the manor, Sir Hereward spoke quietly and close to Mister Fitz, who had been silent throughout the process of freeing the mokleks, his head shifting and his blue eyes constantly searching the Shallows about them as if he had little attention to spare for harnesses.

"What might this Hag of the Shallows be, do you think? And can our hostesses be entirely trusted?"

"Judging by the emanations I perceive, the Hag of the Shallows must be a powerful inter-dimensional entity that manifests here when there is some temporary but regular alignment of the spheres," said Mister Fitz quietly. "As to the Sisters, their order has a good reputation. However, an isolated house like this may not conform to the characteristics of the sorority in general. As always, we must be on guard."

"At least the place looks defensible," said Sir Hereward, as they walked up the ramp of packed earth to the main gate, which was made of the black timber called *urross*, always much in demand for gates and doors due to its strength and resistance to fire. The gate was further studded for reinforcement with steel bolts, and daubed with runes which, to Sir Hereward at least, looked ancient and powerful.

"The sorcerous protections are competent," said Mister Fitz. "Augmented by the powers of the congregation within, they should suffice to keep out a marauding godlet."

"Good," said Sir Hereward with some relief. "That is to say, excellent."

"Yet I am still uneasy," continued Mister Fitz. "I sense the immanence, but I cannot fix upon its location. However, on the balance of probability we should be safer within than without."

Sir Hereward didn't answer, his attention caught by the inner gate, likewise of *urross*, the murder holes in the ceiling of the passage between, and the hotfoot gutters that ran between the paving stones. Not that hot oil above and below would have any effect on your typical godlet, but there were often mortal allies to be reckoned with as well: priests and soldiers and fanatical followers. At least here in a temple building it was to be presumed that the goddess would provide powerful protection against enemies mortal and otherwise, imbuing the stones and mortar with her essence, and her followers with powers of both harm and healing. Though the strength of this protection depended greatly upon the relative presence of the goddess in question.

"Where lies the locus of the goddess Lanith-Eremot?" whispered Hereward to Mister Fitz as the outer gate was shut and barred behind them by two of the priestesses, and others opened the gate within. "Close by, I trust? Not too distant?"

"Two thousand leagues or more, by a straight path," said Mister Fitz. "Longer if a mortal must tread the way."

"A long way for a godlet to exert her power," said Sir Hereward dubiously.

"The distance in this case may not be material to the strength of Lanith-Eremot here. It is possible, even likely, that this place is a point of intersection for a number of different realities, hence the manifestation of the Hag. The natural barriers which resist otherworldly intrusions were worn thin by the conflict between Yeogh-Yeogh and Ryzha, and so interdimensional connections of various kinds will have occurred."

A great hall lay beyond the inner gate, a scene of considerable bustle and noise, evidently in preparation for a feast or celebration, with an array of long tables bedecked with good linen cloth and piled with silver plate. There were many more sisters here, engaged in arranging tablecloths, plate, cutlery, salt cellars, candlesticks, and floral decorations. These buzzing workers wore simple habits of bright silver cloth for the novices and shimmering gold for the full sisters, but there were also many of the warriors about, two score at least of armed and armoured priestesses, who stood against the walls in obvious positions of guard.

One of the silver-clad novices, a comely lass with her black hair coiled on top of her head, approached and bowed to Sir Hereward.

"My name is Parnailam," she said. "I am to show you to the baths we reserve for our male guests, to rest and cleanse yourselves before the feast. I regret, Master Puppet, that we were not sure whether you bathe or not, but various oils and unguents have been laid by that may prove of use to you."

"I need nothing, but I thank you," said Mister Fitz absently. His head was craned back on his spindly neck, looking up at the hammer-beamed ceiling and the dyed-paper decorations that hung there. They were of red and blue, and showed a very male figure with a great phallus entwined by a godlet who was depicted as a kind of black cloud with six, grasping tentacular arms. "Tell me, what is the feast you celebrate tonight?"

"Why, it is the Wedding!" exclaimed Parnailam. "One of our principal feast days."

"And what does the feast celebrate, what does this Wedding signify?" continued Mister Fitz.

Parnailam looked confused.

"I am only a novice," she said hesitantly. "You would have to ask one of the sisters, or the Archimandress herself. We do not participate in the full mysteries. After I show you to the baths, we will have hot spiced milk, sing hymn number five, and go off to bed. I know the full sisters stay up *very* late and are oft tired and cross the next morning."

"Ah," said Sir Hereward. He looked up at the decorations and then around at all the priestesses and thoughts of the coupling nymphs of the Participatory Theatre of Hurshell once more flitted through his mind.

Mister Fitz did not ask any more questions, but strode jerkily along next to Sir Hereward, as if invisible strings pulled upon legs and arms that had become stiff from lack of lubrication, indicating a sorcerous puppet who had lived beyond his mysterious lifespan, the internal magic winding down with every step. He was almost overdoing the deception, thought Hereward, but as none of the priestesses seemed particularly to notice, perhaps the puppet knew best. As he usually did.

The bath house the two travelers were led to was not of the "Most Excellent Supreme Soakwash, Scrub, and Toe Cleanse" class of the Kapoman caravanserais, but it boasted a large circular hot pool with steam rising in wafts, indicating it was warmed either by sorcery or more likely by subterranean fires; a narrow rectangular cold pool to wade up and down in; and a very shallow dish-like pool for soaking feet, this last already infused with pleasant-smelling herbs. Several enormous cushions sat nearby, next to an open cupboard stacked with towels beside a low table on which were arrayed brushes, sponges, and numerous bottles of scent, oil, and cleansing unguents.

"Do you require someone to scrub your back, Sir Hereward?" asked Parnailam, in an innocent tone that suggested she meant precisely that and no more.

Hereward glanced at Mister Fitz, who turned his head very slightly. Not quite a visible shake but a clear indication to the knight that this offer should be refused.

"I thank you, but no," said Sir Hereward. "I must first offer my devotions to my gods before I bathe, and this cannot be done in company. Besides, you have to get to your hot milk."

"Oh, they won't serve the milk till the bell," said Parnailam. "I will wait outside in case you need anything!"

She inclined her head and retreated out the door. Mister Fitz went to it as it shut and placed one wooden hand against the timber, to sense if she was close enough to listen. Sir Hereward put down his saddlebags, put his pistols carefully on the table, unhooked his sabre, and balanced it against the cupboard and then fell back into the largest cushion. Stretching out, he luxuriated in the soft embrace of good goose-feather stuffing, a relieving contrast to the howdah's bottom-numbing accommodations.

But he had little time to enjoy the comfort. Mister Fitz came away from the door and signaled to him to come close. Sir Hereward obeyed, getting up with a sigh to crouch down near the puppet, their heads close together.

"There is something wrong with the Sisters," whispered Mister Fitz.

"What?" asked Sir Hereward. "Isn't it enough to have this Hag of the Shallows lurking about outside, we have to have a problem inside?"

"I am afraid I may have made an error," said Mister Fitz.

"I am quite familiar with both Lanith-Eremot and the Sisters of Mercantile Fairness. There is no wedding of any kind celebrated in the worship of the goddess by either her secular or ecclesiastical followers."

"No wedding," repeated Sir Hereward.

"None," said Mister Fitz. "And the goddess is never depicted as a dark cloud with tentacular arms. Or even as a human female figure. She is normally portrayed as a sort of friendly money-lending monkey atop a pile of coins."

"You think the sisters have transferred their loyalties to some other godlet?"

"Possibly. If they have, most likely it will be to this Hag of the Shallows."

"And the Hag is what you sensed outside."

"Probably," said Mister Fitz. He hesitated, then added, "Though not only outside."

"You sense something *within* the walls?"

"Yes," said Mister Fitz. "And no."

"I fail to understand you," said Sir Hereward stiffly.

"It is both within and without," said Mister Fitz. "I cannot tell more exactly. But given that it is within as well, the Sisters cannot be unaware of it and most likely are complicit in its actions."

"Are you sure?" asked Sir Hereward dubiously.

"No," answered Mister Fitz, shaking his head. "They seem to all my . . . usual . . . senses to be no more or less than they present themselves. But I don't like this wedding business. We should make plans to depart."

"Depart?" asked Sir Hereward. "Need I remind you this is a fortress?"

He stood up and replaced his pistols and sabre, and nervously fingered the heavy wax of the peace seals that kept the old dagger scabbarded and slumbering, content on his belt.

"We cannot sneak out the way we came. Dozens of armed sisters in the hall, the two gates and the guards there . . . how wide was that arrow slit up above, where Withra looked out?"

"You could not pass through it," adjudged Mister Fitz.

"We *might* be able to fight our way out with this," said Sir Hereward, very gently tapping the scabbard of the old dagger.

"A most unreliable artifact," said Mister Fitz. "With only one needle I am not certain I could protect you when it rebounds, as it always does."

Sir Hereward frowned. He knew only an outline of the history of the dagger. But he did know that after slaying a particular number of enemies—a number it alone decided in any given circumstance, without recourse to any outside advice or reckoning—it would return and kill its wielder as well, before resuming its slumber. The only times it had failed to do this had occurred when the wielder was protected by potent sorcery, and in two other singular cases. Once when deployed by the famous inventor Kalitheke, who had launched it from a massive ballista at his rivals in conclave several miles away and had then taken ship for distant parts, the dagger failing to pursue him across the ocean for fear of rust; and the second when it was employed by the incomparable duelist known only as the Swordmistress of Heganarat, who upon the dagger's return after it had killed her faithless husband and her six paramours, parried and danced around the weapon's thrusts and sallies for seven and a half hours before it dropped from exhaustion and demanded its scabbard. The Swordmistress died of a heart attack the next day, but it was still considered her greatest victory.

"Barricade and defend ourselves here till dawn?" asked Sir Hereward, looking around the room. There was only the one doorway, but the door was mere oak and would not hold long against mundane attacks, let alone anything sorcerous or extra-dimensional.

"Even if the entity that comes departs with daylight, the Sisters will still be here," said Mister Fitz.

"The pool is heated," said Sir Hereward. "There is presumably a hypocaust beneath. We can drain it, break the tiles . . . you, at least, might exit through those tunnels."

"Perhaps," said Mister Fitz. "Go and summon our guide. I am sure she will not be far away."

"What do you intend for her?" asked Sir Hereward.

"I will take a little blood and examine the signatures within," said Mister Fitz. "If we find evidence of an unknown godlet we will know the Sisters are under its thrall and must act accordingly. If we do not . . . then there is a chance we will be able to negotiate with them. Lanith-Eremot was ever fair-minded."

"And if we can't negotiate?"

"I still have one needle," said Mister Fitz. "I can get us out, I think. After that, we might have a chance, if we take the lead moklek only and strike across the water. But that is a last resort, for we would certainly be pursued."

Sir Hereward nodded, his face grim. Opening the door, he looked out along the narrow corridor. Sure enough, Parnailam was standing by the doorway to the hall, chatting quietly to another silver-clad novice.

"I fear I need assistance with the removal of my boots," called out Sir Hereward. "Mister Fitz lacks the strength and I have left my jack in one of the moklek bags we didn't bring inside. Could I ask you to help me?"

"Surely, sir," called Parnailam. She came quickly to the door. Hereward stepped aside to let her pass and as she went into the room Mister Fitz jumped upon her back, ran up onto her shoulders, and pressed his wooden fingers into the woman's temples. She gasped and dropped unconscious into Hereward's arms. He laid her gently down on one of the big cushions and shut the door.

As he had latched the door closed, the puppet took a very small but intensely sharp knife and a glass slide from somewhere about his person and nicked the young woman's thumb, catching a droplet of blood. Taking this to his portable sewing desk, a wooden case that casual observers presumed to be an instrument case for a clavichord or something similar, Mister Fitz smeared the blood across the slide and applied a series of alchemical fluids from small bottles. This fixed the blood in place and slowly revealed a striation of colored lines, in the main blue and green with some yellow between, the colors to be expected from a generally benevolent godlet's presence in the bloodstream of one of its devout worshippers.

"Lanith-Eremot," said Mister Fitz. "I don't even need to check the book, I know the signature well. And no sign of anything else. It is extremely puzzling."

"Perhaps the novices and younger sisters are not part of the conspiracy," said Sir Hereward. "You recall they are sent to bed. How long will she slumber?"

"A few minutes," said Mister Fitz.

"If I draw in her companion, and we take their robes, could you cast a glamour upon us?" asked Sir Hereward.

Mister Fitz shook his head.

"Consecrated robes would resist our wearing them, and I dare not waste the power of my needle in small workings. No. Given the signature, I think—"

Sir Hereward held up his hand and jerked his head towards the door. Many feet could be heard, and not the soft swish of novice's slippers, but the boots of armed priestesses.

Knight and puppet moved quickly. Sir Hereward took one corner, leveling a pistol in his left hand and cocking it before also drawing his sabre. Mister Fitz scrambled up on top of the towel cupboard and drew out his last sorcerous needle, cupping it close in his hand, its harsh, blinding light leaking out in narrow, brilliant rays between his fingers.

There was no knock upon the door, but neither was it flung open as at the beginning of an assault. The latch ascended slowly, the door swung open, and the Archimandress Withra looked cautiously into the room, her entire body encased in a pearly nimbus indicative of some divine protective power. She saw Parnailam laid out on the cushion and her face set for a moment, but cleared as she saw the novice's breast slowly rise and fall.

"She lives then," said Withra, glancing across at Sir Hereward. "I felt her slip from my mind, and feared the worst."

"She has taken no hurt," said Sir Hereward. "We merely wished to ascertain her true allegiance."

"And how would you do—" Withra began. She stopped talking as she caught a momentary flash of the violet brilliance contained in Mister Fitz's hand, and looked up and across at the cupboard. Stepping back, a curious expression passed fleetingly across her face, one Sir Hereward could not fully read, for it seemed in equal parts anger, relief, and fear. "Ah, I see. You are not an *entertaining* puppet. My apologies, Magister."

"You know me?" asked Mister Fitz mildly.

"I know *of* you," said Withra. "I had thought you in the category of long-lost legend."

Her tone of voice conveyed respect and a healthy fear. Those who knew much about Mister Fitz's real powers and experience were generally extremely wary of him. Not to mention very polite.

"What exactly is going on here?" asked Sir Hereward peremptorily. He was somewhat miffed that Mister Fitz was getting all the respectful attention. "My companion tells me there is no wedding feast in your sisterhood's usual rites, and he . . ."

we . . . are concerned that you have transferred your allegiance to this Hag of the Shallows."

"Never!" spat out the Archimandress. She hesitated, then added, "However, it is true that we have had to make an accommodation with the Hag. I had hoped to keep you both in ignorance of this. However, clearly this is not possible."

Withra snapped her fingers, and the pearly radiance about her disappeared.

"There is no trouble. Go back to the hall," she said over her shoulder, her words answered by the sound of shuffling boots as a large party of armed priestesses withdrew along the passage outside.

Mister Fitz replaced his sorcerous needle inside his doublet, and Sir Hereward carefully closed the pan on his pistol and uncocked the lock, before replacing it through his belt.

"You made an accommodation?" asked Sir Hereward.

"Not at first," said Withra. "When the Hag appeared some sixty years ago, she was weak, and initially believed to be merely some sort of revenant or ghost, reappearing at the site of her demise. But as time went on, this haunting spirit grew more troublesome, so the Sisters tried to exorcise it, without success. It grew stronger with every year, and a number of serious battles were fought. Though it only appeared once a year and for a single night, these were very costly fights. Great damage was done—this house is the third we have built since the Hag's appearance, you must have seen the remnants of the previous buildings. Eventually, my predecessor hit upon the idea that instead of fighting the revenant, we should placate the Hag by offering up the pretense of worship. It is only one day, after all—"

"Worship would not be sufficient in itself," interrupted Mister Fitz. He jumped easily down from the cupboard and went to stand near Sir Hereward. Though his round head only came up to the knight's belt, he dominated the room. "You must give the Hag something as well. A sacrifice."

Withra nodded reluctantly, licked her lips, and swallowed, as if her mouth had suddenly dried.

"We give her half a dozen men. Weed-stealers, who have been caught by us, tried fairly in Kquq, sentenced to death, and sent back."

Sir Hereward looked at Mister Fitz. A demand for human sacrifice was one of the defining characteristics that would place a godlet on the list of proscribed inter-dimensional entities.

"Do you know who or what the Hag actually is?" asked Mister Fitz. "You must have had many opportunities to take its signature."

"We have," said Withra. She had shrunk a little, it seemed, her shoulders lower. From shame, Sir Hereward suspected. "It is a relict of the malevolent portion of the combined entity known as Yeogh-Yeogh the Two-Headed. It was on this spot that the godlet died, and it is here that it returns on the evening of every seventh day of Rainith, returning to haunt us."

"I am extremely surprised the Grandmother-Marshal of your order would allow your 'accommodation,'" continued Mister Fitz. "Surely greater forces could be arrayed and this relict of Yeogh-Yeogh banished for good and all?"

"The matter was not referred to our principal chapter by my predecessor," said Withra. "She merely reported that the trouble with the Hag was 'settled.' By the time I came here, it had become tradition. It seemed . . . I believed it to be . . ."

"I see," said Mister Fitz. "I suspect if I took *your* blood, the striations would show the influence of Yeogh-Yeogh. However, it is not our duty to chastise you for weakness and poor choices. It is our duty to dispose of the Hag."

"Now, now, let's not rush into things," said Sir Hereward in alarm. "Just remember our current resources! And we have a

very important job in hand, you know, the cannon and . . . we
must get to Jeminero as soon as we can."

"That does not alter our principal duty," said Mister Fitz
in tones that brooked no discussion. "The only question that
remains is how we might best perform said duty."

"I cannot let you try," said Withra hotly, her lips tight. "Our
survival depends—"

"On the contrary," interrupted Mister Fitz. He raised his
voice, and spoke to the air at a point above Withra's head. "I
call upon Lanith-Eremot and all her followers to assist us against
the intruder godlet known as Yeogh-Yeogh the Two-Headed."

"*I* speak for Lanith-Eremot here!" said Withra. "*I* say what
she approves or does not—"

The words died in her throat as the pearly nimbus came
back with a crack like a thunderclap and she suddenly levitated
several inches off the ground. Her head jerked to the left and
right, and back again, and a loud, brassy, and inhuman voice
screeched out of her mouth at an impossible volume.

"I do not approve! I cannot see everything all the time,
but now I do, I most emphatically do not approve of what you
young ladies have done and I require you to put matters to
rights. Help the puppet and his knight, you hear me!"

To punctuate this speech, blood gushed from Withra's nostrils. She fell back to earth, staggered to a cushion, and collapsed
onto it. The nimbus blinked off again, leaving the distinctive
smell of newly printed Ghashiki banknotes, whose ink-makers
used a special mixture of gall-black and balsamic vinegar. Twenty
seconds later, a dozen armed priestesses rushed into the room,
but they had not drawn their weapons. Instead they looked at
Hereward and Mister Fitz wild-eyed, then bowed their heads
and shuffled into a form of repentant choir, no one wanting to
stand out among their sisters.

"Your archimandress will come to her senses in a moment,"

said Mister Fitz, indicating Withra. "It is a difficult thing to be the vessel for a god. How long do we have before the Hag rises?"

"I do not know, Lord Puppet," said the eldest of the priestesses, a woman with a white stripe through the greying hair atop her head, and a scar that continued on from that stripe down the side of her face. "We begin the feast at the eighth hour, and at some point soon thereafter, a black shape arises in the hall."

"Less than an hour," mused Mister Fitz. "Possibly far less, if the Hag is already present enough to feel the momentary intervention of Lanith-Eremot. Where are your prisoners? The ones to be sacrificed?"

"We have a number of cells for penitents that are temporarily put to use for these men," said the priestess. "They are treated well."

"Until you feed them to the Hag," said Sir Hereward sourly. He turned to Mister Fitz. "I trust you have a plan, because I fear I do not."

"I have the inkling of a plan," said Mister Fitz. He tilted his head and slowly looked up and down the length of the knight.

"I already dislike this inkling," said Sir Hereward. "But tell me."

"I am formulating it," said Mister Fitz. He looked at the scarred priestess. "What is your name?"

"Emengah. I am the Bursar of this convent."

"You heard Lanith-Eremot?"

"All within this house heard the Goddess. We stand ready to aid you, Master Puppet."

"Good. First of all, those men must be released and sent away, as quickly as possible. Give them food and money, and tell them to run as if a demon is at their backs. Which might well be true."

"As you command," said Emengah, though not without a

glance at Withra, who was showing signs of returning to consciousness, her fingers twitching and part-formed groans issuing from her slack mouth. "I will see to it now."

"Good," said Mister Fitz. "Take your little novice too, and make sure the young ones are all safely out of the way."

Emengah indicated to two of her followers to pick up Parnailam, bowed to Mister Fitz and Sir Hereward, and exited, the other priestesses following so swiftly they almost trampled over one another in their eagerness to go out the door.

"You intend the men to be a distraction?" asked Sir Hereward. "But we have already been told the Hag can hunt them down . . . oh, I see . . . not a distraction, but a concentration, no doubt. On the one man left close at hand. That is to say, me."

"Yes," said Mister Fitz. "We must focus the Hag upon you, so that *you* are the one she pursues when you flee this house."

"Into a trap," said Sir Hereward. "But what trap could we make in so little time, and you with only one needle?"

"We have the cannon," said Mister Fitz. "And the old dagger."

Sir Hereward narrowed his eyes.

"Pray continue."

"I will go outside now to prepare," said Mister Fitz. "The Archimandress will take you towards the Hag as she manifests, as if you are the first sacrifice. You will break free and flee outside, into the mouth of the cannon—"

"The mouth of the cannon!"

"Please pay attention, Hereward. We have little time. You go into the mouth of the cannon. The Hag will follow. You race from the muzzle to the breech, and at the open chamber, you must turn and throw the dagger, instructing it to kill the Hag. You remember the words?"

"Of course I remember the words, but—"

"Next, you leap out through the open chamber, which I

will then rotate and close using sorcery. I will have cocked the firing pistols already and will pull the cord as I jump—"

"I am to crawl down a fully charged giant cannon with the firing pistols cocked and a carnivorous godlet screaming after me?"

"Are you not paying attention? As I close the breech, you must run and take cover as best you can. Behind a moklek if one is near, I will endeavor to call them. Timing will be of the essence, if the Hag is close enough to escape out the breech before I can close it, or you are too slow with the dagger . . ."

"Why even use the dagger? Surely the cannon blast alone would destroy the Hag?"

"I fear that the explosive power of even that quantity of special powder will not be enough," said Mister Fitz. "We would need the proper projectile as well. However, the dagger might be strong enough to overcome the Hag in combination with the explosion. If we are fortunate, they will destroy each other."

"And if we're not?"

"Our destiny has always been to walk the knife-edge," said Mister Fitz obliquely. "It is a narrow way."

"Is this Hag, this relict of Yeogh-Yeogh, so important?" asked Sir Hereward slowly.

"It was a godlet of the first order of malevolence," said Mister Fitz. "It grew strong very quickly before, invading the essence of Ryzha. It must be dealt with before it can grow as strong again."

"Why couldn't it just be one of those little annoying things that sour wine in a single tavern or make people sneeze at a crossroads," said Sir Hereward, with a melancholy sigh. But he was already reaching inside his shirt to retrieve the brassard. Sliding it up his arm to sit above his elbow, he watched Mister Fitz follow suit with his own armband, and then together they recited the words they knew so well, and had spoken so many times, generally immediately before intense periods of mayhem, destruction, pain, and death.

"In the name of the Council of the Treaty for the Safety of the World, acting under the authority granted by the Three Empires, the Seven Kingdoms, the Palatine Regency, the Jessar Republic, and the Forty Lesser Realms, we declare ourselves agents of the Council. We identify the godlet manifested here as the malignant relict of Yeogh-Yeogh the Two-Headed, a listed entity under the Treaty. Consequently, the said godlet and all those who assist it are deemed to be enemies of the World and the Council authorizes us to pursue any and all actions necessary to banish, repel, or exterminate the said godlet."

Faint symbols began to glow upon the brassards, ancient heraldic marks that identified empires long lost, kingdoms divided and broken, regencies ended, and lesser realms grown even more insignificant. Yet still the Council of the Treaty for the Safety of the World endured, and still its executive agents prosecuted their work. And perhaps, just perhaps, the world *was* made a little safer . . .

"I would not help you, save the Goddess commands," croaked Withra from the floor. "It is mad vainglory, and we will all be slain by the Hag."

"I have heard far worse plans, and taken part in many more badly executed ones," said Sir Hereward, offering his hand to help up the priestess. "It offers a chance to right a wrong, where there was none before."

"If you had taken your bath the herbs therein would have made you simply sleep through the night," said Withra. "We thought your puppet would play for us, and honor the Hag, and keep his counsel, as such players do. No harm would have come to you. Now we are all doomed and the weed-stealers next season will laugh at the fallen house of Lanith-Eremot."

"A faint heart and a weak eye sees doom in everything," said

Sir Hereward. He brought the priestess close and spoke with some considerable menace. "You do your part and stay true to Lanith-Eremot, and perhaps we will all survive, and you can go on chasing the weed-stealers across your shallow lake for years to come."

"I have no choice but to obey," said Withra bitterly. "The Goddess's command sits heavy upon me. Come, I feel the imminence of the Hag."

"Be sure you do as Sir Hereward instructs," said Mister Fitz sternly. He turned to the knight. "I will ensure the gates are open for you, Hereward. Need I say that you must be careful not to trip and stumble, and make the best speed you can?"

"An unnecessary warning," said Sir Hereward. "My mind is well-focused upon the matter. Please ensure you do your part equally well."

"Indeed," said Mister Fitz, and he was gone, moving so swiftly it seemed as if his shadow could barely keep up. There was no pretense now, no clicking, jerky movements. Just the empty air where he had been a moment before.

"Come," repeated Withra sourly, her manner hangdog. "If we are all to die, best we get it over with."

"You will die all the sooner if you do not play your part better," snapped Sir Hereward. He unhooked his sabre and weighed it in his hand for a moment, considering if he could somehow hide it on his person, before reluctantly laying it down and moving his two pistols and the old dagger around to the back of his belt, where they could not be so easily seen by the Hag. "You walk ahead. We will gather some of your soldiers as we go, they can march around me, and I will cross my wrists as if they are bound."

"I hear and obey," muttered Withra. She wiped the blood from her face with her sleeve and stalked from the room, Sir Hereward following very close behind. Despite the command

Lanith-Eremot had laid upon the Archimandress, Sir Hereward thought there was a good chance Withra would try to betray him, and he must be ready for that, or any other development.

There were a large number of the armed priestesses at the end of the passage, muttering together. They fell silent as Withra and Hereward approached.

"Fall in to guard the 'prisoner,'" snapped Withra.

The priestesses didn't move, bar some shuffling in place. Withra's fists clenched at her sides and Hereward heard the hiss of her deeply in-drawn breath.

"Do as she asks," said Hereward quickly, before Withra could speak again. "It is a pretense, no more. When the Hag moves towards me, I will break free, and you must spring away and let me go. Do you all understand?"

The priestesses nodded, but with little certainty. They seemed unclear what to do and there was still only confused shuffling until the scarred bursar Emengah pushed through from behind them.

"You all heard the Goddess," she said sternly. "We are to obey this Knight, and the puppet. We must assist them to the full extent of our abilities and resources."

"So you fancy yourself Archimandress now, Emengah?' asked Withra. "We will do as Lanith-Ermot commands, but I still—"

"You can sort out all that later," said Sir Hereward impatiently. "For now, you will do as I command. You lot, form up around me as a guard. Withra, you go ahead a few paces only. Emengah, have the weed-stealers been released?"

"They have. I have rarely seen such splashes made across the Shallows with their running."

"Then please make sure I have a clear path to run from the hall to the gates and outside."

"The Puppet has already commanded the gates to be held open for you," said Emengah.

"Make sure they are," said Hereward. He crossed his wrists and held them low in front, and began to walk in step with the priestesses who now moved to surround him. "It's the kind of detail I like double-checked when my life depends upon it."

Withra snorted. "Your plan cannot work, Sir Hereward. We will all be—"

"Silence!" snapped Sir Hereward. "Do not speak hereafter, unless I give you permission."

The Archimandress cast a look of burning hate over her shoulder, but her mouth stayed shut. Walking faster, she led the group of priestesses and their ostensible prisoner along the passage, through the door and out into the hall.

There were only gold-clad priestesses there now, no novices in silver. They sat at the tables, eyes scared, the food and wine untouched. Heads turned as Withra, Hereward, and his guards entered, then turned again, towards the tall stone dais at the other end of the hall. Hereward had only glanced at it when they'd passed through before, and had seen nothing unusual. Now, there was a pool of shadow there, an unnatural glob of darkness that defied the light of the lanterns hung above, and the candles in the many-branched candelabra on the tables.

Withra kept walking towards the stone dais. Hereward followed, eyes flickering to the door on the far side, calculating where he would run, the potential obstacles . . . he could feel his heart speeding up, the familiar surge of nervous energy that came on the brink of combat, that must be directed and controlled lest he give way to irrational fear or blustering foolishness.

Ten feet from the dais, Withra stopped and raised her arms. There was a moment of tense hesitation, before all the sisters in the hall save the guards around Hereward threw up their arms as well.

"The Hag!" shouted Withra. "The Hag!"

The third time she shouted, the Archimandress's voice was lost in the swelling roar from her sisters, who took up the chant.

"The Hag! The Hag! The Hag!"

Sir Hereward's flesh crawled as the chant was answered by the shadow atop the dais. It spread wider and then began to rise up, a column of intense darkness. Tiny arcs of lightning flashed around it, and a ring of fog began to form around the base of the dais, drops of dirty water or perhaps diluted blood dripping from the stone.

Withra advanced forward several more steps and knelt down, dropping her arms. As she did so, the chant stopped. There was total silence in the hall. It was so quiet Hereward could hear his own heart beating, beating far faster than he liked. He had to choose his moment exactly, too fast and the Hag might not pursue, too slow and it would catch him—

He started as the dark column moved again, suddenly sprouting four long tentacles and a misshapen lump atop it that perhaps was a head. The tentacles came questing down the dais and advanced across the floor, writhing and turning, emitting small puffs of fog and mist with every coiling movement.

"We bring you a sacrifice!" shouted Withra. "But hear me, Hag! It is—"

Hereward drew, cocked, and fired his pistol before Withra could complete her warning. The sharp report was shocking, seemingly louder than any pistol he had ever fired before. But he paid it no heed, nor did he hesitate to gauge the extent of Withra's wounding. He'd hit her he knew, and she had gone down, the situation assessed in an instant even as he drew his second pistol and fired it straight into the shadow-stuff of the Hag. She was sliding off the dais, her tentacles racing across the floor towards him, moving in sinuous esses like a sidewinder across sand.

The silver ball was swallowed up to no obvious effect, but

again Sir Hereward hadn't paused to see what it would do. Throwing the pistol aside, he jumped to the closest table, ran across the middle of it, kicking dishes, cutlery, drinks, and food aside, and leapt for the door.

Tentacles lashed the air behind his back as he raced through.

"Make way!" roared Hereward, throwing himself forward, putting all his strength into his legs. "Make way!"

Guard priestesses flung themselves against the sides of the passage as he sped past, turning their faces to their wall and praying to Lanith-Eremot as the darkness that pursued him enveloped them. But their prayers were not answered. Bleached bones, shreds of human flesh, strips of leather, and the metal parts of their weapons fell to the floor behind the Hag. When enraged, it seemed she was not particular about only devouring men.

Hereward ran as he had never run before. He pulled at the very air ahead of him as if he could use it to lever himself faster forward, and his knees rose almost to his chest. He skittered around the corner and through the inner gate, and for a fatal, awful second almost tripped on the first blood gutter, only just recovering his balance enough to transform a fall into a diagonal leap forward. Tentacles lashed where he had been, and a priestess behind screamed a death cry so hideous that in normal circumstances it would have galvanized Hereward to run faster still, but now there was no faster. He ran the race of his life.

Water exploded as he burst outside and into the Shallows, great sprays going up with every footfall. It was dark outside, much darker than Hereward had expected, for storm clouds had gathered over the house, blocking out the moon and stars. Yet he could not stop to get his bearings, but instead ran on, trusting to instinct, with an awful sloshing and boiling noise too close behind him the mark of the Hag's closing.

A faint blue light blossomed ahead, like a tiny falling star. It only lasted a few seconds, but the knight knew it for Fitz's aid, the least possible light to conserve the power of his needle. In those moments of scant illumination, Hereward saw the outline of the cannon and knew where its maw lay, almost straight ahead.

Hereward jumped for the cannon mouth as a tentacle grazed his back, the shadow-stuff burning like acid through his doublet and shirt and deep into the flesh beneath. He screamed but did not slow. It was only a glancing strike; the tentacle had no grip and could not pull him back.

The knight went into the cannon like a rammed shot, sliding straight on his stomach for a good six feet before he got his hands and knees under himself and began to scuttle, once again faster than he had moved in such a fashion ever before.

It was pitch-black inside the cannon. Hereward sobbed and cursed Fitz, himself, the Hag, Withra, fate, and all the gods and godlets who'd ever existed as he rubbed the skin off his knees, elbows, and hands in his frantic passage over the thin sharp ridges of the rifled barrel. But he cared nothing for these pains, for the Hag came close behind him. He could feel the dread weight of her, and twice a tentacle lashed across the soles of his feet.

One hundred feet was too far, thought Hereward through pain and fear. He would never make it to the breech, never make it out. The Hag's tentacles would lash around his ankles and drag him back and then, then it would all be over, that fall from the razor's edge that was bound to come one day—

A blue, heatless light shone ahead, outlining an opening above.

Hereward's heart almost burst as he exerted all his remaining strength, leaping up through the open chamber to stand on top of the exposed cartridge, his bleeding fingers tearing at the wax seals and the peace strings of the old dagger, feet jumping and dancing as a single tentacle lashed across from left to right and then right to left, and he almost fell as he got the dagger free, its whiny voice piercing his head as if an icicle had been thrust through his eye and into his brain.

"Who wakes me! Who wakes me!"

"Deal death to my enemies, death to my foes, Anglar-Ithrix I command thee!" squealed Hereward, his voice weirdly pitched from exhaustion and fright, the words gabbled out so fast they were almost . . . almost but not quite . . . unrecognizable.

He threw the dagger and leapt off the cannon, even as the foremost part of the Hag emerged into the chamber, a writhing thing of darkness and fog. The dagger bounced clanging off the bottom of the breech, shouted something peevish, and drove straight at the shadow.

Tentacles writhed to try to fend off the weapon, and then a great tentacle composed of blinding violet light arced over from the cascabel at the very end of the cannon, where Mister Fitz stood, wielding his one remaining sorcerous needle.

This brilliant tendril reached in and rotated the chamber shut in one swift motion, locking the old dagger and the Hag inside.

Evan as it did so, Mister Fitz jumped over the side, letting the three strings that would fire the cannon run through his open hand, and sped to his previously prepared firing position. Though he was far more durable than a human, his papier-mâché and wooden frame being heavily reinforced with sorcery, he still sought shelter behind the moklek he had made kneel down some dozen yards away.

Sir Hereward was not behind the great beast, but there was no time for Mister Fitz to check where he had gone. From the sound of the shouting and cursing inside the cannon, the godlet Anglar-Ithrix who resided inside the dagger was getting the worst of his combat with the Hag.

Mister Fitz lay down and pulled all three strings. Two of the
pistols fired, long trails of sparks spurting up from the cannon.

Then came the long second of uncertainty, the gunner's
doubt. A very long second indeed, almost long enough for Fitz
to pull the strings again in vain hope the third pistol would do
the job, even as thoughts of spoiled powder and blocked vents
whisked through his mind—

The cannon fired.

The blast was titanic, destroying all other sound. A massive
jet of flame enveloped the entire corner of the fortified house,
floor to ceiling. The cannon itself bucked up and backward,
smashing the carts into thousands of pieces, sending wicked
splinters flying in all directions, the great long tube of bronze itself almost dancing on one end before it toppled over and came
smashing down in the Shallows, creating both a minor tidal
wave and a splash so great it was like a sudden, short fall of rain.

Mister Fitz stood up as the rain fell, and looked about for
Sir Hereward. A great swathe of acrid gunsmoke billowed over
everything, obscuring even Fitz's vision. His moklek shield was
trumpeting its pain to its fellows, but the puppet adjudged it was
not badly hurt. He would tend to it once he found Sir Hereward
and ascertained the fate of both the Hag and the old dagger.

Sir Hereward had just kept running until the cannon blast
knocked him over. It took Mister Fitz several minutes to find
him amidst the clouds of thick, acrid smoke from the cannon's
firing. The knight was sitting in the water, looking dazed and
very bloody.

"You did well," said Mister Fitz, carefully checking over
his companion's head, torso, and arms for serious wounds.
"Stand up."

"What?" shouted Sir Hereward. He was deaf from the blast,
and stupid with weariness. Running from the Hag had taken all
the strength he possessed, and then some more.

Fitz heaved him up and supported him when Hereward's knees buckled and he would have fallen again. As he did so, he looked over the lower half of his companion, noting that in addition to many cuts and abrasions, there was a small splinter buried several inches in Hereward's thigh. But it was not bleeding freely, and so it too could wait.

"Did it work?" shouted Sir Hereward. He looked about him, blinking furiously. Even with a good part of the house of the Sisters of Mercantile Fairness ablaze and shedding light, he could hardly see anything through the gunsmoke. He took some comfort from Mister Fitz's cool wooden hands, but less from the knowledge that the puppet had used his last sorcerous needle.

"I am not yet certain," said Mister Fitz, loudly, but not loudly enough for Hereward to hear him. "I still detect some essence of the Hag . . . a small remnant—"

He suddenly let go of Hereward, who promptly fell onto his knees and only just managed to stop himself tilting over face-forward, to suffer an ignominious death by drowning in six inches of water.

Withra was advancing towards them, a gleaming knife in her hand. The left side of her face had been shattered by the silver ball from Sir Hereward's pistol, her cheekbone and part of her jaw bare to the elements, a wound that should have her curled up in agony. But she showed no pain, and when she opened her mouth, Sir Hereward saw why. Instead of a tongue, Withra had a small tentacle of shadow, the very last piece of the Hag still extant upon the earth.

The small, sharp knife Mister Fitz used for dissecting appeared in the puppet's hand. He crouched to spring, but before he could do so, there was the sudden whoosh of a large blade moving very fast, the flash of firelight on steel, and Withra's head parted from her shoulders. The head landed upright in the

water, the shadow-tongue writhing and eyes blazing. Emengah stood above it, the Archimandress's own greatsword held
bloody in both hands.

"We take care of our own," she said wearily. "And all debts
must be paid."

Fitz wasn't listening. His head was tilted, listening to a
high-pitched whistle akin to the cry of a falcon speeding to
its prey. It suddenly grew louder. The puppet lunged forward,
quick as a snake, and snatched up Withra's head, holding the
horrid remnant in front of Sir Hereward just in time to interpose it between the knight and the flying dagger that sped out
of the darkness like an arrow.

Dagger and head meet with a ghastly squelch. The two were
torn from Fitz's hands and went rolling off through the water,
the dagger's imprecations and curses muffled by the shadow that
came out of the gaping jaw and wrapped around the blade. Fitz
started to walk after them, but halted as it became clear they
were not going to stop, but would keep on rolling and fighting
till one defeated the other. Or as was to be hoped, they both
lost the strength to maintain their existence in the world and
were forced to retreat and rejoin the greater part of themselves
in some other dimension.

Emengah walked over to Sir Hereward and grounded her
sword. Behind her, the flames from the burning house rose
higher, and black smoke billowed forth to eclipse the last acrid
swirls of white smoke from the cannon.

"The Sisters of Mercantile Fairness thank you Mister Fitz,"
said Emengah. "And you, Sir Hereward."

Sir Hereward smiled crookedly. He couldn't hear a word she
said, but he knew gratitude and goodwill when he saw it, and
the scarred Emengah with the greatsword in her hands seemed
to him to be fair indeed, a most welcome sight. He managed to

stand up with Fitz's considerable help, and made a fair effort at a courtly bow before he fainted.

WAKING IN DAYLIGHT, HEREWARD FOUND HIMSELF IN A featherbed in a corner of the hall that while it smelled extremely smoky, was undamaged. That could not be said for the other end of the great room, which was open to the sky, allowing the over-bright sun unfettered access past the tumbled walls of blackened stone.

Mister Fitz sat on the end of the bed, sewing up the many rents in Hereward's shirt and breeches. The novice Parnailam, clad now in an ordinary homespun habit, watched his sewing intently, marveling at the tiny, ordered stitches and the speed with which the needle moved.

"Ah," said Mister Fitz to the knight. "You wake. Good morning."

"If you can call it that," said Sir Hereward muzzily. His ears hurt, but at least he could hear again. He was not so sure about his mind, or his memory, and the many pains along his legs and arms indicated he would remain abed for quite some time. "I take it the plan worked as expected?"

"Indeed," said Mister Fitz. "Though there is a slight chance we might have to deal with the old dagger again one day. A very slight chance, in my estimation."

"I hope so—" began Sir Hereward, but he paused and tilted his head, frowning as his ears caught a distant rumble. "Cannon fire!"

"No," said Mister Fitz equably. "Thunder. The rains have begun."

As if responding to this statement, the sky darkened suddenly, the sun vanishing. Heavy drops fell through the open,

destroyed part of the house, and a great fusillade of rain began
to sound on the roof above.

"The Shallows . . . the mokleks . . . the cannon," blurted
Sir Hereward. He sat up and made as if to get out of bed, but
Mister Fitz and Parnailam together pushed him back. "We must
repair, get new wagons somehow, move out before the water
deepens—"

"There is no need," said Mister Fitz calmly.

"Why not?"

"The Sisters are building us a boat, in gratitude for ridding
them of the Hag. We can take the cannon across the Shallows
to Junum, I have a letter of credit at the Bank of the New Ingots
there. We can recruit a century of ox-men haulers to drag the
cannon on rollers. True, there is the small matter of the Loathsome Worms to deal with—"

Mister Fitz stopped talking. Sir Hereward had either passed
out, or was feigning sleep. The puppet took up his sewing again,
Parnailam sitting down to watch once more.

"You are most adept with your needle, Mister Fitz," the
novice said shyly.

"Indeed," said Mister Fitz. His round head turned slowly,
his strange blue eyes met Parnailam's, and his mouth quirked up
in something that was not quite a smile. "But then I have had a
great deal of practice, with many different needles, stitching . . .
and unstitching."

Parnailam gulped, though she did not quite know why, and
soon made her excuses to leave.

Mister Fitz returned to his sewing. Sir Hereward slept.

Outside, a line of mokleks stood happily in the rain, all of
them watching a dented pink howdah float past the tumbled
cannon and drift away.

A LONG,
COLD TRAIL

SIR HEREWARD DREW HIS HEAVY FUR CLOAK tighter around himself and lifted his feet higher, his sealskin boots coming out of the snow with a discouraging sucking noise.

"You're *sure* the road is under here?" he asked, apparently to the empty air, for no one strode next to him, and the bleak landscape of bare snow dotted here and there with dying, stunted trees appeared to be entirely bereft of life.

"Yes," came the short reply from inside the tall wicker basket he carried upon his back. A moment later, Mister Fitz emerged, the hairless top of his round, papier-mâché head flipping back the lid of the basket, which up until two days ago had served to hold the laundry of a country squire. That squire was now dead, along with every occupant of his manor, both human and animal. Since Sir Hereward's battlemount had also been slain by the effect of proximity to the godlet that killed the squire, and the huge riding lizard's saddlebags were unsuitably large for pedestrian movement, the laundry basket had been pressed into service to carry blankets, tarpaulin, carbine, powder, ball, water bottles, and food.

Mister Fitz had climbed inside the basket when the snow got too deep, as he stood only three feet six and a half inches tall on his carved wooden feet. A sorcerous puppet, imbued with magical life, he did not feel the cold but did find deep snow an inconvenience. Not so much to travel, as he was preternaturally strong and could bull his way through the deepest drift, but because he didn't like being surrounded by snow with the consequent diminution of vision.

The snow was not a natural phenomenon. As with the desiccated corpses sprawled about the manor half a league behind them, it was an indication and by-product of the passage of a godlet inimical to both life and the regular weather patterns of the area. The depth of the snow and the heaviness of the fall, as evidenced by the steady flakes now settling on Sir Hereward's woolen watch cap (his three-bar visored helmet was currently tied to his belt) indicated that the godlet and its unwilling and contrary host were only three or four hundred yards ahead of them.

This was the closest the duo of man and puppet had gotten to it after six days of dogged pursuit in increasingly bad weather, and the closest they wanted to get, at least until one of Sir Hereward's cousins got around to delivering the relic they would need to destroy, or rather banish, the godlet.

The whole matter had the air of a mordant family affair, thought Sir Hereward, as he galumphed through the snow, exerting his weary senses to be alert for any sign the godlet might have stopped to lie in wait or had begun to turn back. For in addition to waiting on his cousin to deliver the necessary relic, the reluctant host the godlet rode was Sir Hereward's great-great-aunt Eudonia. A notable witch and thus also an agent of the Council for the Treaty of the Safety of the World, she had been tasked with banishing the newly rediscovered proscribed godlet Xavva-Tish-Laqishtax.

But Laqishtax had proven far stronger than expected and had managed to attach itself to Eudonia's person. As neither witch nor godlet was initially able to subdue the other in a clash of wills, the godlet had sought to grow stronger by sucking the life force from any living thing around that was unable to resist—which was usually everything alive for several hundred yards from its foul presence. Eudonia had countered this tactic by walking them both off into the sparsely populated wastelands of the former Kingdom of Hrorst.

However, at some point in the last week, Xavva-Tish-Laqishtax had clearly found an additional source of power— some poor shepherd and a flock of goats or the like—and had managed to overcome Eudonia sufficiently to redirect their path back out of the wastelands towards the prosperous, well-populated lands of the Autarchy of Kallinksimiril. More grist for the godlet's mill.

The border manor where the godlet had just consumed everything with even the faintest spark of life was but the first of many that lay ahead, not to mention the walled town of Simiril itself. If Xavva-Tish-Laqishtax got that far, and subsumed the life force of not only the inhabitants but also their patron godlet—the benign lesser deity the locals called the Whelper— then it would be almost impossible to overcome.

Hence, Sir Hereward and Mister Fitz stalked Xavva-Tish-Laqishtax at a safe distance, and hoped very much the relic would soon be delivered, so they could attack.

"Kishtyr had best speed her travels," complained Sir Hereward as he stumbled and fell forward into a drift. Standing up to brush snow from his front, he added, "Simiril lies less than five leagues ahead, and I doubt the lake they call the Smallest Sea will slow the godlet one whit. I fail to see why Kishtyr did not arrive last night, or at least this morning. Also, I believe my nose is becoming frostbitten."

"It is no simple matter to retrieve a relic from the crypt," said Mister Fitz in his instructional voice. He had been Sir Hereward's nanny then teacher, and in truth had taught a great many god-slayers over the centuries, so he still veered to the didactic at the least temptation. "Being of necessity items that contain the specially distilled and controlled essence of particularly inimical godlets, the relics held by the Council are secured in a number of different ways. Nothing can be removed in a hurry, it takes several witches several days and is not without hazard. There may easily have been a complication."

"It's been a *week*," grumbled Sir Hereward, quickly wrinkling his nose several times in an attempt to warm it.

"It has been six days and we are some considerable distance from the High Pale," commented Mister Fitz. "Hmmm . . ."

"What was that?" asked Sir Hereward. The puppet's senses were far more acute than his own, particularly for things beyond the ordinary. And even more so when Hereward had a cold coming on. His ears were beginning to be blocked as a consequence of that cold, but he did think he might have heard a distant, fading scream, suddenly cut off.

"Xavva-Tish-Laqishtax has found some more people to consume," said Mister Fitz. "No . . . not entirely, it seems. It has left some fragment of spiritual essence within the husks."

Sir Hereward grimaced at the word *husks* and almost remonstrated with Mister Fitz for describing people in such a fashion. But he did not, for he knew the term was entirely accurate and Mister Fitz did not welcome sentimentality over verisimilitude. Whatever was left of the people after the godlet's devouring passage would indeed be no more than husks, things of flesh without thought or purpose. Unless they were given purpose by a greater power.

"It fills them with its will," reported Mister Fitz. "And sends them against us."

Sir Hereward swore and dumped the basket, unclasping his cloak in the same motion, letting it drop behind. Mister Fitz leapt from basket to shoulder and thence into the snow.

The knight's two long-barreled wheel-lock pistols were already charged with powder and loaded with silver-washed shot, but they were not wound. Sir Hereward wore the spanner on a thong about his wrist and from years of practice flipped it into his hand and began to wind the first pistol even as Mister Fitz pushed out of the drift and swiftly climbed the dead, grey trunk of a tree that up until the god's passage a half hour before had been a luxuriant beech. Its former foliage and much of its bark was now no more than dust below its branches, dirtying the snow.

"How many?" asked Sir Hereward. In a scant minute and a half he had spanned both pistols, loosened the basket-hilted mortuary sword in the sheath at his side, undone his helmet from his belt and slapped it on, and was now extracting his carbine—a more common flintlock—from the basket.

"Eight," said Mister Fitz.

"Unarmed?" asked Sir Hereward hopefully. Those recently dispossessed of the majority of their spiritual essence often retained some bodily memory of how to use arms and implements, which meant they could still fight with considerable competence even when directed by a puppeteering godlet rather than their own will.

"Farmers," said Mister Fitz. "They have hayforks, a scythe, and suchlike."

Sir Hereward grunted and primed the carbine from the small powder flask that slotted into the butt of the weapon. He had seen sufficient mortal wounds delivered by hayforks and reaping hooks to have a healthy respect for even such agricultural weaponry.

"I cannot spare the use of my sole remaining sorcerous

needle," said Mister Fitz. "We may need it to protect ourselves from the godlet's ravening. However, I shall assist as best I may in a more mechanical fashion."

As he spoke, the puppet reached behind his back, and withdrew from a hidden sheath a short triangular blade made to follow the proportion of the Golden Ratio, so it looked rather broader than it should. Some opponents—soon disabused of their fallacious notions—thought such a blade too small to be dangerous, particularly in the hands of a puppet. Most sorcerous puppets were mere entertainers and would not or could not fight under any circumstances. Mister Fitz did not follow that stricture, though it was true he fought hand to hand only when no more elegant alternative presented itself.

"How close?" asked Sir Hereward. He reached up and quickly fastened his helmet strap and turned up the thick, high collar of his buff coat to protect his neck.

"As you see," answered Mister Fitz, pointing.

Hereward could see them now, dark figures stark against the snowy backdrop, moving in the disturbing, stop-start, jagged fashion of the spirit-shorn.

"There are nine," said Sir Hereward, with some surprise, pointing to one far off to the right of the main group.

"That is not one of the godlet's playthings," said Mister Fitz, after a moment's pause. "It is a whole man . . . and he has an aura which suggests something of the sorcerer, to boot. Which perchance explains why he approaches on the diagonal, rather than fleeing as one might expect."

"Should I shoot him first?" asked Sir Hereward. Stray sorcerers of unknown allegiance on the field of battle were generally best removed from consideration in the overall military equation.

Mister Fitz did not answer for a few seconds, his pale blue eyes staring through the falling snow at that distant figure sloshing and leaping through the lesser drifts in an alley between rows of dead trees.

"No," he said finally. "It is Fyltak, the man who calls himself the God-Taker."

"That charlatan!" exploded Sir Hereward. "If he gets any closer, I'll finish him with steel, rather than waste my silvered shot on his—"

"He is not entirely a charlatan, and he may be useful," interrupted Mister Fitz. "In any event, the soul-reaped will be upon us well before he gets here."

"I make no warranty for his life," snapped Sir Hereward. His previous experience with Fyltak the God-Taker was recent, and had consisted of the latter successfully taking the credit for the banishment of the Blood-Sipping Ghoul, a minor but still sufficiently deadly godlet whose nocturnal predations on the burghers of Lazzarenno had actually been put to an end by Mister Fitz, with Sir Hereward taking care of the godlet's hematophagous minions. While Sir Hereward did not want his true business known, Fyltak had messed up their careful plans. The knight cared nothing for the false claims and subsequent rewards. He could not forgive Fyltak's bumbling interference.

"He bears an interesting sword," mused Mister Fitz, sharp gaze still fixed on Fyltak, who was leaping in great bounds through the snow, a blade bare in his hand. "I had not occasion to mark it previously, but I believe it is the source of the sorcerous emanations I have felt before. Not Fyltak himself, after all."

"Hmmph!" growled Sir Hereward. Sorcerous swords were generally even more trouble than sorcerers. Particularly the sentient variety, who were almost always crazed from centuries of bloodletting, or had adopted strange and annoying philosophies about when or even if they would deign to be wielded, and by whom.

The knight looked about for some better shooting position

and sloshed through the snow to climb upon an exposed rock, which on closer examination proved to be a rectangular-shaped obelisk of marble, a fallen milestone of the old Empire of the Risen Moon. Perhaps a good omen as that state was one of the founding members of the Council that Sir Hereward and Mister Fitz served. Or perhaps the reverse, as the empire, like the milestone, had fallen many centuries ago. So had the moon the empire was named after, Hereward suddenly recalled, feeling a frisson of melancholia. It had only been a very small moon, but it had made a very large crater when it fell.

The soul-reaped were drawing closer. They employed no tactics, no stratagems, the godlet in all likelihood simply filling them with thoughts of moving in a straight line and killing everything that got in their way. There were five men and three women, none of them young, for which Sir Hereward was grateful. Even knowing they were already dead in all ways that mattered, it was still easier to give grace to those who had experienced some extent of life.

He raised his carbine when they were some sixty paces away, sighted carefully, and fired. The heavy, silvered ball struck the closest scythe-wielding relict in his chest, hurling him backward as it blew out lungs and heart. The godlet's essence within tried to lift the corpse back up out of the snow, but the silver on the ball had disrupted Xavva-Tish-Laqishtax's hold, and after a few moments of thrashing and reaching, the former farmer lay still.

Sir Hereward placed the carbine down carefully at his feet. There might be a chance to reload. Taking out his first pistol, he took aim again, supporting his shooting arm under the elbow with his left hand, locking in his left elbow as he had been taught long ago. Squeezing the trigger, the wheel spun, showering sparks. The pistol barked its characteristic sharp roar and another silvered ball struck the next closest spirit-shorn, exploding his head like an overripe melon kicked at the market by a disgruntled customer.

"Two," remarked Sir Hereward, returning the pistol to his belt and drawing its twin. Xavva-Tish-Laqishtax's servitors were moving faster now, doubtless infused with more of the godlet's essence as it became aware of opposition. They were jumping high out of the snowdrifts, leaping ahead in great bounds.

There would not be time to reload and shoot again, Sir Hereward judged. He let out a long, foggy exhalation, slowing his breath, which had become quicker than he liked, and took aim once more.

The third shot was not so good, for any one of many reasons. He did not think it was from the fear he kept well clamped within. Sir Hereward was used to fear, and used to managing it, calling on it for energy and direction, rather than letting it use him. He did not trust those who claimed to feel no fear.

In any case, the ball struck the side of a woman who carried a pruning hook, setting her aback several paces but no more. If she'd still been alive, or more alive, the shock would have put her down, blood loss finishing the job in a matter of minutes. But her wounded body was no longer guided by a fearful human mind. She pushed on, leaving a red trail behind her on the snow, her vicious, long-shafted hook raised high.

"Take the wounded one!" shouted Sir Hereward, thrusting the second pistol through his belt and drawing his sword in an oft-practiced movement.

Mister Fitz sprang from his perch in the dead beech, landing on the shoulders of the pruning-fork woman, cutting her throat clear to the backbone, and jumping again almost in one motion. This time he landed in the snow, disappearing under the legs of one of the remaining five attackers, who strode on, only to fall a few paces later, his tendons cut. The puppet reappeared on his back, only his head and sticklike arm visible above the snow, the arm vanishing as he struck down into the base of the fallen man's brain with his short dagger.

Four others came at Sir Hereward, where he stood high on the old milestone. They all bore hayforks, and again showed no trace of tactical thought, colliding together at the front of the stone and thrusting with their weapons, the shafts clashing together. Sir Hereward trod down one fork, dodged another, and thrust first one and then another of the relicts through their eyes. Even as he pulled the slightly stuck blade from the skull of the second farmer, Mister Fitz dispatched the remaining two, stabbing them in the brain stem, leaping from the shoulders of one to the other then to the stone.

Dying bodies flopped in the snow around the duo as the godlet tried to reanimate the corpses. But both Sir Hereward's sword and Mister Fitz's dagger were well washed with silver, and with brain or spinal cord destroyed, the godlet could not take hold of anything to continue the fight.

"Hold hard! I come to your aid!"

Fyltak the God-Taker was still leaping through the snow towards them, waving his sword above his head. He moved very fast, considering the difficulty of the ground.

Sir Hereward grunted, wiped his sword clean on the sack-cloth tunic of the closest no-longer-writhing farmer, sheathed it, and bent down to retrieve his carbine. He reloaded it swiftly, taking cartridge and ball from his belt pouch.

"No," said Mister Fitz. "I think he will be useful."

"I wasn't going to shoot him," lied Sir Hereward. "I am just preparing for the next half-eaten meal Xavva-Tish-Laqishtax will disgorge and send against us."

Though Fyltak arrived far sooner than Sir Hereward had expected, the knight had still managed to reload his pistols as well as the carbine. He had also resumed his cloak and picked up the basket. Mister Fitz rode in it again, his knife once more invisible. He had licked it clean with his blue, stippled leather tongue before sheathing the blade, something Sir Hereward still found somewhat disquieting though the puppet assured him he had no appetite for blood. His tongue was merely an effective cleansing agent and upon occasion, the taste would reveal something of import that otherwise might be missed.

"Thank the kind gods you yet live!" gasped Fyltak. "But know had it been otherwise, I would have avenged you!"

He sheathed his sword and took several deep, racking breaths, indicating what Sir Hereward considered a lack of acquaintance with physical exertion, or perhaps too great a dedication to cakes and ale, though against this supposition he was quite a lean individual.

"I care not for your bravado, Fyltak," said Sir Hereward. "You could no more avenge us against Xavva-Tish-Laqishtax than I could unassisted fly to the closest moon."

"That voice is known to me," muttered Fyltak. He rummaged inside the neck of his somewhat oversized cuirass, to produce a lorgnette on a cord of silk. Placing the glasses on his nose, he gazed up at Sir Hereward, whose face was shadowed by the bars of his visor. The knight noted that looking down at Fyltak the lenses greatly magnified the man's eyes, and were thus presumably extremely necessary and Fyltak should wear them all the time. Furthermore, he probably hadn't seen the detail of the combat that had just occurred, which was useful to know.

"Sir Hereward!" exclaimed Fyltak, letting the lorgnette fall back inside the neck of his breastplate. "Well met, fellow justiciar and executioner of wicked gods!"

"I am not your fellow!" barked Sir Hereward. "You are to me and mine as a . . . a flea is to a dog. Damnably irritating and hard to shift!"

"Ah, the growl of one who has not breakfasted well!" exclaimed Fyltak. "I understand. Nay, I feel the lack myself, but fortunately I bear within this most cunning canister coffee still hot from the kitchens of the Duke of Simiril and within this round tin, pastries fresh-baked from that same kitchen. Allow me to spread a cloth upon this stone and set forth a repast!"

"A man must eat," said Mister Fitz, standing up on the back of the basket. "The godlet has paused in its travel, in any case. We cannot go closer for the nonce."

"Ah, the most wondrous puppet!" exclaimed Fyltak. "Perhaps you might play a cheerful gigue or sing us a roundelay, to lift our spirits while we eat and drink?"

Clearly Fyltak had no conception of what kind of puppet Mister Fitz actually was and had made the common mistake that he was one of the standard performing variety. This further confirmed Hereward's deduction that the man needed his eyeglasses and only pretended to use them as an affectation. A kind of double blind. The knight's mouth quirked at this word-play, and he wished he could share it with Mister Fitz. Though the puppet would doubtless not find it amusing. He considered nearly all of Sir Hereward's jokes and witticisms foolish, or at best, not worth the breath required to make them.

"I fear it is too cold for my lute, and my throat is a little rusty and wants sweet oil," replied Mister Fitz. "Would a poem suffice? I must cogitate a little to create, but I do not wish to hold you gentlemen from your coffee."

"I do not want any coff—" Sir Hereward started to say angrily, but he stopped as he felt the pressure of Mister Fitz's fingers on his shoulder. The puppet saw some use in Fyltak, or in his sword, so with some effort Hereward forced down his ire. Besides, the God-Taker had opened the "cunning canister" and the delightful aroma of hot coffee had reached Sir Hereward's nose.

"I do not normally drink coffee among corpses," continued Hereward, climbing down to sit on his fur cloak at the far end of the stone, as far away as possible from the bloodied snow and the fallen bodies at the other end. "But there is nowhere else to sit in this new wasteland the godlet has made."

Fyltak handed him a steaming demitasse of coffee. Hereward raised one eyebrow at the delicate pale blue and silver porcelain cup, surely not long to survive any serious travel or fighting, and sipped.

Mister Fitz recited his poem as the two men drank.

Soft, the snow falling
Steam spiraling from coffee
The slain cold and still

Fyltak nodded several times in appreciation. Sir Hereward, who considered himself a far more skillful and talented poet than Mister Fitz, privately made a face at his companion that indicated he could do better but would refrain so as not to raise doubts about the puppet's nature.

"Which . . . err . . . godlet is causing the trouble?" asked Fyltak, after a suitable pause to absorb the full beauty of the poem. "There is considerable panic in Simiril, many already flee the town."

"Very wise," said Mister Fitz. He moved closer to Fyltak and reached out with one hand towards his sword, wooden fingers making an understated grasping motion, quickly quelled. Sir Hereward noted this. Fitz really was interested in the charlatan's weapon. It seemed unremarkable to the knight, an old-fashioned sword with a dull blackened steel hilt and from the look of the plain scabbard, a heavy blade made for hacking and slashing, rather than for any finesse with the point, which was very likely dull.

"Your sword interests me," continued the puppet. "I am something of a student of antiquities. I perceive it is of an ancient make."

"What? This old blade?" asked Fyltak. "Been in the family forever, but it's nothing special. I bear it for reasons of sentiment, no more."

"I see," murmured Mister Fitz, bending closer to examine the hilt. Fyltak swapped his demitasse to his left hand and draped his right over the hilt, obscuring the puppet's view.

"As I said, it is quite an ordinary weapon," he blustered. "But tell me of our business! Which godlet is it? What are its powers and weaknesses?"

"Our business!" exclaimed Sir Hereward. He would have gone on, but Mister Fitz glanced at him meaningfully again, so the knight subsided. Fyltak handed him a pastry, which was as excellent as the coffee.

"It is properly known as Xavva-Tish-Laqishtax," said Sir Hereward reluctantly, in between bites, after he saw that Mister Fitz was not going to enlighten Fyltak. Presumably so the God-Taker continued to think him one of the harmless entertaining puppets. "However, it was better known in its heyday as Xavva the Soul-Gorger."

"Ah!" exclaimed Fyltak.

"You know of it?" asked Sir Hereward curiously. The godlet had only been identified by the Witches after some considerable research in their incomparable archives, and that only after Eudonia managed to get a fresh sample of the "spoil" left behind by the godlet's predations, revealing the unique prismatic band of the godlet's sorcerous signature. Unfortunately, after procuring the sample, Eudonia had not waited for the confirmation of identity before taking on the godlet by herself.

"Not as such," replied Fyltak. "That was merely an expression of punctuation, as it were. And its weaknesses?"

"Not very apparent," replied Sir Hereward. He hesitated, wondering how much he could tell Fyltak before he would have to kill him. The man seemed innocuous, an innocent, or near enough. Only his sword made him of some account, though he was either deluded on that score or did not wish others to know of it.

"It must have some weakness," replied Fyltak. "As Hereshmur describes in *Banishing and Imprisonment: Methods for Dealing with Unruly Gods,* all extra-dimensional entities are flawed."

"Ah, a scholar," said Sir Hereward.

"What do you mean?" asked Fyltak, his eyebrows drawing together as he frowned, quick to detect offence or sarcasm.

"Merely punctuation," replied Sir Hereward blandly. "Hereshmur may well be correct, but he is perhaps countered by that famous quotation of Lorquar, Executioner of Gods."

"Oh yes," said Fyltak, nodding.

Sir Hereward, who had made up "Lorquar, Executioner of Gods" on the spur of the moment, kindly did not tell Fyltak so, but ascribed a frequent saying of his own mother to this mythical personage.

"If an inimical godlet's weakness cannot be discerned, does one exist? Act against its strengths for a greater chance of success."

"And this Xavva . . . err . . . godlet . . . what are its strengths?"

"It devours souls," said Sir Hereward bleakly. "It sucks the life out of anything that gets too close, and it grows stronger. Should it garner enough spiritual essence, it will become wellnigh impossible to banish."

"But doubtless you have a plan, Sir Hereward?"

"I have an ally," replied Hereward. "Who is extremely late arriving!"

"And who would that be, sir?" asked Fyltak, drawing himself up and inflating his chest. "For dare I say, an ally already stands before you!"

"Yes," replied Hereward dubiously. "However, the specific ally I await is . . ."

Once again the knight hesitated, reluctant to give this im-
poster more knowledge than it would be safe to allow him
to retain. Fyltak struck an expectant attitude, indicating that
possibly not telling him might lead to death by curiosity in
any case.

"You have heard of the Witches of Har?" asked Sir Hereward. "Agents for the ancient Council for the Treaty of the
Safety of the World?"

"Have I not!" exclaimed Fyltak. "Am I not one of those
agents myself?"

Momentarily puzzled by the double negative, Sir Hereward
didn't respond for a moment. Then he exploded.

"No, you're not, so stop talking nonsense! And before
you go fulminating about the place like a turkey-cock with
singed tail feathers think about what I just told you. A Witch of
Har—a real agent of the Council—should be here shortly, and
they do not take lightly to impersonators. Furthermore, she will
be bringing with her a weapon which we, and by that I mean
the witch and I and Mis—that is, the witch and I—will use to
banish Xavva-Tish-Laqishtax. And you, sir, should immediately
face about in the opposite direction and go as fast as you can as
far as you can and hope that we succeed!"

"You are offensive, sir!" exclaimed Fyltak. "And when this
godlet has been dealt with you shall answer to me for a lesson
in manners!"

"Did you not hear a word I said?" expostulated Sir Hereward. He stood up and thrust the demitasse back at Fyltak, who
reflexively took it. "This is a serious business, not for moon-
gazers and dilettantes!"

"Perhaps we should let the Witch of Har decide who is
the dilettante!" Fyltak snapped back. As he spoke, he put both
porcelain cups back in a well-padded box and slipped it into a
pouch inside his cloak. "A notable such as myself, or a brutish

wanderer who travels about with a capering puppet, aggrandizing himself as a god-slayer!"

Sir Hereward's hand went to his pistol as Fyltak's went to his sword.

"Enough!" said Mister Fitz, very loudly. "The godlet has turned back towards us!"

Fyltak looked to the puppet, but Sir Hereward gazed up to the sky. The snow was beginning to fall thicker and faster, and he felt the air suddenly grow colder, ice forming on his nose and cheeks.

"How far away is it?" he asked urgently.

"Four hundred yards and closing swiftly," replied Mister Fitz. He jumped to the basket even as Sir Hereward leapt from the milestone and began to force his way back the way they had come. Already the path they had made was beginning to disappear under the fresh snow.

"Why do you flee?" called out Fyltak, adding, "Coward!"

"If it gets closer than a hundred yards, Xavva-Tish-Laqishtax will draw the spirit from your body as easily as a man quaffing a pint of ale!" shouted Sir Hereward over his shoulder, not pausing to do so. "Stay and have your soul consumed! Your small life will not be a great weight in the scales! That's if you don't freeze first!"

A few minutes later, he heard Fyltak puffing up behind him.

"So do we simply flee?"

"Going back on its own trail, the godlet will diminish, finding no new life to consume," explained Sir Hereward shortly. "If it follows us for a sufficient time, it may become weak enough to dispatch even without the weapon I await from the Witches."

"It grows cold," said the self-professed God-Taker. His breath came out as dense fog, icicles forming around his mouth as he spoke. "Very cold."

"The cursed godlet is applying its strength to bring an even greater freeze, staking all on this pursuit," huffed Sir Hereward. It hurt to breathe in, the air was so intensely cold. "Fitz! We cannot long go on like this."

"A little farther!" urged Mister Fitz from within the basket. "I am calculating. We must make the godlet use as much of its stored energy as possible, because with only one needle, I cannot hold it off for more than twenty or perhaps thirty minutes."

"Wh-wh-what is this . . ." asked Fyltak, his teeth chattering. He was staggering now, wading through icy, brittle snow that was building higher than his thighs, the air so thick with flakes neither man could see much farther than their own outstretched arms. "Wh-wh-what talk of n-n-needles?"

"The mathematics are simple," continued Mister Fitz, ignoring Fyltak's question. "If the godlet depletes its reserves sufficiently in pursuing us or trying to break down the defenses I will raise, it will not be able to retain control over Eudonia's body. She will reassert dominance and walk away, back along the path they took, where the godlet will only grow weaker. We can follow, await Kishtyr, and proceed as required."

"Wh-wh-what if . . . if it doesn't weaken enough?" asked Sir Hereward. He couldn't stop shivering, and he could barely see now, his eyes thin slits surrounded by ice. "Or we freeze first? We have to stop and shield ourselves!"

"Ten more steps!" commanded Mister Fitz.

Sir Hereward pushed on, but every step took him a smaller distance forward. The snow was waist high and more tightly packed, indicating he had wandered off their previous path. Or so much snow had fallen so quickly it didn't matter where he went. He couldn't hear Fyltak, but then he couldn't hear much of anything, save the echo of his own straining heartbeat. His ears were frozen under his woolen cap, he felt as if the only sound he picked up now was coming from within him.

Dimly he heard Fitz shouting something, and he felt a vibration on his back. The puppet leaping clear of the basket, he supposed. He tried to walk on, but instead he fell face-first in the snow, which was weirdly warmer than the air above it. For a moment he welcomed this, before realizing it was a trap. If he didn't get up again straightaway, he would lie here and freeze to death. Groaning, the knight rose up on one knee and with frantic but feeble swimming motions, managed to clear the snow away from his chest and stand.

Fitz spoke again, a phrase Hereward couldn't properly make out, save it included the word "eyes." He knew what that meant—Mister Fitz was about to use a sorcerous needle—so he forced his ice-ridden eyes completely closed and buried his face in his buff coat sleeve.

Even with this protection, a violet radiance burst through, seeming to illuminate the insides of his eye sockets and skull. Sir Hereward cried out at that, and at the blast of welcome but painful heat. His ears suddenly cleared. He heard Fyltak groaning and Mister Fitz reciting instructions as if they were back in the schoolroom at the High Pale.

"Hereward, Fyltak. Do not move. I have inscribed a sorcerous barrier about us, which will resist the godlet's ravening and also make the air much more clement. But it is of a small radius and should you cross the boundary, flesh and bone would be bisected and death instant."

Slowly, very slowly, Sir Hereward opened his eyes, blinking away the melted ice. He was now standing in a pool of melted snow that was trickling about his ankles, finding its way to the lowest point of the ground nearby. Mister Fitz, sodden to his neck, was crouched next to him, his wooden fingers cupped around a needle that even so shrouded, shone with a light too bright to address save out of the corner of one's eye. A radiant trail, not so brilliant, marked where the puppet sorcerer had drawn a circle around the three would-be god-slayers.

Xavva-Tish-Laqishtax stalked around the circle, ice instantly forming in thick sheets under its feet. Hereward looked at the godlet's current physical form with rather mixed feelings. Eudonia had always hated him, always called him an aberration, even to his face: a boy-child born to a witch, when the Witches only gave birth to girls. She had wanted him exposed at birth on the cliff tops of the High Pale, a fate only averted because Hereward's mother was one of the Three, the ruling council. Eudonia had also opposed his being taught by Mistress Fitz (as she was then), and later had tried to prevent Hereward and the puppet being sent out as companions on the eternal mission to rid the world of inimical godlets.

Hereward feared her and returned her hatred.

But now he also felt pity.

Xavva-Tish-Laqishtax had retained Eudonia's shape, at least in torso and head. But somewhere along its ravening trail it had obviously felt the need for faster locomotion, because there were two extra sets of human legs fused to Eudonia's middle, with repellent growths of flesh and skinless bundles of muscles and nerves bulging out where the godlet had stuck everything together willy-nilly.

Eudonia's harsh, unforgiving face with its ritual scars was unchanged, save that the stubs of sorcerous needles were embedded in her forehead and through both cheeks, all three still sparking faintly with susurrations of violet energy. Clearly she had resorted to draconian measures in an effort to resist the godlet. Looking at her white, rolled-back eyes, Sir Hereward wondered if deep inside she still fought against the extra-dimensional being who had invaded her mind and flesh.

Xavva-Tish-Laqishtax approached the circle, reaching out with Eudonia's hands, only to draw them back as sorcerous energy flared, its fingers smoking and blackened. It paid these hurts no heed, not even dipping its hands in the snow, so the fingers continued to slowly burn, skin crackling back to bone. The awful stench wafted across to Hereward, Fitz's sorcerous defense on this occasion not designed to forestall odors.

"Will the circle hold?" croaked Sir Hereward.

"For a time," confirmed Mister Fitz. The puppet was watching the godlet intently. After a few moments, he made a clicking sound with his tongue, which was pierced with a silver stud, perhaps just for this purpose. "I fear I have miscalculated."

"What?" asked Fyltak, his voice quavering.

"It is more cunning than I expected," remarked Mister Fitz, facing the horrific, malformed thing that hosted the godlet's presence in the world.

Xavva-Tish-Laqishtax smiled at the puppet too widely, the skin around Eudonia's mouth splitting like rotten cloth at each end, revealing bone. No blood came from this new wound. Then the godlet turned and moved away, using all three sets of legs clumsily in a lopsided waddle through the drifts. Snow swirled and followed it, a localized flurry. Though the godlet moved slowly, within half a minute it was lost to sight in the gloom of the perpetual winter that followed it everywhere.

"The godlet's turn and pursuit was a bluff," continued Mister Fitz. He closed his fist completely, concentrating for a moment. When he opened his hand, the needle he held was nothing more than a sliver of cold iron, all radiance gone, and the circle around them faded into nothing more than a line of melted snow. "To make me use my remaining needle in defense. It clearly never intended to press its attack home. Worse, it has more stored energy to sustain it than I estimated, enough to reach the manors on the far shore of the Smallest Sea. There it will gorge itself beyond chance of retribution."

"Yet it is weakened now?" asked Sir Hereward. He was vigorously rubbing his extremely cold nose, so his words were only just intelligible. "There was less snow and ice about it then, as it departed, and it was definitely slower."

"It is diminished," confirmed Mister Fitz. "Our brassards would give us sufficient protection to close with it now and not be frozen. But we still do not have any armament that might force it from Eudonia's body, let alone send it out of this world."

Hereward looked to the sky, shook his fist, and exclaimed, "Kishtyr!"

"Unless, of course, there is more to *your* sword than has been supposed," mused Mister Fitz, his round head slowly turning on his thin neck to fix his gaze upon Fyltak, who stood shivering and wild-eyed at Hereward's side.

"What kind of puppet are you really?" he asked, his voice as unsteady as his shivering body.

"A singular one, made for a most particular purpose: dealing with proscribed extra-dimensional entities," said Mister Fitz. Though he spoke in his usual matter-of-fact tone, there was an air of menace in his next words. "Doing whatever must be done for the safety of the world."

"Mister Fitz is a sorcerer, as much as any of the Witches of Har," added Sir Hereward. "More so, in many ways. Come, tell us about your sword. It might be the only chance for the people whose souls will otherwise be fodder for Xavva by tomorrow's dawn."

"I told you before . . . ," Fyltak started to say, but his voice withered under the combined stare of Mister Fitz and Sir Hereward. There was something about the puppet's piercing gaze, in particular, the man was not eager to meet.

"The sword has been in my family a long time," he finally said. "I don't know exactly how long. We have always known it was made to kill . . . banish, I suppose in actuality . . . godlets."

"Show me the blade," commanded Mister Fitz. He drew closer, while Sir Hereward stepped behind Fyltak. The knight's

fingers closed slowly into a fist, ready to smash the other man
on the side of the head if he chose that moment to try to use his
sword rather than merely show it.

But the God-Taker drew the weapon slowly and held it low
across his body, angling the sword so the light fell upon the
blade. The sky was already clearing, only a few scant snowflakes
falling now, and there was even a hint of the sun's presence in
the west, a kind of golden backlight to the dissipating clouds.
To the east, where Xavva-Tish-Laqishtax was inexorably staggering towards the Smallest Sea, the sky might as well have
been painted with coal dust, being entirely black.

Mister Fitz inspected the sword, peering closely at the
rippled surface of the blade. There were no obvious marks or
inscriptions, at least none visible to Sir Hereward's mortal eyes.
But the puppet saw something there.

"Interesting," he said. "This might actually be one of the
fabled God-Taker swords of sunken Herenclos."

"Herenclos?" asked Sir Hereward. "But that is an abyss, a
molten cleft . . ."

"It was a city once," said Mister Fitz. "Before the earth
swallowed it. The city sat above a deep vent that tapped the
fires of the underworld, which they used in their smithing.
That vent was kept from yawning open by their patron godlet
Heren-Par-Quaklin. When that godlet disappeared, the city
quite literally fell."

The puppet leaned closer still to the sword and touched the
blade with the very tip of his blue tongue.

"Yes," he said. "It is of Herenclos. The last captive of the
sword still lingers within. Greatly reduced, but still with some
remnant power. Perhaps enough."

"Captive?" asked Fyltak and Sir Hereward, speaking together.

"Yes," said Mister Fitz. "The God-Taker swords were not

made to banish the extra-dimensional, but rather to entrap and
use their powers. The smiths of Herenclos were not particular
about which godlets served this purpose, often enslaving benign
entities as well as those proscribed. I do not know which particular godlet lingers in this blade, nor is there time to capture
a slide of its essence . . . What powers does the weapon exhibit,
Fyltak?"

"When I wield it, I can see in the dark," said Fyltak slowly.
"The world around me moves more slowly, I become impossibly
swift and consequently deadly. But this slowing continues . . .
if I hold too long to the sword, then everything about me drags
to a standstill, people and animals. Everyone and everything,
they become as statues and it seems so too does the movement
of the air, for however I gasp and struggle, I can draw no new
inhalation into my lungs."

"So you can only use the sword as long as you can hold your
breath?" asked Sir Hereward.

"Yes," replied Fyltak. "But my family has long raised its
children to practice the arts of the sponge divers of Zhelu. I
can go without new breath for four or even five minutes at a
time. That is why I was given the sword, I was the best of us.
So equipped, I took the name of the sword and became known
as the God-Taker!"

He was evidently recovering his former boisterous self, the
shock of the cold and the close encounter with Xavva-Tish-
Laqishtax wearing off.

"Have you actually tried to use the sword against any godlets?" asked Mister Fitz. "Or did you just merely adopt the
sword's title and not its activity? I ask because the entity within
is very old and somewhat faded, and the sorcerous structures
within the steel likewise degraded. I would presume that the
sword's use against another godlet would result in the banishment of *both* entities and destruction of the physical hosts."

"With this very hand and blade I slew the Blood-Sipping Ghoul of Lazzarenno!" exclaimed Fyltak.

"No you didn't," said Hereward crossly. "Remember who you're talking to."

"That would be wise," said Mister Fitz. "For any number of reasons."

"Oh, yes, that's right," said Fyltak. He looked nervously at the puppet. "In truth, while I have slain a number of . . . I suppose you might call them hedge wizards and shop sorcerers, I have not yet had the chance to test my mettle against an actual godlet."

"Hedge wizards I am familiar with," said Sir Hereward. "What by Hroggar's beard is . . . what is a shop sorcerer?"

"You know, someone whose powers come from sorcerous trinkets they have purchased," said Fyltak. "Invariably they are scoundrels seeking an easy path to power."

Hereward blinked at this assessment from a man whose own sorcery derived entirely from a sword he had inherited.

"Though you have not proven its worth against a godlet as yet, I think the sword may still be strong enough to do what is needed," said Mister Fitz. "We had best take it and test this assumption before Xavva gets too far ahead."

"Take it? None but I can wield this sword!"

Sir Hereward glanced aside at Mister Fitz, who gave the slightest shake of his head, forestalling the action he knew full well Hereward wanted to undertake: smack down Fyltak and take the weapon.

"Well then, you had best accompany us and wield it against the godlet," said the puppet. He jumped to the basket on Hereward's back. "Let us go, forthwith!"

They had barely gone three steps when Fyltak moved past and began to walk half-backward so he could face knight and puppet, talking all the while.

"Ah, while of course I wish to take action against this vile godlet," said Fyltak. "What with the cold, and the . . . er . . . spirit-gorging . . . do you have a plan on how to proceed, taking these things into account?"

"It is weakened," said Mister Fitz. "We have sorcerous brassards that provide some protection against such things as Xavva-Tish-Laqishtax. We will don them at a suitable proximity."

"Oh, the agent's brassard!" exclaimed Fyltak. He reached inside his cloak and drew forth a broad silk armband some five fingers wide, embroidered with a symbol of great familiarity to Sir Hereward and Mister Fitz, that of the Council of the Treaty for the Safety of the World. Though the symbol did not glow as it should from the sorcerous thread used to sew it, it was unquestionably genuine and merely quiescent.

Sir Hereward stopped, boots crushing ice emphatically.

"Where did you get that?"

His face was set and hard, his eyes narrowed, his body tensed to take action. The brassards were supposed to fall into dust if they left their owner's possession for more than a night and day, and were carefully handed down from one agent to the next, often as a deathbed ritual.

Once again, Mister Fitz touched Hereward's shoulder, restraining the knight from sudden, lethal action.

"It is also a family heirloom," said Fyltak, oblivious to his danger. "With the sword. Though the old tales say it should light up, brighter than a lantern."

"It will," said Mister Fitz. "May I hold it a moment?"

Fyltak passed the brassard to Mister Fitz, who tasted the silk with his tongue. A ripple of light passed through the silken threads, fading as the puppet handed it back.

"Curious," said Mister Fitz. "It is very old, not some recent find, Hereward. Fyltak must indeed be a descendant of some

long-lost agent. The brassard will answer to the invocation, in
due course. Come, we must hurry!"

They marched on, the weather around them returning to
its more natural state, the air warming and the snow melting.
There was still a clot of darkness ahead, but clearly Xavva was
saving its strength, for the black cloud no longer stretched across
the horizon but was concentrated in an area of a few hundred
yards about the godlet.

A few times they caught sight of Xavva itself, for they were
descending a broad slope towards the Smallest Sea and there
were several sections where it was quite steep and the height
extended their view, cloud notwithstanding. But always the
snow swirled and closed about the godlet, so they saw little beyond that it was still using three sets of legs in an ungainly motion that provided slightly slower locomotion than the pursuers
could manage on their own better-twinned pairs of legs.

"The Simirila have thrown down the bridges," remarked
Mister Fitz, who could see more clearly through the snowy
cloud. The Smallest Sea was little more than a lake, dotted with
many islands, which were connected by a multitude of bridges
of many different makes and load capacities, forming a veritable
maze of water crossings that usually required a local and not
inexpensive guide to navigate, particularly if requiring bridges
that might support wagons or draft animals.

"We will catch it on the shore, then," said Sir Hereward.
"What do you intend? Don the brassards and close? We two
distract Xavva as best we may while Fyltak takes off Eudonia's
head with the God-Taker?"

He spoke lightly, but with the clear knowledge that the
godlet was almost certainly still potent enough to draw out
the life essence of any or all would-be distractors, regardless
of the protection offered by the brassards. The only question

would be if the godlet could do it quickly enough to avoid the banishing stroke from Fyltak's sword.

"I fear the lack of a bridge does not halt the godlet," replied Mister Fitz, blue eyes bright. "It is making its own, of ice. Come, we must be on the ice it makes before it melts again!"

Sir Hereward broke into a run, the basket bobbing up and down on his back. Fyltak ran at his side, exhibiting none of the puffing and blowing he had done before when they had met him earlier that day, adding credence to his story about how brandishing the sword slowed all around him, including the air.

There was a layer of ice on the muddy shore, which cracked under their bootheels, but the broad swathe that led out across the water looked considerably thicker, much to Sir Hereward's relief. He paused by the shore to drop the basket before testing the ice with his sword. It held against several blows, and he stepped out upon it, causing no cracks or disturbing movement. Despite the thick ice underfoot, it was not particularly cold.

"Xavva expends much of its strength upon the ice bridge," said Mister Fitz, bending down to inspect the newly frozen surface of the lake. "That is good. It is only fifty or sixty yards ahead of us now. Come, don the brassards. We shall do as you suggest, Hereward, the two of us distracting it for Fyltak to make the banishing blow. Fyltak, you must strike for the neck and take the head off with a single blow. Can you do that?"

Fyltak licked his lips nervously, then nodded. He hesitated further for a moment, then drew the lorgnette out of his cuirass and wrapped the cord around his head to keep the lenses balanced on his nose.

"Not the best eyes," he said. "But I can do what must be done. I am Fyltak the God-Taker!"

"After this, you will be indeed," muttered Sir Hereward, who was pulling his brassard over the sleeve of his buff coat, not an easy operation with fingers still numb from cold. He thought, but did not say aloud, "If you live."

"Remember to drop the sword as soon as the stroke is through," instructed Mister Fitz. "Now, slide the brassard up your arm, and we will do the declaration as we hurry along. Repeat what Sir Hereward and I say. Are you ready?"

"Yes. I . . . I am ready."

Knight and puppet spoke together, with Fyltak a few moments behind. The symbol on their brassards shone more brightly with every word, the God-Taker's no less brilliant, for all its antiquity.

"In the name of the Council of the Treaty for the Safety of the World, acting under the authority granted by the Three Empires, the Seven Kingdoms, the Palatine Regency, the Jessar Republic, and the Forty Lesser Realms, we declare ourselves agents of the Council. We identify the godlet manifested on the ice ahead as Xavva-Tish-Laqishtax, a listed entity under the Treaty. Consequently, the said godlet and all those who assist it are deemed to be enemies of the World and the Council authorizes us to pursue any and all actions necessary to banish, repel, or exterminate the said godlet."

When they finished the declaration, Fyltak had a broad smile upon his face.

They had been walking while they spoke, but now Mister Fitz urged them to move more quickly.

"Faster! The godlet sprints for an island, and the fools have only thrown down the closer bridges!"

The puppet ran ahead, bending almost double and using his hands as well as his feet, his spindly limbs making him all too reminiscent of some injured spider that had lost half its legs. Sir Hereward galloped after him, both pistols drawn, with Fyltak close behind, who had not yet drawn his sword.

As they ran, the snow cloud ahead dissipated, pulling apart

to become mere streaks across the sky. They saw Xavva clearly, a hundred yards short of the closest island. But it was not moving straight for the shore. Two of its legs were trying to take it back the way it had come, and the others were straining to go forward, resulting in a crabwise, sprawling motion.

"Eudonia has risen within it!" cried Mister Fitz. "Quickly now!"

He matched action to his words, drawing his triangular blade to send it whirring through the air as fast as a crossbow bolt. It struck one of the added-on legs above the knee, inflicting a terrible wound, but not severing it as he had hoped. The knife, deeply embedded in bone, stuck there. Fitz reached inside his sleeves and drew two more blades, longer and sharper versions of the sorcerous needles he more commonly used.

Sir Hereward paused, went down on one knee, aimed for a second and fired both pistols at the midsection of the godlet. One ball whizzed past. The other struck, but as far as he could tell had no effect. The knight threw the pistols aside and drew his sword, charging onward with a wild shout he hoped would serve to distract the attention of the godlet from the real attack, delivered by Fyltak.

Who slipped over on the ice and fell, the God-Taker sword sliding from his grasp.

At that moment, Xavva stopped, reached down to break a splintered piece of fallen bridge out of the ice, and turned to its pursuers, raising its makeshift weapon over its head. An oak beam longer than Hereward was tall, this terrible club was liberally dotted with iron bolts, and a single blow would doubtless be fatal.

The godlet advanced on Hereward, who slipped and skidded backward in an effort to arrest his forward momentum. Mister Fitz circled around the godlet, knives ready, but even if he could successfully close, it was doubtful sharp steel could do more than irritate it.

Fyltak got to his feet. His lorgnette had fallen off, but he still spotted his sword upon the ice. He staggered over to it and lifted it with both hands.

But the godlet paid him no attention, apparently completely fixated on Sir Hereward. It was only as it got closer he saw that Eudonia's eyes were open now, albeit crazed and washed with the violent violet light of remnant energy from the sorcerous needles.

"Aberration!" spat the witch's mouth. Clearly, the godlet was no longer fully in charge of the body, but this was not the hoped-for improvement Sir Hereward and Mister Fitz had counted on, as his great-great-aunt's animosity to the boy-witch had remained when so much else of her personality had been eroded in the long contest with the godlet.

"Aunt Eudonia!" cried Hereward. He retreated again, but he could feel the ice cracking and shifting under his bootheels. Now the witch was back in charge, the godlet was not freezing the water. "I charge you to assist us as an Agent of the Treaty!"

"Vile spawn," muttered the witch, following these words with a sudden smashing blow with the bridge timber that sent a fountain of exploded ice up into the air. Hereward leapt aside as the club came down, and scuttled sideways for more solid ice, but his foot broke through and he fell forward. Twisting around, he raised his sword in a futile attempt to block a further blow, just as Mister Fitz jumped to the witch's shoulders and plunged his needles into the witch's insane eyes.

Eudonia—or the godlet, or both—screamed. But it was a scream of rage rather than pain. It threw the timber away, narrowly missing Sir Hereward, and one hand grabbed Mister Fitz and hurled him away too, far away, over the ice and into the water.

Sir Hereward freed his foot and crawled on his elbows and knees over the ice, faster than he had ever crawled before. Half

of him hoped the godlet or Eudonia or Xavva or whatever the
thing behind him currently was would follow and be distracted,
and half of him desperately hoped it wouldn't.

At the edge of the island, he hit mud instead of ice, rolled
over, and looked back. Xavva *was* following him, blind face
pressed close to the lake surface, nose sniffing, hands reaching,
head twitching from side to side as it sought to catch sounds as
well as scent.

Fyltak was behind it, moving with a peculiarly swift and
liquid grace, the God-Taker sword raised high, the brassard
bright upon his arm.

"Eudonia! Xavva! Over here!" screamed Sir Hereward, as
he drew himself to his feet and readied himself to run as best
he could.

The godlet sprang up too, its legs bunched to spring forward, just as Fyltak swung his sword. The blade met the thing's
neck and cut through with a sound like the mainmast of a great
ship snapping in a hurricane or an overpowered siege cannon
blowing itself apart. The blade burned away like a powder trail
as Fyltak finished the cut, but the head toppled from the neck
and rolled across the ice, which in that same moment was crazed
with a thousand cracks.

Fyltak dropped the sword hilt, emitted a euphoric shout, took
one step, and fell through the ice into the Smallest Sea. A moment later, the unnaturally chilled waters also claimed the God-
Taker sword hilt and burned-out stub of a blade, and the body
and head of Eudonia, with or without the godlet still within.

Sir Hereward took three swift steps into the now-open water, which was littered with tiny chunks of ice similar to those
chipped into the cool drinks of that same city of Simiril which
lay ahead and supplied Fyltak's coffee, but he stopped when
the water came to his waist. He was too heavily clothed and
booted to swim, and the water was very cold. Besides, there

was a small chance that Xavva-Tish-Laqishtax was not in fact banished after all.

He looked around for Mister Fitz, fully expecting the puppet to have swum ashore. The puppet had done so, but Sir Hereward was shocked to see Mister Fitz's upper body in its dripping blue jacket was canted to one side at an odd angle. Though made of papier-mâché and wood, the puppet was constructed of sorcerous versions of said materials, which were extraordinarily difficult to damage. But here he was, most evidently damaged.

"You are injured!" exclaimed Hereward, rushing to his side. But the puppet waved him off.

"It is nothing," he said. "Merely the alignment of a joint in my spine, which I will adjust as soon as my sewing case is replenished. Have you seen any sign the godlet persists? Movement under the water?"

"No," replied Hereward, turning to gaze upon the ice-cube-spattered waters. "Yes! There!"

A shadow was moving under the water. Sir Hereward and Mister Fitz drew back as it broke through the surface in a sudden explosion of ice cubes.

Fyltak stood there, huffing and blowing and shivering, before quickly wading in to be greeted with a comradely backslap from Sir Hereward, who was rapidly readjusting his views on his unlooked-for ally.

"I thought you drowned for certain!" exclaimed the knight. "In cuirass and boots and cloak, no man could swim ashore!"

"Nor could they," coughed Fyltak. "I walked upon the bottom of the lake. I told you I was trained in the arts of the sponge divers of Zhelu."

"And I am glad of it!" exclaimed Sir Hereward. "Ah, did you perchance see anything of Xavva-Tish-Laqishtax while you were down there?"

Fyltak jumped and twisted about to look behind him.

"No!" he cried, suddenly shaking even more. "I had thought . . . It is banished is it not?"

"I am not certain it is," replied Mister Fitz. "The water clouds my sight . . ."

The lopsided puppet shifted clumsily, turning his whole body rather than just his head, to gaze upon a stretch of water some fifty yards distant.

"It is still here," he said. "Greatly diminished, but still here."

Even as he spoke, a ghastly, headless thing crawled out of the lake on all fours. It had lost not only its head, but the extra legs as well, torn off in the explosion caused by the conjoining of godlet-possessed sword and the entity within Eudonia's body. Despite raw gaping wounds at neck and hip, no blood flowed.

It did not attempt to stand, but moved fully onto the land, pausing to shake itself, an unnerving sight given that it had no head.

"What . . . what do we do?" asked Fyltak.

"Move away quietly," said Mister Fitz in a whisper. The puppet followed his own advice, stepping out swiftly and surely though his torso remained twisted. "Tread lightly, breathe shallowly, stay calm."

"But it has no head, it cannot hear . . . or see us," said Fyltak as he too hurried away, glancing anxiously back over his shoulder.

"There are other senses," replied Mister Fitz. "I fear it will be swift, once it locates us. But if we make that bridge, perhaps we can lure it into the water once more . . . Hereward! Why do you stop?"

Fyltak ran on for several steps, only stopping when he realized Fitz had turned back. Puppet and knight were looking to the sky, but Fyltak could not tear his gaze away from the headless, broken thing that was now scuttling like a spider in a zigzag, backward and forward where Fyltak had first left the water, somehow finding a trail of energistic scent or something of that kind.

Suddenly, a vast shadow passed over men and puppet, accompanied by a long, falling shriek of titanic proportion. Fyltak thrust his hands against his ears and cowered down, all courage leeched away by this new addition to their woes.

But Sir Hereward kept looking up, a smile lifting the corner of his mouth. A moonshade swept past overhead, its enormous leathery wings spread wide, a hundred and twenty feet or more. It turned its big-as-a-house, furred, bat-like head down and fixed Sir Hereward with one sharp black eye, an eye greater in diameter than the knight was tall. Opening its pink-lined, sharp-toothed, elongated jaw, it gave vent once more to its greeting call.

The witch who sat securely on the tall chair on its back, seemingly grown of the same shiny black bone as the creature's spine, added to the creature's screech with a jaunty wave. Sir Hereward smiled, for though she was very late, Kishtyr was one of his favourite cousins, and a former lover besides, who might well be one again. The Council back at the High Pale would not be expecting her to return for at least another week.

But far more significantly, Kishtyr was suitably equipped with both a god-slaying relic and a full sewing desk of sorcerous needles. The husk of Eudonia and the diminished extra-dimensional entity Xavva-Tish-Laqishtax within would offer her no challenges. She would swiftly banish the godlet and give whatever might remain of the woman peace.

Hereward lost his smile at the thought of Great-Great-Aunt Eudonia's head still somewhere out there under the lake's clouded surface. Pierced by three sorcerous needles and infused with an indomitable will that would not even surrender to a godlet, it was possible that Eudonia still lived—after a fashion—inside that sunken head. Kishtyr's task might not be as straight-forward as he had supposed, and worse, she might enlist him to go fishing. He most certainly did not want to hook and land Eudonia's separated head . . .

"What is that?" asked Fyltak, creeping up to man and puppet. He could see that whatever it was, its arrival had disturbed the remnant relict of Xavva-Tish-Laqishtax, which had retreated back to the lakeshore and was now trying to bury itself in the mud, presumably in an effort to conceal itself from this new, airborne nemesis.

"It is a moonshade, bearing a Witch of Har," answered Mister Fitz, responding literally, as was his wont. "The long-awaited Kishtyr, in fact."

The huge flying creature turned about to land on the longer and broader shore on the northern side of their current island. Despite their enormous size, moonshades were nimble and agile flyers, and could set down in a space only a little longer than their own length. Once landed, they could fold their wings up remarkably small, as this one was in the process of doing. They were in fact deceptive in their size, being mostly leathery skin and thin bones, with a little black fur dabbed here and there. Though, even when all was said and done, it was still a monster roughly the size of a watchtower laid on its side.

"More to the point," said Sir Hereward, dragging the smaller man upright and draping his arm over his shoulder in a comradely fashion. "The moonshade and the witch who rides it represent an opportunity which I believe we should take at once."

"An opportunity?"

"To shuck off our cares and responsibility, and hie ourselves to yonder Simiril, where I will purchase both of us some more of that excellent coffee."

He paused and added with a wink to the puppet: "And some sweet oil, for I, for one, would like to hear Mister Fitz sing!"

CUT ME
ANOTHER QUILL,
MISTER FITZ

UT ME ANOTHER QUILL, MISTER FITZ, IF YOU would be so kind," said Sir Hereward. The some-time knight-artillerist's hands were blotched with ink rather than the more usual powder or blood, and the quill he was gazing at ruefully had lost its point entirely.

"That is your second within the hour," said Mister Fitz, who was perched upon the neighboring desk, rather than at a stool like Sir Hereward. But then the sorcerous puppet stood only three feet six and a half inches tall on his carved wooden feet. "Can you not sharpen your present pen?"

The scrivening room was dusty and dark. A single arrow slit in the far side failed to admit much in the way of daylight, and there was only a single candelabra of three branches on Here-ward's desk, though the candles it held were pure beeswax and quite bright as candles went. Mister Fitz, of course, could see very well in the dark, and in fact the blue-painted pupils of the eyes in his pumpkin-sized papier-mâché head had a faint glow of their own.

For the purpose of keeping their activities secret from the general populace, their chosen place of work was high in the southwest tower of the Archon's palace. There were guards in the chamber below, who fetched and carried whatever documents Mister Fitz requested from the chancery over on the eastern side of the palace.

Both the knight's and the puppet's desks were laden with thick rolls of faded yellowish vellum, and knight and puppet each had a roll unfurled before them, revealing them to be tax records. They were making lists of selected names drawn from the roll on sheets of more modern, clean white paper. Sir Hereward's page was rather spoiled by blotches, though his fist was otherwise neat enough. Mister Fitz's list was impeccable and much longer, and any scriptorium would have enlisted him at once, though scriptoriums were not what they once were, since the advent of printing a century or so before.

"You have the sharper knife," grumbled Sir Hereward. "Furthermore, my present quill is too brittle and second-rate to take more sharpening, and it has slowed me abominably."

"How many names have you writ?" asked Mister Fitz. He took a tiny triangular knife from some hidden sheath behind his head and expertly shaped and slit the end of a goose feather, the blade so sharp it parted the quill without any resistance at all, as if the puppet sliced the air. "A noteworthy number, I hope?"

"Certes! Nine . . . no . . . ten that are possible. And you?"

"Sixty-two," replied Mister Fitz dryly. "As the complete census, across twenty-nine rolls, contains in my estimation in excess of eleven thousand personages, your progress and contribution to our task will clearly be minuscule."

Sir Hereward got up from the desk and bowed to the puppet.

"Most excellent calculation, good puppet," he declared, waving his hand in a series of descending flourishes. "What I doubt is the method overall. Why do we not simply walk through the city and look for anything that might suggest the presence of the dragon? If there is a dragon."

"The records I found in the Library of Karrilinion strongly support the presence of a dragon here, and more importantly, its treasure," said Mister Fitz. "But we will not find it by walking around. This dragon has managed to hide here for at least three hundred years, suggesting it is not entirely foolish. Unlike others I might mention. I know your expertise is with gunpowder and shooting off guns and so forth, but even so, I trust you have heard or read something about the extra-dimensional invaders commonly called godlets?"

"A little, I suppose," grumbled Sir Hereward. "What has that to do with anything?"

Mister Fitz's question and Hereward's answer would have surprised and perhaps amused anyone who had significant dealings with the duo in the past, since Sir Hereward and Mister Fitz were agents of the Council of the Treaty for the Safety of the World and, as ever, were engaged in their seemingly eternal quest to rid the world of exactly those illegal godlets and other proscribed extra-dimensional invaders Mister Fitz had just mentioned. But neither the Archon of Nikandros nor anyone else in the city-state knew this. Or so Hereward fervently hoped.

"I shall enlighten you," said the puppet.

Sir Hereward sighed and slumped back onto his stool, not needing to feign his resignation. Mister Fitz had been his nanny long before becoming his companion in arms, and the sorcerous puppet very frequently lapsed into the didactic persona of Hereward's school years.

"The beings commonly called dragons are a peculiar class of extra-dimensional entity. They can assume a variety of physical forms, given sufficient raw material to do so, including the classical winged reptilian, but also that of a man or woman," continued Mister Fitz. "When they take the shape of an everyday

person, their otherworldly essence is cloaked and hidden, and so
would appear neither more or less than any other citizen of this
fair city. In other words, there would be nothing for us to see.
No horns, no tails, no strange eyes—"

"Yes, yes, all right," said Sir Hereward, but this did not stop
Mister Fitz.

"They do not necessarily have a predilection for consuming
young maidens, nor do they flamboyantly display their hoards.
They do not breathe fire, at least not when hiding in mortal
shape. They do not—"

"Enough!" cried Hereward, holding his hands up in surrender, accidentally splashing a large drop of ink on the original roll,
requiring immediate ameliorative work with sponge and knife.

"So walking around the city would achieve nothing save
the gratification of your senses, which I perceive is the true
reason you wish to do so, and also why you play the laggard at
this work."

"Oh, very well," said Sir Hereward, giving up on his efforts to remove the ink stain as hopeless. "How about we leave
this musty alcove to look into the first seventy-two we have, a
goodly number to begin, I say."

"Because as soon as we do, word will spread of our activities," said Mister Fitz. "This should be obvious even to you,
Hereward. If the dragon hears rumor the Supreme Archon has
sanctioned investigations into all those who possess a stock of
gold amounting to more than ten thousand staters, they may
well flee to some previously prepared retreat, before we are
ready to pursue them. And as I need not remind you, I am sure,
locating that retreat is our chief consideration, for that is where
the dragon will have amassed their primary treasure—"

"Which the Archon is going to confiscate," interrupted Sir
Hereward. "I still think we should have held out for more than
a quarter share. After all, we found the tablets at Karrilinion—"

"We? And a moment ago you suggested there is no dragon."

"All right! All right! But my joints grow stiff and I have aged a year in the two days we have spent here already. Let us divide and conquer, as Narbonius declaimed in *The Death of Many*."

"You know the historical Narbonius divided his forces and they were defeated piecemeal?" asked Mister Fitz. "When Kidenses wrote the play, she chose to change the actual events."

"No," admitted Sir Hereward. "I mean, the play is the thing. Who remembers the history?"

"Narbonius was a fool," grumbled Mister Fitz. "He was well advised, but chose to disregard what I . . . that is to say, I have read that he turned against his advisors."

"Ancient history!" said Sir Hereward. He scowled at Fitz and changed the subject, his voice growing louder. "I wonder if we renegotiated—"

"Six hundred and seven years ago," mused Mister Fitz, but he had lowered his voice, almost whispering to himself. "Four months and three days. Shortly before noon. Battle was joined thereafter and Narbonius slain shortly after sunset, an arrow in the back as he fled the field."

"As I was saying," declaimed Sir Hereward. "A quarter share seems little recompense for not only bringing news of this dragon, but also all this busy work here—"

"I have cut you a new quill," said Mister Fitz. "Pray continue more speedily."

Sir Hereward sighed, took the quill, and returned his attention to the roll in front of him.

"You know that once we start examining all these rich people, there will be an uproar," said Sir Hereward. "They'll presume the Archon plans a new tax. There will probably be a revolt."

"There will be no fuss," said Mister Fitz. "If you had bothered to listen when I explained matters to the Archon, the list

of those possessing a sufficient stock of gold is only the first
step, an indication, if you will. Once we have those names, we
must cross-index them against the registry of births, deaths, and
disappearances, to discern any unusual pattern of inheritance.
This, I expect, will deliver only two or three people to look
into more closely. The Archonate is to be commended on the
excellence of their records."

"You were nattering away for hours," said Sir Hereward. "It
was very dull. Besides, the Archon doesn't like me."

"I doubt the Archon has any feelings for you one way or
another," said Mister Fitz. "She is a very sensible woman. Pray,
do get on with the task."

Silence reigned in the chamber, save for the occasional
sound of a pen scratching a new name, until the great bell in
the central tower began to sound the turning of the sun, when
it reached its zenith and began to fall again. Or as those in the
North called it, noon.

"We should have just done this in the chancery," said Sir
Hereward, flinging down his quill again. "An airy, well-lit
chamber, all records close at hand—"

"And many of the clerks young women for you to attempt
your charms upon," interrupted Mister Fitz. "We are better
here, in seclusion, where none may know of our task, or suspect
the existence of a dragon's treasure."

"I'm not convinced there is a dragon after all!" announced
Sir Hereward, rather loudly.

"Shush!" snapped Mister Fitz, with a meaningful glance at
the door. While it was of solid oak, it had swollen from disuse
and occasional inundation due to the inadequate roofing of the
tower against the monsoonal weather of Nikandros, and did not
properly close. There was a three-finger-wide gap at the bottom, so it was quite possible the two guards could hear every

word, even from the chamber below, and definitely could if they had crept up the steps to eavesdrop.

"What? They're the Archon's Chosen, aren't they?" blustered Sir Hereward. "Fine soldiers. Loyal. Not to be swayed by thoughts of treasure."

"Hereward. I have told you before, we must keep this matter close, you need to curb your natural tendency to conversation. Now, the sooner we press on, the sooner finished."

Hereward mumbled something.

"What was that?"

"I merely wondered how long this current task might take," said Sir Hereward. "Not in so many words."

"A reasonable request," replied Mister Fitz. "By my computation, presuming only a slight increase in your contribution, we will be finished with the tax rolls in another eight days, and can then move on to the cross-indexing, which will require nineteen to twenty-one days—"

"A month!" roared Sir Hereward. "A month stuck in this dark, mildewed chamber! I can't do it! I need air and light . . . I . . . I need a drink!"

"Sir Hereward!"

But the knight-artillerist paid no attention to the puppet. He stood up, knocking his stool over backward, and stormed to the door. He wrenched at it uselessly once, then again, before finally getting it open. Mister Fitz watched him with his strange, painted blue eyes, but said no more. Sir Hereward grunted something and went down the steps at a dangerous speed.

Mister Fitz waited a moment, hopped down, and went over to push the heavy swollen door closed with an ease at odds with his small stature and the limbs of thin, polished wood beneath his loose scholar's robe, which was the same color as the stone of the tower. The door shut, he crossed the chamber, picked up a leather satchel, and swung it over his back, before swiftly climbing up to the single arrow slit, those same slim wooden fingers piercing the mortar between the stones like hammered iron pitons. Reaching the window, the puppet lifted the hood of his robe over his pumpkinlike head, and climbed outside.

Sir Hereward, taking the more conventional steps, arrived at the landing below where the two guards were stationed. He almost collided with one of them, who had either been listening or perhaps merely looking up, curious as to the source of the commotion. She stepped lightly out of the way, and Sir Hereward slowed down to stand between the two guards, his fists clenched, nostrils agape, breath snorting, all too like a fractious bull.

"Is there some trouble, Sir Hereward?" asked the woman. Her name was Aryadny and she was the senior of the two guards, and far more dangerous in Hereward's reckoning than Zanthus, despite the other guard being younger, at least a foot taller, and considerably heavier, in muscle not fat. Both wore the close-faced bronze helms, gilded scale mail, and plated leggings of the Archon's Chosen, and both carried short-staved demi-halberds, but Aryadny also had a punch misericorde at her belt, and she moved with the sinuous grace that suggested frequent use of the narrow-bladed weapon. She was more of an assassin than a soldier, unless Sir Hereward missed his guess.

"Your pardon," said Sir Hereward. He took a deep breath and let it out slowly. "That clerkly puppet irks me! I swear his blood is ink, and of course his head is made of paper!"

Aryadny laughed.

"A dry stick, sure enough," she said. "Very different to the musical puppets I've seen. They are full of japes and jokes, and sing and play most beautifully."

"I'd like to see one of them," said Zanthus wistfully. "Do you think old . . . whatshisname . . . Futz . . . would give us a song?"

"No," said Sir Hereward. "A crow could sing better. A stone would! Whatever ancient sorcerer put him together made him solely to burrow in books and scrolls, and write damn fool lists of no consequence."

"You make an odd pairing, Sir Hereward," said Aryadny. "I mean, a mercenary officer, skilled with cannon and the like. Why do you truckle under an inky old puppet?"

"I don't truckle," protested Sir Hereward, but with good humour. "As you said, I am a mercenary. In high standing in the western kingdoms, I'll have you know. Ask anyone."

"The western kingdoms lie a thousand leagues distant," said Aryadny.

"What's that to do? In any case, I work with Fitz because he pays very well, and has a nose for . . . let's say a nose for even better pay. I aim to raise my own company of great guns by next spring, and that will not come cheap."

"It's true we offer the best prices on bronze or iron guns in the known world," said Aryadny, with a look that suggested she now understood Hereward's motivation for being in Nikandros far better than she had a moment ago. "My cousin's a cannon-founder, a master of the Guild, should you wish an introduction. Doubtless he would offer attractive prices for a man known to be in the Archon's good graces."

Hereward nodded thoughtfully.

"I may well ask that of you, once our work is done," he said. "I thank you. But right now I need a drink to wash the dust from my throat. Can you suggest a tavern with good wine for a discerning soldier such as myself?"

"Sign of the Black Sun," offered Zanthus.

"I think Sir Hereward would prefer the Windflower," said Aryadny. "It has the superior cellar. Perhaps even wines from the western kingdoms."

"Whichever is the closer will serve," said Sir Hereward.

"Or you could simply visit the buttery within the citadel, close by the gatehouse," said Aryadny. "We serve our noble visitors a pleasant zinthen, a wine you may know."

"Oh, aye, a white grape, somewhat sour for my taste," said Hereward. "But it would quench my thirst, which I confess is mighty. Yet if there is a finer vintage to be had . . ."

"Then the Windflower should serve you well," said Aryadny. "It lies on the wall between the Upper Third and the Middle. From the main gate of the citadel, you should cross the great court and take the varden marked with the bronze statue of a bull—"

"The varden?"

"Our name for what you might call an alley, or perhaps a lane of steps," said Aryadny. She continued with a long list of directions that Hereward kept asking her to repeat, though he had them memorized on the first recitation.

He had also closely studied the map of the city Mister Fitz had purchased before they took ship at Sarg Sargaros, so Hereward already knew what a varden was, and had a good idea of the layout of the city.

Nikandros was built atop a wedge-shaped stone mountain that formed an island off the coast of Er-Nikandros. The narrow point extended several leagues out into the sea, and atop this was the Archon's citadel, fourteen hundred feet above the water. As the arrowhead broadened and descended towards the mainland, it was filled in with the houses and shops of the rich or at least well-to-do. This was the Upper Third, though in fact it occupied less than a quarter of the city's rambling acreage. A high wall separated the Upper Third from the Middle, which was terraced into five main sections, the lowest terrace some five hundred feet below the wall.

A great crevasse—bridged at over a dozen points—separated the Middle from the Levels, the generally flat outer area domi-

nated by forges, foundries, and the metalworking industry that
was the source of Nikandros's wealth. The Levels extended
to the base of the arrowhead, where the peninsula joined the
mainland, and was enclosed at its extent by an ancient wall and
beyond that by more extensive and modern defenses of ditch,
bastion, and ravelin, all suitably equipped with fine cannon of
the city's own making.

Because it was built into and upon a mountain, the streets
of Nikandros were generally narrow and involved a lot of steps.
But only the broadest thoroughfares, and there were few of
these, were known as streets. Most of the ways were very narrow, never went in a straight line, zigzagging back and forth as
the slope required, and these were known as vardens.

The other thing Hereward already knew was that a dark,
steep, constantly turning varden was the ideal spot for ambush
and murder. Though there were plenty of places like that within
the citadel as well, Hereward thought, and he hoped Mister Fitz
was right about certain aspects of the plan they had set in motion.

"So I turn right at a barber's with the tree in the tub by its
door?" he asked.

"No, left at the barber's, which has the sign of a copper
comb," said Aryadny. "After that, right at Pharem's fruiterer—
she has the tree in the tub as a sign."

"Ah, yes," said Hereward. "I fear all the scribing in that little
room has mazed my mind. Left at the barber's, with the copper
comb, right at the tree in the tub, go straight on and down the
steps with the rotten railing—I'll be careful of that—and then
when I get to the courtyard with the old cannon, there are various vardens, and I take the second from the left."

"No, it's the third varden from the place of various vardens!" exclaimed Aryadny.

"I can just ask directions," said Hereward. "And if I see
some tavern on the way, perhaps—"

"No, no, the Windflower's wine is far superior to anywhere else," said Aryadny. "You know, I think I should accompany you."

"What! You can't—" Zanthus started to say, but Aryadny held up her hand.

"I'll send up Mennos to take my place," she said. "After you, Sir Hereward."

"I will be able to collect my weapons?" asked Sir Hereward. He had surrendered them when they first arrived at the citadel, but he didn't want to go wandering about the city without being fully armed. Or that was the impression he wanted to give.

He had a dagger in each boot, of course, another up his left sleeve, and the locket he wore around his neck did not contain a portrait of a loved one, but rather opened to reveal a very small moon-shaped blade, sharp as a razor.

Then there were also the curious gold earrings he wore, shaped like long bones. They were hollow, with little holes drilled through them. Charming pipes the length of his little finger, a solid weight of near pure gold. Not exactly weapons, but they had a purpose.

"Your baggage is held at the main gate," said Aryadny. "Of course, if going into the city, you may take up sword and pistols. Though you will not need them, provided you stay out of the worst parts of the Levels."

Still Hereward did not move. Aryadny shrugged and went ahead, sweeping down the stairs with the ease of a native Nikandrosite, for whom steps were more natural than a level floor. Hereward did not immediately follow, taking a surprisingly large silver flask from the pouch at his belt to indulge in what appeared to be a long swig.

"You cannot wait for the wine, Sir Hereward?" asked Aryadny politely, looking back up the steps.

"This is a medicine," replied Hereward, wiping his mouth.

The smell of powerful brandy rolled off his breath. "A nasty concoction for an old wound in . . . in my hip . . . that niggles at me betimes."

"I trust it will not grow worse," said Aryadny. "You are not troubled by all our steps?"

"Not at all!" declared Hereward, bounding down after her. He immediately stumbled, recovering himself just in time to avoid cannoning into Aryadny, though she had stepped aside in any case. She was very light on her feet, further confirming Hereward's assessment of her as an assassin.

"Or perhaps a little," confessed Hereward. He belched brandy fumes and started off again, more slowly. "It is true I have never been confronted with such an array of stairs and ramps and steep changes of altitude."

"Nikandros is unique in many ways," said Aryadny. "But then you are also a novelty to us, a visitor from so far away. Do you really think there is a dragon here?"

Hereward pretended surprise, stumbled again, and clutched at the wall to save himself.

"What . . . why . . ."

"We are the Archon's Chosen," replied Aryadny. She paused to open the door at the base of the stairs, admitting welcome sunlight. "Naturally we have been informed of your purpose here."

"I see," said Sir Hereward, following her out into the narrow courtyard that led from the isolated tower to the palace proper. "I had wondered if you'd been told. I am not personally convinced there is a dragon, but Mister Fitz has found old documents that purport otherwise, and I have to confess that clerkly old puppet is very good with documents. And he has found dragons before."

This caused Aryadny to almost stumble herself, on perfectly flat paving stones.

"He did?"

"Without profit to us," grumbled Sir Hereward. "I had to kill it before it could lead us to its hoard."

"You killed a dragon?" asked Aryadny. "Might I ask how this was done?"

Her tone did not so much suggest curiosity as disbelief, but not in an offensive manner.

"It's easy enough when they're in mortal form," said Sir Hereward, puffing out his chest and assuming a rather pompous manner. "Though 'tis true they cannot be slain with any ordinary weapon."

"How then?"

"Fitz is a clever fellow, for all his other defects," said Hereward. He stopped to take out another, smaller flask from his pouch and drank from that as Aryadny waited patiently. "He found me something that would do the job."

"Some particular weapon?" asked Aryadny. "I confess I did wonder about one of the items in the small arsenal you brought ashore."

"Ah, noticed it, did you?" asked Hereward, tapping his finger with his nose, apparently forgetting he held the small metal flask. He flinched as its stopper almost went up one nostril.

"I would say it is unusual for an artillerist and exponent of gunpowder weapons to entertain the use of something so outmoded as a crossbow," said Aryadny. "I think anyone would have noticed that."

"Well spotted, well spotted," said Sir Hereward. He took another drink as Aryadny opened the door at the other end of the courtyard. "But it—hic—isn't the crossbow, as such. No, the secret lies in the quarrels!"

"The quarrels?" asked Aryadny. She frowned. "I do not recall seeing any."

"They're in a case," said Hereward. "A case, made special, lined with lead to keep them quiet."

"Keep . . . the quarrels quiet?"

"They've got imps in them," confided Hereward.

"Imps!"

"That's what I call them," said Hereward. He returned the small flask to his pouch and fished around for the larger one, removing it with an air of triumph. "Fitz found them— the bolts, I mean. Dug 'em up somewhere. They talk. Mutter. High-pitched little voices. Imps. Apparently that's what it takes to kill a dragon. Worked on the other one, anyway. Oh gods, more stairs."

"There are always more stairs in Nikandros, Sir Hereward," said Aryadny. "This is something of a secret way to the main gatehouse. I would like to look at these imp-haunted bolts, if you don't mind."

"Didn't think we came up this way," said Sir Hereward. He tripped, fell against the wall, and rebounded with the air of a man who thought the wall was at fault for being there. Somehow he didn't drop his flask.

This stairwell was very narrow, the ceiling was low, and unlike the fine stonework everywhere else in the citadel, the passage that stretched down and down and down, lit only by the occasional torch in a bracket, was the original rock of the mountain, rough-worked, as attested by the many chisel marks.

"No, this is a direct passage. We generally prefer our visitors to take more pleasant paths," said Aryadny. "But I fear this is a long stair, and dull, without windows or outlooks. Perhaps you would tell me how you came to slay your . . . ah . . . first dragon. Where was this dragon, as it happens?"

"Oh, far off," said Hereward. "Can't tell you. The puppet, he swore me to secrecy. Might go back and search for its gold someday. Only when he found out about the dragon here, that had to come first. He says it will have a much bigger hoard!"

"Why is that?"

"Oh, the one we got was youngish, or so Fitz told me. Only a hundred or so. The one here is much older. Least that's what the puppet says. Busy old fool."

"You think the puppet is wrong?"

"Oh, probably not, but his ways are tiresome," complained Hereward. He paused on a step to vigorously shake his flask, sighing as he heard no answering gurgle. "Won't let me drink. He found the other dragon without all this fussing about with musty old tax rolls. Shepter's blood! How many more steps are there?"

"It is not far to the gatehouse now," said Aryadny. "It is a shame you could not find your first dragon's hoard. Was there a great area to search?"

"Half of . . . half of the county," said Hereward. "You said there was good wine near the gatehouse? The buttery? I've a mind not to bother traipsing down any more stairs. My hip, you know."

"Oh, yes, the buttery would be much easier," said Aryadny. "And you won't need to pick up your weapons."

"Fine, fine," said Hereward. "Lead on."

"I am leading on," said Aryadny, in a puzzled tone. "We're almost at the lower door and then it is but a hop and a skip to the buttery, so to speak."

"Good," cried Hereward. "I need a drink! Many drinks!"

But Sir Hereward drank only two glasses of very sour wine before collapsing face-first on the table with a lengthy, snoring grunt. Once planted, he concentrated on breathing noisily through his mouth, and began a meditative exercise taught him long ago by his mother, one of the Mysterious Three who ruled the Witches of Har. His sense of himself retreated into a deep, inner place, where he could observe his own body but would not immediately react to any stimulus.

He lay there for a minute or two before he felt Aryadny prod him hard in the ribs with the pommel of a dagger. It hurt, but he did not let himself flinch, instead simply stopping his breath for a moment before letting out a donkey-like snort of the kind someone dead drunk might make at sudden pain.

Next, Aryadny's clever fingers cautiously opened his pouch, taking out the contents. He heard coins on the tabletop, followed by the soft whirr of the stopper being unscrewed from his large flask, followed by a deep sniff.

"Strong stuff," Aryadny said to someone else, who chuckled. "I'm surprised he made it down the narrow back stair."

"Talking all the way," said the other person. A man, whose voice Hereward had not heard before.

"You got it all?" asked Aryadny.

"I hear, I remember," said the man. "She'll be interested, for sure."

"Go recite it to her then," said Aryadny. "I'll get this drunken blowhard taken back to the guest chambers."

"What about the puppet?"

"He scratches away in the tower," said Aryadny. "Very single-minded, sorcerous puppets. He'll keep reading and making notes until he's stopped. Go on."

Almost as if he watched it happen from some distance, Hereward felt himself lifted up by strong hands. He made no effort to hold his head up. It lolled backward and he almost choked on his own tongue before someone lifted his neck and he was able to take another gargling breath.

"How'd he get so sodden so quickly?" muttered an unknown woman, one of Hereward's bearers.

"I'd say he's a drunkard who's been holding out," said Aryadny. "Until he couldn't. Knocked back at last three gills of a fierce spirit."

"Surprised he isn't dead," muttered another voice. "We'd best lay him down so his vomit goes out, not in."

"Yes, you had," said Aryadny sternly. "She will want to see him later, I'm sure."

"Where are you going?"

"To get his weapons. He has sorcerous quarrels that must be destroyed. Go on, you have your orders!"

Hereward waited in his trance state for a good hour after he was carefully placed on the floor of his guest room, arranged so that he would not choke and die. It was surprisingly restful, and in a disassociated way he wondered why he had not kept up with all the daily meditations he'd been taught by his mother and aunts and Mister Fitz, though of course he had many other daily exercises to pursue. Sword work, shooting with carbine and pistols, wrestling, sleight of hand, trigonometry, and ballistics . . .

When he heard the bell from the central tower strike the third hour of the falling sun, Hereward opened his eyes and looked about the room. It was the pleasant guest chamber he'd been assigned. It had a window with nine panes of glass that looked out to the sea, a plain but more than serviceable bed with a feather mattress, and a chest for clothes. The door was shut, and there was no one else there, so he carefully got to his feet and sat on the bed.

"How travels the bait?" asked Mister Fitz, climbing in through the window. He shut it behind him carefully, then sat atop the chest, his leather sewing bag on his shallow lap, so the sorcerous needles within would be close at hand.

"Slowly," answered Hereward. "I am fairly sure it is not Aryadny, but she is certainly in the employ of the dragon."

"She would not have left you if she was the dragon," said Fitz. "They cannot resist the lure of another dragon's hoard; she would have made you give up all you know. And she would have taken the earrings."

"There was someone else, slinking behind us on the stair," said Hereward. "Some sort of spy, ears flapping. He has gone to tell 'her' everything I spoke of."

"Then matters will be soon in train," said Mister Fitz. "You have done well, Hereward."

"I trust you will be prompt," said Hereward. "And what if she has minions hard by? Aryadny is a killer if ever I saw one, and she will be swift with that misericorde."

"No dragon would chance a mortal hearing the where-abouts of a hoard," said Mister Fitz with calm certainty. "She will question you somewhere undisturbed by others."

"I hope you're right," said Hereward. He made a face and wiped his mouth with the back of his hand. "I also hope I never have to drink any more of their disgusting wine."

Mister Fitz did not answer. His perfectly round head rotated on his neck like a globe upon a well-oiled stand, and his leather ears pricked up.

"Someone comes," he said.

Hereward dropped to the floor, stuck his fingers down his throat and managed to regurgitate up a loathsome, alcohol-stinking puddle near his mouth. He drew back from it, wrinkling his nose, then gasped as Fitz pushed his head completely into the vomit before hiding under the bed.

The door opened, and several people marched in.

"Faugh! What stench!"

"Clean him up and get the cordial down him," instructed Aryadny.

Hereward felt himself lifted up onto the bed, a cloth was wiped across his face, his mouth was forced upon, and a stream

of something even viler than Nikandrosite wine was forced
down his throat from a skin under pressure. He coughed and
gasped and opened his eyes.

"Sir Hereward!" bawled Aryadny, close to his face. "You
have an important audience! The cordial will clear your head."

Someone clapped an open hand against his stomach. Hereward breathed in and inadvertently swallowed the foul brew.
He knew what it was from the taste alone—oil of gnashtur
mixed with the juice of erskberries—even before he felt the
horrible, hollowed-out sensation which rapidly spread through
his entire body. While it had the virtue of removing drunken-
ness, it also delivered an immediate, peculiarly nasty kind of
hangover. Very unfairly in Hereward's case, since he had no
more than one swallow of brandy from his trick flask, a mouth-
ful of stomach-lining moklek milk from the small flask, and the
two glasses of wine.

"Urgghhh," he gasped. "What?"

Three of the Archon's Chosen were standing over him.
One gripped his left arm, the other the right, while the third
stripped his boots from him, quickly followed by his belt,
pouch, and dagger, and then his coat and shirt, along with his
other knife. The large pendant on the necklace at his throat was
examined, found to be a blade, and removed as well.

Fingers plucked at his ear, but stopped as Aryadny spoke.

"Leave the earrings. They're gold. She'll want them."

Hereward roared and struggled as his undershirt was lifted,
and kicked at the third man, sending him reeling back.

"Have no fear, Sir Hereward!" soothed Aryadny, who was
standing by the door. "We merely wish to ensure you have no
hidden weapons."

"How dare you!" roared Hereward. "I'm a guest of your
Archon!"

"Be easy," said Aryadny. "Allow him up, gentlemen."

Hereward staggered to his feet, and swayed in front of Aryadny, his shift billowing about his knees, his stockings around his ankles. No one noticed the wide garter on his left leg which had also fallen, after all it was only a piece of cloth. The men who had held him down stayed close, but it was Aryadny he watched, her and that thin dagger.

"I shall explain two possibilities to you, Sir Hereward," said Aryadny, smiling. "The first is that you allow us to blindfold and lead you to an audience, which I assure you will be of profit; the second is we beat you a little short of senseless—for you will need to talk—and carry you there, and doubtless it will be of less profit. I give you the choice."

"Bah! The Archon will hear of this," said Hereward. "I choose the first of your so-kind alternatives. Who is it I am being taken to meet?"

"You will see," said Aryadny. "When the blindfold comes off at our destination."

They blindfolded the knight and led him quickly out into the hall and immediately through a secret door that Hereward had not known existed in the opposite wall, into a space where they were crammed together while Aryadny opened another door, from the sound of it one with a complex or little-used latch.

"Head down," she instructed. "Pull up his stockings. There are steps, Hereward, lift your feet. Up."

They climbed for some time. Hereward counted steps, for form's sake, rather than any real need. At the two hundred and six mark, they stopped and he felt the warmth of the late afternoon sun on his face, and saw the edge of its light stealing in around his blindfold. From these things, he deduced they were outside, and atop one of the towers of the citadel—and he had a very nasty feeling everything was about to go hideously wrong.

"Leave us."

The voice was a woman's, and sounded calm and even kind. There was a general shuffling around Hereward; the hands that had held his arms were gone, and he heard his captors walk away and a door shut.

"You may remove your blindfold."

Hereward pulled off the blindfold. It was very bright, and he lifted his hand to shield his eyes. He was not atop a tower, as he'd thought, but on a demi-lune or miniature bastion out-thrust from the mountain of rock at its highest and most narrow point, with the sea below, the sky above, and all of Nikandros behind it.

The woman who had spoken, who for a moment he'd thought might be the Archon herself, was not. Which was a re-lief, because if she had been the Archon, the whole plan would have turned towards disaster. This woman had the same air of authority, and was similarly middle-aged, dark-haired, and olive-skinned, but she was older than the Archon. She sat on a carved stone bench and was eating olives, spitting the pips over the railing to fall the fourteen hundred feet to the sea.

As Mister Fitz had said truthfully earlier, there was nothing physically obvious to indicate she was a dragon, but Hereward had no doubts as to her identity, even before she spoke.

"You have found what you are looking for," she said. "Or rather, part of what you seek. I am the dragon of Nikandros, but you will never have my treasure. Nor will you slay me. Your 'imp-infested quarrels' have been taken to the great smelter in the Levels and melted down, the pathetic entities within re-leased. Your life is naturally forfeit. However, if you will tell me where you slew this other dragon, and where its hoard might lie, I may spare you."

"That seems a fair offer, milady," said Hereward. He sat down on his bottom, extended his legs, and pulled off his stock-ings, including the wide garter on the left.

"What are you doing?" asked the dragon. "If you hope to fashion a garotte, you are even more of a fool than I anticipated."

She put down the olive she was about to eat and stood up.

"Oh, no, milady, they were uncomfortable," said Hereward. He stood up, slipped the broad garter—an armband really— over his wrist and up on to his bicep. Then he tugged the earring from his left ear, lifted the small bone to his mouth, and blew upon it. No sound came out, not even a butchered single note.

"Are you mad?" asked the dragon. "Or still drunk?"

"I might be still drunk," admitted Hereward, backing up to the door. Reaching behind him, he tested the ring to open it and found it wouldn't move.

"Even in this weaker human form, I can rip your heart from your chest in a trice," said the dragon, flexing her hands to show him some long and very disturbing fingernails. "But I will start with something softer and easier to detach if you do not tell me what I want to know. Where is this other dragon's hoard?"

Hereward made a whimpering noise and blew on the golden bone again.

"Your eyes," said the dragon. "I will pluck them and eat them like those olives. What was the dragon's name?"

"I don't know. Mister Fitz knows," said Hereward. He gave up on the door and edged along the wall. But there was nowhere to retreat in the small demi-lune. There was the locked door behind, or over the walls to certain death far below.

"Sorcerous puppets are notably resistant to torture," said the dragon. "They simply don't care. Whereas you, I am sure, care greatly."

"I do, I do," said Hereward. He lifted the golden bone in his hand and blew on it for the third time, without result.

"Is that little golden pipe meant to do something?" asked

the dragon. She tilted her head. "I sense no magic in it. Only gold, leavened with a tenth of silver."

"Yes, it is meant to do something!" declared Hereward. Unwisely, he added, "Distract you."

"From what?" asked the dragon, and then she moved incredibly swiftly, flinging herself down as Mister Fitz appeared over the wall, leveled one of his sorcerous needles, and unleashed a bolt of blindingly violet sorcerous energy.

Unfortunately, through a space in the air where the dragon no longer stood.

Hereward dived to the floor. Black blotches were floating in his vision, but he managed to see the dragon roll hard against the stone bench, even as Mister Fitz leapt onto it, readying his needle again. But the puppet lost his footing as the dragon heaved herself against the solid slab. With the shriek of stone on stone, it slid aside to reveal a deep hole, the entrance to some secret shaft. The dragon threw herself headfirst down it, legs flying.

Hereward caught her foot, but he could not hold her. She was far heavier than any normal person her size, and gravity did the rest. The dragon slid down the hole and Hereward followed.

The escape passage was an oiled slide, a narrow tube. After the initial short drop, it ran at a forty-five-degree angle for a hundred feet or so before it suddenly corkscrewed down in a series of giddying turns.

Hereward gripped the dragon's ankle with one hand, and with the other touched the garter turned armband, gabbling out the necessary recitation, coupled with shrieks and cries as he was flung about by the sudden turns and the dragon managed to land a kick.

"In the name of the Council of the Treaty for the Safety of the—ow—World, acting under the authority granted by the

Three Empires, the Seven—curse you—Kingdoms, the Palatine Regency, the Jessar Republic, and the Forty Lesser Realms,
I—arrgh—declare myself an agent of the Council. I identify the
dragon manifested as Harquahar-Drim-Jashar—ow—a listed
entity under the treaty and an enemy of the World, and the
Council authorizes me to pursue any and all—damn it—actions
necessary to banish, repel, or exterminate the said entity!"

The dragon screamed something back at him and kicked
him again, but it had little effect. It hurt, of course, but she
couldn't get the leverage to deliver a decent blow while they
were sliding so swiftly.

Hereward tried to look behind to see if Mister Fitz had
jumped after him, but he was falling too fast, sliding up and
down and around the well-oiled escape tube. He desperately
hoped the puppet was very close indeed, for even with the ac-
tivated brassard providing some minor physical protection,
the dragon probably could rip out his heart when they arrived
wherever this slide ended up.

The ending up happened rather more suddenly than Hereward expected. One second he was being flung around another
corkscrew turn, and then in the next the slide slanted steeply
upward to check the velocity of the sliders, went slightly down
again, and spat out the dragon and Hereward onto the floor of a
vast cavern. This was well lit by many small holes in the ceiling
and upper third of the walls, allowing the afternoon sun to poke
dozens of brilliant fingers in to light up what would otherwise
be a dark and dismal cave.

Hereward rolled away as soon as he landed, and sprang up,
not quite as easily as he'd intended due to the oil he was covered
in. But he managed to stay upright and be as ready as he could
be to fight the dragon.

But she did not instantly attack him, as he expected. Rather
she stood staring at the centre of the cavern, where the sun's rays

flickered over a scene of destruction. Dozens of empty chests were thrown together in a pile, surrounded by a nimbus of at least a hundred flat and flaccid leather moneybags, their draw-strings loose and every which way, looking like a mass beaching of sea-stingers cast upon an unforgiving shore.

"My . . . my treasure!" she wailed. "My gold! My lovely, lovely gold!"

She turned on Sir Hereward and hissed, revealing long, daggerlike teeth he hadn't noticed before. They were even more disturbing than her talon-like fingernails.

"Where is my gold?"

"The Archon took it earlier today," said Hereward, backing up. His eyes flickered from side to side, looking for a weapon, and also, rather hopefully, to the escape slide. But he couldn't see anything useful, not even a stone, and there was no sign of Mister Fitz. There were probably trapdoors that closed behind the first escapee, or something of the sort. Any well-planned escape slide would block pursuers. He'd been lucky to hang on to the dragon.

"The Archon?" asked the dragon, as if she couldn't believe it.

"Mister Fitz and I were never interested in the treasure," said Hereward, hoping to keep her talking rather than ripping his heart out. "Only in you, Harquahar-Drim-Jashar."

"What? Who?" asked the dragon. She had half turned to look back at the empty chests again. Her shoulders sagged, and she seemed older somehow. In fact, she looked just like a ship-wreck survivor. Hereward had seen this kind of shock before. He'd been shipwrecked himself.

The knight touched the brassard on his arm. The arcane symbols glowed more brightly, the violet light harsh in com-parison to all the rods of soft golden sunlight slanting down from outside.

"You are a proscribed entity, Harquahar-Drim-Jashar," he

said. "We are agents of the Council of the Treaty for the Safety of the World."

The dragon turned back to him. She frowned in puzzlement.

"Who? I'm not Harquahar-Drim-Jashar."

It was Hereward's turn to droop slightly.

"Wh-wh-hat?" he stammered.

"I'm not Harquahar-Drim-Jashar," said the dragon. She stepped closer, but did not raise her taloned hands, and her teeth appeared to have retracted to more normal human dentition. "My name is Jallal-Qreu-Kwaxssim. I am nowhere near as old as a Jashar. They're ancient."

Hereward stepped back, glancing at the slide exit again.

"I see you have to answer to a puppet," said the dragon, stepping closer again. "And belatedly I recall stories of scarred women who slay godlets and the like. But you are a man. And surely, this is all ancient history, and I am not who you are hunting, anyway."

"I don't answer to a puppet," protested Hereward. "And not all the agents are women—Oh!"

Mister Fitz came flying out of the slide, a sorcerous needle cupped in his hand, its blinding light contained. He landed easily, skidded far less than Hereward had, though he was just as oily, and spun about. Fierce light bloomed as he opened his fingers to unveil the needle.

Hereward dived away from the dragon, but she had already launched herself towards him. He felt her snatch the earring from his right ear; there was a flash of sorcerous energy, immediately followed by the harsh rumble of falling rock. He crawled away on his belly and elbows, blinking away afterimages of violet light and coughing up stone dust. All the while desperately hoping the dragon wasn't about to land on his spine and wrench his heart out through his back.

When the heart-ripping didn't happen after three seconds, he rolled over and pushed himself up, to look frantically in all directions for the dragon, who was not immediately visible. Hereward could see only Mister Fitz, standing in the middle of the cavern, his head tilted back, no sun-bright needle in his hand.

"Did you get her?" he gasped. The object of Mister Fitz's sorcerous blasts was to unstitch the dragon's connection to this universe, which would banish her back to the dimension from which she had trespassed. If he had succeeded, there would be nothing left.

There was nothing left, Hereward was relieved to see.

Until Mister Fitz pointed up.

Sir Hereward narrowed his eyes, looking towards all those tiny, sunlit holes in the cavern's upper walls and ceiling. A golden dragon in the classical reptilian guise, though only the size of his little finger, folded back her shimmering wings to shoot through one of the holes. She spread those wings on the other side to catch the sea breeze that came every afternoon to blow the foul smoke of the foundries on the Levels far from the city.

Hereward and Fitz caught one more slight glimpse through another hole as she spiraled upward and away.

"I didn't know they could shape themselves so small," said Hereward. He looked at the empty chests. "Why bother with all this, then?"

"She would have to give up nearly all of her energistic energy to take so small a size, and with it went much of her invulnerability and combative prowess," said Mister Fitz. "Though not banished, she will not prey on any more large, blond-haired men for a considerable time, presuming she is ever able to amass sufficient gold to grow. So I suppose we have not entirely failed."

"What!" exclaimed Sir Hereward. "You never mentioned . . . I thought it was young maidens—"

"Hereward," said Mister Fitz, adopting his didactic voice. "As I am not an entertaining puppet, you are not a trained actor. Our plan depended on you presuming yourself to be not immediately at risk. Need I say more?"

"You could have told me," grumbled Sir Hereward. "By the way, she said she wasn't Harquahar-Drim-Jashar, she's Jallal-Qreu-Kwaxssim."

Mister Fitz's head slowly rotated to fully face the knight.

"Hmmm," he said, after a long, drawn-out moment of silence. "I need to check that name. It was most likely an attempt at misdirection. Though occasionally two dragons will join forces . . ."

But he spoke to the air, for Hereward was already looking for the way out.

THE FIELD OF
FALLEN FOE

HE SUN EXACERBATES THE BONES, WHICH EMIT A deadly miasma," explained the guide, pointing at the sullen green clouds that drifted across the plain, writhing around, above, and between the massive, brilliantly white remains of the long-dead monsters who had died there several centuries ago. Thousands of these skeletons were dotted about the vast field, an unnaturally flat square a little over a league on each side, the entirety ringed by low hills.

"As you have contracted the guild's weather-witch, a north-westerly will come soon and will clear enough of the poison to allow passage, with suitable precautions. Our witch will then send clouds overhead, lest the sun begin its work on the bones again, while also ensuring that while it is cloudy, there is no rain."

"Why?" asked Sir Hereward uneasily, clutching at the rail. He, Mister Fitz, and the guide were atop a slender watchtower made of lashed-together poles of hoopoo wood, and the whole thing was swaying even in the absence of a breeze, all too like the mast of a ship. Which wouldn't have bothered Sir Here-ward, as he was an excellent sailor. But the tower wasn't the mast of a well-founded vessel. Rather, it was a rickety affair atop a rocky hill overlooking the Field of Fallen Foe, and he suspected neither its construction nor its foundations were particularly reliable.

"If it rains, the bones are excited in a different fashion, and disgorge a liquid poison which mixes with the water to create rivulets of death," said the guide. She tapped the badge on her tunic proclaiming her to be a senior member of the Guild of Guides to the Field of Fallen Foe. The badge was gold, and looked heavy, indicating guiding parties into the field of poisonous death was more prosperous than might be presumed. This particular one had seven small, bright stones set in it, that the gullible might believe to be diamonds, but to Sir Hereward's trained eye were only glass. "Though overboots, as well as masks, will be supplied by the guild, they only go so far."

"Naturally," muttered Sir Hereward. He glanced down at Mister Fitz. The sorcerous puppet was gazing into the green fog, his strange blue eyes almost luminous. He was wearing a false papier-mâché nose over his own, a non-magical construction, unlike his own ensorcelled skin. The false nose was very long and pointed, with flared nostrils painted a lurid red. Sir Hereward had introduced him as a specialized puppet made for tracking, not one of the more usual entertainers.

The latter part, at least, was true.

"Fitz, are you sure we need to—"

"Yes, master," replied Mister Fitz, looking up at the knight. He moved jerkily, as he generally did around outsiders, to lull them into thinking he was badly made and weak. "It definitely went into the field."

The puppet turned to the guide. He pitched his usual speaking voice higher, and quavered on some of the words.

"You have said the clouds are flammable, but if that were

so, there would be more evidence of fires, or some continual conflagration, yes?"

"The exact nature of the miasma has defied many an alchemist, save the guild's own. We have penetrated its secret," answered the guide. Though the woman remained as expressionless as ever, Hereward caught the faintest sideways flicker of her eyes, an indication of some lie or half-truth. "The clouds *are* flammable, and for that reason we forbid naked flames and anything that might too easily strike a spark, such as powder weapons. However, our sorcerers have exerted an influence so that when such ignition occurs, the fire does not spread. There is a local explosion, a fireball of some prodigality, but it does not ignite nearby densities of the miasma. It does, of course, kill whoever sparked the fire."

"Interesting," said Mister Fitz, once again staring down at the swirling clouds of poison. He made loud sniffing noises, almost snorting, his bulbous head jerking up and down. Sir Hereward hoped the prosthetic nose was as firmly fastened as the puppet had promised. The guide moved away, as far as she could on the flimsy platform.

Sir Hereward sighed deeply. Unlike Mister Fitz, he did not find the field of deathly gas and the monster skeletons interesting. He found them alarming and annoying. He sighed again, gripped the railing as the tower swung in the breeze, and wished his aunt had found him harder to locate, because if she had, he would not be here.

EVERYTHING HAD BEEN GOING SO WELL FOR A CHANGE. He had just been paid off from his last contract, a straightforward and peaceful ten weeks spent as the master artillerist tasked with overseeing the emplacement of new cannon in the rebuilt south

bastion of Pecall-Torin, a lively city untroubled by any proscribed godlets or malign entities.

Gold in hand, Hereward had looked forward to staying on
in Pecall-Torin for several weeks. Time to read, and eat ex-
travagantly, drink wine, gamble a little and pursue an architect-
wizard, one Suryane Diramolo, who was in charge of rebuilding
the bastion and had worked closely with Sir Hereward—and
who had let it be known she might welcome cooperating more
closely still with him on personal matters when their mutual
task was done.

But all that had been taken from him, just as everything
began to look so promising.

Suryane had accepted his invitation to play a game of Starmount and Moonshade (often known elsewhere as "Kings and
Fools"), an accepted tactic in the convoluted courting practices
of the region. Sir Hereward had put two heavy gold nobles into
the willing hand of the innkeeper of the Striated Pardecoup
where he lodged, and ordered a meal of seven removes, with
a flask of an almost transparent Alastran white wine to be set
in ice, and two flasks of a particularly fine vintage of the ever-
popular wine commonly called oxblood, to be opened and allowed to draw breath.

Hereward and Suryane had opened the ritual of seduction
with the game, using a particularly fine set of jade and gold–
chased pieces on a polished board made of five timbers, most
notably walnut and fruitwood, which Fitz had procured from
somewhere when Sir Hereward said he wanted to brush up on
his playing. Fitz was far better at bartering—the knight always
overpaid if he was left to his own devices—and so Hereward
was rarely allowed full control of their shared purse.

Naturally, the puppet knew Hereward wanted to practice
because he hoped to entice Suryane to his bed, and the knight
had to win at least one campaign to advance his suit. But the

puppet had raised no objection, and he even went so far as to play several games the day before with the knight without being *too* scathing about Hereward's strategies and lack of ability to mentally picture more than ten moves ahead.

But the courting game had barely begun—only the first, careful mouthfuls of the Alastran wine drunk and Suryane having made her opening move (the orthodox steepling of her second moonshade roost) when disaster struck. Or perhaps *misfortune* was more apt, *disaster* being at that point too strong a term. Sir Hereward had reached for his foremost Dverzlak, to push it forward where it could intercept the launch of moonshades (again an orthodox response to the steepling). But even as his fingers closed on the horned beast of jade it rippled under his fingers, losing solidity. Its long backbone of thorns, ready to fire at aerial opponents, shrank into its body and the whole piece began to assume a new shape, that of a human or humanoid.

"What's this?" exclaimed Suryane. She pushed back her chair, and straightened up, ready to move. "Cheating already?"

"Not by me," said Hereward cautiously, snatching back his hand. He let it fall by his side, fingers close to the hilt of the misericorde in his boot-top. But Suryane seemed genuinely surprised and was making no threatening motions, no spellcasting gestures or the like. Besides, the former Dverzlak was beginning to assume an actual face, one that was beginning to look rather familiar. Even familial.

"Fitz!" called Hereward. He inclined his head to Suryane, a regretful motion. "I am sorry, Mistress Diramolo. One of my aunts has tracked me down and will doubtless shortly be listing my many faults and shortcomings, and in the midst of that, some sort of family message. We must postpone our . . . game."

"This is not a sorcery I know," said Suryane. She glanced from Hereward to Mister Fitz, who stood in the doorway, a box of rosewood and gold under his arm. An innocuous container, or so it seemed to outsiders, but it was Fitz's sewing desk and at present was fully stocked with the sorcerous needles with which he could unstitch or repair things both of this world and the extra-dimensional.

"There is evidently more to you than merely an artillerist, Hereward. And to you, Master Puppet—I sense some powerful sorcery emanating from that box, the layers of lead and bone behind the wood notwithstanding. You are not an entertainer puppet after all, are you?"

"I am not," agreed Mister Fitz. "But you need not wield your sharpened measure-stick nor call upon the power of your thumb ring, Mistress Diramolo. We are not your enemies, nor of Pecall-Torin. Indeed, unless I am mistaken, we are about to be ordered to go elsewhere." He addressed his companion. "Your Aunt Rapalle will manifest within minutes, Hereward."

"Rapalle?" Diramolo asked. "An unusual name. She is named after the fabled Witch of Har, I take it."

"Not exactly," hedged Sir Hereward. "It would be best you depart, I'm afraid—"

"She *is* a Witch of Har," said Mister Fitz, whose inability to lie and desire to offer instruction were of equal strength in his makeup. "One of the Mysterious Three of the High Pale—"

"Fitz," interrupted Hereward. "Suryane, you should go *now.*"

Suryane sat down instead.

"But I am fascinated. The Witches of Har are more than legend? And one is *your* aunt? In the stories they only had girl-children, though. No men at all, yes?"

"I am, as in so many ways, an exception," said Sir Hereward, with the faintest tone of melancholy. "Now, please go—"

"Too late," said Fitz. "Rapalle is almost manifest."

"I beg you do not move or speak," hissed Hereward urgently. "Rapalle will not take kindly to the presence of an outsider."

Suryane nodded very slightly, and remained still.

The little Dverzlak figurine had completely changed, jade and gold melting and reforming to become an angular woman of advanced age. She wore boots, leather shorts that extended past the knee, and an armoured coat of many metal paillettes. Her head was half shaven, the left side bare, and even in miniature the scars on her face and scalp were very visible. She held a sorcerous needle in her right hand.

The needle flared, so bright Hereward had to look away. When he looked back, the figure had come alive, Rapalle replacing the needle in a purse at her waist. Having done so, the figurine looked up from the board, directly at Sir Hereward. Her face, no longer carved jade with golden eyes, shone like moonlight on a lake, cold and mysterious.

"Hereward! Attend me!"

"I *am* attending, Aunt," replied Hereward, rather mulishly.

"Is Fitz there? I have limited sight through this working."

"I am here," said Fitz, climbing up on to the table before leaping to Hereward's shoulder. He sat there, wooden legs dangling down the knight's chest, his arm lightly wrapped around Hereward's neck. The knight noticed Suryane shiver at this, but he liked it himself. Fitz had been his nanny as a child, and was almost the only person in the High Pale who had consistently paid him attention, cared for him, and taught him what he needed to know to stay alive.

"Good. The star pool indicates you are presently in the town of Pecryll-Tollen, correct?"

"Yes," answered Fitz. "It is called Pecall-Torin now, however."

She ignored that. "There is a locality some twenty leagues distant from you, commonly called the Field of Fallen Foe. A mortuary of dead Kymberbeasts, summarily executed by the godlet Oraxyll-Pra-Rannill, itself later absorbed by a superior entity. This is background, you understand. The matter at hand is that at long last we have found evidence that Scromris-Paszell-Entercret survived the encounter with Laiselle. That is your late great-great-great-aunt, Hereward, not your living cousin. A recent successful divination confirms it went to ground in the Field of Fallen Foe several hundred years ago and remains there still. You must find and end it."

"Scromris-Paszell-Entercret," said Fitz, "is not proscribed."

"It killed Laiselle!" snapped Rapalle. "Its existence is forfeit!"

"Laiselle incorrectly identified it," said Fitz calmly. "She was the aggressor. The godlet merely defended itself. In fact, it fled, and I believe has caused no trouble in the four centuries since. Nor did it in the thousand years before. It has always been classified as benign."

"We made you too much the stickler, puppet," said Rapalle. "The matter has gone before the Three, it has been decided. Regardless of its prior classification or Laiselle's error, no extra-dimensional entity may escape punishment for actions against agents of the Council of the Treaty for the Safety of the World. You understand the instruction, Hereward?"

"Yes," said Hereward, shortly.

"And you, Fitz?"

"Indeed," said the puppet.

"Then carry it out," said Rapalle.

"How is my mother—" Hereward began to ask, but the jade and gold figurine was already melting into an ugly blob, which sank some distance into the board, emitting an acrid twist of smoke. It did not reform into the Dverzlak or anything else. The whole set was spoiled; the game—and the seduction—doubly so.

Suryane scratched the long scar that ran across her forehead. The result of some falling masonry in her early apprenticeship, she had told Hereward, before she fully learned the mystic arts involving stonework, and could not be harmed by such accidents. He, of course, raised among scarified women, found it adorable.

"The stories made the Witches sound more noble," she said. "Slaying only malignant godlets."

Hereward frowned, and did not reply. Mister Fitz jumped down from the knight's shoulder and advanced to the table, reaching up to pull the melted piece out of the board. It was stuck, and came away accompanied by several long splinters.

"A pity," said the puppet. He dropped the misshapen blob and picked up another piece, one of the two Scryllintars, the sinuous flank guards whose coils could entrap three pieces when fully extended. "This was made by Felice of Konqwal, I have never seen another such set, in all my travels."

"So you go to the Field of Fallen Foe?" asked Suryane. "There to dispatch some harmless little godlet that has likely slept amidst the noxious vapors some hundreds of years, doing no one any harm?"

"Noxious vapors?" asked Hereward.

"Poisonous airs that stem from the rotting bones of thousands of dead creatures," said Suryane. "Some with precious gems for eyes, if the guild that controls the Field is to be believed. They guide parties in, demanding swingeing payments to do so. But I have never met anyone who came out richer from the Field of Foes than they were going in. No one from Pecall-Torin would be so stupid, but they still get custom from far places, people who have heard of ruby eyes and choose not to consider the more dispiriting facts. So, I ask again, are you going to the Field to slay some harmless godlet?"

"Yes," said Sir Hereward. "We are oath-sworn to do so."

"Then I think the less of you," said Suryane haughtily, and swept from the room.

Hereward sat heavily in his chair, and reached for the flask of Alastran wine.

"I will purchase riding beasts," said Fitz. "Do not drink the oxblood too, Hereward. We should depart at dawn and I do not wish said departure to be accompanied by your groans and pitiful requests for remedies."

TWO DAYS LATER, THEY WERE IN THE ENCAMPMENT OF THE Guild of Guides, on the lower slope of one of the enclosing hills, below the wavering tower. Hereward no longer had any of the payment he had received from Pecall-Torin, the gold had all gone on the hiring of a mask, thigh boots, and glow-stones, in addition to the services of the three guides. These were apparently indispensable, even though Hereward had assured them his hunting puppet with the enormous nose would guide him to their desired prey, who had hidden amongst the sprawling expanse of bones. He did not tell the guides this prey was a godlet, instead claiming it was a monster long sought after, whose head would adorn the great hall of a heavy-pursed collector who had hired Hereward and Fitz to bring it to her.

"Allow me to examine your mask, Hereward," said Mister Fitz. The puppet, of course, did not need one, since he did not breathe and the quality of air he inhaled in order to talk was of no consequence.

"All our masks are of the best," said the chief guide, who had asked to be called "Seven," the others being "Fourteen" and "Thirty-Six." The latter wore silver badges, which had no fake diamonds set therein. Sir Hereward noted these two guides were of a hulking, brutish sort, and given the similarity of features, were probably brother and sister. They wore boiled leather cuirasses and their masks hung from their belts, ready to don. Both wielded massive glaives, too large to be easily scabbarded, so they held them ready at all times.

"So it seems," said Fitz. He examined the exterior of the

mask carefully. It was of the kind in common use by plague doctors, a long-snouted device made from a single piece of leather, the pointy end packed with a filter cut from the hardy lungs of the mountain moklek, the much smaller and more energetic cousin of the beasts of burden commonly used upon the plains. Behind the filter, there was a section stuffed with nodules from the marine weed known as airpop, which, when fresh, slowly exuded breathable air and so would refresh and augment the cleansed air drawn in through the moklek lung filter. The eyepieces were round lenses of thick glass, very well-made glass without imperfections, but tinted slightly yellow.

"Yet," continued the puppet. "There is a very fine crack close to the chin in this one, which will slowly admit the vapors it is supposed to keep out, bypassing both filter and airpop. Sir Hereward will take your mask, Seven, and you may procure another."

"What?" asked Seven, taking the mask. She held it close to her eye. "I see no crack! We are very careful with our masks!"

"My eyes are, perhaps, more perceptive," said Mister Fitz. He opened them wide, and they seemed more blue than ever, and colder. "Swap masks, if you please, or we cannot continue."

"Your hunting *puppet* is mistaken," said Seven to Hereward. She held out the original mask to the knight. He refused to take it, stepping back.

"Fitz is a master hunter," said Hereward easily. "This naturally includes oversight of all the equipment of the hunting party. I will have your mask. You can use that one, if you believe Fitz is wrong, or fetch another."

"I will get you another mask," said Seven.

"I want yours," replied Sir Hereward. His hand fell to the hilt of his mortuary sword, and he briefly regretted that his wheel-lock pistols were locked away in a chest secured on the back of his riding beast, which was chained nearby, in accordance with

Seven's earlier warning that nothing that might spark the vapors could be taken into the Field.

"This is your assigned mask," said Seven.

"But I want yours," repeated Sir Hereward. "And furthermore, I now have doubts as to your good intentions."

Mister Fitz swung the rosewood box he wore as a backpack around to his chest, the lid slightly open. Seven held the defective mask in front of her, in such a way that it hid her left hand from view. Hereward had previously noted she wore a throwing knife on her left hip. The other two guides lifted their huge glaives a little higher. There were no other guides currently in the camp, or at least none visible, with only a small stone hut to hide in, and the open shed where the riding beasts chewed on the long strips of dried meat that hung from the feeding rail.

"We decide who enters the Field of Foes," said Seven. "And who comes forth again. As you doubt us, we will not guide you, nor permit your entry. But I will allow you to leave. Mount your riding beasts and depart!"

"And the gold I have paid?" asked Sir Hereward mildly.

Fourteen and Thirty-Six took two lumbering steps closer, glaives held high.

"Forfeit for your boorishness," said Seven. She lowered the mask, to show the throwing knife was already in her hand. Only it wasn't a throwing knife, but a disguised pistol, the flintlock cocked as she drew it from the cunning sheath.

"We are three, and you are alone," continued Seven, ignoring Mister Fitz. She smiled, the first time he had seen her do so, and raised the pistol to aim at his face.

Hereward dived to one side, drawing his sword as he came down on one knee, immediately springing up and forward into a lunge, piercing Fourteen above the thigh, immediately withdrawing the blade for a lightning-fast slash to the right wrist of

Thirty-Six, cutting it to the bone before the guide could swing
down her cumbersome glaive.

There was a gunshot along the way, and a moment of intense radiance behind Hereward that blinded both lesser guides,
giving him the two or three seconds necessary to stab Fourteen
in the eye—the desired two inches and no more—twist his
sword out and repeat the process on Thirty-Six, who was already screaming and clutching at her nearly-severed hand.

Both fell slowly and heavily, like sawn-through trees, to lie
twitching in the bloody dirt for their remaining few minutes
of life.

Sir Hereward spun about to face Seven, blinking away the
dancing motes in his eyes caused by the brilliance of Fitz's sorcerous needle. He was ready to strike if necessary, but it wasn't.
Seven had been almost completely vaporized. Only a lump
of molten gold that had been her badge remained, between
her boots, the feet inside burning like the wicks of strange,
footwear-shaped lamps. The awful, but unfortunately familiar,
stench of charred flesh assaulted Hereward's nose.

"I think they wanted to ambush us after we had found our
notional prey," said Fitz. "And sell the 'trophy' themselves, to
add to their profits. Better to force a confrontation early."

"I too had my doubts," said Hereward. He looked down at
the three dead guides and slowly wiped his blade clean on the
cloth he kept for that purpose. It had once been snowy white,
and now after many, many washes, was a strangely attractive
shade of pink.

If only they had kept their word, held to the agreement,
they would be alive. So simple, and yet so difficult, at least for
some people.

"Was the mask really cracked?" asked Sir Hereward.

"Yes. You would have felt faint within minutes of entering
the field, unconscious soon after, and dead within the hour."

The puppet pulled off his enormous prosthetic nose and threw it in the top of the nearer burning boot, where it too began to crackle and flame. "Are you significantly wounded?"

"What?" asked Hereward, and only then felt the pain. He craned his neck to look at his left shoulder, where the buff coat was torn open, blood slowly staining the heavy material. He probed the hole with two fingers and felt the wound.

"The skin is barely broken," he grunted. "I will cleanse and bind it up later, there is no urgency. Are there are many more of these cursed guides about? What of their weather-witch, where is she?"

Mister Fitz's spherical head swiveled completely around for a full view of their environs, a most disturbing action. It was like a globe being slowly spun on its axis, something that should not be done by an even somewhat human-looking head.

"There are two other encampments. One on the southern side, and one on the eastern side of the plain. I daresay they will soon venture out to see what has occurred, as they watch us from their towers. But I do not think there is a weather-witch at all. The Guides presumed too much on their visitors' ignorance. I have been here before, and I also consulted the owner of a most excellent and recent almanac of the region before we left Pecall-Torin. At this time of year, the nor-wester rises every morning, blows for several hours, and then fails, at which time the overcast reforms, but the vapors on the ground take much longer to do so."

"And the rain?"

"Very unlikely to occur."

"But it does cause the poison to flow in rivulets of death?"

"It does," agreed Mister Fitz.

"I do not trust these boots," said Sir Hereward, stamping his feet in emphasis. "Perhaps I can fashion some stilts from the timbers of yonder shed; I have not forgotten the trick of walking with them. You remember the circus of Jonghame? I sometimes think I should have stayed with them . . . what?"

Mister Fitz's head had rotated around again, to look behind him into the depths of the poisoned field.

"What?" repeated Sir Hereward.

"It will not be necessary for us to enter the Field," said the puppet. "Scromris-Paszell-Entercret is coming out. It must have sensed my sorcerous action, as it is a kind of entity most sensitive to the use of an energistic needle."

Hereward started, peered at the green-tinted fog, and perceived a directional eddy, the vapors parting as if before something large and purposeful. He fumbled the pouch at his belt open, took out the brassard, and slid it up his arm over the sleeve of the buff coat, wincing as the action made his wounded shoulder twinge.

Mister Fitz did not take out his own brassard, nor open his sewing box to arm himself with a new needle.

"Fitz!" spat Hereward. "Your brassard! We must speak the invocation!"

"That will not be necessary," said Mister Fitz calmly. "Scromris-Paszell-Entercret knows I am here from the particular stratum of my sorcery, just as I know of its presence from the prismatic spoor present in the vapors. It will not attack us; it merely wishes to communicate with me."

"But we're supposed to . . . to . . . ," stammered Hereward. "The Three gave the order!"

"Hereward, you have known me your entire life," said Mister Fitz. "You surely know by now that my nature is fixed. I was made to undertake certain actions of supreme importance for the safety of the world, and I fulfill my makers' intent. But I do not, and will not, exercise myself to carry out instructions that are not congruent with that purpose."

"But what do we tell Rapalle? She's bound to enquire sooner or—"

"I will take full responsibility," said Mister Fitz. His voice was both strangely lighter and more definite. It was the voice of Mistress Fitz, when the puppet had been Hereward's nanny.

"Oh, all right," said Hereward, his creased brow smoothing in relief. "But what if it does attack us? How can you be sure—"

"Scromris is a benign entity," said Mister Fitz, with absolute certainty. "In fact, for many centuries it performed an important role in the maintenance of the city of Bazynghame."

"Bazynghame? Barely a city, and full of coin-clutchers. You recall they tried to hire me to train their guard, but only offered—"

"The city was much larger then, and more prosperous. Laiselle did them great damage when she drove out Scromris-Paszell-Entercret, thinking it was another, actually dangerous entity."

"It must be at least *somewhat* dangerous if it killed Laiselle," said Hereward dubiously.

"She was pursuing the fleeing godlet, fell off her battle-mount, and hit her head," replied Mister Fitz. "She was chewing rhyss seeds."

"You were with her," said Hereward, in sudden understanding.

"I had been sent to bring her back to the High Pale," replied Mister Fitz. "But I was too late. I followed her from the city, I saw her fall, but there was nothing I could do. The rhyss would have killed her anyway, in a day or two. She was ingesting at least two handfuls a day by that stage."

Hereward nodded slowly. It was not unusual for the agents of the Treaty for the Safety of the World to seek remedies to counteract the stresses of their calling. Most worked alone, and had no one to share their secrets and fears. Though unlike him, they were allowed to return to the High Pale from time to time, to see family and friends. Not that he felt any particular urge to submit himself to the predictable critique of his every action of the last fifteen years if he did return. Arguably his best friend from his youth was already at his side and his mother and aunts had never shown him any particular affection, regarding him more as a flawed tool than anything else.

"And here is Scromris. I trust you will not take action against it yourself, Hereward?"

"Me?" protested Hereward. "No, I trust your opinion, Fitz. Besides . . ."

He stared at the enormous insectile creature that was emerging from the miasma. It was as big or bigger than a moklek, and resembled a cockroach in its dark armour and questing feelers, but it had shorter legs and many more of them. It scuttled forward and stopped some ten paces distant, its frond-like antennae twitching.

"I doubt it would be any use," he finished.

"Indeed," said Mister Fitz. The puppet walked forward and stretched out his little wooden hands, palms up. The godlet's feelers descended, the puppet closed his fingers on them, and they stood there for some time, in evident communion.

Hereward wanted to step away, to go and fetch his pistols from the chest on his riding beast. The other encampments were some distance away, but there could be guides already in the Field for all he knew, and some way of communicating with them. Still, he didn't move.

Fitz let go, stepped back, reached into his sewing desk, and took out the Scryllintar from the Starmount and Moonshade set. He set the little figurine down in the earth in front of the monstrous godlet and stepped back.

"Turn around, Hereward," he said. "And shut your eyes."

Hereward spun about, raised his forearm to his face, and

pressed his shut eyes hard against his sleeve. Even so, the flash
was blinding, brighter even than Fitz's needles. The knight kept
his eyes closed and his arm up for several seconds, until Fitz
spoke again.

"It is now safe," he said.

Hereward lowered his arm, and once again blinking away
floating dots and sparkles, turned around.

The massive insectoid godlet had disappeared. The Scryllintar figurine had grown. It now stood as high as Hereward's
waist and with all its segments fully extended was some dozen
paces long. It had also come fully alive, its many legs shivering
in anticipation of movement.

"Go well, Scromris-Paszell-Entercret," said Mister Fitz.

The godlet, in its new Scryllintar form, performed a sinuous
flex and raced past Sir Hereward, who couldn't help but lurch
back and cry out. It ignored him and continued on and away up
the hill, pausing for a moment to smash one of the supports of
the lookout tower, which came tumbling down in an avalanche
of hoopoo wood.

"The transition of material form will muddle any scryers
for a long time to come," said Mister Fitz. "So Rapalle will *not*
enquire, or not for many years. Tell me, you have powder and
slow match with you?

"Um, powder and slow match," repeated Sir Hereward
slowly, staring up the hill. The godlet had left hundreds of tiny
glowing footprints in the earth, though the closest were already
fading.

"Hereward?"

"Yes, I have my usual store. Only a small barrel, mind you,
a quarter keg. It is stowed in the panniers of your beast, as it
happens. What do we need it for?"

The puppet stared into the Field.

"Two parties have left the encampments and converge upon

us," he said. "Four from the south one, five from the east. They are masked, coming through the miasma at the run. Presuming no increase of pace, they will all be here in just over one quarter of an hour. How long will it take for us to get well down the other side of the hill behind us?"

"Ten minutes, at the jag," replied Hereward. The riding beasts were gentler, slower cousins of the battlemounts he preferred, but their paces were the same. The jag was roughly the equivalent of an equine gallop.

"Then cut your slow-match for eleven minutes. How long is that?"

Hereward calculated in his head, then did it again to be sure.

"My current stock of slow-match tests at thirty-two seconds the foot," he said. "So that is twenty feet, seven and a third inches, using the Mergantz measures. But surely—"

"That should suffice to ensure our safety, if the air remains still. Fasten the slow-match to the barrel in the proper fashion, and I will take it to the fringe of the miasma. Then, immediately after the fuse is lit we must make as much distance as we can, certainly to interpose the hill, at the least."

"But Seven said any spark or fire would be contained by their sorcerers," protested Hereward. "The chance of getting all the guides in one small explosion is slim. Surely it would be better to simply flee now?"

"Seven lied," said Mister Fitz. "About very many things. The entire field will go up. Greater fires have been suppressed only by the presence of Scromris-Paszell-Entercret. This was its municipal function in Bazynghame, and many times it prevented conflagrations that could have destroyed the city, and indeed did so, after the godlet's expulsion. Come, we are wasting time."

Hereward looked over the vast field of highly flammable

fumes for two and a half seconds, his jaw hanging down. He was an artillerist and well-versed in the making of explosives. He liked explosions, but was also very much aware of their destructive power, and he had once seen a swamp redolent with marsh gas go up all at once. He wasn't sure if his eyebrows had ever properly grown back from that.

The Field of Fallen Foe was bigger than that swamp, and there was a lot more poison vapor floating above it then there had been marsh gas.

He ran to the riding beasts, feverishly rechecking his calculations both for the length of slow-match (made and tested by himself, and while more accurate than most, might be off by as much as twenty seconds) and the possible scale of the explosion that would ensue when the powder barrel ignited the gas. Or perhaps even when the slow-match burned close enough to the vapors . . .

THE RIDING BEASTS SCREAMED AS THEIR RIDERS WHIPPED them with the loose ends of the steering chains, keeping them to the jag. They were on the far side of the watchtower hill, but Sir Hereward did not let up, standing high in the foot-steps and shouting encouragements to the beasts that were almost as loud as their shrill screams.

"One minute!" shouted Mister Fitz, who needed no time-piece for perfect chronological accuracy. He stood entirely on the saddle, his feet wedged in a crossband. He plied his chain ends no less vigorously than Hereward, displaying a strength that he usually disguised.

"That depression to the right!" answered Hereward, steering his beast to a wallow or dried-up watercourse. It was less than two feet deep, and broad, but it would offer some protection. "Get the beasts down and we go behind!"

But even as the beasts jumped the crumbling bank and were slowed by the sandy bottom, the world behind them exploded with the coming of a new and brighter sun, followed only a second later by a massive blast of almost unbearably hot wind that flattened both riders against the necks of their beasts, peppered them with fortunately small clods of earth, and set the mounts into a full stampede that could not be checked no matter how fiercely the riding chains were pulled against the choking neck rings.

For several seconds, Hereward feared his mount would fall, but somehow it kept running, at a pace born of pure panic well beyond a jag. But glancing aside, he saw Mister Fitz leap from his beast as it fell over its own forelegs and went crashing down. Deafened by the blast, Hereward did not hear the awful crack, but he was sure the mount had broken its neck.

He hauled on the chains again, at first to no effect. But as the air stilled, the echo of the blast ebbed, and the riding beast's muscles gave out, it finally slowed. Hereward turned it around and headed back, though it could only manage a lope, and then not even a walk, so he had to dismount and guide it carefully from the side, watchful of the usual attempts to bite off his head.

But the beast was too exhausted even for that. When they got back to the body of the other mount, it laid itself flat on its belly and howled in misery, though whether for its own state or the loss of its companion, no one could tell.

A massive column of intensely black smoke rose beyond the hill. With no wind, it went straight up, only beginning to spread out in the much higher airs where the wind never ceased. It made almost an anvil shape, and soon would occlude the sun.

Mister Fitz had taken off the dented panniers and was sitting on top of one, inspecting his left hand. One of his cunningly jointed fingers was splayed out at an obtuse angle. Fitz was rarely injured, his wooden and papier-mâché frame being heavily reinforced with sorcery, but it did happen every now and then.

"We are both injured," stated Sir Hereward.

"My finger is of little consequence," said Mister Fitz. "I can repair it in a day or two, though I will need to procure certain materials."

"I fear my own wound is worse than I thought," said Sir Hereward. "Given you are also injured, I suggest we need somewhere safe to undertake treatment, and then some time to fully recover. The nearest suitable town is, I believe—"

"Pecall-Torin," interrupted Mister Fitz.

Sir Hereward inclined his head, in part to hide a small smile of self-satisfaction.

"Well," said Mister Fitz. He bent his head too, in thought.

Though Hereward could not know it, the puppet was thinking of Laiselle, and other agents, even longer ago, who had unrelentingly pursued their sworn duty and had buckled under the weight of it, to the detriment of the mission. They would have benefitted from some time of careless relaxation.

That was all. Hereward would be more effective, should he be allowed to forget even for a little while the work that must be done.

Fitz told himself he was not influenced at all by any other considerations, and so did not realize that it was possible for a sorcerous puppet of his nature to lie, if only to himself.

"Why not?" he said, and hopped down from the pannier.

ACKNOWLEDGMENTS

I OWE A PARTICULAR DEBT TO ERIC FLINT, who published the first of these stories in the online magazine *Jim Baen's Universe*. I had sold Eric a SF story and he asked me to submit more; "Sir Hereward and Mister Fitz Go to War Again" was the happy result. If he hadn't asked me, maybe it never would have been written. Eric was a tremendous supporter of other writers as an editor and publisher, in addition to being a very fine writer himself.

I am also very grateful to the editors who published subsequent stories featuring my artillerist and puppet duo, and welcomed further entries in the series. Thank you Jeff Vandermeer, Ann Vandermeer, Jonathan Strahan, Lou Anders, Melissa Marr, Tim Pratt, G.R.R. Martin, and the late and very much missed Gardner Dozois.

Thanks are also due to William Shafer and Subterranean Press for the lovely limited edition hardcover of *Sir Hereward and Mister Fitz: Three Adventures* back in 2013, which introduced many more people to my pistol-toting and sorcerous needle–wielding heroes.

When I realized I had enough of these stories to make a full-sized collection, I was momentarily discouraged by the task of bringing all the final, published versions together to show prospective publishers. But this was swiftly overcome by the excellent work of Peter M. Ball, who extracted the texts, wrangled the formatting, and got it all together.

As always, my agent Jill Grinberg and her team at Jill Grinberg Literary Management are owed a massive debt of gratitude, as are Fiona Inglis and the crew at Curtis Brown (Australia).

David Pomerico was the first publisher to take on this collection, responding with tremendous enthusiasm to the existing tales and the prospect of a new, ninth story. I greatly appreciate his energy and professionalism, and the dedication of the whole team at Harper Voyager. Likewise, many thanks are due for the sterling work of Marcus Gipps and Gillian Redfearn at Gollancz for the British edition; and in my own country, I am very grateful to Eva Mills and the home team at Allen & Unwin, for the Australian edition.

Everyone does, of course, judge a book by its cover. I am very fortunate to have a great one here, with the illustration by Damonza and design by Jean Reina. Thanks to Mike Hall for the map illustration.

And, as always, none of my work would be possible without the love and support of my wife, Anna, my sons, Thomas and Edward, and our dog, Snufkin.

CREDITS

Stories originally published in the following publications:

"Sir Hereward and Mister Fitz Go to War Again"	*Jim Baen's Universe,* edited by Eric Flint, 2007
"Beyond the Sea Gate of the Scholar-Pirates of Sarsköe"	*Fast Ships, Black Sails,* edited by Ann VanderMeer and Jeff VanderMeer, 2008
"A Suitable Present for a Sorcerous Puppet"	*Swords and Dark Magic,* edited by Jonathan Strahan and Lou Anders, 2010
"Losing Her Divinity"	*Rags and Bones,* edited by Melissa Marr and Tim Pratt, 2013
"A Cargo of Ivories"	*Rogues,* edited by G.R.R. Martin and Gardner Dozois, 2014
"Home Is the Haunter"	*Fearsome Magics,* edited by Jonathan Strahan, 2014
"A Long, Cold Trail"	*The Book of Swords,* edited by Gardner Dozois, 2017
"Cut Me Another Quill, Mister Fitz"	*The Book of Dragons,* edited by Jonathan Strahan, 2020

ABOUT THE AUTHOR

GARTH NIX has been a full-time writer since 2001, but has also worked as a literary agent, marketing consultant, book editor, book publicist, book sales representative, bookseller, and as a part-time soldier in the Australian Army Reserve.

Garth's books include the Old Kingdom fantasy series: *Sabriel, Lirael, Abhorsen, Clariel, Goldenhand,* and *Terciel and Elinor*; SF novels *Shade's Children* and *A Confusion of Princes*; fantasy novels *Angel Mage, The Left-Handed Booksellers of London,* and sequel *The Sinister Booksellers of Bath*; and a Regency romance with magic, *Newt's Emerald*. His novels for children include *The Ragwitch*, the six books of The Seventh Tower sequence, The Keys to the Kingdom series, and *Frogkisser!* His short fiction includes more than sixty-five published stories, some of them collected in *Across the Wall* and *To Hold the Bridge*.

He has also cowritten several books with Sean Williams, including the Troubletwisters series; *Spirit Animals Book Three: Blood Ties*; *Have Sword, Will Travel*; and *Let Sleeping Dragons Lie*.

More than six million copies of Garth's books have been sold around the world, they have appeared on the bestseller lists of the *New York Times, Publishers Weekly, The Bookseller* and others; and his work has been translated into forty-two languages. He has won multiple Aurealis Awards, the ABIA Award, the Ditmar Award, the Mythopoeic Award, a CBCA Honour Book, and has been shortlisted for the Locus Awards, the Shirley Jackson Award, and others.